A FOREST, DARKLY

A. G. SLATTER

TITAN BOOKS

A Forest, Darkly
Print edition ISBN: 9781835412565
E-book edition ISBN: 9781835412572

Published by Titan Books
A division of Titan Publishing Group Ltd
144 Southwark Street, London SE1 0UP
www.titanbooks.com

First edition: February 2026
10 9 8 7 6 5 4 3 2 1

A CIP catalogue record for this title is available from the British Library.

EU RP (for authorities only)
eucomply OÜ, Pärnu mnt. 139b-14, 11317 Tallinn, Estonia
hello@eucompliancepartner.com, +3375690241

Printed and bound by CPI Group (UK) Ltd, Croydon CR0 4YY.

‘The Summer Husband’, which has been integrated into this novel, was first published as a short story in Issue #2 of *ParSec*, Ian Whates (ed.), PS Publishing, 2021.

A version of the extract from *Mother Muriel’s Tales of Gods and Unearthly Things* originally appeared in the limited edition novella version of *The Tallow-Wife*, published by FableCroft Publishing, 2017.

The tale told in Chapter Twenty-Four was originally published as ‘The Juniper Tree’ in *Lady Churchill’s Rosebud Wristlet #18*, July 2006, Kelly Link and Gavin J Grant (eds).

To the very wonderful Terri Windling for your brilliance, kindness and generosity. An inspiration before we ever met, now a forever-after friend.

Homes in the Great Forest – in it, around it, even several leagues from its very outer edges – are wont to have protections not found in other regions. Carvings of tutelary spirits, either one or two, are generally affixed to dwellings, hewn above lintels, around door- and window frames, sometimes into the very doors themselves, even on stoops. In locations where the populace is particularly superstitious – or particularly experienced with such things – each door and window and chimney has this talisman. There's such a cottage at Briga's Leap, in the west. It's deserted, now, and a curtain of leaves and vines of brightest green hangs on either side of the front entrance, but the two heads (foliate) carved into the doorframe by he who made this tiny house (himself now dust and forgotten) are not hidden.

In spring, pink and purple flowers (of a variety unknown elsewhere) bloom and the twins are crowned with delicate blossoms. Their features are strikingly similar, but for their expressions: she to the right wears a benign smile and graces the world with a gentle, knowing gaze; her sister to the left presents an astonishingly baleful glare. Her face is older too, as if she has lived a life, seen too much, given too much, had too much taken from her. Received too little in return.

Above, in the centre of the lintel is a third head, entirely covered by foliage, and seen only if one digs around (as your correspondent did). A child this one, expression clean, innocent, guileless. Concealed as she is, her secret remains: that she still bears what the others have either never had, or lost through the workings of curious fingers, rough hands, the elements and years: horns. On her forehead they sit proudly, budding, but definite.

Although the twins have been called "green women" or "green maids" – conflated perhaps with the myth of the Green Man – they are perhaps nothing to do with him. The horned one above surely is not. She is a hind-girl.

Hind-girls, creatures who reject the roles the world would give them, who will live beneath no roof nor within any walls, who dance along the narrow forest trails. Sometimes they throw their heads with such abandon that the antlers of one get caught in those of another, but their feet are sure on paths of beaten earth for they know such ways of old.

The twins, however? Perhaps they are indeed green women? They say that, once, there were many scattered through the Great Forest. Some say she – or they – disappeared, wearied by the ways of the world, or simply that she – or they – hibernates at whim, or when she feels a need, or when things become too dangerous for her to roam her forests.

MOTHER MURIEL'S TALES OF GODS AND UNEARTHLY THINGS

(UNPUBLISHED, ORIGINAL MANUSCRIPT ACCESSIONED TO THE LIBRARY OF THE UNIVERSITY OF WHITEBARROW)

1

I don't generally, as a rule, get lost.

Or at least not in these woods, or rather my part. I know them, as the saying goes, like the back of my hand. I've wandered here for the better part of two decades, learning their paths, open or otherwise, the hiding places above and below, where its pools and ponds and rills wait and run, where the herbs and mushrooms grow best and thickest, where the oak saplings are at their finest and strongest, where sun and moon fail to shine and where they sometimes brighten both day and night. Unsuspected barrows and highest tors that poke above the tree canopy, stone circles where magic more ancient than memory sleeps until it's woken, places where older gods wait, grown still and stiff with passing time, forgetful of their purpose. Or so it's said. Never met one myself, or not to my knowledge.

Yet here I am, adrift in a dappled clearing that I cannot seem to escape. The day passing me by in leaps and bounds as I tread in circles, a penitents' path I neither willingly joined nor suspected. Some sort of faery trap into which I tripped and all the profanity in the world cannot cut me loose. A fly in a spider's web. How long's it been here, waiting? Who laid it? *Here?* So deep and dark, so far off the beaten trails where even I'd not have come, except I was following that bloody hare for my stew pot, and hasn't it had its revenge? Disappeared before I could even draw my bow…

Trickster thing.

Or merely an animal that's smarter than me.

The latter is most likely.

I'm not normally so careless, but something gripped me and I ran along with it; I stay fit with work around the holding, tramping the forest and foraging for ingredients medicinal and flavoursome. But I'm no great huntress – meat comes to me in the snares I set, the villagers and rare travellers who bring offerings for aid, for medicaments, for readings to guide their future or find direction – but such barters have been rare in recent days and my snares empty. Mostly, I provide *small magics* only because it's never a good idea to let people know exactly what you can do. Something I didn't realise when I was young, which is precisely how you *(I)* get into trouble. But in my middle years… well, I'm not normally such an idiot. Yet here I sit, having given up on trying to walk my way out of this blasted circle because all paths lead me back to the centre.

At first glance I'd thought it merely a disturbance in the ground, dug up by badgers or the like. At second glance, a penitents' path such as one finds in the great cathedrals. Third and final (and too late) glance – the only one with proper attention paid, I recognised it for what it was: a maze, ploughed into the forest floor, left like a raised scar, the rough spiral pattern turning back and forth on itself, but with no exit. I'd already stepped over the outer border and was stuck in its warp and weft. And I'd run so far from home, so far from any chance of my shouts being heard had there been another person in my cottage (which there's not); so far I'd gone past the Black Lake, even, a place I seldom visit more than once a year.

Around me, the forest, dark and quiet – not a peep from bird or bee, fox or badger; no giggle of a stream running nearby, nor even wind skipping through the branches though I can *see* it moving the leaves. So: an enchantment here, and not a good one. I scan the undergrowth, the trees, looking for any sign of something that might be watching me and waiting for a moment's inattention, but there's nothing out of the ordinary, other than the sense that this is a trap laid with intent. Not necessarily to trap *me*, but anyone or anything foolish enough to wander this far from the village (so perhaps *me*, dumber than a hare). Or even those from any of the outlying cottages, the few tiny forest farms. When will its maker come back? How many such traps await? How often does whoever or whatever set it check it? Or is that person or creature a long-gone thing, and only these snares remain? Or do they bide their time?

Not knowing is frustrating and while the years have taught me better to keep my temper (or at least hide it), I've been sat in this cage without bars for almost two hours according to the movement of the sun. The rage isn't a sudden thing, although it feels like it could be, except I know it's been building, fuelled by vexation, that sense of being held against my will. And the memory of that very thing happening has left a mark, indelible, a well from which fury can and does bubble more and more frequently nowadays and, with a profanity, I draw my iron knife and plunge it into the heart of the maze. Blessed iron, so thoroughly grounded, so thoroughly mundane that anything eldritch cannot bear it. So weighty that it drags the unreal into the real world, makes it visible. Solid. A hittable target.

I feel rather than hear a roar, a growl, and I'm up immediately, sprinting for the edge of the circle. Then, at last, I break out, my steps no longer magic-led back into the centre. Free, I turn and spit into the trap. *So there.*

In that moment, I feel the weight of a gaze, pushing the air downwards, seeking and searching – when it passes over me I'm fool enough to breathe a sigh of relief that I've been *missed*. Which is when it doubles back, that strange gaze, and falls like an avalanche, pins me to the earth, lies upon me like a night-hag trying to steal my breath. I'm very still, although it's not as if I have much of a choice.

Abruptly, the weight's gone. It stayed long enough to make a point, but not long enough to kill me. No. It just wanted me to know that I'd been *found*.

* * *

The closer I get to home, the better I feel, although simultaneously more irked. I can't deny that some irritation stems from the fact that, usually, I'm the worst thing in the woods (bears and wolves notwithstanding) and I like it that way. The further I am from that particular patch of the woodlands, the safer it seems; I'd wandered much further than I'd meant to, and I might be fooling myself, but my cottage is warded and protected against any number of threats. It's a secure place. Whatever waits out there would be hard pressed to get in.

I hope.

Maybe it'll forget me.

Maybe something else will take its attention.

Maybe it's time to run.

That thought grates.

I ran once before; I ran so far and for so long.

This was where I came to rest.

This was the place that welcomed me and let me forget the things I'd done.

I'll not give it up, or at least not easily.

Whatever's in the forest can't be worse than what I fled.

What I did.

Thus, I will stay. I'll pretend it never happened, and life will continue as it has for the past twenty years. Yet as I approach my cottage, with its barn and gardens and tiny fields for just enough crops, I hear voices, arguing, and it suddenly feels as if this day is the start of worse ones to come.

* * *

Bright blonde curls, summer-blue eyes, a heart-shaped face and trim figure, wrapped in a travel-stained sapphire silk brocade dress, heeled boots with bows and golden cloak – the girl is not exactly dressed for camouflage. Even with limp locks, grit on her skin, shadows under her eyes and reeking of perspiration, she's a beauty, sitting on a bench seat in the little rose garden, staring across my holding, gaze fixed on the pond and the stream that flows into it. Her companion, her minder, throws exasperated glances at her as we speak, and this woman – whom I've known a very long time, and to whom I owe much – tries to convince me that this girl must be my next fosterling.

As yet, I've not let them into my home. My white-washed cottage, its angles slightly odd. The interior bright, surprisingly roomy, kitchen, bathroom, sitting room and workroom on the ground level; a cellar below that. The first floor has two bedrooms, and a third in the attic. It's a sanctuary, and I'll not easily let others over the threshold.

Witches in trouble oft find their way to dark forests and this is one of the darkest. One of the largest, hence "the Great Forest". A good place to hide. We live away from the churches and the god-hounds who serve in them. We keep ourselves hidden as well as we may; we're self-sufficient, making what we can, trading with the tinkers who roam the countryside and sometimes venture beneath the trees for what we cannot. Or bargaining with the isolated farmsteads or villages where our talents are needed (potions and powders for sickness and health, fertility or otherwise for women with already too many mouths to feed, or solutions for wives with husbands not man enough to behave like decent human beings). We're easier to find than doctors in such remote spots, and more reliable, for what we do *sticks*. No placebos come from the hand of a hedgewitch or henwife.

It's grown too hard to live in the cities, too hard to hide what we are, and even those of us who don't make weight on the witch's scale, those untouched by power, light or dark, still aren't safe. It's too hard to be a cunning woman or even a simple henwife when either term might so easily be pronounced "witch". Out here we can be safe – we can't all have the privilege of the Briars of Silverton. We've been hunted, yet we survive and sometimes parents and friends who love more than they fear send girls like this one to women like me. Sometimes girls like her go back home eventually; sometimes they can't.

This one, Rhea, can't apparently, and Fenna has spent the last ten minutes trying to cajole me into helping. To open my home. She speaks at normal volume, the girl hearing everything that's said about her, some of which is not flattering, and this tells me Fenna is at the end of her tether, and any thought of protecting feelings has long fallen by the wayside.

'Mehrab, please. Yes, she's sulky and stubborn, but she's also afraid. Give her a week, she'll settle. If she doesn't then send her away. Once she realises there's this or fending for herself, she'll buckle under.'

Will she though?

I look from Fenna with her greying hair with a thick white streak at the widow's peak, hard lined face, dark cloak over trews and shirt of browns and greens and greys – a woman who knows how to blend in – to the girl with all her golden beauty; weigh the trouble this will cause me. I've not fostered in some years, have become used to solitude and my own ways. Grumpy and impatient, I've been quite happy sinking into this stage of life. This Rhea looks like hard work.

'Where's she from?'

'Lodellan.' Something in her expression tells me there's more.

'How bad was it?'

'An insistent suitor.'

'And?'

'Later,' she says in a low voice. I look at the girl on the bench, patting the fat tabby cat that had wandered out of the forest.

Mr Tib stayed, though not invited to, even after I treated him roughly to make sure he was no shifter. I did name him, and that's my own fault for giving such encouragement. I raise my voice a little: 'Girl, what can you do?'

A defiant gaze turns on me; she holds one hand palm up and in a trice there's a single blue flame of witch-fire dancing there. Mr Tib hisses and scarpers – not from the craft, but the flame, so close. She holds my stare, does this Rhea, and I know I should say *No.* I should say *Take her elsewhere, Fenna!* But I don't. There's something in her face that reminds me of another's – not the looks, no, but the expression, the *air.* A sadness at the heart of the insolence. (A voice in my head whispers *Be bold, be bold but not too bold*, and another replies *Be as bold as you like!*) It reminds me of my debt to another, unpaid. The force of that failure presses the words 'All right' from my mouth and makes me nod. I can't help but think it's the worst decision I've ever made – but I know that's not true.

2

It's still early spring and there's a nip in the evening air so I build up the fire in the sitting room. Fenna takes the long sofa (a tapestry of roses and unicorns, many cushions, not exactly comfortable but I imagine a novelty for someone who's constantly travelling), and I my usual wingback chair with the knitted rug rolled into the curve of my back for support. Aching joints, tired muscles and creaking bones have become my constant companions in recent months. Them and the hot flushes, periodic forgetfulness and the rage. The spectacular all-consuming fury that comes over with little warning – as it did in the forest this morning – at the slightest frustration of my wishes.

I know it's the changing of my life's seasons, shifting me to autumn. It happens to us all, women, but I don't have to be happy about it. There are things I do not miss, like the red flux and its attendant pains and risks. No children will come from me, and I might no longer turn all heads (I'm vain enough to have enjoyed that), but there are benefits to passing without notice. I'm not done yet, not with life; I no longer bleed, and my blood is my own now.

I read once of an old woman mourning her loss of beauty, her youth. Written by a man, he put words into her mouth, and grief, had her wail that she was a swan swallowed by a dragon. That the dragon of old age with all its folds and scales and ruination had devoured her loveliness, that swan trapped inside. This I'll tell you: I had youth and sufficient looks and the influence that comes with them – yet all are fleeting, ephemeral. But the other thing? The power that lives inside, that can't be seen except by my actions and my will? That power's eternal. *That's* the power of the dragon. The dragon didn't swallow the swan but rather came forth from it, has a power the swan could never wield, a fire that would singe feathers and roast tender meat. Some days I envy young women their looks and grace, but I have dragon-fire and no one can take that from me, neither by injury nor time nor the hand of man. I know which I'd rather have.

'What was that?' Fenna's looking at me over the top of her mug of warm honeyed rum; I hope I wasn't talking aloud. The habits of living alone can sometimes be incompatible with company.

'Muttering. Sorry. Too long on my own, must remember how to be a proper person.'

'Were you ever that?' She laughs and farts as she does it.

I wave a hand to dispel the stink. 'Probably not. And did you die at some point?'

She snorts, then sobers. 'Sometimes I feel that way, I get so tired.'

'How much longer, do you think? Doing what you do?' I've known Fenna for twenty years, she was the one who guided me here when I needed help, and she's a good decade older than me at least. When I had to hide… she doesn't know all of the details and nor should she ever, but she knows enough. That I was on the run, that I couldn't risk being found and, even then, she was helping women like me. 'Will your apprentices continue?'

'There's two or three I might rely on.'

'So few?'

'Many have been lost.' She sighs, continues, 'The women I help are dangerous or seen as such. They're pursued so viciously and anyone aiding them is at risk.'

'Yet no one's betrayed you?'

'My girls. My apprentices… Those who've been caught have taken their own lives rather than be dragged to the church prisons and tortured.' She grins. 'And they've taken as many god-hounds with them as they can. I hear, in the aftermath, what happens – whether it be fire or flood, or a concealed knife. Somehow, I always hear.' She closes her eyes briefly. 'And I'm not the only one. There are others who walk the paths and gather our lost girls.'

The girl, Rhea, went straight to bed after dinner, sulked her way to the small attic room that's kept for guests and the occasional refugee witch. She said barely a word to either of us, managed to mutter *thank you* when the shepherd's pie was served, but not much more than that. I clear my throat, eyes lifting skyward. 'What more do you know about this one? A flammable suitor, you said?'

'Insistent and flammable. All I know is that the father made the match, and the girl was not amenable. And the suitor thought to convince her…'

'Ruin her for anyone else?'

She nods. 'Her mother knew about her daughter's talents, also knew enough to be able to contact a Visiting Sister. They got her out of the city, and onward.' Fenna shakes her head. 'She's not said much but I fear the father would have handed her over to the church to save his own hide and reputation.'

The Visiting Sisters are so-called, for what man takes an interest in a woman's relatives unless they're there to cook or clean or bed him? Thus they pass beneath notice, dismissed as easily as women's words are as gossip. Unofficial, whispered, a thread and a lifeline. For a long time unsuspected, until recent years.

'She passed through more than two dozen hands, an atlas-worth of towns and even more villages, walked through forests untravelled, along rivers to break the scent if – when – they come with dogs, and spells were laid in her path to send any pursuers astray. All before she came to me. The trail's as broken as it can be.'

I shake my head, a little morose. 'You can't vouch for the quality of those spells or the ones casting them.'

'Mehrab, if you doubt everything and everyone, you'd never help anyone. You may as well give up and lie down, waiting for death.'

'We're all just waiting for death.'

'Gods, you're cheery! What happened?'

I pause, poking at the tender spot inside me, the prideful part. 'In the woods, today. I chased a hare, deeper than I've ever been. The creature disappeared, but I found – was caught in – a trap. Cut as a penitents' path in a clearing – held me like a cobweb holds a fly.'

'So far out?' She shakes her head. 'Did you see anything?'

'No. But I *felt* something, some awareness of me.'

'How'd you escape?'

'Rage. I'd thought to try and re-carve part of it, dig the channels so the magic flowed differently, but I threw a tantrum instead, stabbed my dagger into the earth at its centre.'

'Iron?'

I nod.

'Odd. Odd place to set such a trap. The hare – ordinary or otherwise?'

'Couldn't tell you. Didn't seem anything peculiar about it, but how can one tell a shifter-witch from its animal shape? The whole point's that they're indistinguishable, so unless you see one mid-change…' *Or you can get your hands on it,* feel *its bones and being.* I shrug. 'But it moved fast, and I followed longer than I usually would have.' I think back to how I felt, to the searing hunger as I ran. 'But I wanted the damned thing, I wanted to catch it, kill it, a burning desire all out of proportion with anything I've ever felt' – or in a long time, at least – 'and so I kept going. The usual aches and pains didn't stop me. I felt… younger.'

And I only realise these things *now.* Now that I examine them – the arrival of my unexpected guests distracted me from considering earlier – and if Fenna and Rhea had not been here would I have given the incident in the forest further thought? Or would it have drifted off, the spiderweb thread of memory dissolving?

'Something laid long ago? The trap? Forgotten and unsprung?'

'Until me.'

'Until you.'

'Cannot say. I'll avoid that part of the woods in future.' I sigh. 'And where to next for you, Fenna?'

She shakes her head. 'I think north. There's word that the Darklands have changed – rumours trickling down that the Leech Lords are gone. Gone in one night, so they whisper.'

'How? Who might have done that?' I frown. It seems unlikely. Too great a thing to have happened, quickly or otherwise.

'I know. Hence my going north. I'll see the Briars in Silverton first, maybe they know something.'

I nod. Ructions in the Darklands, traps in the forest, a new fosterling. This morning the world seemed so simple, hidden here deep in the woods. Nothing and no one to bother me. Then: that hare crossing my path. Me, filled with the lust of the hunt, the certainty that if I didn't take that creature for the stew pot then starvation would be upon me. Yes, my snares have been empty; yes, the offerings from the village have been fewer – but it's the start of spring, there's less need of me, no colds and agues at the moment. Soon, however, birthing will begin and I'll be called. Hunger is not so close to me – in the cellar are bottles and barrels of preserved food – starvation is not anywhere near. Why was I so sure it was?

I don't share these questions – don't need anyone deciding that living out here is affecting my mind, that aging is taking my faculties so soon. These thoughts are my own and I'll keep them to myself, at least until I have answers.

'Ah, well,' I say. 'We're not strangers to strangeness.'

'No, we are not.' She sniggers. 'But speaking of strange…'

I raise an eyebrow.

'To the west, there's a great kingdom – years ago the ruling family was overthrown, all slaughtered, it was thought. But now…' Fenna waves a finger at me, making sure I'm listening – '*Now* comes a princess, her face all scarred, claiming to be of "the blood". Now comes the princess who was hidden and forgotten. Now comes the one who will claim her throne and restore the family line.'

And I try so hard not to react. I try to freeze my limbs and my features, to not stiffen in my chair, to not gasp or cry out. I try not to show that this has any effect on me, on this day which has been filled with outlandish things. I needn't have bothered. Fenna's not paying attention, she's draining her drink; she'll want another soon so I force myself upwards, go to the kitchen and heat more honeyed rum.

My hands shake as I do so, listening to her chatter trickle through the doorway. The tale told often for years, then as those years grew longer and further from the source, told less and less. A tale that travelled quite a distance – the savagery of the slaughter, the flames that rose over that city of renown, the losses sustained, the riches gained, the new rulers never quite able to keep hold of the crown and replaced by successive pretenders over and over. The latest one the longest lasting, a wielder of sword and whip, the most brutal yet.

And now, a princess, her face all scarred…

I shake my head. Not my story. Nothing to do with me. I let her words wash over me, pretend I cannot hear. I will not think on it.

3

Fenna left before dawn, without saying goodbye to Rhea, which appears to have made her even more sour than yesterday. Though the girl didn't seem overly attached to her minder, perhaps being passed from hand to hand, in constant motion, is discombobulating and losing even the slightest connection is upsetting. In fact, I *know* it is, so I try to be kinder over breakfast, which has no effect whatsoever – I'm treated to one-word answers and grunts that I'm quite sure her rich parents didn't teach her or, if they did, never intended her to use in any situation because for all intents and purposes she was raised to be a *lady*.

It's only when I finish my porridge, wash my bowl and cup (leaving her to hers), and check the contents of the small backpack I prepared last night (hatchet, length of rope, rolled leather kit of medicinal items, a water skin and a ploughman's lunch) that she shows some interest. She follows me out the front door, hesitating on the threshold, sounding childlike as she asks, 'Where are you going?'

'To the woods, I've things to do.'

'Can I come?'

'Best not.' I can't think of anything worse than mother-henning this brat when I'm trying to concentrate. 'Stay here and settle in, rest. There'll be work to do if you're willing – and even if you're unwilling, work is the price of your safety. Many have deemed you worth saving and put themselves at risk to do so. If you're going to be in my home, then you'll be helping around the place.'

'I want…' She stops and I can see the effort it takes her not to demand. To say *please*. 'Please. I want to go for a walk that's not a forced march for my life. I will help, but… today I want to *stroll*. I want to explore. And… I don't want to be alone.'

I decide against taking the bow today, ensure the knife's in the sheath on my belt, and hitch my skirt up to one side to make the walking easier. My trews need mending and I wonder if the girl's got any skill with a needle; it's something I hate doing. I'm careful not to look at her as her voice trembles until she clears her throat, speaks firmly once more. 'Please.'

'You can come along if you promise to do as you're told. No questions, no arguments.'

She nods without hesitation.

I point at her fine dress, dirty as it is. 'That's all you've got to wear?' I know it is; she arrived in it, no pack or other baggage. 'We'll have to see to that soon.' She clutches at her fine blue skirts and I recognise the gesture – the idea of letting go of the last connection to home feels like a physical blow. I'm taller than she, my clothes would hang on her like a child playing dress-ups. There'll be something we can take up, perhaps, but not right now. It was months before I burned my finery, before I could bring myself to let go of those silken rags. 'Don't worry, we'll clean that up, make it like new. You won't lose it.'

She nods. 'Thank you.'

I look at the shoes peeking from beneath the hem of her skirt: terribly fine though worn-looking. Her only choice – my feet are much bigger than hers, so my second-best boots won't help. She'll just have to cope. 'I'll have the cobbler make you a sturdy pair of clod-hoppers. They'll be ugly but will see you through winter and any further travels, should you need to flee.'

The joke falls flat as she pales; clearly the idea of taking to the roads again is not appealing.

'Come along.'

But as I close the door behind her and turn towards the path that will lead from my holding and into the woods, I see someone standing just beyond the tree line. My heart thuds, thinking of yesterday deep in the woods, of the sense of being *found*, and hold my breath. Then the figure steps out of the shade and resolves into a man and a woman peering over his shoulder before her shadow separates from his and they both walk reluctantly towards the gate in the white picket fence. I move to meet them, urging Rhea to go back in the cottage.

Up closer, I recognise them: the bakers, Anselm and Gida Hadderholm. They live in the village almost an hour's walk away – Berhta's Forge – far enough for it to be an effort to come here, and the village itself far enough from civilisation that no church has ever been built there. No bells ever to ring in the Great Forest.

'Hello, Gida, Anselm,' I say gently. Even in places where churches and god-hounds are few and far between, people can be tentative about coming to see a witch in the woods. 'How can I help? Are you unwell?'

Anselm's hulking, bearded, a smattering of flour still in his hair, small puffs of it across his dark jacket as if he dressed in a hurry and his wife was too distracted to dust him down, or no longer loves him enough to do so. As I recall they're a loving couple, no violence between them. She's small, delicate, seeming to curve in on herself; sometimes that's aging but many women learn to take up more space rather than less. Perhaps in this case it's something else.

Anselm shakes his head. 'We can see you're about to go out' – a convenient excuse to not cross my threshold – 'and we don't wish to trouble you, but—'

'—our daughter's missing. The youngest,' Gida interjects, her pitch high, sharp. 'And we cannot find her. We hoped you—'

'—we can pay.' Anselm's pulling a coin purse from his pocket, waving it in my direction like a carrot to a donkey. Not the sack or basket of bread and cheese or game that's my usual payment-in-kind. 'We can pay for your help. Only we thought you might be able to see her? See where she's gone?'

They've not brought things I can actually use because, for some reason, they think this is a gold coin service. That its value is beyond that of food (which is foolish – what can I use coin for out here?). Holding up a silencing hand, I ask, 'When did she disappear? Where was she last seen?'

'Three days ago. Ari went to collect mushrooms.' Gida's wringing her fingers now, fit to twist them off though I don't think she's aware of the motion.

'And you've been searching?'

Anselm nods. 'No sign.'

'What was she wearing?' I address Gida – many fathers are

barely able to recall their children's faces, let alone clothing.

'A blue shift. A red cloak. Her grandmother made it,' sobs Gida. 'She loves the colour so, my dear girl.'

Neither of them have paid attention to Rhea – whom I note has *not* gone back inside – until now, and the haunted stares make me think their Ari is another bright girl who likes to stand out. 'That's my cousin's child come to visit,' I lie. 'How old is Ari?'

'Eleven next month. Dark hair, brown eyes. Not tall. Takes after me,' says Gida around the eruptions of hiccups she's developed in trying to suppress her weeping. I try to remember if I've met the child, but there's only a hazy recollection of the older children, all moved away now to larger towns or small farms in the forest, with their own families started.

'Did she go past Falda's holding? Or Brecca's?'

'Falda's. The mushrooms were growing by the pond there – the far bank.' Hastily said in case anyone thinks they'd sent their child to steal from another's land.

And not so far from the village. 'You've spoken to Falda?'

They nod. 'Except she wasn't home – was at the smithy, having her horse re-shod by Faolan.'

The name makes me twitch. 'Who saw Ari last?'

'Caraid Cawes' children, we think. They saw her walk past while they were playing on the common. No one else has spoken up.'

Or no one else who'll admit it.

The Hadderholms have always been polite when I've been in the village, bought some of their pastries as a treat, dropped my wheat at the mill next door run by Anselm's sister. Gida herself has visited the cottage on her own, sat at my table, drunk my tea, taken what medicines I've offered, asked me to read cards for the future of this endeavour and that. This, however, is the first time Anselm has come to the woods, and there's a sense they're here out of desperation; he's searched as far as he's brave enough to, now wants me to do better. I wonder, if Gida were alone, would she come inside?

'I'll keep a look out today when I'm in the forest.' Although why she'd have come this far is beyond me, but it occurs that no one's brave enough to search *this far* into the forest. 'If I can find no sign, I'll scry tonight.'

'Why not now?' demands the baker and I glare.

'I'll forgive you that, because I know you're worried for your child, Anselm.' I say this to remind him that I'm a witch and I know his name, and my kind might use such a thing for good or ill. 'Scrying requires much effort, and it costs me dearly.'

'We can pay!' Again, the purse is waved at me.

'It's not a matter of money. I'll take no payment for this. Now, do you have something of hers for me?' Gida pulls a handkerchief – white and embroidered, a fine thing, a name-day gift – from inside her cloak and hands it over. 'Thank you. Go home. I'll come to you when I know anything, whether it's good or bad.'

'When?' cries Gida.

'When I can.' I hold up a hand once more. 'As soon as I can. Gida, you've trusted me before. I bid you do so again.'

I can see their reluctance, but in the end they leave. They move off, re-join the path that leads into the forest, that will take them back home, to a house that's emptier than it should be, to rooms that echo not as they should.

* * *

'Will you be able to find the child?'

I'd almost forgotten Rhea was trailing behind me. I'd waited until the couple had disappeared into the undergrowth before trotting off in the opposite direction. Hadn't mitigated my pace to account for Rhea's pretty, pointless shoes; so, I slow down, and she falls in beside me, where the path is wide, puffing a little.

'I don't know. I'll try. I've another task today that cannot wait, but I'll keep an eye out. You should too – you need to get to know the forest for however long you stay. I can't chaperone you every hour of every day.'

'I don't expect you to!' Defensive.

'It's easy to get lost is all I'm saying.'

'Shouldn't we be searching where the child was last seen?'

As if I'm going to take her into the village so soon. I shrug. 'Search parties have been doing that for three days. If they couldn't find her close to home then she's wandered farther afield, either by her own will or not.'

'If not?'

'Then perhaps none can find her.' I shake my head. 'There may well be no sign of her out here.'

'What about that trap you were in? That you told Fenna about?'

I look sideways at her. 'Someone's got big ears.'

She reddens but doesn't break eye contact. 'My mother always says the only way to learn anything useful is to listen.'

'Wise woman, your mother. Just remember that eavesdroppers hear no good of themselves either.'

She snorts.

I go on: 'Since you were listening, you'll recall that trap might not be newly laid. Could be old, old, old. Something from a decade ago, a century, more. People leave behind layers of their existence, which are easier to see in cities, but in forests? More easily concealed here because of regrowth, because there are fewer folk around, and things can lie undiscovered for a very long time indeed. If Ari fell into such a trap – just as if she drowned in a lake or fell off a cliff or into an abyss, or broke an ankle, a leg, too far for anyone to hear her cries? We'll likely never know.'

'And if you scry? Will you *know*?' She sounds eager and I wonder how much she's been taught, about her own power, that of others.

'Perhaps.' We come to an intersection with our path. 'For now, there are lessons to learn. See the trunk of that tree at your left? Yes? See the leaves? Look at them carefully so you recognise them. Feel the right side of the trunk, about head height – mine, not yours – what's there, beneath your fingertips?'

'A carving – an arrow!' She laughs, pleased with herself.

'Lesson number one: whenever you come to a crossroad like this? In my part of the woods? There'll be an arrow as a guide. If you can't find one then you've strayed – retrace your steps. Eventually you'll be able to make your way without them, but for the moment they'll help keep you on the path.' I nod. 'Come along. More to do.'

4

'You need to make sure they're not too green, but not too brown either,' I explain, but the girl's not listening, not really. There's a pond in the middle of the grove, tremendously still, and she's staring into it. I'm about to snarl, instead I take a moment to watch her when she's unaware.

Curls lifted by a spring breeze that's still got the echo of last winter behind it, eyes bright, hands at her face, touching the skin briefly – then she shakes as if waking. And I'm suddenly certain it's not vanity, this gazing at her own reflection. It's wonderment that she's still alive. Her hide's intact. She's not been hanged or burned, drowned or pierced so many times her outside cannot keep her innards where they need to be. Perhaps she's thinking of how the all-too-insistent suitor turned so quickly crisp.

I clear my throat, am glad I didn't simply snap at her. We've gotten on well today thus far. There's nothing worse than living with someone whose breath you want to stop, and if I can't bear her, nor she me, she'll have to find another fostering, another teacher, and frankly most of my kind look askance at one who's been passed on, especially when so much depends on it. I remind myself to be patient.

'Rhea?' Yet I can't resist a little sting, no matter how gentle my tone. 'Kindly do me the courtesy of paying some attention.'

She startles guiltily. 'I'm sorry, Mehrab. I was just…'

Rhea chooses not to explain, perhaps thinking there's nothing she can say that won't sound bad; instead she clasps her hands in front of the fine fabric of her skirts, setting her chin at the slightest of angles, and doing her best to make me believe she'll follow my lesson. I stare for a few moments longer, knowing the weight of my gaze is burdensome, bright green and penetrating, then shift sidewards so she can more clearly see what I'm doing.

'You *need* to make sure they're not too green, but not too brown either,' I repeat, and she nods. 'Too green means weak and whippy; too brown means inflexible, already on the way to half-dead.' She nods again. 'The choosing takes time, or it should, if you wish to avoid an unpleasant season. Indeed, a series of them if you keep choosing poorly.'

Pointing to the sapling which is on the edge of my favoured grove – they're well watered and get just enough light through the canopy – I continue: 'This one? Right here? Too thin. To the untrained eye, it looks elegant, slender, but trust me, it's naught but frail.'

Rhea leans closer, fixes her gaze to where my fingers direct. I do my best not to notice how many age spots litter the backs of my hands; hers are so white, plump. I hate her just a little, though I try not to, truly I do. I swallow it down, bile-bitter. 'See this bend, this angle? Note how the crook is a little too deep; too easy for fractures to begin there. Once they start, there's nothing you can do about it. Things will grow out of true, and it'll always be feeble.'

I step away from the reject, move further in, slipping between the bigger trees with their rough bark, spreading branches well above my head. Too old, these, too well established, too much *themselves*, unlikely to be bent to another's will or be reshaped, at least not without consequences. But I've taken most of my previous harvest from this copse (not the *other*, not any longer), and the feel of them is right. They've served me well more times than they've failed. Just need to find the correct one for this season.

Behind me I hear Rhea stumble and swear. Her dress will be catching on outstretched branches, the smooth soles of her city shoes not finding grip on uneven ground; rocks and pebbles and roots are hazards for her. I'm sure she can dance a carola like a princess, catch the eyes of lords and earls and god-hounds with such leanings (at least until they realise what she is), but she cannot walk a steady line in the woods. This amuses me far too much and I don't like my own meanness, it feels like acid and I've never been partial to things that burn, inside or out.

Pausing, I wait for her to catch up. A fresh breeze wings through the boughs, rustles leaves, makes the trees loom almost as if, well, alive, but more human-alive, I suppose. I feel like our presence has been noted (yet not in a malign fashion). 'You need to watch where you're going, Rhea. At least at first. It's not like city streets, friendly to your feet.'

'Lodellan cobblestones aren't in the least bit friendly,' she snaps.

‘Never been there myself,’ I answer lightly. It’s true, I was born elsewhere, far across the sea, in another great city, had a life there until it became too dangerous for a variety of reasons. I remind myself that criticism isn’t helpful, that I’ve lost the habit of being around others, of softening myself for them. ‘Watch first, feel with your soles; eventually you’ll learn how to balance. It’ll come as naturally as breathing.’

‘Thank you, Mehrab.’ Her tone’s a little forced; the effort of being gracious is telling. For both of us, I suppose. I wonder once more how long she’ll last here.

We step into a patch of light and savour it; the warmth is wonderful after the cool shade. Both of us raise our faces like flowers. The moment passes when a cloud covers the sun. I shiver and Rhea follows suit. This is another clearing – several clearings in the one large grove, turned into compartments by the walls of trees. The opposite side is where we’re headed; I point. ‘That looks promising.’

When we’re standing in front of the next sapling I nod and smile. It’s the right height, too; I have my requirements.

Rhea tilts her head, slits her eyes at me. ‘It looks the same to me as all the others.’

‘And so it will, for a while, but you’ll learn.’ *You’ll learn or it’ll be lonely, hard-working summers and cold, cold winters for you.* ‘You’ll recognise them when you see them.’ I gesture. ‘Now, this one is different. Not so elegant, no, nor so slender, but see? Joints all sturdy, no places where hairline fractures might easily occur; certainly not as pretty as the other, but what use is pretty when strength is required?’ I couldn’t help that one, so I smile to soften the edge.

I remove my backpack, lay it on the ground, then roll my shoulders slowly, feel them warm up, windmill my arms, loosening the muscles. When a sweat breaks beneath the bodice of my faded green dress, I pull the hatchet and a blue whetstone from the pack – even though the blade is already sharp enough to split a hair. I slide the stone over the metal a few times for form's sake, hopeful that Rhea will take note of the habit and adopt it. 'I'm careful with my tools; I know if I take care of them, they'll take care of me. It's the same with all witching.'

'This is witching? I thought we were getting firewood – a long way from home.'

Home. I think we both pause at that slipping from her lips.

I put the stone away, lean forward and run my fingers down the sapling, thrill to the feel of not-quite-smooth-not-quite-rough bark (*Skin*, I think, and my heart beats a little faster). 'This one. Green enough to bend, brown enough to be stable; biddable, tractable; ready to withstand any kind of weather, but the worst of gales.'

'It seems a lot to ask,' Rhea says, a smile in her voice.

'My demands are not unreasonable,' I say and we laugh. 'It's *just* right.'

I take my hatchet, shiny and silver, swing back for leverage, then forward, aiming at the base of the young tree, just below where the feet will be.

* * *

It's slim still, and relatively light. Easy enough to hoist onto my shoulder and carry home, switching sides when I need to. I could make the girl do it, but she's not sure enough in those shoes. No point in having her drop it. It's not like it's a delicate thing, but still. I like to work with the best materials. Needless to bruise it before the time's right. And no point in making either of us think I'm getting too weak for physical burdens. Still, I make her take the backpack.

These trails are narrow and Rhea has to follow behind, no space for companionable conversation. Her chatter has died off anyway; she's getting tired, I can tell. It's been a long walk, and not a restful stroll for which she'd hoped. Or perhaps it was what she needed – time outside not spent running for her life. Possibly she'd not expected it to take so much of the day, the there-and-back of it, and the meal I'd packed to be too small between two. Still and all, we'd found a blackberry patch, some wild raspberries, and cherry plums which added a sweetener to the bread, cheese and salted meat. Not a huge meal, no, and her stomach's growled latterly. So has mine, and I think longingly of the pot of stew I left on the hob for dinner.

We talked for a while about what I will do with this sapling. We talked too about the process of scrying because we've seen no trace in our wandering of a small lost girl, no sign or indication that she might have passed this way. We talked about what I'll need her to do for me when I'm done with the dark mirror, and I warned her of what might happen. She grew silent then and changed the subject soon after. I asked about her parents, and while she would speak of her mother, she baulked at mentioning her father, which lends weight to Fenna's belief that he would have sacrificed his daughter to save himself. I think Rhea knows it now but had no inkling before – that she was a father's darling until she acted on her own will, did not obey his wishes, put his plans at risk. Not the first woman to find out the hard way that a father's love can be very conditional. Not all fathers, no. Didn't know my own, dead before he had a chance to disappoint, although others have told me theirs were not entirely awful.

It's getting darker but even beneath the trees the light stays a little longer on spring days. Still, I'd like to be home before dusk nips too greedily at our heels, so I walk faster. Rhea curses under her breath, but she won't like being stuck in night's forest any more than I do. When the path begins to broaden, she comes abreast once more and surprises me by saying: 'We should keep searching for the girl.'

I shake my head.

'But we've hardly done anything!'

'*You've* hardly done anything. I've kept my eye out all day, seeking broken twigs and disturbed underbrush, footprints in damp earth and dry, for some flash of pale skin or red cloak in places they don't belong!' I stop, exasperated. 'Darkness is falling. There are rivers and lakes unsuspected, deep and wide, rock-filled and so cold they'll steal your life between one breath and another. There are wolves and bears and worse – how do you think it will help anyone if you stumble into a den or a pit or a hunter's snare? Do you think I haven't also been checking for traps like the one I was already caught in? Don't be an idiot, child, your death aids no one, nor does mine. Self-sacrifice without purpose, without caution, is sheer stupidity.'

We glare for a few moments, then I set off again. I expect her to hang back and sulk, except she doesn't. She catches up again and keeps pace. I wonder if she's considering what I said or plotting revenge. About ten minutes later, from the corner of my eye I see her arm lift, hand outstretched, fingers pointing. 'More berries!' she cries, as if I've not recently snarled at her, and scampers forward. Stops.

Upon reaching her, I see what she mistook for a solid patch of cowberries or raspberries, perhaps. Up close, it's clearly none of those. A scrap of fabric, the length and width of my hand, not overly large, a darker red limning the jagged edges. Ripped from a cloak of fine crimson wool, perhaps, something knitted by a loving grandmother for a granddaughter who liked to draw the eye. I'd brought us back a different route to teach Rhea another way, and in hopes we might, perhaps, find something of Ari's passing or fate – and lo, here it is.

Or rather, here is an artefact. Can we be certain it's Ari's? Yet how many fragments of scarlet wool might be here in these woods? So distinctive?

A sign, then?

No more story to it than a broken twig – it might show a direction, but it tells no true tale, no details. It might as easily have been dropped from above, from a bird's claws. Still I nod at Rhea. 'Gather it up and bring it home with us. It'll help with what I need to do.'

5

'Ugh. Disgusting!'

Rhea has a hand over her mouth, and I can't blame her. She watched as I carefully laid the sapling on a rack in the small purpose-built room at the back of the barn where it will dry. When I closed the door and shot its three bolts, I made her promise not to go in, not even for the slightest, quickest of peeks. 'If you do, it'll be ruined. Needs to stay in there for two full days, no more, no less, and an opened door will change the temperature, moisture will get in and mould will quickly ensue. And then I'll have to start all over again and I'll not be best pleased with you.'

Had we not spent so much time in the woods yesterday, I'd have started this task when we returned, but it was full dark by the time we stumbled home, and my limbs and joints were aching. Nor did any energy remain for scrying. Today has been spent in activities I'm sure she feels are a punishment for something she didn't do. I had her help me remove the wooden lid on the old trough in the little yard behind the barn and the stench is almost overpowering; so it should be given it's been fermenting since last year's use.

The smell rose in clouds like the souls of the earth-bound released. I did tell her to stay back but she's got a cat's curiosity and will apparently only learn through painful experience; right now she's leaning forward, staring down. Experience has taught me to tie a cloth soaked with lavender oil over my mouth and nose. The trough is filled with an unappetising mixture of urine, manure, water, wine, and more than a little blood from creatures foolish enough to catch themselves in my snares, and a little of my own. A similar concoction to that which others might use to grow homunculi.

'How long?' she asks, waving a hand in front of her face as if that will help.

'Two months. The Church'll tell you their Lord created the heavens and the earth in seven days, but that sounds unlikely to me. Takes a woman nine months to gestate… I think that's just men trying to one-up everything when they know full well they can't birth anything but ideas.' I take up the long wooden paddle and begin to stir the liquid, which bubbles and pops, releasing even more odiferous gas.

Which is unfortunate for Rhea since she's mid-snigger and gets a mouthful of the foul air rising from the surface of the *broth*; gets a lungful too and stumbles away, coughing. Neither cows, nor sheep, nor goats and certainly not Fyren the ancient draught horse come near this corner of the yard at this time of year. Sometimes the cat will hang around for sheer perversity, but he doesn't remain long, preferring to curl in the sunshine or chase mice in the barn.

'Careful,' I say idly, breathing oh-so-lightly as I work. No fire required for the mixture creates its own heat. I'm sweating, this close to it, stripped down to my shift, and the cotton's sticking to me like a second skin in the midday sun. 'We've got to do this for three hours every day of the week. It needs to be attended to for two-thirds of spring, Rhea, so you'd best get used to it. Wrap a cloth around your face next time since you didn't listen to me when I said to step back.'

There's no answer, and I can hear her gagging, trying not to puke, but soon enough comes the sound of vomit spattering the dirt; a waste of breakfast. 'Sit and rest. Don't go passing out on me because I'm not leaving this task for hell or high water.'

She grumbles, says something under her breath, something I don't need to hear to get the gist. There's the creak of the wooden bench as she settles, and I take a quick glance over my shoulder. Behind her is the tiny rose garden I like to keep, the earth covered in thick green grass, rolling up and down over the tiny mounds of the little cemetery of favoured felines and others. Pale pink roses form a halo around her head. A sheen of sweat glimmers on her top lip and forehead. Even ill Rhea looks pretty.

'My, my, that is an impressive shade of green and no doubt about it,' I say. I shouldn't be so cruel or arrogant – the first time I made this blend I did exactly the same thing, only there was no one here to watch me hurl my guts. She'll be regretting her choices, I've no doubt, all the ones that led her here.

I give her an hour, while I stir the miasmic mix serenely as if it's not making my eyes water. Revelling in the strength of my body, my stamina. There's something satisfying about the action, about creating for myself, investing this time in my future. I assay some questions about her life before all this, more details about her flight from Lodellan, but she still hacks and coughs on and off, making conversation hard. So, for a while I sing — I've a sweet voice, at least, if not a nature to match — then, bored, begin to tell her tales.

'While I might be the only witch to do *this*, it's said the first one was born, not made. That it walked from the forest one day and took a wife. It's said that their children could pass unseen in the woods, could melt into the trunks of the greatest of trees and slumber for year upon year. Some stayed there, some woke and wandered, but when they returned to the place of their birthing nothing remained of their old lives, nothing that made a memory spark, so they soon found new oaks and yews and larches to sink into. It's said if you come across a woman in the woods with flowers in her hair, she's not a mortal creature.'

'So,' Rhea croaks, 'no one taught you this?'

'No one. I… thought of it myself. Dreamt it myself. Remembered the stories and wondered if there might be something I could do. After Yrse died.'

'The one who was here before you? That's the name Fenna said.'

I nod. After Yrse died. After Faolan…

My arms are aching from the repeated motions, my joy in the activity worn down, so I harry her. 'C'mon. Up! I'm not feeding and sheltering you so I can do all this myself.'

No grumbling this time and I don't bother looking over my shoulder. I simply expect obedience, and she appears at my elbow, apron wrapped carefully around her lower face, eyes slanted up at me, only a little resentful. I nod.

'Another hour, then lunch.' Handing over the paddle, I

relent: 'The hard work we do now ensures that when summer comes, Rhea, our lives will be easier.'

* * *

At dinner, Rhea's appetite makes a valiant return and she eats well. I do not – an empty stomach is best for what I'm to do. I won't lie – I'm glad to have her company while I do this. It's not entirely necessary, but on my own, it's much riskier; and the toll on the body is greater than when I was younger.

In the sitting room, I sit cross-legged on a cushion in front of the hearth. I hang four chains from a hook inside the chimney, then link their free ends together so that the shew-stone can be suspended. I've let the flames die down, but the heat radiates still and the highly polished mirror – obsidian, best for scrying – warms rapidly. On occasion, I've trekked through the forest to the Black Lake, used its oh-so-still surface to see what I want, but not today, not now, not for this. Not after the last time.

I pour a little water onto the stone, add a dash of attar of roses. The smell wafts up immediately and I pull the blade of my knife across my forearm, let the blood drip into the water and oil, paying the red price. The substances mix without any assistance, forming a smooth reflective pane. I take the scrap of red fabric Rhea found in the woods – bloodied and dirty, it'll be more powerful than the clean handkerchief Gida brought – cut away a corner and throw it onto the coals, watch as they and it begin to glow.

Glancing over at Rhea, sitting straight-backed in the armchair, watching me like a hawk, I say, 'Remember: no more than a minute,' then grab up the green apothecary's bottle from the hearth stones and drip one single drop onto my tongue. Essence of nightshade, carrying within it death and delusion, but also visions and dreams and the gift of far-seeing. If you know what you're doing. If you're careful. If it's one of your talents.

I stare at the shew-stone, marvel at how it looks like a pond undisturbed. Soon it changes from the darkest red-black to the dimness of the night-forest silvered by the moon. Without warning, I'm no longer in the cottage but flying above the trees, the air cold and crisp against my skin. I'm both moving and not. Somehow, I'm looking over the entirety of the forest from its edges to its centre, and I'm sitting on a spider's web spread over the treetops, connected down its trunks, into the very earth, into the undergrowth and blades of grass, every droplet of water in every lake and pond and puddle running off the River Ayda. I feel the heartbeat of every beast in the great dark woods, every snore and breath in the village, in every outlying farm and isolated hut and cottage like this one. But I'm seeking a particular breath, a particular heartbeat, that of a girl I may or may not have met, of the girl who wore this red cloak, the smell of its burning scrap of wool almost overwhelming the attar of roses, the rising smell of my own blood slowly cooking.

Then I'm falling.

I'm falling like a bird shot from the sky, I'm shaking in a fit, there's froth in my mouth, vomit rising, my eyelids opening and closing so hard I should be able to hear them.

And Rhea's voice, shouting in my ear '*Mehrab! Mehrab! Mehrab!*' Her hands on my shoulders, fingers in my mouth, prying my lips open despite the foam and the vomit, as she pours in a cup of curative then holds my jaws closed until some of it makes it down my throat and I pass out.

* * *

When I wake, I can smell myself, sweat and vomit but at least not piss. Not shit. There was that much control left to me at least. I'm lying on the floor, the cushion under my head, a crocheted rug over me. And, under the cushion, I realise, Rhea's lap. When she sees my eyes open, she starts to cry.

'Oh, thank the gods. I didn't know what to do.'

My throat hurts as I try to clear it. Waking in company after scrying is definitely better than alone. Patting her hand, I slowly sit up. 'You did,' I rasp, 'what I told you to. Thank you. I'm alive.'

'Barely.'

'Don't be melodramatic. I'm a little worse for wear but otherwise, I'll survive.' I shake my head, regret it. 'However, you might understand now why I'm reluctant to scry, at least as a first choice. And how much harder it is if I'm alone?'

She nods, wipes her tears away, then hands me a mug of honeyed rum. 'You should eat. I kept the stew on the hob.'

'Soon,' I say, not quite able to bear the idea of food. 'When you scry – and not all of us can do it – it's not only exhausting, it chips away part of your soul. While you're looking into the mirror, sometimes other things are looking out. Being noticed isn't always a good thing.' I think but don't say, *And when you've done dark deeds, you might attract dark things.*

'Did you see her? Did you find Ari?' she asks.

Sadly, I shake my head. 'No.'

'What's that mean? Did something go wrong?'

'It means there's no trace of her in the forest. She's not here, which means she's not alive.'

‘What if she’s outside the forest?’

Again, I shake my head. ‘It takes a month to get from where the village lies to the nearest outskirts. That’s on horseback. The girl’s been gone three days, four now. If she were alive, I’d have found her. But there’s no trace, no pulse, no thread of life or breath, and scrying doesn’t work for dead things – leastways not my version of it – so I can’t even tell her parents where they might find her body.’

6

'But why can't I go with you?'

I think Rhea would stamp her foot if I were not currently tracing around it on a piece of scrap leather. I click my tongue, and she obediently puts the right foot next to the outline and I draw again. Holding up the leather, I admire my handiwork.

'Because it's too soon, even out here – someone will still be looking for you, somewhere. The Visiting Sisters have done their very best to cover your tracks, but you can't ever let your guard down.' I don't tell her that constant vigilance is wearing and wearying because she'll feel it soon enough. 'Anselm and Gida have seen you. That's sufficient. I've told them you're my cousin's child – the easiest lie is that of a big family, and the tale I've woven for myself is that of a woman with a large and scattered family. People get used to hearing of this relative and that, and they generally don't pay much attention. It's a long while since I've had a fosterling, many weren't ever seen in the village – but you'll stand out in memory. Give it a month, let's see if anyone comes sniffing around, before I introduce you to anyone else.' I roll my eyes. 'Before the next young man decides he'd like a piece of you.'

She huffs but doesn't contradict me. 'What am I to do all day without you?'

'It'll be five hours at most.' I laugh. 'And you will spend three of those hours stirring the trough.'

'The shit bath!'

'Yes, the shit bath. Three hours. Constant stirring, slow and steady, ensuring you dig to the bottom to get the sediment to rise. Wear a mask – the lavender oil is best for covering the smell.' I rise, my knees protesting. 'Then make yourself some lunch, eat it in the sun – Mr Tib will come slinking around, I've no doubt – and when you're done, come inside. The dough in the blue bowl should be risen – knead it well, then put it into a greased pan and bake it for twenty-five minutes. Let it cool on the windowsill. Then…' I wave a hand vaguely, '…read a book, draw something, darn socks, fix the rip in my trews, nap, whatever you want except for wandering the forest or going into the village. There are books to read and learn from. Don't leave this holding. Not without me. Not until you know the place better. I'll be very cross if I have to go looking for you or drag your carcass back for burial after you've gaily got yourself killed.'

'Yes, Mehrab,' she grumbles.

I stretch, bending backwards, palms against my lower back; the spine gives a satisfying crack and everything feels a little looser, a little more comfortable. I roll up the outline of her feet and stuff it into the satchel, along with pouches of ground herbs, some small vials of liquified things, and a list of items I'll need to barter for or buy. 'I'll be home well before nightfall.'

'What if you aren't? What if you don't come back?'

'Then I'm dead.' I speak before I think and it's only her

stricken expression that makes me pause. The child's had her life entirely uprooted, her mind is directed towards unexpected catastrophes, and they're all she's looking for now. This may also explain her intense desire to find Ari, a child she's never met – most of us, I think, will reach for the illogic of *if I save another, I can save myself.* 'I'm sorry, Rhea. I didn't mean to be unkind, merely flippant. I will return – but if I don't then this cottage is yours. Stay here. It's safe, or as safe as anywhere can be for the likes of us.'

And I find myself hugging her as if she's my child to comfort.

I'm the one who breaks away first, grabbing up the satchel and hooking it over my head so it lies flat against my back. 'Don't forget: three hours of stirring shit.'

* * *

Birdsong and sunlight are my companions on the walk. Those and the chant of the river running beside this stretch of the path. The spring breeze is cool and rattles the branches. On my own again I begin to feel more myself, relaxing into my old shape. Two and a half days of companionship is taking its toll – not Rhea's fault, nor even Fenna's. Mine. I've become so used to my own company that even the knowledge of another in my space is grating. It won't last, I'll grow accustomed to it, or I won't. Those who preceded her – Melda, Aythe, Gele, Lisabeth, Uriela – were younger, children really, while she's almost eighteen. They were disinclined to question, fearful enough to listen and learn. Not all children listen, of course, and I think about Ari – did she stray from the path?

In the general way of things, children go missing, no matter how vigilant parents might be. Children have gotten lost for centuries. The village however, as I recall, has been safe, or seemed so. Yrse I'm sure said the same thing. Of course, some have died of illnesses, of accidents occasioned by idiocy or misfortune, some of punishments too enthusiastically administered – but none have wandered from Berhta's Forge and never come home, not in the twenty years I've lived in its environs.

When a child disappears, it might be animal predation. It might be a killer hiding in plain sight of neighbours and friends. It might be someone seeking a slave, a child-wife, child-husband, someone on whom to vent frustrations. None of their reasons are ever good. Sometimes for revenge or merely a meal. Sometimes an old god roams, looking for a treat, for a new lease on life; yet mostly they stay hidden in the darkest hollows.

But yes, in the general way of things children go missing… elsewhere.

There's the tale of the village of Iserthal, once a prosperous place, now a ruin no longer even noted on any but the most ancient of maps. Its children were taken but not by a god, or not a proper one. A plague maiden, who swam up through the frozen lake in winter and stole them all away. There's a whisper, though, that two were spared but of them there's no trace…

There's the legend of a giant swan that floated down the River Bale close by Angharad's Ruin and coaxed three children onto its back and promptly floated off again. Not a trace of either the trio or swan was ever found.

The story of a witch who built a cottage of sugar to lure children inside so she might thereby be furnished with her dinner. They say her own offspring had been lost in one of the devastating famines that swept the land, when bands of men who filed their teeth to points roamed and plucked tender children from their homes. It never made sense to me that the witch would do what had been done to her, but then grief is an unpredictable thing.

The recountings of the old days of the battle abbeys, when archbishops and mother superiors both would "recruit" children found running in the streets without a parent, sometimes simply standing in their own gardens, all taken off to be trained in the church militant.

And the story of a man who came in the guise of a friend at the dinner table and in the cold hours stole away the offspring of a great lineage. It's never been simply the children of the poor and undefended; great houses and castles, grand families and the rich and powerful have also had their future purloined and never recovered. Perhaps a small sad pile of bones found here and there, perhaps a memento, a trophy returned and left on a doorstep to be found in the morning and break a heart. Or a flayed skin hanging from a tree, a dream-catcher woven of a child's hair and hung in a window A scrap of woollen fabric draped on a bush…

I shake my head, come back to myself.

My pace has increased as my thoughts have galloped and as a result, I've made good time. Standing on the outskirts of Berhta's Forge, I take a deep breath, calming myself against the unwonted press of people, and the news I must deliver. When I step over the boundary, I feel the earth shift a little beneath my feet as I enter someone else's demesne.

* * *

There's only one real road leading into Berhta's Forge – as in a road intended as such, packed down hard and maintained – but many paths in and out, many smaller thoroughfares that wind through the forest and lead to other farms, the bigger orchards, bigger crop fields, the wood mill a little downstream, to the preferred swimming location and thc other more secret ones, the spots where some still do their washing. To get to the main road that leads to the few other towns and villages buried in the Great Forest you've got half a day's ride on our "proper" road.

No wall or fence around the village, it's remarkably unfortified, relying mainly on its remoteness from anything and anyone; even groups of brigands either avoid it, can't find it or simply think it not worth the bother of raiding. Sort of an insult but also a protection.

There's a distinct lack of a castle or true grand manor, and no church, which means no place where holy treasures and relics might be found. The place is small, out of the way, so far from Lodellan as to be too inconvenient to worry about – and the folk hereabouts tend to worship older, greener gods even if they're smart enough not to make a great showing of it. Every home has a green woman carved somewhere on its façade, no matter how small she might be.

Festivals cycle in with the seasons, with harvests and solstices, with the days when veils between worlds are thin and the dead might pass back and forth. All in all, the best sort of place for a witch to live; near those who are less than devoted to the church and whose home remains uncontaminated by god-hounds, even though they're still afraid of us. Of me.

It's a pretty village, I suppose – I can't help but compare

everywhere to the grand city of my birth, no matter what happened there – and well laid out. Built by the banks of the River Ayda, there's not much stone hereabouts, or not so easily acquired, so most houses are either of wattle and daub or wood, rough-hewn or polished, depending on the prosperity of the owner.

Thatched roofs are all overgrown with flowering vines that have wormed their way inside and are sometimes trained around a ceiling rose or hanging light, over a mantlepiece or a bedhead or canopy. The only building mostly of stone (by all accounts brought in on carts at great expense by a long-ago ancestor) is the home of Thaddeus Peppergill, the headman, alderman, mayor or whatever title he might fancy on whatever day. Not a bad stick, just a little jumped-up, a little promiscuous, but he does care in his own way for the seven hundred or so souls under his hand.

Roughly u-shaped with a market space in the centre around the well, and the first boundary is mostly shops – butcher, seamstress, cheese-monger, apothecary, general groceries. The blacksmith is one terminal, the inn marks the other. At the far end, the base of the u, are the bakery and millhouse – a joint venture between Anselm and his sister Sanne (as big as her brother, unmarried with no wish to become otherwise) with living quarters upstairs – right on the riverbank, with the water to keep the millstone turning day and night, and a mill pond that runs off the river, still and surprisingly deep.

Beside the inn is an expansive green for common grazing, for ballgames and chasey, for festival feasts and sacred burnings when it's time for such things. Behind this is the first row of houses and holdings, somewhat higgledy-piggledy with yards and gardens of different sizes, but generally orderly. Nestled in here is the school that children attend until they're twelve, when they go to apprenticeships or farm work or family businesses or some few away to study. Behind are more such houses, and more rows and more – the homes getting smaller and less impressive the further out one goes, but the barns and outbuildings growing proportionally larger.

Architecture's not an outstanding feature, but it's picturesque nonetheless. It is, now, a town. A village when I arrived, but Berhta's Forge has grown. No one has yet thought to begin calling it "town", and I don't like to acknowledge it because I know that the larger the place becomes, the more people it will attract for various reasons – and the more dangerous it will become for me and my kind. There are shops with glass in their windows rather than simply a small circus of market stalls; there are specialist goods sought after by other towns and cities; more merchants visit by the year. Eventually, a church will be built, old ways will be stamped out or co-opted; Thad Peppergill will find himself set aside on feast days and solstices, no longer leading ceremonies. A god-hound will take his place, will harry folk to come to worship a jealous god, to obey without question, to allow no patience with difference in order to survive because god-hounds have never understood tolerance. Yes, the day will come when I must leave, but until then I'll call this place a village.

I don't use the main thoroughfare in; my path lets out at a far corner of the green and I'm thus able to avoid the smithy as I step into the small bustle of bodies going about their business, and make my way towards the bakery and mill. Part of me would prefer to do this task after my others; part of me would like to put it off as long as possible, but I'd not want grieving parents to think they'd been put last. As I push through the crowd, I feel the buzz as I'm recognised, as folk step aside to make way, murmuring greetings. The air feels heavier and the noise levels lower, eyes feel almost as a weight on me. When I was younger and didn't know any better I used to let this upset and unsettle me, being noticed, being different. Now every part of me is carefully schooled: my expression remains pleasantly remote, or remotely pleasant, my posture is very straight, shoulders back, my gait smooth and even, almost a glide, my chin tilted up just enough to border on imperious. There's a fine line between respect and fear, and it's the work of a lifetime to maintain the balance.

At last I'm at the yellow door to the bakery, hand raised to knock; the sound of the waterwheel dipping and splashing into the river and the simultaneous rumbling of the grindstone inside the mill next door fill my ears loud as can be. Finally, I force myself to rap on the wood.

The door's opened so quickly I almost topple in. Gida takes one look at my face and bursts into tears, falling forward. I half-carry her back inside, into the large bright kitchen where all the baking takes place, and coax her onto one of the high stools around the long table. I can smell yeast and sugar and the scent of warm bread. The light is so strong that it seems to wash Gida out completely; for a moment she's a blank white oval. I'm bending towards her as she weeps, trying to calm her, when I'm plucked upwards by an elbow, my joints straining.

Anselm drops me as I shout, and bawls: 'What did you do to her?'

'Nothing! I'm here at your request!' And the fact I spent my evening throwing up more than once from the aftereffects of the nightshade only to be met with this welcome does nothing for my temper. Taking a deep breath, I remind myself they've lost a child.

Gida gasps out, 'I saw her face and I just knew…'

I move away from them towards the sinks and the big window behind that looks out over the river, stare at the smooth flow of water while the sobbing slows, while Anselm croons to his wife. There's a kettle on the stovetop that feels hot enough to be recently boiled and, in a cupboard, I find a ceramic teapot and mugs, old enough for the glaze to have crackled. Retrieving chamomile leaves from my satchel, I make tea, don't let it steep too long, then hand mugs to Gida and Anselm. 'Drink.'

They both obey. The baker, with a hangdog look, apologises. I take one of the tall stools and indicate that he should sit beside his wife.

'The day you came to me, I searched and found no sign until late in the afternoon, and that was just a scrap of her cloak. Last night I scried for her presence, across the forest.' I still looked ill this morning, pale, eyes bloodshot, so the physical cost of the experience remains writ on me. 'I'm sorry, but there was no trace.'

'What are you saying?' Anselm begins to rise from his seat – I cannot tell if he is immediately trying to be threatening or it's simply a function of his size. Nevertheless, I lose my temper.

‘Ah, gods-shit, man. Sit down. I swear I’ll set a pox upon you! I’ve tried to help! I didn’t lose your child for you – that’s your own sin to bear!’

Anselm deflates, sinking down, seeming to become half his actual size. It was cruel, but I won’t be blamed for what’s not my fault, and my voice is calmer when I speak. ‘I’m sorry. You know I’d find her if I could. If she were still alive. There’s no more I can do.’ I hesitate. ‘There’s… there was blood on the scrap of cloak – perhaps a wolf, or bear, recently risen from hibernation and starving. You’d best warn others just in case, make sure children aren’t left alone, that they’re home before dark.’

From my pocket I pull the embroidered handkerchief that Gida gave me, return it to her. Watch her fingers pluck at it, until she says, ‘Do you have the piece of her cloak still? Can I have that?’

‘It was consumed in the scrying.’ A lie – the last scrap is secreted in a drawer in my workroom. It might be useful yet for something or other, filled as it is with a grandmother’s love and loss, the child’s joy in it, and her death. Besides, if I give it to her, she’ll spend her years mourning over it in a way she won’t with that pretty square of cambric. Best she not have anything to waste her tears on; they have other children and grandchildren who need her attention and I’ve seen more than one parent neglect those who remain for mourning the memory of the lost.

Anselm tries to offer payment as I leave; I tell him no. Not because of a failure but because it simply wouldn’t be right. Outside, I steady myself in the bracing air, trying to shake off the grief welling in the rooms behind me.

7

I drop the pattern in to Edric the Cordwainer, who looks pleased to see me; perhaps business has been slow. He supplements his income by the manufacture of bags and belts, saddles and bridles, straps and aprons; any purpose or shape to which leather can be bent. The shop is small, an outpost of the felt-makers' building, really. (Felt is one of the items produced in Berhta's Forge that goes out into the world in bulk, commanding high prices, turned into protective vests and tunics for soldiers, horse blankets, hats, boot lining, jackets to ward off winter, and padding for any number of things). I choose a buttery tan leather – I'd not thought to ask Rhea what she'd prefer, but since I'm paying for them, she'll like it or lump it – ask for the soles to be thick and the lining of sheepskin. I tell him they're for a young cousin because he knows my feet aren't that small, and I pay the price he asks even though it makes my eyes water as it doesn't pay to insult the man who makes your footwear when winter's as cruel as it is in these parts.

At the seamstress's shop, I exchange pleasantries with Mistress Godiva, and a little gossip: Rosina Tolkas's daughter is pregnant, and Rosina demanded payment from the boy's father in the form of one of the cottages the family owns. Godiva says he gave in less out of shame and more from a desire to no longer be yelled at. Good for Rosina, I say, and Godiva agrees. Edberg Zimmer, his wife gone to her well-deserved rest, has been trying to talk one of twelve village widows into marrying him (one at a time, not all at once, moving on after each rejection); alas for his plans none of them are foolish enough to accept his proposal. Why would they inconvenience themselves? I ask and Godiva agrees. And Ceryth Danby's got her ninth child on the way and doesn't know what's causing it. Someone should tell her, I say, and Godiva agrees. When I ask about Ari's disappearance, she can offer no more than I already know, but she murmurs, *Poor Gida*, and I agree. When I leave, it's with two lengths of cotton – a sunflower yellow and an azure blue – and only the vaguest idea of how to turn them into dresses. I get them cheaper in return for a love potion (for her husband's flagging libido) and a tea to help her sleep.

Though the bell above the door rings cheerfully when I step into the apothecary's lair, the store remains empty for long moments. I take in the myriad shelves and jars, coloured vials, scales, alembics, mortars and pestles, sacks and pots of all manner of liquids, lipids and medicinal pounce and leaves, twigs and poultices. The light is low so as not to upset the delicate balance of the merchandise.

In the end, I call, 'Reynald, if you don't appear this second, I'll steal something.'

From deep in the back, behind walls and curtains, I hear the clatter of shoes, the tinkling of light fixtures set too low for the height of the man who works here, and I hear cursing. Profound and impressive cursing which ends on a mild 'Don't you dare, you light-fingered witchy bitch.'

Reynald Alberic, slender and elegantly dressed in shades of dove-grey not really compatible with a profession involving powders and bubbling liquids, steps through the doorway like a stork being born – if storks weren't hatched but rather entered with all the aplomb of a chorus girl on stage in Seaton St. Mary or one of Bellsholm's finer theatres. Yet he's no dancer, but the person who formulates and mixes *materia medica* for those like me and for others, far-flung, who call themselves doctors. Reynald has a keen mind for the chemistry of ingredients, for their alchemy. We work with similar intent, he and I (though his skill is the greater), but only I will be condemned if something goes awry; apothecaries live, witches die.

His means of distilling essences are better than mine, the equipment more finely tuned and expensive, so I'm glad to trade with him: raw plants of rare sort for the processed liquids of another – he prefers not to have to gather ingredients out in the woods. His husband, Lucien, runs the Fox & Crow Inn across the way. I've also found Reynald to be my best source of useful gossip.

'Shouldn't leave customers waiting like that,' I say as he busses my cheek, once, twice. Such fancy manners.

'Indeed not when they're as old as you and like to expire at any moment.'

'Rude. You'd make an excellent frog.'

'Then who'd provide ingredients for your worst concoctions and best elixirs?'

'You're in luck, I still need you,' I grumble and open my satchel, withdrawing the dozen pouches of fresh and dried leaves, petals, herbs, mushrooms and grasses that grow in various locations in the woods, mostly hidden, hard to get to and known only to me. Pink bleeding heart, purple strangleweed, yellow Belver's hemlock, creeping gloriana red as blood, pale monksbane fungus, green weld and St Bathild's lace the colour of mud.

Reynald draws in a sharp breath, delighted. 'Oh, bless you, Mehrab. Perfect and timely.' In return, he dives behind the counter and swiftly resurfaces with a series of labelled small blue bottles filled with concentrates, their stoppers sealed with wax. He proceeds to wrap each one in tissue paper to pad them for the journey home – substances I don't especially want carelessly spilled – enquiring as to my health and wellbeing, and I after his. He hands them over with glee; no coin ever passes between us for this barter is far more useful, more profitable.

'Can I help you with anything else, Mehrab?'

'The child who went missing, Ari Hadderholm?'

He nods. 'The baker's girl. Such a shame. Quite a nice child.'

'Did you see her the day she disappeared?'

'Not that day, no.'

'Another?'

'Most days because she and the other urchins gather on the green when they're out of school.' His smile droops. 'Poor mite. I don't hold out much hope.'

And I don't tell him any different because the tale will soon spread from the Hadderholms' bakery, grief lit and flying like wildfire in a field. 'And no sign of her anywhere?'

'Lucien hears things; people talk over their meals, drinks. There were footprints leading to the pond by Falda's, then some on the other side as if she'd taken a dip. Along the northern trail and into the common orchard, across to the opposite fence then gone. Like she'd been plucked up and carried off.'

'Poor mite,' I echo. 'Nothing else of interest?'

He appears to hesitate, and my interest is piqued.

'C'mon, Reynald, spill it.'

'Promise you won't be mad?' He's not really fearful, but definitely reluctant, and I don't think I've ever seen him like this in the years I've known him.

'Promise – within reason.'

'Best I can hope for.' He sighs. 'Faolan's wife died two months ago.'

Despite my best effort it seems the shock shows on my face. Not the news I expected. Not sure what he expected from me, but he goes on quickly as if to forestall a reaction: 'You've not been into the village for the last few months, and it didn't seem like something you'd want anyone rushing to tell you…'

I shake my head. 'No. No, you're right. No reason to tell me at all.' I do not ask if the blacksmith is well. I will not. I had nothing against the woman, though there was so much… history there. The feelings are so old; they should not sting. I'm precise as I pack the wrapped vials into the satchel, careful as I sling it over my shoulder. My voice is level as I ask, 'Do you have any special requests for the next harvest?'

He hands me a list on a fine piece of paper; I peruse it, nod, and bid him farewell.

* * *

Outside, the traffic has thinned with villagers going home or to the inn for a midday meal. My tasks are all done, so I could begin the walk home and be returned by early afternoon. Or I can walk the path to Falda's holding, to the pond and around it, then into the orchard to see what I can see.

At Falda's cottage, I speak to her as she leans against the doorframe, one babe on her hip while two others play by the hearth. She doesn't ask me in, nor do I request it. While she's sympathetic about Ari's loss, her tone tightens when she mentions the child hunting for mushrooms on her holding. Says she wasn't even aware of her presence until the parents came knocking. Falda doesn't strike me as the sort of person to do away with a child over stolen mushrooms or anything else. I thank her and assure her that I'll steal nothing while looking at the orchard.

There are no prints in the dirt as I pass, not now, not of hers, or none that are recognisable – too many searchers have gone this way on too many heedless feet. On the far bank of the pond, there are very few mushrooms, only the old, withered.

In the shared orchard, I look at the apple trees, think how in early winter the villagers will gather here, pour cups of warm spiced cider onto the roots of the oldest trees as a gift to whatever old things might live in their trunks. Briefly I wonder if something went wrong with last year's offering – I don't attend, am not invited – and some discontented sprite decided to pluck their own offering. But it would have been a long time to wait, though, from ritual to revenge, especially when children cut through here all the time. Why would Ari come here after the mushrooming? And how'd she get to where I found the scrap of her cloak?

No trace of her footprints, but I follow those the searchers left, which lead me to the three-planked wooden fence around the gathered fruit trees. I think about young girls, myself at that age, the freedoms I stole. Ari would have walked the fence. Not just clambering over it, but balancing on the narrow top board, arms held out, cloak streaming behind like wings. She wore it even in spring because she adored it so. While I don't doubt she was loved, she was the youngest child, the last at home. A child in a house where no one paid her much attention…

I scan the ground inside and outside of the fence to the right. Nothing. Then to the left. No footprints, no. But a red strand of wool caught on the fencepost, and a scattering of mushrooms on the ground outside the enclosure. Withered, several days old. Dropped as if when the one carrying them in the folds of her apron was snatched away – and up. I look at the trees outside the orchard, thick-limbed yews and oak and lindens – one linden in particular, spreading so far like a complex series of bridges. A child – limber and agile – might easily jump from the fence to the nearest branch, might walk among the trees for ages before having to touch the ground. Might not leave a trace for a long while or way.

* * *

No children play on the green as I pass by and I don't have the energy to knock on doors, asking questions of those who may or may not have seen anything. Perhaps parents are being cautious, keeping their offspring inside. I've had my fill of human contact for the next while and so set off towards the break in the undergrowth where the path leads back to my cottage. I'm almost there when a voice breathlessly calls my name. I sigh and turn.

Lutetia Arnold is a woman both round and angular (at shoulder and hips), both motherly and spiky. She's worn down by the worry of the only child still living in her home, Kian, a mostly grown son. The eldest two have families of their own and have been urging her for some time to evict their brother for the sake of her health. But she's overly kind and doesn't want Kian's feelings hurt. Kian at least has gotten gainful employment at the sawmill.

'Mistress Mehrab, I just heard you were here. I'm so sorry to—'

'How can I help, Lutetia?'

'My lad, two days ago he fell off a cart at the mill, been hobbling and moaning ever since.'

'You should have called for me sooner,' I say. Her husband Goscelin died a few years ago for he'd have no truck with a witch, insisting on tying a rune-carved amulet over the wound and going about his business without bandages or cleansing. I recall his death because I remember every unnecessary one.

The woman goes red. 'That's what I told him. He said I was over-reacting.'

'Show me.'

Back across the green, across the market, between houses, two, three, four, five rows back, to a neat and plain cottage with wisteria growing over its front door. Inside, Lutetia leads me to a bedroom on the ground floor. The lad in question – over twenty – lies on a bed, feverish and pale against the bleached linen.

I throw back the sheets and look at the legs poking from the hem of his nightshirt. The right is twisted, red and swollen. I don't feel especially like comforting the idiot. 'Oh gods. I can tell just by looking that's fractured, boy. You're not being tough and strong, you're being stupid. You won't heal properly, you won't be able to work, and your mother will see out her much-shortened life taking care of you.'

I could have been gentler but there are other things that need my attention. 'Lutetia, give him a good measure of rum or whiskey, whatever's the preference.'

While she bustles to the kitchen, I sit on the mattress beside Kian and place hands on him, letting my consciousness flow through the skin, into the flesh and muscles, the blood and to the bone, find the break, not clean, a hairline fracture down the femur. 'I'll not lie to you: this is going to hurt.'

He gets a little paler and knocks back the glass of very dark rum his mother produces, still giving me resentful glares. I make a cut on my palm for the red price, return both hands to his thigh, to where the fracture calls, and I mutter an incantation beneath my breath to help focus my power. Even with my eyes closed, I know he's gritting his teeth because I can hear the grinding as he tries not to cry out. In under a minute, he gives in and bellows until he passes out. Then I'm free to finish knitting the bone together as surely as if I'm placing stitches on a tear, gentling the traumatised flesh and muscle around it.

When I finally open my eyes, I'm shaky, sweating. A glass of that same dark rum appears in front of me, and I throw it back, followed by a piece of apple loaf. It's still a few minutes before I can get to my feet. 'He'll wake soon enough, sore, but able to walk and go back to work. In future, send for me.'

'He didn't want to bother—'

'If he wants to die like his father, it's his choice.' I shrug, and while Lutetia was not the least bit grief-stricken over her husband, I think she'd miss this son for reasons best known to herself. She's a decent person, keeps a kind eye on her neighbours, delivers bread and bottled fruits, leaves food at the doors of new mothers and those recently bereaved. 'But for the love of all the gods, Lutetia, stop coddling him or he'll never leave the tit.'

* * *

It's a little later than I'd planned when my own cottage is at last in sight.

Before I go in, I check the trough in the courtyard. Its lid is on and the paddle's damp from use. All the animals are chewing contentedly; eggs have been collected. The roses have been expertly trimmed, the clippings added to the compost heaps. I nod approvingly.

When I open the front door, the smell of baking bread and a hearty soup wafts out. Suddenly I'm so tired and so grateful that I could cry. I'd never have thought the delicate Lodellan lass with her dancing shoes could have cooked anything that smelled so mouth-wateringly good. Nor that I'd be so glad of her help and company.

8

'Be careful,' I say, trying to keep a sharp tone from my voice. Perhaps my mask dulls it; any road, the expression in her eyes doesn't change, remains focused on what we're doing.

I've never done this with help before. Never done it with a witness either, never tried to teach someone else to do this brand of magic. None of my other fosterlings have been here at the right time; they've only been with me in the cold months when the last of this work gets turned to kindling. I might have refused to explain it all to her, to this girl who's trying her best – admittedly not something I'd thought to see – I might have kept it all a secret, working out in the barn on my own and bolting doors, spinning wards across them, but then what's the likelihood of her not snooping around? Gods know I would – they tell us curiosity kills the cat, but a smart woman knows that knowledge is her best defence. She's clever and questing. Oft-times, our more annoying quality is also our best, so I may grumble at her questioning, but I'm also pleased by it. I wonder if any of my teachers thought the same of me?

So, I'm instructing her as best I can; the others were fit

for only small magics. When I asked her what she knew, her reply was shame-faced: 'I have no spells. I've never learned anything like that. Just the fire – it's mine. It comes with my temper, with my fear, but only if I concentrate. I can't make anything else happen.'

Untrained then. 'No matter – everyone's different on the witch's scale. I can teach you spell craft, things that'll be useful in your days to come.'

'Thank you, Mehrab.' And for the first time she sounded shy. I tell her that with a power like hers, witch-fire that she might draw on all day, she could try a Briar Witch trick and begin each morning with a small bloodletting, paying the red price ahead of time. It doesn't really make sense for my kind of magic, but for hers it should make things easier. Faster. Especially if she's needing to defend herself.

The sapling, after its week in the drying room, has been anointed with a peculiar mix of powders and a little oil to make the wood more absorbent (which surely seems counter-intuitive). When it goes into the bath, I need it to soak in as much of the vile liquid as possible – but also not to take on its stench. Hence, the oil is aromatic, strongly so.

'Ouch!'

'What?'

'Splinter,' Rhea grumbles, but she's smart enough not to drop her end of the sapling – it's become unreasonably heavy, which is the weird way of things – and keeps moving with the peculiar gait of someone terrified of dropping a precious burden. Her backward steps are precise, measured.

When we're next to the bath, I say, 'Don't just toss it in.

That's only going to make the liquid splash up, and we don't want that on your skin or your newly made dress. Or on my skin for that matter.'

Neither of us is an especially able seamstress but armed with that knowledge we were very attentive to the task and seams were double stitched for strength. The frock will win no prizes at a fair, yet it does what it's supposed to, which is ward off nakedness and she says it's comfortable. There's another dress pinned for cutting out too, and an old dress of mine, long unworn, to be repurposed into trews for her, but by consensus it was decided we both needed a rest before tackling those. Time for the needle- and pin-holes in our fingers to heal.

Slowly we lower the sapling into the broth, which burbles and bubbles. I step away quickly because experience has taught that those burbles and bubbles can send liquid flying, and Rhea has learned to listen to me on this subject at least.

'And you said no one taught you this?'

'No one,' I say, surprised to sound nervous; I've never spoken of it before. 'Not every woman's a witch and not every witch is a spells-woman. Some work by ritual and wish, the small magics of hen- and hedgewives. Some have greater talent, can produce larger effects. Some have a gift – like yours with fire – and that's all they ever work with.'

'Do you have a gift?'

I ignore the question. 'Some simply use what's written in a tried-and-true book, passed down, never experimenting. Some are committed to their own workings. Some of us navigate by trial and error.' *And ambition.* 'A constant process of experimentation, trying to further our abilities to match our imagination.' I clear my throat, putting something into words for the first time: 'I'd always been interested in how things become other things, how flesh and substance might be manipulated. So, I pondered what I wanted, what was of most use to me. I tested various techniques, crafted and adapted spells until something worked the way I wanted it to.'

It sounds so simple, so normal. No hint of what drove the urge. Or of the things that went awry.

'Do you do that often? Experiment?'

'Less nowadays.' *Nothing to prove, now.*

'What's the greatest thing you ever did?' Her eyes are shining like a child's hearing a story.

I grunt, lie. 'This. I thought one day how useful it would be to have someone around to help with the heavier work. I didn't always have fosterlings, and they weren't always up to the hard labour of hauling and lifting. I didn't want to take on a lad because lads become men and cannot be trusted.' I shrug. 'So, I began *playing* with this – there are spells in other books, other grimoires, there are things that are a little bit of this. I just… joined them together.'

'Did it work the first time?'

'No, it did not. A grand failure, an explosion, very messy.' I hold the hair away from the left side of my neck, show her the scar from a jagged piece of flying plank. 'Had to rebuild the barn – which is, not coincidentally, why I now do this work outside – but it taught me things. And I had the chance to design a structure that met my needs better, isn't as simple as most of them are.'

'The drying room?'

'The drying room.'

'What's next? More stirring?'

'More stirring. Off you go.'

* * *

The next few weeks drift by, broken up by stirring shifts, and lessons in enspelling shoes and cloaks for decreased visibility so one might pass safely by a threat, or sneak somewhere one isn't meant to be. I've given her one of my unused journals so she may begin her first grimoire, and set her books to read and learn from (honestly, I don't have the patience to begin at the beginning). She asks me questions when she fails at a task and I talk her through what went wrong – all failure teaches something, and humility is valuable for a witch to learn; without it, you might think yourself a god, and that way lies madness.

We've settled into a comfortable routine. During the day, we attend to the sapling and then hunt up the plants and fungi on Reynald's list; sometimes she helps mix philtres or grind and combine dry ingredients to stock my own stores and staples. In the evenings, one of us will try to pry details of the other's past; it's become a game of sorts. Only little things have been extracted, nothing of import. The only disruption to life has been the discovering of offerings on the doorstep, every few days for the past fortnight.

Sometimes berries and other forest fruits, sometimes roots dug from deep in the woods, vegetables I do not grow and sprays of herbs and leaves; a few hares, a brace of partridges, a fat duck. Nothing out of the ordinary except at no point have we ever seen who left them.

No knock on the door, no one to say, 'Thank you for what you've done' or 'I would like to buy a service'; no note. Just waking in the morning and finding a benefaction on the stoop as if it's an altar. I've told Rhea not to eat any of it – not yet, not until whoever is bringing it presents themselves too, and makes a request – because eating implies an acceptance of a bargain, the details of which we are not aware. So, everything's been piled into baskets in the coolness of the cellar, waiting.

I wasn't too worried, at first, because the wards around my holding were intact. I'd checked them after being caught in that spiderweb of a trap, and I walked the boundary every few days to make sure they remained thus. So, nothing that wasn't meant to be there could come to my threshold.

No, I wasn't too worried until today and the appearance of a parcel wrapped in what looks like old shroud-cloth, greyed and not-quite crumbling.

I don't bring it inside, but crouch at the stoop (knees protesting) and unwrap a corner, just enough to glimpse what lies within – smooth pale skin, neat cuts at the joints, no odour of decay or not yet at least. Or not detectable. And its inner wrapping of red wool.

'Rhea!' She comes when called. 'Get the baskets from the cellar, quick as you can.'

I tap my pocket, make sure the tinderbox is there as ever. A hunter, perhaps, might leave something after an especially good hunt, a particularly large buck or bear, even one of the bigger wolves (though they are stringy and the food of the desperate). It's springtime and animals are plentiful, largesse can be borne. But a hunter would be unlikely to wrap his gift in shroud-cloth and a red woollen cloak. Or an ordinary hunter at any rate.

Tenderly I rewrap the thing, but only after Rhea's gasp tells me she's seen the meat too – haunch? No, shoulder. I cannot bear to look any longer – then carry it to the far border of the eastern field, to the clear land between my holding and the tree line. I ignore Rhea's questions and she stops asking. At the circle of cindery earth where I burn rubbish, we tumble the fruits and vegetables, the game, from the baskets, and on top I place the shroud-cloth-covered bundle. Break branches and twigs from a fallen tree and build the framework for a fire. When that's done, I set it all alight. The blaze is good and hungry, the flames orange-blue.

Rhea pipes up again. 'Was this why you wouldn't eat anything that was left for us?'

I nod. 'Imagine how we'd feel if we had, then *this* arrived? If, in our acceptance of the offering was an implicit acceptance of a bargain? Waiting made it show its hand.'

'It was the child, yes? Ari?'

'I think so. Unless another's gone missing, wearing a red cloak.'

'How will you tell her parents?'

I pause, considering. 'I won't.'

'Why not? They deserve to know—'

'I've already had to tell them their child is dead. To tell them now that part of her has been left on my doorstep? That she's being proffered like a sweetmeat? To have them question why something felt it could do such a thing? Worse, to have them think it's a gesture another thought I might *welcome*?'

I shake my head. 'Rhea, you'll learn that sometimes it's safer not to admit everything.'

'But—'

'What will it profit them to know their child was carved up? Bad enough they might imagine her torn by an animal, her bones lying in some lair or den, her flesh gone to feed young. But for me to appear and say, "Here she is, or part of her – look how tidy these cuts are!" That would be torture, Rhea, a torment.' I push out a breath, exasperated. 'I've lived here for twenty years and I can tell you that the villagers, my neighbours, still don't trust me, not really. They come for aid, I've saved them and their children many times over, but there's still a tiny doubt in the back of their minds; they still fear that I will someday turn and do them ill. Good witch, bad witch, it doesn't matter. I remain *witch* and that terrifies them.'

She's silent, struggling. The girl will not survive if she doesn't learn to lie or at least dissemble a little more readily. Finally, she says, 'Why burn it all? Out here?'

'This is an unequivocal *no*. No to the offering, no to the bargain, no to the trap laid in the guise of generosity. Showing that we'd rather turn it to ash than accept.'

I scan the trees, the shadows and shades between their trunks, the chinks in the undergrowth, looking for eyes that watch. A surge of rage – that feral, primal rage – takes hold once more and I shout 'No!' at the forest. Birds, disturbed, fly up from the branches, a storm of indignation speckling the bright sky. I stare a few more moments, daring whatever is out there to step forward, show itself in the light and declare its intentions.

Nothing happens, except some of the more stubborn birds resettle on their perches, reproachful caws and squawks ringing in the air. I wait until the fire burns down, until everything is glowing coals and wafting ash, then send Rhea for a bucket of water to dampen the last of the heat. The smell is terrible. Corrupted. Not a sweet savour at all. I gather up the emptied baskets, link my arm with Rhea's and walk her back towards the cottage. I don't hurry, don't want to show any sign of weakness or panic or fear.

'Be watchful and wary, Rhea. Don't go anywhere on your own, or at least not without a weapon.' I remember the girl's fire at her fingertips, think she'll probably be fine, but this evening I'll make talismans for pockets, perhaps sew some dried sage and lavender into hems and collars. 'If you see anything, hear anything, tell me immediately. And don't mention what happened today, not to anyone.'

'What if there are any more offerings?'

Slowly, I shake my head. 'I don't think there will be. Not after that.'

'How will it know? Is it watching us?'

'Might be. Or other things are and they'll tell *it*.'

'And what is *it*?'

'Your guess is as good as mine at the moment.' One last defiant look past the boundary, to the forest, and I think, *I've faced worse. I've been worse.* 'Come, inside now.'

But I don't mention to Rhea that whatever it is has somehow come past my wards.

9

When I finally get to sleep that night, I think I've put the memory of the offering – carnivorous and cruel – away from me. Buried it. My dreams, however, show the lie of it.

I'm a child in a red cloak, plucked from a fencepost just when I imagined myself free. Though I feel a child's fear, my thoughts are my own, steady, adult, imagining what it might be like to be weightless and untethered from life in the tiny village, from a mother who lost her temper too often at my insistent questions, from a mostly inattentive father. Parents who'd had me too late, when they thought their parenting days done, that their attention might only be divided between their own interests and grandchildren who could be handed back. This, I think, is why the parents were so strangely guilty – not because of a greater love for this youngest child, but for whatever irritation her existence caused them. An afterthought, an annoyance, a child with demands that felt like too much when they'd thought to have quieter days.

Will they admit it to themselves? Unlikely. Perhaps it would feel too much like taking blame and few are willing to do such a thing. Most prefer to blame others, punish them even though such action never results in relief, only makes something dark and foul grow in the soul.

I shake myself awake and go sit in the window bay, watch the rose garden beneath the quarter moon, everything a little silvery-dark. My hands ache, the knuckles cracking as I clench and release. The rosebushes sway like dancers; they're never without blossoms, not through any great magic, or rather effort, of mine; from my inadvertent losses, yes. The moon's briefly obscured by the shape of an owl flying by. I think of other nights of my life when I've sat somewhere watching this same moon, in all her moods and phases. Even as a child, I'd climb to the roof of our ramshackle home (a single room, divided only by the functions we assigned to it, the privies communal things at the end of the alley) because if I sat there long enough she'd pass overhead and I could see her even in that city of high towers and almost buried harbour-side slums, we so far down by the river, the buildings built up the slopes and into the cliffs, climbing like vines. Beneath the moon, I could forget. Beneath the moon I felt the flow of a power that I didn't know truly or understand, then.

I think of my mother favouring my sister; anything pretty that fell into our deprived lives was given to Esther, nothing for me, no spare brightness or colour. I wonder, if she'd paid me some attention, my mother, would I have wandered off that night to be lost in the streets of that great city where I began? (Where, even now, a new power rises.) Running, truly, to find the moon on a dark night because it was overcast and I wanted so much to see her, so I ran, trying to find her, to catch her and bathe in her light because it was the closest thing to a gift I ever knew. Got myself lost.

Lost and then found by a woman who was seeking a child such as I, with a black hole for a heart and magic lurking in her veins. I think of all the glorious – bright, pretty, colourful – things that came from *her* hand and made it easy for me to stay. Elevated. More than an apprentice, not quite a daughter, to the court witch, the high sorceress who taught me more than I'd ever likely have learned in the ghetto, the slums, that rookery of my birth. More than I'd ever have learned at my mother's knee except that I was less loved. I'd have been married off – not for any care about my future but for the coin I'd bring in from a bride price. I was lucky, I suppose, that she hadn't already sold me for worse.

But the high sorceress, tall and stately in her black and red robes with her silver hair braided and wound like a crown on her head, with her eyes so ebon and her lips so crimson in a snow-pale face? She taught me no fear – no empathy either. No conscience. I had to grow that for myself and it's still a stunted thing.

* * *

The flames change on command.

First a single bright flare in the centre of her palm. Next, separating to run along each finger and the thumb, to dance at the tips, then back again. Rhea's been here for weeks now and her control has increased with practice. At first, she whined about the rote nature of the training, but I think a sense of achievement has settled into her, something she's not had before – and the activity provides a break from gently turning the sapling twice a day. I suspect her greatest achievement to date was to be beautiful. This power, though? It's hers, she's in control of it, it will not dim with age. If it becomes greater, that's to her credit. Beauty can only decay.

'Good,' I say from the bench (the cat sits not too close and I don't deign to reach out). 'Now, the target.'

The target is a large wooden rectangle in the middle of the courtyard, soaked with water to minimise the chance of a blaze, although the witch-fire can burn through many, many things and we're careful to keep our distance from the trough of simmering excrement and sapling soup. Rhea doesn't question or complain, merely takes aim and shoots a constant stream of fire at the circle carved in the centre. There's smoke and steam but for the moment the dampening works.

'You're learning very quickly. And you had no training before?' She's such a quick study it's hard to believe.

'None. Only my mother telling me to hide what I was.'

'That's the song of many mothers. They think they're protecting us.' Of course my own mother said and did no such thing; the abilities I manifested weren't easily seen and it took the high sorceress's coaxing to bring them out.

'I know she was afraid.' Rhea shrugs. 'Rightly so apparently.'

'Now, stutter it.' The flames become intermittent, a perfectly timed rhythm of on and off.

I find myself nodding. 'Well done, Rhea. Very well done. That's it for the day.'

She smiles, pleased with herself, proud. Then she frowns. 'But what will I do with it, Mehrab? This power, what's it for?'

This gives me hope; so many don't question it. If they do,

their answer is 'For *me*.' And they spend their lives pursuing gain based in that puissance, in making sure no one else ever gets a chance. Using the power to dominate. I wish I'd thought to ask that question when I was young.

'The main thing is to know that you can defend yourself and anyone you choose to love. We're too vulnerable as women. We can't rely on men to protect us – and as witches? So few are willing to step forward to help us. You simply need to be able to protect yourself and to know that you can.' I pause. 'I think that fear leaves when you're certain you can look after yourself. Or at least it diminishes to a level that's manageable – that doesn't overwhelm you, that can act as an early warning. Most folk die because of fear; it paralyses them, stops them from fighting. They fear themselves dead and then become so because they lose their grip on being alive.' I shake my head. 'Don't let panic get a foothold.'

'You're very calm,' she says.

'Hard-won.'

She nods slowly, stares out into the trees, measuringly. 'No more offerings.'

'No,' I say.

'Not since the burning.'

'No.'

'Do you think it's gone away? Whatever it was?'

'I don't know. I haven't seen anything, haven't sensed anything. Perhaps it's given up or made a strategic withdrawal to regroup. Still got your charm?' Rhea pats a pocket to show the little pouch of herbs is there as well as the sprigs of sage and rosemary in our hems. 'Stay alert. Come along. Dinner time.'

* * *

'How old is the forest, do you think?'

I'm stretched out on the long settee, Rhea's curled in an armchair, Mr Tib balanced on the curved back behind her. There's a small fire lit – a spark from her fingertips and a laugh when I'd sought out the tinderbox – just to take the chill off the night air. When summer proper comes, we won't need it, but spring still likes to flirt with winter's breath, just to remind folk that she'll come again. This has become our habit of an evening, to sit and chat, a mug of honeyed rum or mulberry mead in hand, unless we're too exhausted or I'm concentrating in the workroom and have insufficient patience. We've settled into a rhythm much more quickly than I thought we would – indeed, I didn't think we'd ever find an ease in each other's company. It's a good reminder that I'm not always right and sometimes people must simply accommodate habits and quirks. Not always. But sometimes.

'The forest is far older than us, older than people. The woodsmen cut down trees, count their rings and call its age – surely there's the oldest tree ever, the most ancient of them all, somewhere in the deepest depths of the forest. But what's the point of learning its age if you can only do that by killing it?'

'What indeed?'

'And we act as though we're separate from it, as if we just live here with no connection to the woods, but some say the first people were born of the trees. That trunks opened like caskets to let them out when they were ready. Or that the birds and animals dropped from the branches as strange seeds and grew in the primordial mud to become two-legged things that spoke.'

'Like the sapling in its soup of shite?'

I nod. 'Like the sapling in its soup of shite.'

She unfurls herself, goes to refill our glasses, then returns to her position. The cat gives a haughty look as if she's inconvenienced him.

'They say when those first folk were birthed, they strayed. Strayed from their mothers, thought them worthless, took it into their heads to find another use for those organs of the forest. Thought it not enough that they'd been given life by the trees, that those trees weren't doing as much as they could. That they should have more *purpose*. So, the people hewed and hammered, made houses of their wood – their parents – burned their bodies for warmth. They no longer slept in the branches nor returned to the boles; they mated with each other, producing more and more offspring with less and less sap in their veins, less connection to where they'd come from. And the trees stopped birthing humans, having seen it at last as a terrible idea. Can't blame them.'

'Is that true?'

I laugh. 'It's a "they say". Maybe a little part is true, but it's wrapped about in other tales to make up its bulk. Yrse told it to me when first I came here. The story sits differently on every tongue, tastes different, and every tongue adds a little something to the tale, so it's constantly forming and reforming, some parts added, some parts left behind.'

'Tell me more.'

I dredge up memories of other recountings: some from those my mother told for my sister's pleasure and which I stole in the listening; some from the high sorceress when she waxed expansive, sharing more than just lessons; some gathered from different places and faces over the years. 'I've traversed deserts where the trees themselves burn forever – or at least beyond the memory of the living. Not their outside, no, but internally – get close enough and you'll see the glow of their red-hot core, the very coals of them.' I shrug. 'Sometimes I wonder if witches like you have somehow come from trees like that. If we did indeed spring from them, some of us at least.' I take a sip of my drink. 'They say a tree, if bathed in enough blood – those on and around battlefields – might come to crave it. The blood. It's rumoured there are groves, sacred and otherwise, where the trees lay in wait for unsuspecting victims, most often animal but a human is a cause for celebration. They say that when these groves are discovered, they're destroyed because such things, sentient and bloodthirsty, cannot be allowed to thrive. Cannot be tolerated. And their keepers – for sometimes there are people who bring fresh meat to their charges – are thrown onto a pyre made of those very trees.'

'So, from birthing us to eating us?'

I shrug. 'There's always an element of consumption in old tales, don't you think? How many are told of families that, in times of famine, devour their own? Or those who, loyal to their kin, ambush travellers to provide themselves and loved ones with meals.'

'A bit desperate.' Rhea pulls a face.

'I think that's the point. And we never truly know what we'll do in extreme circumstances.'

'Mehrab? Any further thoughts? About what left the offerings on our doorstep?' *Our*.

I have suspicions and I hesitate before sharing. If I'd not already had two glasses of mulberry mead, I might have kept them to myself. 'There were older things, things that were here before us – the trees weren't the only beings to produce uncanny fruit. And the trees might not have been the first things here; something brought them forth.' Without warning, the cat leaps from her chair to mine, no sign of effort, and curls himself over my feet; I don't react. Cats are such queer things. 'The old ones? Some still remain, some sleep and wait. Most are gone, dead or elsewhere. We're just the next iteration of them, I think – worse and weaker but sometimes better and kinder. One thing's for sure, they don't like us as anything except fodder. We're nothing but game to them, those few that remain; we're here to be hunted and consumed. It's fortunate, then, there aren't too many of them left. Those that are here, hide, weakened by age and natural decay; even gods die in one way or another, little by little.'

'Have you met any?'

'No. Perhaps. They leave snares, though, on forest floors,' I grin ruefully, 'beneath the surface of lakes and ponds, tiny sparks that burst into flame without warning, air that suddenly turns poisonous or so wild that it carries a full-grown cow or bear or person away.' I empty my drink. 'And there are tales of tricksters for whom it was never enough to simply steal children – nothing would suffice except to have parents hand those children over. A sort of tithe. There are rules, you see, to the giving and taking of such things – if a child is given, a parent has no recourse; if a child is stolen, there's a debt that mounts against whatever takes them and eventually, it will be tallied though it might take aeons. Some gods don't care, some gods do. The cunning ones know that the smaller their debt, the longer they can reign, the longer they can do whatever they wish either in shadow or light. Some get around it by sending the children back, changed.'

She's silent for a while, then says very quietly, 'Do you think Anselm and Gida handed their daughter over?'

I shake my head. 'No. They weren't the most patient parents, but I don't believe they gave her up. Their grief was genuine, and the guilt. And they'd not have come to me for help. Why set a witch to investigate when you know you're responsible?'

'So, whatever took Ari, why leave offerings for you?'

'I don't know.'

'Did it take her *for* you? As a sacrifice specifically for you?'

'I don't know.' *And I don't want to think about it.*

10

'*This* is the hardest part?' Rhea asks as I straighten.

My spine aches, I've been leaning over working for too long. Pressing out a painful hiss of a breath, I nod. Every year it hurts more, so every year the need to do this is greater. 'I know it's hard to believe after weeks of stirring that trough, but yes.'

Five days ago, we lifted the sapling from its bath and laid it in the drying room again. The timber had swollen, absorbed the nutrients of the admixture – a sapling no longer, but a log essentially, its circumference wider than my waist, my shoulders, my hips. For four days, it lay out to dry, the excess moisture leaching away. Yesterday, I began the task of carving and reshaping – wood is always harder to change than flesh. Here in the barn, he's lying on a table formed of two trestles and another old door, repurposed. My tools sit on the bench running along one wall, knives, chisels and gouges, the hatchet again, blades and hooks, adzes and veiners, of various sizes and for various purposes. Rhea has watched with increasing interest as I've toiled, roughly at first, splitting the trunk into legs, then higher, two arms, higher still a ball of a head. At the end of yesterday, a rudimentary man lay before us, then we left him overnight to settle, to prove.

My sleep was dreamless as the dead last night, and I woke refreshed despite the ache in my muscles from the constant labour. This morning, Rhea's positively feverish with enthusiasm. I've already threatened to lock her up if she doesn't stop buzzing about. Undeterred, she keeps pacing around the table, looking at my creation from every angle.

'You're very good,' she says admiringly.

I shrug.

'I mean it, Mehrab! And this… this feels like big magic. No one ever taught me anything, before you, and the fire simply came to my call. All the other things you've shown me have been – no offence – quite mundane, small. But this—' she spreads her arms wide to show the magnitude '—this is life! This is grand and great. Creation!'

I can't help laughing at the unbridled eagerness. 'No offence.'

She pouts, puts her hands on her hips; those hands, much less pale, a little less plump after weeks of chores; not like mine, though, not yet. Not until she has to start this kind of activity. The advantage of the soft young wood is that any splinters are supple. 'Don't laugh at me when I'm so admiring!'

'I'm sorry. I'm sorry – but no one's ever seen this done. I've never instructed anyone in this. I'm not used to reactions or an audience.' And I laugh again. How far have we come from my unwilling agreement to foster her, to me showing her this secret like she's my child and this her inheritance? 'Your first will be the ugliest, unless you've any artistic talent?' She shakes her head regretfully. 'Ah, you'll survive. A bit of ugly won't hurt you. You'll learn, with time, what you like, what you can do, what you can put up with. All mistakes make for experience.'

I shrug, step back to get a better look. The face is still basic because I've taken my time with the body – as ever, I have my requirements, my tastes — and I must admit to some pride in this year's effort.

Stiff as a board in front of us he lies: broad-shouldered, deep-chested, long-legged. His surface is damp, sticky as moisture leaks from where I've shaped him; it will dry into a smooth resin after I rub him smooth with fine sand from the bed of the stream. Rhea nods at the apex of his thighs. 'You've put some care there.'

'And you will too, one day. The trick is to be tender and remember that the length you make it is the only length he'll ever have so don't go cutting too short assuming there'll be the growth of a man of flesh and blood. Summer husbands don't work quite that way.' It takes some effort to tease the cock free of the swollen trunk – that's what the immersion in the trough mix does, makes the wood swell, bulk up, even though it's been cut from its source, so there's substance enough to work with. 'It's an artificial life, of course, eldritch and unnatural, limited, but life nonetheless for a brief span.' I gesture, say confidentially, 'Once upon a time, I used to make the effort to carve a bed of hair, *down there*, something for it to rest upon. Realistic but fiddly and ultimately unnecessary – who looks, after a while?'

She gives a jerk of a nod. Maybe she'll do the same thing when it's her turn. Maybe she'll learn the hard way, literally, as I did.

'And do you… you know, just…'

I look at her, blink for a moment, then realise her meaning. 'Oh. No. No, no. If that happens, it happens. They're to help with the holding, the harvest, the planting, anything that needs doing around the place. To make life easier, especially as I get older. If something *else* happens, well it happens, but sometimes there's no… spirit in that direction. There must be willingness on both sides. Otherwise, no.'

I think about the loneliness that brought about the making of the first one. I think about the hole inside me left by betrayal. I think, perhaps, there was madness behind it, at least at first. The wish for company, the need for a labourer, the idea that I was in control of the seasons of such a thing. That I was creating a tool, so to speak, and nothing more. 'But as I said, if something does happen, you don't want to find you've made something that… falls short.'

Switching topic, she observes: 'There's no stench.'

We'd poured the remains of the soup into a hole and heaped earth over it; it will feed the rose garden, indeed is one of the reasons for the year-round flowering. 'No. I'm careful about that. The right mix of oils works wonders.'

'How much longer?' Rhea asks, taking the ladle from the bucket and carefully sprinkling some water over the body to make sure it doesn't dry out too soon.

These past days, she's been much more helpful and biddable, eager to please, taking better notice when I speak about powders and potions, sitting by the pond to practise her art, glaring at the float in the middle of the water, where she can set it aflame with little consequence – an upgrade from the target which finally burst into flame despite all our dampening precautions. She does things around the cottage without having to be asked; has fitted herself into the life here. I think, now, she will do well enough, that I can equip her with the skills she'll need to survive when she goes back out into the world to make her own way.

'How much longer?' she repeats, impatient.

'A few more hours after lunch.' I'm tired and I should rest or I'll get careless. I want to see his face, but it needs to be right. 'Tomorrow morning. I'll finish then.'

* * *

Even though I sleep deep and dead, I wake exhausted, because the work isn't simply a matter of carving a thing. It involves spells and the chanting of them, the cutting of them into the summer husband so they slow what time inevitably brings. To buy me the months I need for harvest and sowing, for cutting and stacking the woodpile for winter, clearing the undergrowth around the cottage, checking the roof is sound, that the tiny cellar is dry and the stream hasn't tunnelled its way back to the old leak from years ago when the place flooded and I knew nothing about it until I went down the stairs and found a bath awaiting.

By the time it's done, I'm almost cross-eyed and can barely stand. He's ready, though, and beautiful in his own fashion. The fine detail is clear and I've made his eyes and lips, chin and cheeks, nose, forehead, jaw, ears, the semblance of hair, just the way I want them. And, as I said to Rhea, if something's to happen you want *this* not only to be equipped but appealing.

'The cup,' I say and my voice is rough, throat dry. Rhea's quick to hand me the clay goblet. The contents laps at the lip, a viscous mix of rabbit's blood and sap, with a little nub of living clay dissolved therein (I've kept a store for years, purchased from a red-haired travelling woman who had the secrets of mud harvested from graveyards, rich and foetid with the essences of life and death). The slit I made for his mouth, carved out into a void (but no tongue, never a tongue, never again), is waiting and I pour the elixir in.

And because I'm exhausted, I'm sloppy.

Fumes rise where the liquid meets the wooden lips. I, heedless as Rhea was all those weeks ago when we soaked him in the trough, take a negligent lungful of the vapours. Reeling away, I cough, choking, spluttering, stupid as an apprentice.

Rhea, distracted by the transformation of the block of wood on which I've lavished such attention, does nothing more than raise her hands vaguely in my direction. But she doesn't come to my aid, stays where she is, transfixed by the summer husband. I understand, in spite of everything, for even though I've seen it so many times, I'm never *not* enchanted, never *not* fascinated by what I've wrought. By the fact I managed to turn my skills to this, to adapt.

Yet this time I miss it altogether, the transformation, the *becoming*, as I try to get my breath back, try to clear the tears from my eyes. And I forget, as I cough and splutter, the first rule of making a thing (of making any sort of child): always be the first thing it sees; only by this means can you ensure its love. But I'm not the first thing he sees, am I? And it's no one's fault but mine, because I'm in a corner, throwing up. So to not witness it even once feels like a grief that will haunt me forever, but it's not the worst part of it.

The first thing the new summer husband sees – the product of my hands, my sweat, my blood and magic, my tears and spit – is *her.* Rhea, with her blonde locks and her bluer than blue eyes, her trim figure, peaches and cream skin, leaning over him with wild fascination.

* * *

Sitting outside on the bench in the rose garden, trying to get my breath back. To clear my lungs, to swill out the taste of vomit with the whiskey Rhea brought me when she could tear herself away from the summer husband. *He's* still in the barn, still supine, too new to know quite what to do until he's told. The girl's beside me, chattering, asking if I'm quite well, and all I can think of is that she's champing to get back into the barn. Then she's tapping my shoulder, hard, and I pay proper attention to her.

'Mehrab. Look.'

I follow the direction of her nod to where the path feeds out from the forest or leads into it depending on which way you're going. The hulking shape of Anselm stands there, hesitating, almost as if he's hanging, suspended in the shadows, unwilling to step into the patches of sunlight that dapple the way to my garden gate. I raise a hand to beckon, then wipe my mouth with the self-same hand.

When he's close enough for me to make out his expression, I say, 'I know I look like seven types of shite right now, but you look infinitely worse, Anselm.'

Which is probably not the gentlest thing to say to a man who lost one of his children not so many weeks ago, but my stomach is battling with me still and it makes me curt. But he simply nods, refusing to meet my eye. 'What is it, Anselm?'

He clears his throat, looks at me at last. 'Our Ari's back. But… she's not the same.'

11

'How long's she been back?' I ask at last. Walking towards Berhta's Forge, neither of us has spoken for the last ten minutes, me still uncertain of my stomach, he wrapped in his thoughts. Anselm had waited patiently while I bathed the stench from me, drank a ginger tea. Wet hair soaking through the back of my fresh dress, I'm not looking my best or most imposing. I told Rhea to wait in the cottage, to stay out of the barn; I put the bar across the doors just in case this summer husband happened to come to himself faster than others – they're often different, each one. But the average? He won't be mobile for another day; birth is exhausting. I personally would like to be in my bed, sleeping off my pains and disappointment and pulling my energy back.

He clears his throat. 'A week.'

'And it didn't occur to you to let me know?' I can't keep the peevishness from my tone. Again, they've delayed in sending for me. These past weeks when I've gone into the village to collect Rhea's new boots and occasional supplies, Reynald's whispered there's been no trace of the child, although her mother's been seen wandering the forest paths, still seeking. For one part, I think, there's still a lack of trust, a modicum of fear when it comes to the witch in the woods. For another, I'm out of sight, out of mind, unless they want something. That has its advantages of course. If you're not on people's minds, they're not thinking either good or bad things about you. They're less likely to blame you for something. Mostly.

'We were just so relieved to have her back.'

I note he doesn't say "happy". That's the guilt speaking. *Don't let her be gone and leave us with the burden of knowing we didn't care enough. Love enough.* 'And?'

'At first it was little things, mannerisms, habits. We thought – Gida says it's the time she's been away. Gida says that people change when they're away from family and children are more changeable than adults. Then the way Ari speaks – the accent odd sometimes, the word choice not like a child's. Words I had to ask Faolan the meaning of.' He seems to struggle to continue. 'We're both sleeping badly – deeply but badly.'

'And?'

'And we wake in the night and find her standing at the foot of the bed, just watching. Staring. Gida says sleepwalking's normal. That's all.'

'But?'

'Sometimes I think her eyes shine like they shouldn't, not in the dark.'

'And?'

'She's started cursing at her mother, me too, if she doesn't like something. Things keep getting broken, small things with sentimental value – a vase that belonged to my mother, a drawing by our oldest son, a hand-embroidered apron, even the highchair that's been in Gida's family for almost a hundred years. We use it when the grandchildren visit. Came home to find it almost in splinters one afternoon, and only Ari had been there that day. And the handkerchief we gave you? To scry? Found scraps of it in the hearth, mostly burned, but enough left so we'd know what it was.'

'Maybe Ari's just feeling lonely and looking for attention?' I offer, weakly.

He shakes his head. 'Her best friend won't have anything to do with Ari anymore. She and Tieve were thick as thieves.'

'Two months is a long time for children – perhaps Tieve's made new friends? They've grown apart?'

'But I've seen Tieve run away from my daughter, seen the fear in her face. Gida says it's our punishment for being poor parents.' He clears his throat. 'But we weren't so bad, didn't beat her or abuse her. Maybe not as attentive as we should have been – it's hard, when you think you're done with breeding, you know? That you've got some freedom… But Gida says it's our burden to bear.'

'Sounds like Gida's saying a lot of things.'

'She… she doesn't believe there's anything wrong. Won't believe it. She's treating the child like a princess instead of—'

'An irritation?' I'm swinging between some sympathy and none. Making a child feel like an inconvenience is a terrible thing, yet so many parents wonder why their offspring turn on them as adults (I speak from experience). Anselm colours, a dusky red, and I go on, 'Exactly what do you think I can do about it?'

'Talk to Ari? Children listen to you – scare her.' He shakes his head. 'Or talk to Gida and make her see sense. She,' he coughs, 'doesn't know I've come to you.'

I cough too, swallow, taste the bitterness of the elixir's fumes once more. My eyes water at the strength of the memory. We don't talk for the rest of the journey.

* * *

'What are you doing here?' Gida raises her voice. She's standing in the kitchen, was staring out the window at the river when we arrived, took some long moments to realise she wasn't alone.

'Anselm was kind enough to let me know Ari's returned. What wonderful news. You were so distressed when you came to ask for my help.' A reminder, not so subtle, that I'd already been brought into this. That I'd made myself ill in their service, taken no payment for it.

'Oh. Yes. In the excitement we forgot to tell you.' The glare she gives her husband is searing; there'll be more raised voices not long after I leave.

'And is she well, your Ari?' I sit without being asked, elbows on the tabletop, heedless of the floury surface; the smell of baking bread doesn't tempt my appetite and I still feel queasy. Anselm sits across from me and Gida reluctantly follows suit. Both of them look exhausted.

'Healthy as a horse.'

'And did she say where she'd been all this time, with so many people looking for her without success?'

'She doesn't remember. Except for falling from the fence around the orchard' – I think of the lack of footprints – 'and waking in the darkness. In a cave, she said. Then she slept again, woke and slept again. When she woke next it was to find herself in a grove of trees. She's been walking home ever since.'

'She must have been very deep in the woods. North or south? East or west?'

'She couldn't say.' Gida's tone is growing sharp. But what child of Berhta's Forge can't tell their compass points from the position of the sun or the moss on the side of a tree?

'What did she eat?'

'Berries. You know the woods are filled with them this time of year, so many varieties. She dug roots as well – she's clever my Ari, knows how to feed herself. All village children do, all those who were born *here*.' This last is said tartly. This reminder that I was not born here, and twenty years later that lack is still not forgotten.

'All that time on berries. She must have returned very thin.'

'Very thin, I'll give you that. But she found tubers and the like, drank from streams.'

'I'd like to see her, Gida, even though it sounds as if she's in rude health, and I know you care devotedly for her.'

Gida's mouth moves without opening, as if she's fighting to keep her reply in, and I have to bite down on a grin. Laughter would do no good. I simply gaze at her until she realises she's got no good reason to refuse, and she turns and calls, 'Ari, my dove, will you come down?'

And Ari steps so quickly into the kitchen that it's clear she's been listening from the staircase that leads up to the living quarters. In the seeing of her I finally recognise the child; she bears a vague resemblance to the image I'd conjured in my mind those months ago when the parents came to see me and I could not really recall a face. Shortish, dark hair in tight braids, blue knee breeches and a white shirt, leather shoes with laces, and she's wearing her fine red woollen cloak, inside. I recall her nodding to me whenever she passed, smiling shyly when I visited the village, the bakery for bread and rolls fancier than I was prepared to make; a quiet, polite child. But now, the set of the chin is different, a haughty angle, an insolent cast to the brown eyes. As if her absence has been accompanied by a personality change. Much as her father said, I suppose.

'Hello, Ari. It seems you've had quite an adventure.' I'm usually wary of speaking down to children, but irritating someone can often make them show their hand.

She nods, doesn't answer.

'Ari.' Anselm's voice is louder than is required, a tense wire plucked.

'Yes,' says the child, as if dribbling out a taste she doesn't like.

'And you're quite well? Despite nothing but berries and roots?'

'And eggs. Sometimes I'd find nests with eggs in them. I'd eat them raw – nothing to cook them in, you see.'

I nod. 'Do you recall how you got so far into the woods?'

'I—' She tilts her head to one side as if listening. 'No. I was playing in the orchard, on the fence. I'd picked the mushrooms, but I didn't want to go home and something happened,' she squints trying to recall, 'I dropped the mushrooms and thought how angry Mother would be, then…' She shakes her head. 'All I remember is waking in the dark many times, until one day I woke in the light, in a clearing, and started walking.'

'And you knew which way to go?'

'I can find my way in the woods.' Scornful. Probably right; most children know how to get their bearings, to wind their way home. And contradicting what her mother told me – possibly what she'd told her mother.

'And you didn't see anyone else? The whole time?'

She shakes her head. I gesture for her to come closer. She hesitates, then concedes. I examine her hands and nails, the palms with their map of lines so intricately drawn. Next her face and throat, along the hairline and at the back of her neck in the little dip where skull sits so neatly on spine. I'm tempted to hold tighter, dig deeper into the very being of her, but that will hurt her, she'll scream, and her parents will say how I injured their child out of spite. It's not worth it. When I'm done, I sit back in my chair and nod. 'Thank you, Ari. You've got your cloak on, going out I take it.'

She nods. I gesture towards the door, whether it's my place to give permission or not, and the child skips away. I wait until the front door opens and closes before looking at her parents, pronouncing calmly: 'Nothing wrong that I can see. You're very lucky to have her back.'

Gida nods, sullenly, although she looks a little relieved. Anselm, beads of sweat on his brow, walks me out. In the front garden, he gives an anxious look. 'Well?'

I shrug. 'There's nothing physical that I can point to. You may just have to come to terms with the fact she's behaving badly because she was on her own for over two months and no one rescued her. She feels abandoned and she's going to punish you for that for a while. And remember she was on her own and survived without help – that's a hard-won independence right there, Anselm. She might forgive you eventually, might behave better. But it will take some time.'

He stares, disbelieving. 'So, you don't think there's anything wrong.'

'I didn't say that. Until there's proper evidence of something worse than bad behaviour there's nothing I can do. Keep an eye on her, send for me if there's anything concrete.' I touch his arm, find him shaking. 'Give her some time, Anselm. Practise patience. Keep an eye on Gida, though, she seems brittle.'

However, as I'm walking away from him all I can think of is Ari in her red wool cloak. Her perfectly lovely, perfectly intact red cloak. No sign at all of the piece the size of my hand that was torn from it, that bore traces of blood. The scrap of fabric that sits in a bottom drawer in my workroom at home. Or the piece that wrapped the chunk of unidentified *meat* that was left on my doorstep.

* * *

There's a group of children and a dog playing on the common, a little desultory this warm afternoon as they kick a ball around. As I approach, they stop moving, wait for me to speak. Five of them, three girls, two lads, maybe eleven to fourteen. Some on school recess, some snuck away from apprenticeships, I assume.

'Do any of you know Tieve?' I ask, and as one they shrug. I wonder at this. 'Does that mean you don't know her? Or she doesn't want to be found. Or you don't want her found?'

A long-legged boy with tousled black hair steps forward, the oldest of them perhaps, gives an aggressive little bounce as he stands in front of me. The dog – a dark grey lurcher of a thing with more than a little wolfhound in her blood – follows him closely, leans against his leg. His hand drops down to pat her head, and eyes close in contentment. I'm still taller and if he thinks I'm easy to intimidate, he's got another thing coming. There's something familiar in his features but I can't place him. The others cluster behind him like chicks.

'What do you want with her?' His voice breaks between two notes, on a cusp as he is. I hide a smile.

'I want to talk about her friend Ari.' His expression shutters, as do the others', and I know enough about people to understand I'll get nothing from them, not today at any rate. Pushing will only make things worse. 'If you see her, please pass my message along, that I would speak with her. At her convenience.'

The lad nods, still suspicious, but at least he mutters with more politeness, 'Yes, Mistress Mehrab.'

And I give a sketchy curtsey, which makes them laugh, relieving the tension. I offer the dog my hand to sniff and she lets me pat her before I move off, murmuring, 'Good girl.' Most adults would insist, start yelling, and nothing's more likely to make children obdurate than that. Most adults too. Best I can do is sow the seed.

Witchcraft isn't just potions and powders and spells. It's whispers and gentleness, giving folk a sense they're free to share their secrets with you – a feeling of a door left ajar, open without obligation. It's listening to what's not being said as well as what is coming from someone's lips and watching in case words do not match deeds. It's knowing that every lie told will eventually reveal itself and the person who told it.

Not everyone understands this.

12

Pondering the mystery of the child who's no longer missing and the issue in my home of Rhea and the summer husband; of the loss of connection to something I've made by the labour of my own hands, something that happens every year with a comforting regularity, upon which I've come to rely. I'm so distracted I don't notice the direction I've taken through the village. Normally I make a point of going the long way around so I don't pass the smithy, but my mistake becomes obvious when there's the call of a voice I've not heard in a few years. It's amazing how long you can avoid someone if you – and they – try hard.

'Mehrab. What brings you to my door?'

'A mistake. It's always a mistake, Faolan.' I don't pick up my pace lest he think I'm fleeing, even though I want to bolt. I force myself to meet his gaze as he stands there by the forge, sweating and soot-marked, a great hammer in one hand, tongs in the other, gripping a ploughshare blade which he plunges into the wooden slack tub. I watch him through the steam rising from the surface of the water.

He hasn't changed. How long's it been since last I saw him

this close? Two years? Three? Mid-fifties, thick silver and black hair, a neat beard, muscles into the end of next week. Brown trews, leather apron. His skin light brown, ash smeared on his forehead and cheek, beads of sweat on his naked chest. The long, raised scar that runs from the top of his left collarbone across his chest and ends just above the tip of his right hip is still visible despite my best efforts.

My skin prickles as he stares at me. Finally, he nods towards the children still playing on the green. 'Saw you talking to my son.'

Now the familiarity of the features makes sense. The bouncing on the balls of the feet, the low-level aggression. Insecurity. I think how Faolan's wife had come to me when she couldn't conceive… The boy's partly my fault, then. Poor motherless lad.

'Saw you talking with Anselm, too.'

'I'm amazed you get any work done, spending so much time watching others.'

He grins and I concede, 'He's got some concerns for his daughter.'

Faolan nods.

'Have you noticed anything? Has your son?'

'Why would he tell his father anything?' Dismissive, as if it's just a light truth and not a hint at a deeper hurt. 'Nor do I follow the comings and goings of children.'

'Someone should around here…' I turn, look at the group breaking apart, moving off to various homes. His hand against my elbow, a shock runs through me this time. He moves as quietly as ever.

'I miss you, Mehrab.'

I can smell him, the sweat and the scent that's particularly him, a sort of sweet pine; it conjures up memories that bring a blush to my cheek, a rush of blood to other parts, and for a few seconds I'm back there, long ago, grass beneath me and Faolan obscuring the sun and moon. It would be so easy to melt back into that feeling. Before… before…

'You should have thought of that years ago when you decided to take a wife.'

'You didn't want to marry me.'

'Marriage makes chains. As we were, was all I wanted.'

'Perhaps your desires aren't the only ones that matter, Mehrab.' His grip tightens but not painfully so; he leans in, lips moving against my ear. 'We wanted different things – except for each other. We never stopped wanting each other. I wanted you to wife.'

'You wanted a possession.'

'My wife…' he begins, then drops off, looking away, lets me go. 'You're flushed, Mehrab – are you well? Will you come in and sit for a while? There's dandelion tea or something stronger, if you wish.'

'I do not.' Curse myself for sounding like a pinch-mouthed spinster, a dried-up nun; prim and prudish. He leans against one of the massive wooden posts that holds up the roof of the smithy, an expression of defeat. I move off, don't look at him so he can't see the fleeting wings of disappointment I know cross my face.

'Orin says the girl's changed. Doesn't play with them so much anymore. Has become unpleasant.' His voice halts my steps. 'He looks out for them, the other children, my lad. Can't settle to one thing, horses or smithing, but he does look out for the youngsters.'

'Has he said anything about Tieve? The best friend?'

'Only that there's been a falling-out he didn't quite understand. The ways of women.'

I grunt in irritation; shoot a glare at him. He laughs and it irks me out of all proportion.

'Mehrab. Mehrab, when will you stop being angry at me?'

'When you're in the earth, perhaps. And perhaps not even then. I'll dance on your grave so loudly you'll hear it under all that soil.'

He laughs even harder. 'Remind me to have a funeral pyre instead, then you'll burn with me, you old witch!'

'Less of the old, thank you very much.' And a laugh forces its way out of me. I step away lest I start to recall why I loved him. 'Get back to work, old man.'

* * *

Walking home, I think more on the problem of Ari.

There are stories, of course.

Double-walkers or double-goers that appear to a person as an omen of death. Or as a dark echo of that same person, doing things the real version never would. A haunting of self, sometimes as a punishment for sins unforgiven or unrepented. Or a "first-comer" that does whatever the person does – sometimes walking ahead of them, just a few seconds, almost like a blur of movement, a prediction. A fetch, a ghost of a living person. Whatever they are, they're never regarded as good omens. They are not helpful, not like household spirits or creatures like hob-lads, or beekies.

But.

But, but, but…

Those doubles, those reflections or echoes, all exist when the original is around – either seen together, or in different locations at the same time – the entire point is to exist simultaneously, to be seen and *known*. There is torture in that, a plucking at someone's sanity. However, the double is always merely an echo, a shadowy thing, a reflection – if touched, hands pass through them, the body disappears like a cloud disturbed by a breeze.

Ari, however… the child was not wispy, there was no give in her flesh, or no more than a human normally displays. So, might she be something else? Perhaps?

A changeling.

A replacement. Something left behind, made of other flesh – a cuckoo in the nest. There are tales of such things, of trolls leaving their offspring in cradles, of fae whose babies need mortal milk to survive, to strengthen them in the way fae mothers cannot. Both troll and fae changelings are made in infancy; the former will be a most grizzlesome, gluttonous child, but the latter very quiet and only will be shown up if iron is applied to its flesh – but I didn't think Gida would appreciate me drawing my iron blade on her daughter.

Sometimes a "stock" might be left, a child carved of wood to resemble the stolen one – held too close to a flame and the thing will twist and turn and burn. A troll-child left behind to wreak havoc – such tales are plentiful, even royal families have suffered such things. Sometimes a distillation of brewed eggshells would force the thing into its true shape – either drinking it or simply the smell of it.

But, but, but…

Why? No child has gone missing from the village in the twenty years I've lived here. Yrse told the same story, no such losses in her lifetime. Been lost, yes, for a while, but always found quickly and safely. That's not to say there've been no deaths, but those have been from illness or accident. So, why now? *If* something's happened. *If* it's something unnatural. Yet I could feel nothing wrong with the child's flesh, the little examination I was able to make.

There's another explanation, there must be.

A child's resentment at parental treatment, a confidence blooming of having survived on her own, punishing behaviour. A new cloak, knitted at speed to make up for everything. A guilt gift.

What if it's not that simple?

What if it *is* that simple?

I will not hurl an accusation that could be baseless – my kind suffer that too often, and it takes so little to ruin a life, to send someone to the gallows or the waters or the flames. Anselm will watch his daughter; he knows where to find me. In time, the atmosphere in the baker's home will calm, tensions will lesson, the child will either return to her sweet nature or she won't – and if she doesn't? Well, that's no concern of mine.

I fear my own home is about to be of sufficient concern to me.

* * *

Deep in my thoughts, it takes a while before I realise two things: the usual bird sounds are lacking while conversely, there is a single constant noise becoming louder. A padding somewhere behind me. The rhythm is off, not simply a one-two, one-two pattern of something going on two legs. But extra beats. One-two-three-four – hard to distinguish unless you know what you're listening for, but it is distinct. Wolf or bear, bear or wolf. Not horse, nor deer. Stealthy, tracking.

My options are limited. Climbing a tree solves the wolf problem briefly, but a bear will come right up after me. The stream to my right is too narrow to use to break my trail, too shallow to hide in. Desperate times…

My iron dagger is sharp and the nick on my palm is almost painless. I choose an oak (old, less likely to cling), and smear blood on its bark, whispering the words to grant me passage as I run my pointer finger down the bole. My nail bites into the wood, and I use both hands to pry the trunk open. Inside the hollow widens, sensing my need, and I clamber in, pausing only to turn and pull the tree closed behind me, leaving only a single knothole. I try not to think about the tight space, about lying in a belly as if swallowed. Try not to think about the old tales of witches sealed inside sacred oaks and set alight.

Instead, I concentrate on the restricted view through the knothole, watching the path a few feet away from me; one hand wraps around the talisman in my pocket. The sound of footfalls is deadened by my cocoon. I lean forward, the tree – the scent of sap so fresh and sharp – hugs me; I force myself to breathe.

A dark grey shape passes by and, involuntarily, I jerk away; there's nowhere to go. I half expect whatever's outside to circle back, for a giant eye to press against the hole, begin tearing at the tree…

Ten minutes later there's nothing, no further noises. Unless it's lying in wait. But I can't bear this hidey-hole any longer. I try to find the seam, the place I unpicked, and for long, long seconds my fingers can't find anything, nothing except a smooth, slightly sticky surface. So long that I begin to think this is my end – after surviving everything else I've been through – in the guts of a tree trunk; that I'll starve and rot and desiccate *here*, and no one will come looking for me. Rhea will be left with a summer husband and no idea what must be done at the end of his season. Village folk will sicken and die with no one to offer aid. And all I am and all I might become will be lost.

Then my fingertips snag on a line, almost perfectly straight, the scar left by my knife. I speak the words of opening, and light pours in through the gap like water. Cleansing. And I tumble out like a child hiding in a cupboard for too long, gulping in air as if I've been drowning. I lie on the leaf litter of the forest path too long, especially if something is lurking. Fortuitously, there's not. Nothing, except returned birdsong, the scrimbling and scrambling in the undergrowth of things with fur, harmless things. But no sense of oppression, no weight of attention on me.

I rise and set off towards home, nervous as a cat, listening carefully for anything out of the ordinary.

* * *

When I step out of the forest onto my holding, I see Rhea leaving the barn, dropping the bar back in place. She spies me and waves as if she hasn't been caught doing exactly what I told her not to. As I get closer, her smile fades and I think how forbidding my expression must be, all the disruptions and discombobulations of this day writ large.

'What did I say?' I hiss, grabbing her elbow and pulling her towards the cottage. Her feet barely touch the ground and I'm aware of my height and strength, of her lack. I think about the fire that comes when she calls, but I'm too angry to be cautious. 'What did I say?'

'Not to leave the house.'

'Not to leave the house. Not to go into the barn.' I reef open the front door and push her inside. My right hand goes to the face of the green woman; the familiarity of the gesture calms me somewhat. 'Why didn't you listen?'

'I was… curious.' She throws herself onto the armchair, sulky as a child.

'You know what's said about curiosity and cats?'

'Cats have nine lives, don't you know?' she snaps back.

'How many do you think you've lost so far? How many close calls, how many escapes? Count those and you might decide to be less profligate with your remaining chances.' I shake my head, pacing back and forth in front of the unlit hearth. 'And, Rhea, you are not the only one at risk here if you're careless. Me. I don't flaunt my workings in front of the village, I never show anyone what I've made. Never show a summer husband! Never give anyone a reason to destroy you, certainly not because you couldn't be bothered to control your whims.'

'Mehrab, I'm sorry—'

'Will you be sorry when we're dancing in the flames or at the end of a rope? When they decide to swim us in a drowning pool?'

Those blue eyes fill, the bottom lip trembles, and I'm sure she looks fetching even when in floods of tears. Another rage rises in me that isn't her fault; for a moment, I'm so jealous of her youth and beauty I could spit. With restraint, I remind myself she's not responsible for that any more than she's responsible for anyone's reaction to her face. Beauty is luck, a gamble, and brings as much ill as it does good; and I had my share of it. I steady myself. 'Weeping doesn't work on me.'

Rhea gives me a sulky look but dashes the tears from her cheeks with angry wipes, sniffles. I remind myself how young she is; that she's been separated from everything she's known, family and friends; that she's settled here surprisingly well; that she's been helpful. That this infraction is quite small and I am overreacting.

'Rhea, if I tell you to do something it's not out of whimsy. Being aware of how easily life can change is the one thing that might keep you safe. This is a witch's life. Unless you go deeper into the woods, off the paths, and never have anything to do with humanity for the rest of your life, you will always need to be vigilant.'

'Why didn't you go deeper into the woods?'

'I did! When Fenna brought me here, it hardly ever saw a visitor apart from Yrse's fosterlings. The village was smaller, but there's more traffic now because the smith doesn't just shoe horses but breeds them, his metalwork and weapons are in demand. The Audelay sisters' tapestries and fabrics are sought after. These seem such small things, but they draw attention – at the moment things are sent out, but eventually… eventually folk will come in and then we will be noticed if we're not clever and cunning.' I sigh. 'Places like Berhta's Forge have neither doctors nor churches, so we can thrive here. Eventually, though, others will come. When they grow bigger – and trust me, this place *is* growing bigger – those are two things that come seeking a foothold.'

She hangs her head. 'I *am* sorry, Mehrab. I'm… so used to thinking about myself and no one else. I can't say I'll ever be perfect, but I am trying. I am trying to be less selfish. You're right. I was bored and curious. I wanted to see him, to know more…'

I clear my throat. 'It – he has a purpose. He has a season. He's an instrument. A time will come when you make your own, perhaps, wherever you wash up in life, if you need such a tool – but you need to learn how to create, how to manage and how to *end* such a thing.' Shaking my head, I finish: 'And the time will come when his season is over. Then you will have a task you will not like, but which must be done.'

wonder if that was the beginning, so small a drop, yet the very first taste.

I set him to collecting branches and logs that have already fallen – it seems cruel to ask him to cut down trees, although I do make him chop whatever's already dead and stack it into the woodpile against winter's breath. He carries water to the garden, feeds the pigs and goats, sheep and cows; the two oxen do not like him, but the old heavy horse seems to find him acceptable – although if not watched carefully it will try to nibble at the green growth of his hair. If you don't look too closely he's not that much different to a muscular young man, tall and broad; it's only when you focus that you notice the blunt features, the grassy tint to his skin and the entirety of his eyes. I send him onto the roof of the cottage and the barn, too, to check for leaks and any thatch that needs repair, have him dredge the pond and clear the reeds (and lay them out to dry), dig a channel to allow fresh water to flow in from the stream, and another for it all to flow out again so the supply is continually renewed.

I have Rhea pruning the orchard, but when I'm distracted with the summer husband, she trims the smallest apple tree too enthusiastically and I fear whatever it puts forth will be very poor indeed – or entirely non-existent. With a deep breath, I begin to teach her as I should have in the first place with a practical demonstration. Her next effort is better. I whisper an apology to the poor scalped first one, though, and promise it a wassail cup when the time comes, just as the oldest tree is given. I carve a small rune at the base of its trunk, and feed it a few drops of my blood while I sing a spell to help it grow back mightily. In winter, Rhea can have her head in the pruning of the older trees; they'll be dormant, and it won't matter then. But she must be tender around the young ones; it's not lost on me that I might also take that advice too.

Some days we pick so many berries – blackberries, raspberries, elderberries, gooseberries and rowanberries – that we have to make three trips to carry all the baskets home. The bottles line up like legions and I can't help but think that if we run out of everything else, at least there'll be a surfeit of jam. The summer husband takes to shearing the sheep surprisingly quickly; there's an efficiency to him that's commendable. The animals are quiet in his hands as he clips the wool away; I gather it up and in the evening Rhea spins it into thread, and the whole cottage smells like lanolin. She's surprisingly skilled but shares that her mother was a wool merchant's daughter, so that makes sense. I'll take it, eventually, to Misses Audelay in the village to weave it into cloth on their looms.

The hay and wheat will be harvested some weeks apart; the former will be baled and stacked in the barn for the animals, the latter bundled into sheaves to dry, then winnowed and threshed, and I'll take the sacks of grain to Sanne at the mill for grinding into flour. It's the only thing I can't do by myself if I absolutely must.

I do my best to lose myself in the work, and for the most part, I succeed. Days go by, feeding into night and back again. I *wish* I could say I think only about what needs to be done around the holding in the cup of summer's palm, in order to prepare us for winter. This time should be one of deep satisfaction at organising my life, providing for myself, my fosterling.

But.

But.

But I hear them in the darkness each night though I told her he was to stay in the barn. She speaks, he does not (cannot); his noises are barely more than grunts, branches knocking against each other in the wind. All I can think is that I wish she had a little more consideration. Well, not all. I think how I wish her ill, how I wish her gone, how I wish him *kindling.* I wish them no joy of each other, though they take it and give it. I wish that she'd let loose a spark and set him alight.

Every day is a challenge to keep my temper when one of them does something wrong. Or not even wrong, just something I would not have done. Or differently, because one always experiments to find a better way or a way that suits one best. It's exhausting, reminding myself of this daily, saying *Be patient. Be kind. Be reasonable.*

I wish.

I wish.

I wish.

And if wishes were horses then beggars would ride.

I wish I were a better person, that I could shrug this off, be generous about it. Gods know I'm trying.

And I know there's no point in screaming at her, no point weeping and wailing. She didn't do it on purpose, there was no intent on her part, only my own carelessness when I made him. No point in anything when he'd loved her from first sight (though I can't help but wonder would he still have done so, even had he seen me first? Would she have managed to circumvent even *that* magic?). No point in putting her out, sending her away, being petty and *small*. He'd only follow and that would complicate matters further, the pair of them wandering lost in the woods.

Yet I cannot help the whispers in my mind that don't drown out the murmurs from her room but rather amplify them. He was meant to be *mine*. That's why he was made. That's why all summer husbands are made for we women on our own. We provide for ourselves; the things we cannot easily get are created by eldritch means, even husbands. And even if there'd been no spark between us, he'd have been my company, my reliable worker for his season. I cannot help but think this is another thing, this adoration, that's come easily to her.

I wish I were a better person.

Worse still: Rhea insisted on naming him despite my warnings that it's something I'd learned long ago not to do (a named thing is harder to let go of). She sings it in the dark hours, and it finds my ears with the same harsh clarity as a beacon light blinds the eye. I cannot avoid it, even in my sleep, and upon waking I feel my head is full of the sound of her voice, the sough of his name.

I think of another appellation, flung into the darkness many years gone by, with the same urgency but by my voice. I think of the strangeness of my own name being sounded out by underdeveloped lips and tongue, not quite as it should be, but close enough, strange enough, to imprint forever on my heart, my mind, my conscience… the places where all my sins hide.

And I grit my teeth, for it's all I can do, and wait for the time to come.

* * *

One morning, I return from downriver where I've been fishing – seven fat trout lie in the bottom of my basket, occasionally twitching still. One will go in the pot for tonight's dinner, the rest will be salted and dried to be stored. I find Rhea standing in front of the cottage, staring up above the lintel over the front door. Arlo is out in the wheat field, weeding.

'What are you doing?' I grumble at the girl.

She points at the carved head. 'What's that? I've never seen them anywhere else before.'

I can't help but think she hasn't travelled much; then again, the main places I've seen them are rural. Not a feature of the cities, which are no great devotees of pastoral lore and ways.

'Some would call it a green woman,' I say shortly.

Every house in the village, no matter how mean or how fine, has a foliate head as decoration. Some above the doorframe, some to the side, the braver (or more foolhardy) have them on the fence or hung on a tree in the yard. Everyone knows you want the protection as close to the house as possible, preferably touching the walls. Some few are simply bearded men's faces poking from a frame of leaves, others have a more distinct womanly cast; a very few have vegetation (sometimes purely fruit, sometimes vegetables, sometimes a mix of both) disgorging from the mouth, sometimes corn cobs from the ears. This one is female, has nascent horns, more hind-girl than green woman, but I've actually *seen* hind-girls, never a green man or woman. Doesn't mean they don't exist, just means I've not witnessed any sign of their existence. Perhaps they've already been and already gone, things that have passed from the world.

Rhea gives me a shrewd look; it appears she's become keen

to the nuances of my tone. I shrug. 'There was a green man when I arrived here – the old woman who was here before me had one. When she was gone, I decided I preferred the idea of this looking out for me. Edo the carpenter made it for me.'

'The horns?'

Again, I shrug. 'Part green woman – the symbol of the earth, rebirth, the natural rhythm of things – part hind-girl, women who choose their own fate, make their own choices and leave old lives behind.' Where I come from, we have no hind-girls. I heard the tales of them *here*, saw them *here*, when I first arrived. Chose them as my north star when I was in need of a direction, of a guide, of a beacon to walk towards; a reason to go on, to have hope.

'Are there any summer wives? I think a female version of Arlo would look like this.'

The observation irks me. 'No summer wives, not that I know of.' But I wonder if anyone had thought to make a wife of such a thing. Others have taken so many other things to wife – foxes, seals, bears, wolves, badgers – stealing their skins and leaving them stranded in the shape of a woman, so why not? At least the summer husband is reshaped only for a season, and his end is a natural one.

I thrust the basket at her, say, 'Scale and gut these,' then continue on into the cottage, fighting my own dark thoughts.

14

At least there have been no more visitations, not that I can sense, no more offerings left on the doorstep either as gifts or lures, no more sense of a pursuit when I enter the woods. I wonder if the presence of the summer husband is what keeps the other thing (or things) at bay – the strangeness of the one repelling the other. I would make new wards if I knew what might lurk in the shadows, but I don't. Not specifically, and while oft-times general protections keep all manner of creatures out, there are some that exist by their own rules – and one needs to know those rules before one can guard against them.

No visitations, no, but when I do manage to slumber (to stop my ears to muted whispers and sighs and moans from the attic room above – how glad I am she refused to move into the spare bedroom opposite mine) I begin to walk in my sleep. Not something I've done in a very long time, and I hate it. Hate the sense of being out of control, of a tiny part of my mind rebelling. Sending me awry unconsciously while not sharing the rest of the plan with me – the motivating desire buried deeper than I can access. Or perhaps that part of me simply knows that I'd say *no*.

The first night, I woke at the foot of my bed, reaching for the door handle. I stared at the windows, the night-darkened glass, searching for I-didn't-know-what. Putting it down to a one-off, my mind disturbed from the events of past days, I returned to bed.

The second night, I woke at the front door, my hand on the key to turn it. My eyes flew open; don't know what woke me. I wonder if it was the cold metal of the key, the sensation enough to shake me from my trance.

The third night – tonight – I wake only when my foot touches the waters of the Black Lake. I've not been here since the night when the god of the hunt went by.

Weeks before Rhea arrived, before the day I was trapped in the penitents' path, on a full moon I went to the Black Lake because curiosity had gotten the better of me once more. Despite the number of years since I fled, I still wonder about the kingdom I left behind, those who remained, the others who did not. The acts I committed then, in my youth when I knew no better but should have – no. When I did know better but chose to act otherwise because what I desired, what I pursued, moved me more strongly than right action. Or perhaps I *thought* it was right, then.

Those nights, perhaps once every few years, I have gone to the Black Lake to use its undisturbed surface as a scrying mirror, to watch the entire city spread across the smoothness of the water, to seek that face I… When I want a greater vision than that offered by the scrying mirror, that is where I go. And that night, curiosity struck keenly, disguising herself as grief, perhaps – or perhaps she truly is grief, perhaps that's her truest name – and I crept along the hidden paths to find the liquid obsidian waiting for me. Using the Black Lake for this purpose is foolish and difficult – it demands too much blood, really, another reason not to do such a thing except years apart – but there are days when the yearning to see it all, the whole broad spectrum of the city (what's become of it – what *will* become of it) is too much and I'm willing to pay that red price.

I'd only just sat by the shore, begun to open the cut in my forearm when the crashing of something in the undergrowth reached me. Horses and stags, unearthly shouts of men who no longer belonged to the earth, and howls of wish-hounds and hunting dogs. Too soon the noise was upon me and the leader of the hunt reined in – yet he was *alone.* All that noise of a gaggle of hunters and mounts and pursued beasts? Here there was just this one being; as if the cacophony that accompanied him was a memory only. A ghost of itself.

Beneath the moon sat half a man upon a skeletal beast. When I say "half a man" I mean not the top or bottom halves, but the left half, the sinister side; somehow staying on that saddle, somehow remaining on his bony mount. And the substance of him flowed and shifted like smoke, sometimes forming the other half of him so that I gained an impression of how he might look if whole, but the right never stayed, only blew back like smoke from a fire, was swallowed once more by the left, and any impression I'd had was quickly gone, as if the memory could not remain.

I'd heard tales since childhood of the one who led the hunt – or the ones, for such stories travel across countries, across seas, of a man or woman who leads the pack; there's more than one master or mistress of the chase – but I'd never *seen* such a thing before. Not in any other place I'd lived or travelled, not in any other forest I'd traversed, and not in *this* vast forest in the two decades I'd lived here and roamed its byways. Had heard histories and recountings, certainly, about how men had joined the chase at the hunt-master's invitation and in the end found the quarry to be their own wife or child; or men who'd run when confronted by the riders and hounds and been driven off cliffs or into mires; of women who'd been taken away on the saddles of otherworldly beings and never heard of again; of children who'd either charmed or been harmed by the leggy wish-hounds, adopting them as pets or becoming food for the beasts depending on their nature. Always a tale of a band, yet there was a single creature.

The rider before me stared and stared for an unbearably long time as if he knew me, and when he at last made to urge his mount forward I did the only thing my mind could grasp at and leapt into the Black Lake. Whatever dwelt there could not be worse than the thing that stalked back and forth on the bank while I swam down, down, a'down holding my breath until I thought my lungs would burst into a flame fit to burn water. When the moon passed behind a cloud, I surfaced far out, did my best not to gasp for air, not to swallow it greedily so the sound of it would travel back to what sought me on the shore.

And I stayed in that lake for hours because the master of the dark hunt did not leave until dawn threatened, pale streaks across the sky, and then the rider finally wheeled his horse and plunged away into the green to escape the day. And I was aware all that time, or so much of it that the difference doesn't matter, of something else in the lake with me. Beneath me and circling, never visible and never making contact, but I knew it was there. I *knew* it was there – mer, kelpie or other water-horse, mari-morgan, wicked jennie, rusalky, nelly longarms, merrow or water-bull; all aquatic, malign or mischievous in varying degrees – but it was still preferable to that bizarre and fractured dark thing that had lurked. Death by them would be quick, or I might even defend myself as only I could. But that thing waiting, beneath the trees, pacing back and forth? Whatever came from it would be slow. Somehow, I knew that.

I remember, now, the cold of the water when I finally climbed out, the chill of my soaking clothes and hair as I walked, the forest floor against my naked feet because I'd taken off my shoes to begin the ritual and left them when I'd taken to the water. And they were no longer waiting for me. I spent days in bed – it was at the end of winter, unseasonably warm, and the reason I'd survived the plunge into the lake – but I'd caught a bad chill and it was only the medicinal tisanes of my own making that made me well again so soon.

But tonight? How did I get back here? How long did I walk so far in my sleep?

I remember the odd sense of the water against my skin, soaking through the fabric of my trews and cloak. I grasp now at the skirt of my long nightgown and find it… not entirely wet.

Not wet.

I pinch my upper arm, hard.

Wake at the sharp pain.

I'm standing knee-deep in the pond in the front yard of my holding. There's no moon except a crescent sliver, the rest swallowed by the night. Nothing more than another sleep-walking episode. How far might I have gone, though?

'Mehrab!' Rhea's voice comes to me from a long way off. Grows louder. 'Mehrab! Mehrab! Are you all right?'

I'm shivering and shaking despite the humidity of the night, the warm wind blowing through the crops, the trees, rattling the doors and roof of the barn, making the rose bushes dance, the bells in the field jangle. Suddenly my joints ache, and the fog rises in my brain and I can barely remember my own name. My temperature rises, rises, rises and I feel like I'll burst into flames, that there's a fire beneath my skin. And, above all, I feel *old*.

Rhea helps me back inside and I don't have the strength to push her away, no matter how much part of me wants to. The only thing I'm certain of is that this sleepwalking is not natural; it's a summons, a pull, and I must do something about it.

* * *

In the morning, I'm stiff and sore, as if I'd run a league but there's no chill this time, no sign of anything lingering. When I come down to breakfast, I find it already prepared. Rhea has made porridge, sweet and buttery the way I like it, she's brewed a strong dandelion tea, and there's bread cut thick and being toasted over the fire. One of the new raspberry jams is waiting, as is a pat of butter.

'Thank you,' I say and sit. Through the window I can see the summer husband already at work digging a new garden bed in the potager.

'How are you feeling, Mehrab?' Her careful tone irritates me more than it should, as if I'm a frail old woman, with one foot in the grave. I pause before answering, gather the threads of my temper and tie them tightly together.

'I am perfectly well, Rhea. Ridden by the mare of night, is all. Dreams of old days and faces long forgotten. A life lived very differently.'

'Where were you born, Mehrab? I can still hear, ever so slightly, a trace of an accent. Only on certain words, and only when you're tired.' The change in topic is welcome, the subject not so much.

That stops me in my tracks. It hadn't occurred to me that the girl might observe me the way I do her, cataloguing each glance and gesture, giggle and twitch, seeing what's repeated, habitual, until I can almost predict her actions, her questions and replies. It *does* occur to me that I've underestimated Rhea. That I should be more careful. That I should have some respect for her – she might not be the idiot child I predicted. 'Not here,' I say shortly. Then relent, 'In a country to the west, far over the sea. And I left a long time ago and don't wish to discuss the matter any further.'

'But you *were* like me. On the run – that's why you left your home and family?'

Home was my suite of rooms in the palace, the grand villa I was awarded for services rendered to the royal family. Family? My mother and sister I'd long ago lost track of, left behind in the slums by the harbour when I ascended, stolen away by my mentor. And that mentor? The high sorceress, in a country where we were tolerated far better than elsewhere (here-where); she was the closest thing I had to true family, I suppose. She wasn't always kind but there was always a reason for her cruelty, and that I understood. But she kept me safe and fed, she taught me the magics I know today, helped me develop the power that took me to the heights of wealth and influence (and down to the hollows of the earth once more); she taught me enough to know how to experiment with my other forms of magic. How to make my reach exceed my grasp, and how to regard all failures as a means to learn. She was the one who'd instructed me on how to leave – who'd warned me always to be prepared for the day the sky falls in, as it inevitably will, to varying degrees – which meant I was ready the day the walls were breached, and the beautiful city began to burn. When I—

No. Don't think about that.

'I was like you, yes. No more questions, Rhea. Not now. Not today.'

She obeys, though I can tell she doesn't want to. But she keeps busy, pottering around the kitchen, cleaning up after herself before sitting down opposite me and eating her own bowl of porridge (*This one is juuuust right*). I stare out the window for a good few long minutes, my mind untroubled in the quiet of the cottage. I become so relaxed that it takes me a moment to realise someone has materialised out of the forest, at the mouth of the path that leads to Berhta's Forge. I stand so quickly my chair tips over.

'Rhea. Someone's here. Hide Arlo. And yourself for good measure.'

'What will you—'

'I'll distract them. Hurry – out the back door, not too far into the woods, and don't leave the border of the holding.' I head for the front, hoping we're quick enough.

15

Luckily my visitor is hesitating, making her uncertain way towards the cottage, so I with my long strides manage to intercept her before she comes too close. I know of old that the line of sight from that path to the fields is obstructed by the barn, so she won't have seen Arlo. As long as Rhea is careful about where she takes him, as long as she's swift – into the woods, hopefully, down by the stream – no one should be any the wiser. I don't look over my shoulder to check, don't draw attention anywhere else, merely pin a broad smile on my face and nod at the child coming towards me and call, 'Hello.'

The child's wide-eyed, scraggly red-haired, thin-limbed. There's a purple bruise along her chin, blossoming up to her right cheek. My hand itches to reach out and examine the injury, but she looks skittish, likely to flee at any sudden movement, so I knit my fingers together in front of my skirts, calm and untroubled. 'I'm Mistress Mehrab. Do you need help?'

The girl nods, hesitantly.

'Is it Tieve, then?' Has my patience paid off at last? Rather later than I'd imagined, but still a result.

Again, she nods, says timidly, 'Yes.'

'Can I offer you some tea? Perhaps breakfast? There is sweet porridge and fresh cream.' The child looks half-starved, so this offer seems a good one. She grins, relieved whether at the offer of food or tea I cannot divine, but sweep one hand towards the front door anyway. 'You may enter, or I can bring your breakfast out here if you'd prefer to eat in the garden? The fresh air?'

Giving her a choice is important, I sense, but I also think her curiosity wins out. She wants to see the witch's cottage; my, won't she be disappointed to see how ordinary it is, all light and bright and airy? Perhaps I should decorate with bats' wings and cobwebs?

* * *

Settled at the table, Tieve eats with spectacular speed, burps and turns bright red with embarrassment.

I smile as I take a seat across from her, my own cup of tea warming my hands. 'Take your time, there's no hurry.'

'Mam says I've bad manners.'

'Nonsense. You're hungry is all, I can tell. But I don't want you to make yourself sick. There's no need to hurry, no one will take your food and there's more if you wish.' Her smile breaks out at the promise. 'Do you have brothers by chance?'

She rolls her eyes. 'Seven.'

'Hard to get enough food when they're around, I imagine.'

Another nod, chagrined. 'There's not much anyways and they eat first. Mam says the boys need it most because they have to work in the fields.'

It sounds like her family's among those with too many

mouths and insufficient skills for finer work or even much land of their own, so they're at the mercy of those who employ them for hard physical labour. The sort of family that sometimes doesn't survive winter months intact. 'Well, you're welcome to visit here. There will always be bread and butter to break your fast, something to drink, and a fire to warm yourself by.'

Which seems a lot to offer so quickly when I hardly know this child, but there's something haunted about her (do I see something of myself in her eyes?), and I cannot leave a child whose mother puts her last to hang in the wind. She thanks me, then finishes her meal at a normal pace. When she's done, she politely refuses a second helping. But I'll make a parcel of sweet buns for her to take when she goes, and a few copper bits to hold against a rainy day, a few more to buy bread from Anselm (and perhaps I'll have a quiet word that he shouldn't be letting his daughter's best friend starve, even if they no longer speak).

She asks to use the privy, then returns, wiping damp soap-scented hands on her tunic. When she sits, Mr Tib jumps up onto her lap and she seems delighted.

'Just don't let him on the table,' I say, despite the knowledge of a losing battle with the cat. 'Now, why have you come to see me, Tieve?'

She doesn't look away, instead holds my gaze and speaks clearly and firmly. 'Orin said you'd been asking for me. And about Ari.'

I nod. 'But your friends let me know you didn't want to be found.'

'No.'

'You're here, so something's changed.'

'Ari's been my friend since we were very small. If I'd wished for a sister, she'd be it. But… she doesn't want to play with me anymore, and I don't want to play with her.'

'Why's that?'

'She's different. She pinches other children, slaps them, pulls their hair. Only the worst ones will play with her now. The ones that like to hurt birds and cats and foxes.'

I point to the bruising on her face. 'Did Ari do that to you?'

She shakes her head. 'But she egged on the one who did. A boy, Jory.'

I rise, go to the workroom and bring out a blue glass vial. She permits me to rub the cream onto the bruising, and I'm careful not to hurt her. 'This has essence of calendula, arnica and witch hazel suspended in lanolin. It should help improve things very quickly.' I put the cork back in the neck of the bottle. 'Take it with you, you should get another five or six applications out of it.'

Her hand darts, out then back, empty. 'I can't pay you.'

'Well, let us barter then. Information in return for treatment. Fair?'

The hand returns, I place the vial into the centre of a slightly calloused palm, and her thin fingers curl around it. 'Fair.'

'Can you recall anything strange the day Ari went missing?'

'Nothing. We were supposed to play in the afternoon after she'd done her chores, were going to meet by the well, and I waited. I waited a long time and then got angry because she didn't come. I went to the bakery, but her mother didn't know where Ari was, and she got angry too. I think she'd lost track of time. Then she yelled at Mr Hadderholm and they both got angry. That's when I went home. The searchers went out not long after that, and we young ones all had to stay locked in.'

A natural reaction, the assumption that another child might be in danger. Especially living in the forest where children are such sweet meat for so many things lurking in the shadows, and sometimes walking boldly in the light.

'And you didn't see her again, not until she returned at the end of spring?'

'Mam told me Ari was back. How happy her parents were – but, Mistress Mehrab, they'd barely paid any attention to her before.' As I'd suspected. 'Now, they're so nice to her and she's been so mean to them.'

'And when did you see her?'

'As soon as Ma told me, I ran to the bakery – but she just looked at me like she didn't know me. Or didn't care.'

I wonder if Ari – the old Ari – had sometimes fed her friend fresh stolen bread, enough to help the girl be not so thin. However, the weeks of Ari's absence and the subsequent ones of her indifference meant Tieve was half-starved. 'And she's been cruel?'

Tieve nods, looks away. I don't need any greater detail, I can imagine from those bruises. 'And why did you come to see me?'

'Another child's gone missing.'

* * *

A little boy this time, younger than Ari, only three and barely able to toddle a circuit of his parents' very large garden. The son of headman-mayor-what-have-you Thaddeus Peppergill and his wife Deva – another couple who'd been childless until she'd come and begged for my help. Prosperous people with business interests, who organise the caravans that move the various products of Berhta's Forge out of the Great Forest and into larger towns and cities, and also bring other things back, either useful or frivolous, for those whose purses stretch to such fripperies. Sold in the small Peppergill emporium: cosmetics, the latest fashions, jewellery, sweet treats, strange alcoholic brews more exotic than those made in the Fox & Crow, the stills in most back gardens, paintings and carvings in marble and other semi-precious stones – as if there is a competition for such things in the middle of the woods.

The place is not large enough to warrant either church or god-hounds, but the commerce Thaddeus pushes is the thing that will one day bring them. For the moment, he is the one to conduct wedding ceremonies and funerals, but eventually the church will come and bump him aside. Doctors will appear and begin to spread lies about the witch in the woods. Everything will change in Berhta's Forge.

But not yet.

Not yet.

It's late afternoon by the time I take Tieve back to the village; the idea of letting a child wander in the woods on her own strikes me as the height of foolishness. I could have insisted she stay the night, but if anyone thought her missing it would set off another panic. She's clasping the cloth-wrapped bundle of sweet buns as if they're a treasure.

When we're about halfway there, I hear the crack of a branch somewhere behind us, so loud, then utter silence, as if someone or something has frozen mid-stride. I think about the black thing that stalked me weeks ago, but this doesn't feel the same or sound the same. Besides, I don't have time to hide as I did then and I don't want the child to see me do it, so I urge her up the trunk of an ancient spreading yew. I reach upwards, grab a handful of leaves – its berries would be even better but it's too soon for those to be out – so I scrunch the leaves, drop them where I stand and then climb the trunk as fast as I can. Not a spell, no, but if I'm right, whatever's coming will react to the scent of the crushed leaves.

I swing up beside Tieve, put a finger to my lips. *Quiet.*

The yew's a tree for the dead; it often takes its place proudly in graveyards, roots winding their way through ribcages and skulls. But in forests such as this, creatures will come to its foot to die; they sense a sacred place, choosing to fertilise it with their deaths. The essence of dying is absorbed, making its leaves and berries not only poisonous to the living but also acting as a deterrent to those who hunt them. A distraction. The smell of the already-dead can throw them off the scent of those yet-to-die.

Peering down, the multitude of branches and foliage obscures whatever comes along the track, then lurks and circles at the base of the trunk – and what I see is a bright red flare of fabric. A cloak. A red riding hood. A quick glance at Tieve shows her hand over her mouth, her eyes big as the moon as she recognises her friend. She probably realises, as I do, that Ari had followed her. The child below makes a discontented sound, a sort of growl, and swirls away from where the crushed leaves lie; heads off in the direction of Berhta's Forge.

Her reaction to the yew decoy makes me suspect Ari couldn't cross the boundary of my holding. I hope not. I hope Rhea is safe, that she stayed within my borders; either way, I don't believe Arlo would allow anything to happen to her.

We stay in the tree for another fifteen minutes, perhaps – not that I'm scared of an eleven-year-old, but of what one might think she can do after stalking an adult – then climb cautiously down. As we continue along, I pluck long grasses from the undergrowth, twigs and leaves from rowan and elm and even spot some of the rare hairless nettles that don't sting, and as we go I weave together a little doll, give her a rowan-berry cluster for a necklace. I prick my finger and dab some crimson onto the crown of the little thing's head and whisper a protection spell.

'Here.' I hand it to Tieve. 'Keep her secret, in your pocket all the time, especially if you must travel this path again to see me. It's to help you pass beneath notice.' I wonder if I should enspell her shoes too, but the doll should be sufficient. 'Remember, hide her. She's yours.'

Tieve gives me the glance of a co-conspirator and hides the doll away in the pocket of her rough pinafore. 'And don't tell anyone about what we saw.'

'Didn't see anything,' she says airily.

'Good girl. Now, let's hurry along.'

16

The lad's disappearance had been discovered early this morning, Tieve said, the village alerted by his mother's screams. That was when Tieve took it upon herself to come to me because she figured sooner was better than later, after what had happened with Ari.

Once there was a child who went a'wandering into the woods, down its paths and then off them, setting foot onto mossy slopes and rocks, forging through undergrowth and brambles, feasting on berries and nothing else. Certain that the deepest part of the forest held no dangers, only the siren-song of the trees, calling.

I think of my mother's voice, low and soft, telling this tale to my sister one eve. I wrack my brains trying to recall the ending, but the memory's murky, something I've given up or suppressed – something I didn't like and preferred not to hang onto. Something other than the trees was calling, perhaps? Something other than a gentle creature? Something with appetites? The child never left the woods, that's the only thing of which I'm sure.

I think of Yrse, the old woman who lived in the cottage before I did, the one Fenna deposited me with. The one I ignored when she warned me against so many acts, including going to Faolan's bed, then against caring for him in addition to fucking him. She was right and I've hated her for it. But by the time her predictions of heartache came true, she was dead and gone, and I was left with no one to beg sympathy of, no one to complain to – although I did, sitting by the grave I'd dug for her in the rose garden, where smaller ones would be later sunk to keep her company. She'd never mentioned children going missing, not in her time, and she'd been the witch by Berhta's Forge for almost sixty years. Born in the village, raised there, moved into the forest with a woodcutter husband in her youth, buried him among the trees not long after (*Not the man I thought he was* she sang to me once in her cups) and then remained there with only occasional guests in the form of runaway rebel witches. Her own powers were very small – she was a potions woman, though, handy with those medicinal and healthful, occasionally destructive (*But only ever for good purpose, to save a woman or a child*). The greenwood had been, for her, quiet and restful, a place of refuge.

Then I came, her last fosterling, a little like Rhea though older, not necessarily any wiser. Angry and hurt and fearful, used to power and all it had brought me, full of imperious habits, but finding myself unable to use my magic the way I had. Obliged to hide everything I was because it was too dangerous to show everything I could do. Eventually, I settled in. After Faolan and that debacle, I settled better. Made a new home, made my own peace with the villagers, showed them I could be trusted. But I was never one of them, not born here; a foreigner forever.

'Mistress Mehrab.' Tieve's tone is soft, her small hand on my arm insistent. 'We're here.'

'Oh. Thank you.'

'I could tell you were elsewhere.' The child looks solemn.

'Thank you for pulling me back to earth.' I need my wits about me; it's one thing to be lost to the world when I'm on my own or even with Rhea (who's grown used to my habits) and quite another to wander into the village looking like an idiot. Not a good idea. 'And now, Tieve, it's time for you to go home. And not a word of defiance – it might not help for folk to know you came to me.'

Reluctantly, she nods. 'Yes, Mistress Mehrab.'

'Don't forget to keep that poppet safe and secret. Take her with you everywhere and avoid Ari as best you can.'

She nods again and slips away. I wait beneath the trees until she enters a small cottage, one of those in the back rows of the village. What must it be like to live with seven brothers? Fighting off a shudder, I make my way to the marketplace, which is empty, as is the green. Stores and stalls are shuttered, and all is silent. I imagine that most of the adults are out searching the woods.

I make my way towards the Peppergill manor, the largest house in Berhta's Forge. I notice, as I always do, that there's no green woman at the door – she hangs as an ornament on the large ash tree by the picket fence. Patiently, I begin rapping and am eventually rewarded by a red-eyed maid, very young, opening the door. She hesitates.

'I'm here to speak with your mistress,' I say firmly. 'Since I'm assuming the master is out.'

The girl steps aside, allowing me to cross the threshold, then leads me along a corridor to a spacious dark-panelled parlour, curtains and sofas and chairs finely decorated in shades of yellow, patterned in roses and daisies. Clustered in the room are women I recognise as the foremost matrons, wives of men of various standing and others who are the mistresses of those self-same foremost husbands. Gathered with them are children, aged from babes-in-arms to perhaps fifteen, girls and boys looking surly. Elsewhere in the village there will be other children shuttered in their own homes in the care of mothers, older siblings or grandparents unfit for traipsing forest paths. Some, for whom no one cares, will be doing as they please. I wonder if Tieve's mother has been waiting anxiously; I wonder if she's yelling even now at her daughter.

Deva Peppergill sits in a tapestry-covered chair shaped not unlike a throne, gold and silver threads picking out more roses, more daisies. Unlike most of the other women in the room, she's not weeping, although her long face is the colour of milk, not helped by her greying hair. The child – Matthias – was a miracle; she and Thaddeus had spent many years trying for a baby, and although Thaddeus managed to father offspring on any mistress he took (at last count there were six girls and three boys all bearing his large brown eyes and thick hair, just not his surname), his wife seemed impregnable. Until they – she – finally came to me, five years ago, all unwilling to have truck with a witch, but spilling out how other women had come to me and borne offspring. That they'd urged her to come to me, even Faolan's wife.

It was a near squeak of a thing, with her almost fifty then, but with some of the strongest fertility potions and spells I could muster, and a little something else, Deva finally fell pregnant. Though they both dote on the boy, neither likes to be reminded that they needed aid; and Deva doesn't like to think of a time when it was whispered that her husband would likely put her aside for one of his fruitful paramours. Yet I can't help but wonder, if Tieve hadn't come for me, how long it might have taken before the Peppergills thought to do so – would they have learned from the Hadderholms' lesson? Or thought themselves better and let that longed-for child disappear through pride?

'What are you doing here?' Deva Peppergill's tone is unfriendly; perhaps that's my answer there.

'Hello to you too, Deva.'

'Hello. What are you doing here?'

'I heard Matthias has gone missing. I thought perhaps I could help.'

'You didn't manage to help Anselm and Gida,' she hisses at me. I wonder at the vehemence – she and Gida are not especially close. Gida doesn't even begin to approach the status required to take tea in Deva's elegant parlour. A shared loss, then; a shared grief. Resentment. Idiocy. 'Thaddeus is leading search parties.'

I ignore the accusation. 'No one came to me when Ari went missing, not for days. I can't work miracles, or at least not all the time.' I drop my gaze to her stomach, remind her that she wouldn't have that child if not for me. She flinches. 'Yet you all expect them. So, tell me: when did you last see your son?'

'When I put him to bed last night.'

'You did? Or the nanny?'

'I did. He's *mine*.' Over her shoulder I see the maid servant who'd let me in; she gives a slight shake of the head. Deva won't want *me* to know she's handing off care of the child she wanted so badly.

'Of course.'

Even though the others, the richer ones, do exactly the same thing. None would admit they don't tuck their little darlings into bed at night, sealing them in with a sweet kiss to the forehead, perhaps a story before slumber. No. The nannies and serving maids do these things, telling the little ones the tales they grew up with, little snippets of superstition, folk and fairy lore, warnings about the creatures that creep about in the dark looking for tasty treats, how they shouldn't let a foot or hand hang over the edge of the mattress lest it prove too tempting for the things that live beneath the bed, that only come out after sundown – the night-tenants, as my mother called them, those with dominion over the dark hours. The children of the rich are frequently raised by the poor, yet familiar fears are carried in our blood just the same, planted there before we can properly speak, sung to us by the voices of those who guard our bedtime. 'And the house was undisturbed? No sign of anyone entering? No strange noises heard after lights out?'

Deva shakes her head, twists her hands, one around the other. Still hasn't risen from her throne.

'I wish to look at his room,' I say and nod at the serving maid before her mistress can think twice and gainsay me. The girl is swift, leading me to the staircase and up, along a landing and into a large room filled with toys and books; wooden swords, carved horses, cast metal soldiers gaily painted in uniforms few military men would wear; I palm one for scrying. An enormous bear sits in a rocking-chair in one corner. I check the windows, find them all locked – the room stuffy and warm – and look at the bed, pulling back sheets lest there be a sign of blood or violence there. In the ceiling, no trapdoor or skylight that might be used as another entrance or exit. Nothing under the bed either, and the floors are solid when I stamp on them; same with the walls, no secret panel, nor passages.

Tapping a finger to my chin, I ask the girl, 'What's your name?'

'Cylla.'

'His room's not locked at night, Cylla?' I ask.

'No.' She adds hastily, 'I sleep downstairs, next to the kitchen. For his first three years I slept here, on a pallet in that corner. Then, a few months back, Master said it was time the boy learned to be on his own because we women were making him soft.' She bites her lip. 'The mistress loves him, only – she's tired. She's older for a mother and well, tired. So, I put him down in the eve and get him up in the morn, but she's with him the whole day, otherwise.'

I understand what Deva is going through, her time of life is the same as mine, except hers is complicated by a young child demanding attention when she's barely able to meet her own needs. I'd wondered, when she came to me, whether it was a blessing or a curse to help her bear a child at that age – but I wasn't prepared to make it easy for Thaddeus to set her aside, marry a mistress and write to the Archbishop of Lodellan begging a declaration of legitimacy for the relevant offspring. At the time, it felt like I was saving Deva from a precarious enough existence, that the child might just buy her some security. I didn't need to like her to want to help her.

'Cylla, return to your mistress, tell her I will have other questions in a moment.'

The girl's obedient and she goes. I'll likely only have a little time; from my pocket, I pull a long lozenge-shaped clear crystal on a string, something I retrieved from the workroom this morning, and hold it up, swinging the crystal in ever-increasing circles. If something magical and malign has been in the room, the crystal will become a dark purple.

I hold the crystal high so it catches the rays of sun from the windows, then chant, a thing that's as much a prayer as a spell (I've never been entirely sure of the difference between the two). Walking slowly around the room, the crystal echoes me, calling back softly and a little sadly it seems. While a pale green rises in its depths, there's no sign of the deep purple I was expecting. Finally, I give up. The green mist fades as does the song of the crystal.

The colour means nothing but contentment. A contented child inhabited this room. So, he wasn't taken. He *walked* out – toddled – under his own steam. He's so little, but I've never seen that stop a child. If he wanted to leave, if he thought something interesting waited outside? He'd have made his careful way down the stairs and out. He's tall enough to reach the doorhandles, big enough to turn them. Of course, it's entirely possible something *called* to him from outside – just as it did me – didn't need to enter the house to lure him forth, didn't need to pass under the gaze of the green woman that hangs from the tree branches in the front garden.

I make my way to the bottom of the stairs, where Deva is waiting, the other women a frozen wave behind her. I touch the older mother's arm.

'Nothing came into your house. So, Mattias left by his own will. Tonight, I'll scry, see what I can discover.' Even as I say it I shudder at the idea of undergoing that ritual again. Briefly, I consider going to the Black Lake this time, then I recall the things in the woods, the blood the lake will demand, that Rhea will need to get me back to the cottage on her own – or with the aid of the summer husband, which irks me quite irrationally. 'I'll return in the morning as soon as I can with any news – and if the child is found in the meantime, I expect to be advised as soon as possible. Am I understood?'

She nods, a short sharp gesture, and Cylla opens the door for me. I push my way through the crowd of women, and they part reluctantly as if letting me go is not what they wish to do. I'm down the front steps from the verandah and almost at the garden gate when I see a small brown bundle curled in the base of the ash tree, beneath the green woman that twists and turns in the breeze. Camouflaged a little, but I swear I'd have noticed it when I arrived! My heart leaps towards my mouth and it's all I can do to keep my stomach from following it. I swoop on the bundle, mind filled with thoughts of the red cloak, the red-wrapped parcel, that *slab* of child left on my doorstep. I reach out and grasp at the thing, more roughly than I should, and it gives a surprised squawk. I lift it up and the brown blanket falls away to reveal Matthias Peppergill in blue pyjamas, very grubby, a little smelly, clutching a knitted bear of golden-brown wool, but very much alive.

17

With the child deposited safely back with his mother and nursemaid, with loud thanks and quiet apologies ringing in my ears, and my forearms festooned with baskets of bread and fresh produce, sweet soaps and cheeses, I turn towards home. Yet by the time I get there, all these gifts will weigh me down and I'll be exhausted; I'm not the witch I used to be. It's probably time to make my life a little easier; my old feather-foot won't be around forever, and he's not fit for riding, hasn't been for years; getting him into the plough harness requires a long negotiation.

No sign of Faolan lurking, but in the main enclosure behind the smithy, out of the stables, are his pride – the forge work is his labour, breeding horses is his joy. Baskets at my feet, I lean my forearms on the top rail of the fence and admire the mares. One in the back corner, darkly dappled, most dignified and disinterested; three others all heavily pregnant, black, white, red. All beautiful. The black creeps closer but not close enough to be petted. I fish a ripe peach from one of the baskets and take a bite – it's a little tart still, perfect. The black mare paces over; I hold the fruit out to be snatched from my palm. She dances away, snorting with glee. The other two seemingly have no interest in risking their dignity even for a treat.

'Well done. Sorrel usually won't come near anyone except me.'

'Do you ever get any work done?' I don't turn to look at him until I sense his presence right beside me. I must be buoyed by the finding of Matthias Peppergill because the blacksmith's presence barely annoys me.

'Not when you're around. Fortunately, that's not often. Or rather fortunately for the purposes of my work ethic, less so for my amusement and distraction.'

'Gods, if I were an idiot I'd fall back into your bed with that talk. Such charm!' The words burst out and I don't mean them to; he only grins. I jerk my chin towards the mares. 'When are they due?'

'A month, for the red and Sorrel; the white, Birch, another month after that.'

Idly, I say: 'I'll be needing to replace my old feather-foot soon, I think.'

'You want to turn one of my very fine beauties into a cart horse? Plough horse? Have you gone mad?' His offence is genuine.

I laugh. 'No, I'll need a heavy horse for that, but you don't have any of those.'

'No, but I can find one for you, though. Bargain for a good one.'

'What cost?'

'A kind word, Mehrab, perhaps a smile.'

'Too expensive by half.' I snort. 'I might take one of the foals when they're old enough, though. For riding.'

'Taking up hunting, Mistress Mehrab?' He nods at the mare nibbling at my hair. 'Sorrel and Birch's offspring might be gentle enough. The red? Blister? Unlikely.'

'Blister?!'

'Well, she was Rowan but I called her Blister because she's fast and unpleasant. My lad's the only one she likes. He's got a rare gift with horses, shame he can't settle to anything.'

I laugh hard, feel a muscle in my stomach pull a little. I don't say that my hips and knees and ankles are getting tired of the walk into and out of Berhta's Forge. That it's time I gave myself a rest. 'What if I am taking up hunting, old man?'

He bows. 'Ah, now I've learned that the answer is "none of my business", old woman. I can keep the finest foal aside. And I'll talk to Gaderian Beck up north at Sarith's Ford – I'm up there soon – about another heavy horse for you – you don't want one too young for plough and cart, too flighty, too much trouble to train, you want them working right from the start.'

'Thank you. I'd appreciate that.' The black and white mares begin to prance, finally coming within reach, nuzzling at their master's neck, and the tips of my fingers – still wary, still teasing; the red maintains her distance. I can't help but smile. There's enough money hidden around my holding for a horse or several. If I'm honest, there's enough coin and gems buried to buy a castle, all carefully hoarded, by me and my predecessor. Safer than a big city bank, the forest earth. No one looks for it there. And fleeing witches, rebels and mothers and maidens, crabbed crones, all need coin at some point.

'Doesn't solve your current problem, though.' He gestures at the baskets at my feet.

'No. It doesn't.'

He nods towards the dappled mare. 'Take Rosie. I'll saddle her.'

Before I can argue, he's in action, talking the whole while so I can't get a word of an argument in edgewise. I am, for a change, too tired to bicker much. Soon I'm seated on the broad back of the mature mare, baskets and sacks hung about her like festival decorations.

'She's calm of nature, won't startle, and fast if need be – for short spurts, mind.' I wonder if he suspects something's wrong in the woods. That things have been looking for me there. No. No reason he should. He's just being charming, in hope of a later benefit, as was his way once; idly I wonder when he'll begin to play the merry widower of Berhta's Forge. I'll take this benefit now, be picky about how I pay him back when he calls in the favour – as is my way.

'Thank you, Faolan. How will I get her back to you?'

He grins. 'Keep her until harvest home. I'll have a feather-foot for you by then that you can ride around like a queen in a sedan chair.'

'What about you?'

'You want to ride me around like a sedan chair?' Mock surprise. 'Well, it's not the most flattering—'

'What'll you do without Rosie?'

'Ah, not to worry. Plenty of horses here in the stables; got another half a dozen out to graze with Orin in the forest. I'll not go short.'

I nod, urge the mount towards the path that'll take me home. 'Then thank you again.'

'And I'll see you at harvest home?'

I don't reply, but grin knowing he can't see me.

'Mehrab? Mehrab?' His chuckle is loud and rolls after me.

* * *

I shouldn't let Faolan help me. I shouldn't even be thinking of him, let alone owing him favours. Then again, he is the only source of horses for leagues and leagues, and I do not propose to leave the forest – or even go just as far north as Sarith's Ford – to buy one. I remind myself of the hurt and burn of being cast away by him. I wonder, again, if I'd had a child – been able to carry a child to term – would it have been different? Would he have stayed? Would we have lasted? I let my mind wander paths it's not been allowed on for long years.

Then I stop.

I remind myself of his wife, the woman he chose over me. Younger than I was, far less worldly, less questioning, far less independent. Like most women in places like this, she took all that such a life offered: a husband, children, housework, cooking, perhaps grandchildren, then death – although in her case, death came sooner than expected. And if she'd wanted anything different – yearned, dreamed – she buried those desires lest they interrupt the flow of existence. She knew of me, resented me because I'd been first – it's only a natural thing – but she still came to me when she couldn't fall pregnant, just as Deva Peppergill had. Children are an anchor for women such as they. Easier to help her than Deva, with youth on her side, but in the end there was only one child. Orin. And I'd never seen her again, not even to hear her say thank you. Easier to help such women when I couldn't do that for myself.

So, I remind myself now: he did not choose me. He is not mine. He hasn't been so for a very long time, if indeed he was ever mine at all.

Still…

Harvest home.

On the green, dancing and feasting after the last of the wheat is taken to the mill for grinding and turning into flour before being returned to each householder for the coming wintertide, and spring and summer after that. The burning of corn-dolls, the roasting of meats and vegetables, a round of meeting and mating inside and outside of matrimonial bonds with not much offence caused. An event which I've never attended, except my first year in Berhta's Forge, under Yrse's watchful eye – or at least until she fell asleep under a tree after too much mead. I think about Faolan, the contours of him, the feel of his skin, where it's lighter protected from the sun by his clothing, the scars from stray embers, careless knife cuts and occasional hammer bruises; the marks where horses have taken their ill-temper out on the big man who's nothing but gentle with them.

I shake my head. My attention is needed on the path homeward. I remind myself I've had several near scrapes in recent weeks, although to be fair this morning's was merely a stalking child. Mooning like a lovesick girl won't keep me safe. So I think again about all the wrongs done me by Faolan, how my heart was broken to hear him say he would be married but not to me (even though he had asked, and I'd refused). That he believed, though, that we would continue as we had been, but because I wouldn't give him children (couldn't carry one to term, and he'd not noticed, and I'd kept the secret of each miscarriage), he must have a wife. A proper wife. And I, with no desire to ever marry, suddenly found an utter bereftness inside me that only hatred could fill, especially when I saw the girl he had replaced me with, in looks a younger version of me, sweet of face and voice. How I avoided the village and her until the day she appeared on my doorstep, begging aid – and then again after that, avoiding the smithy and any place I might see either her or him. Quite the feat, for all those years, to know nothing about them, to never enquire after their health or otherwise, for no one in Berhta's Forge to ever offer gossip about them.

The memories work, and by the time I reach the cottage, I'm in a much worse mood, resenting the loan of the horse, the talk of buying a foal, of him bargaining for a heavy horse on my behalf. Of having to speak to him again, of returning Rosie, of harvest home. When I dismount, I see Arlo and Rhea coming out of the trees. I wonder if they've hidden there all day. I'll warrant no work's been done, and even though I know it's irrational – I told them to hide – I'm irked. I remind myself that one of the unforeseen advantages of the summer husband is that he's kept Rhea uninterested in the village. She no longer asks about accompanying me and no one's seen her except Anselm and Gida, and they think her family.

'Mehrab! What happened?' Rhea rushes up, trailed by the summer husband; her expression is one of relief. 'Are you all right? Whose horse is this? Who was the child?'

She rattles out her questions rapid and staccato as a

hailstorm – I think the fact that her summer husband cannot speak is wearing, the conversation a lack. Rather than answer, I say: 'Arlo, the vegetable patch – there'll be ripened things that need picking before the birds find them. Off you go now.'

I say it as I have to previous summer husbands over the years – possibly even more politely since this one's not really mine – and they've all obeyed with alacrity. Today it's the garden, in a week more it'll be the wheat needing to be scythed, gathered up, tied by Rhea and me in the wake of Arlo's cutting, ready for threshing. A week after that, the hay must be cut and baled and stacked in the barn. The small fields grow enough to see two to three mouths through winter snows, and enough set by for spring and summer, but it's the job of several days to harvest and thresh it, then put it in sacks and load it into the cart, hitch up old Fyren and coax him along with the right treats into the village mill. There's a schedule to be adhered to so we don't get behind, don't miss the best chance for harvest, at least a dozen other tasks needing to be done. And, in spite of my temper, I've said it casually, kindly enough; bitten down on my ill-humour for it's not their fault I'm in a mood, not this time at least. Not to start with.

And *this* is the work he was made for, his very reason for existing. When he looks away from me to Rhea for her word, it's such a tiny thing, such a slight gaze, such a glancing blow, but it has the effect of a punch. He does as he's meant to, but it's at *her* command, not mine.

It's all I can do to keep my temper, to throw Rhea the reins and tell her to take care of poor Rosie while I heft baskets inside.

18

That night, I take precautions against sleepwalking – either from the impetus of my own troubled mind or from the call of something out among the trees, something that thinks if it can't get to me, it will draw me to it. I do what I should have done on the second night, even the first, but I hadn't realised then what was happening.

I take a tall glass of water and drink it down, then I refill it and sprinkle salt over the top and dried lavender leaves, and a pinch of grave dirt. I push the glass under the bed, as close to the middle as I can get. The events of the day have worn me out, so I have no trouble falling asleep. In the morning, the water in the glass is black, shimmering and churning just a little: *aqua nocturna*. The water of nightmares, an ingredient witches will pay dearly for – I don't recall my nightmares, I slept very well, and now their essence lies in a glass. I decant it into a bottle before breakfast; I've no doubt I'll find some use for it – or Reynald will gleefully pay good gold for it.

* * *

The ritual continues to work and I'm back to remaining in my own bed during the dark hours, and I can focus more on the training sessions that have been scarce in past weeks. Between the labours leading to harvest, the habitual everyday tasks, and the hours she's spending with the summer husband, time for magic lessons has been a rare commodity. Evenings are shortened by exhaustion, the opportunities for, or willingness to, chatter or concentrate are low, and some nights now I don't even hear their whispers and soughs.

So, this morning, when the summer husband is occupied with threshing the wheat in the barn, I take the opportunity to see whether Rhea's skills have deteriorated. Today's target is two planks attached to a buoy anchored out in the middle of the pond, which bobs and dances a little with the current from the stream. It looks a little like a person. I'm pleased to note that Rhea's aim remains wonderfully accurate. The thing goes up like a church martyr dowsed in oil.

'Well done,' I say, nodding approval.

Her face is gleeful as she laughs. 'Looks like the prince the day I burned him!'

I freeze. She covers her mouth, too late, the secret let out.

'What did you say?'

She doesn't reply, but takes her hand away, lips pursed tightly as a gate locked after the horse has bolted.

'Rhea, I'm serious. One does not burn princes lightly.'

Rhea glances away, sulky.

'What did you do?' I insist. 'Burning a suitor is one thing, a merchant's son, a what-have-you no matter how rich. You might still escape that. But—'

'Mehrab—'

'Child, you'd best tell me. You're under my roof. My protection – and if you've brought such a risk to my house, you owe me the truth.' I clench my fists, then hiss: 'Parents of princes don't give up hunting their son's murderer no matter the circumstances.'

'He has no parents,' she mutters. Then she slumps to the grass on the bank of the pond, hands over her face. No tears, though, no sobs, just a weary sigh. I sink down beside her. Vaguely, I hear Rosie whicker in concern from her enclosure; she's sociable with people and both of us are generous with treats. Not at the moment, however.

'Tell me.' I pull the hair from her face, the hands from her eyes.

She hesitates, as if gathering thoughts she's made a point of forgetting. 'He is – was – the Prince of Lodellan. My father, ambitious for more than just an increased fortune, finagled an invitation to the Winter Solstice Ball. The Princess Royal, ancient and wrinkled as she is, has run it for decades, and it's still the event of the year. Many matches are made, the Princess chooses her next lover or lovers, the Prince too.' She clears her throat. 'He's been without a wife for twenty years, after the last one went mad – or rather, they're still married even though she's been locked away in a sanitorium run by the Sisters of St Abbe in Wulfhere's Bend.'

'Go on.' It's all I can do not to wave my hand: *hurry up.*

'But word had come that his wife was dead at last – eaten her own tongue or something equally awful. Rumours abounded. Only her demise was a certainty. So, word had it – so many words! – that the Prince would seek a new wife. Possibly more offspring – his heirs had not fared well, taken by Lady Death one way or another.'

'I'm amazed he'd not continued to use the old wife or have her set aside by the lords of the church. Surely dispensation would have been easier.'

'My mother whispered he'd have been rid of her except she's the mother of his children and once the great love of the Princess Royal's life – and *she* was loath to let the woman go…'

'Ah. So, at last the Prince of Lodellan was free, and your father all ambition for elevation and armed with a beautiful daughter…'

She gives a side-eye glance, head tilted. 'Thought you didn't know my story?'

'It's the same story, over and over, only the names change.'

'Cynical.'

'But correct.'

'Mehrab, I knew none of this. My life was perfect – as long as I hid my strangeness – there was nothing to complain about, I was spoiled as any daughter can be – what did I care for the goings-on of others? Yes, yes, get that look off your face, I know I'm an idiot.' She sighs. 'The invitation to the ball arrived with great pomp. Father promised a beautiful new gown, there'd be nothing like it in the whole world, and I'd be free to dance and dance and dance to my heart's content. Imagine, all those glorious shiny creatures in the gems and frocks, those handsome men and boys, all so gaily flirting.'

'Did you not imagine a husband, though? That one would be provided for you?'

'A husband, yes. A prince, no. I'd not thought to look so high. I'd seen the spouses provided for some of my friends from Miss Belle's Ladies Finishing Academy – made Father promise me a better one, a handsome one.' She laughs, bitterly. 'Had he been a young man? Closer to my own age? Perhaps I'd not have minded quite so much. But he was older than my father. Wrinkled and crabbed, his hair all white like spun straw, violet eyes rheumy, and a potbelly pregnant as a sow. He's ruled the cathedral-city for so very long. *Had* ruled.' She shakes her head, shudders. 'I couldn't bear the idea of him climbing onto me, into me…'

'And at the ball?'

'My father made an introduction, dangled me in front of that disgusting old man like a treat. I was polite but offered no encouragement, yet the very next day he began to pay court to me. There were other girls there, many prettier than me, but apparently indifference makes one irresistible.' She shakes her head again. 'Gifts arrived at all hours, flowers and perfumes, gowns and jewellery, puppies and kittens, sweetmeats and fine wines. The house was filled to bursting and I began to send things back because I'd realised there would be a price to pay for all those pretty things.'

'You could have become the Princess of Lodellan.'

'I couldn't and can't think of anything worse. A bird in a gilded cage, humped by that old man every time his physicks gave him a virility potion? Caught in a trap by any children I might have?'

'You could have bided your time, waited him out. Hurried him on his way, perhaps?'

'Would you?' She glares at me. 'Would you bed a relic all for the sake of a title? A crown?'

I pause. I think about the things I did do, those that gained me something, those that netted nothing, and the reasons for them. But not that. 'No. I wouldn't have.'

'Then kindly don't think so lowly of me.'

'My apologies. Then what happened?'

'One day he came to visit himself. Demanded to know why I continued to return the gifts. Who did I think I was? Did I think myself too good for his royal blood?' She sighs. 'He was insistent. At first, I was gentle, considering him an old man, harmless, and then – then he was not harmless, and his pants were around his ankles and he was lifting my skirts and—'

'Fire?'

'Fire.'

'Did the Visiting Sister know any of this?'

Tears now, rolling down her cheeks. 'My mother didn't tell her those details and urged me not to do so either. She said… she said I had to get out of the house before Father came home, otherwise I wouldn't survive.'

I take her hand, squeeze it briefly, let it go. 'It's hard to realise that a parent you thought doted on you has merely been coddling you like a hot-house orchid for their own benefit. I'm sorry for that. But you're lucky in your mother.' And I wonder what's happened to Rhea's mother, if she's survived or been punished in her daughter's place, offered up to the Princess Royal as a sop. Truly we're isolated here, that word of the Prince of Lodellan's death hasn't reached us. 'The Visiting Sisters risked so much to get you here. I hope for all our sakes,

Rhea, that they covered your tracks well. Princes do not burn without consequences.'

'I'm sorry, Mehrab. I'm so sorry. I didn't want to burn or drown or hang… Please don't send me away. Please.'

'No. But I wish you'd told me sooner. Remain wary, keep an eye out for strangers, for god-hounds. Don't wander far from the cottage. And you can't go into the village. Only Anselm and Gida know you're here.' I consider what I need to do about the Hadderholms and their knowledge; probably best not to draw attention to Rhea's existence. Drop into conversation that she's gone back home to my distant cousins? Can I make them forget they ever saw her? Possibly. Or should I simply deal with both *permanently*? My mind shies away from that avenue as once it never would. I've changed, lived here too long to blithely decease my neighbours, those who've relied on me, helped me. I shake my head and rise, slowly and with some undignified grunting as my joints object. 'Keep training. One day you might need to defend us both.'

'And Arlo,' she says, innocently.

For once, I'm not irked at her. I understand, now, why the summer husband is so important to her. He's gentle, he's not a typical male, he'd never force himself on her; and his silence is appealing when men talk so very much about so very little and for so fucking long. She might not be able to converse with Arlo, but she can hear her own voice for a change.

'Mehrab?' I look at her, standing beside me, expression so beseeching.

'Yes?'

'You have my secret. When will you share yours?'

I hesitate, consider confession, wonder if it is indeed good for the soul. Shake my head, then point at the target, smouldering out in the pond. 'My secrets are too many to recount. No one's earned the right to them. Back to your task.'

Her face falls, disappointed and hurt. The truth is that if she heard everything I'd done, I fear her good opinion of me would not long survive – and I'm surprised to find that matters to me.

* * *

'Where do the hind-girls come from, Mehrab?' Rhea's sitting at her books tonight; I made her send the summer husband up to her room to make sure she concentrates on something other than him. *Murcianus' Magical Creatures* is open in front of her.

I shrug. 'I've never seen them anywhere but this continent.'

'How many times?'

I pause. I'm grinding herbs for a delivery to Reynald; the last of his wished-for fungi have sprouted and they must be turned to powder quickly or their power's lost. 'A few or five? They're migratory, travelling in herds. No one, as far as I'm aware, has bothered to track their patterns or how the herds form.'

'There's an old story. "The hind-girls dance along the narrow forest courses, throwing their heads with such abandon that sometimes the antlers of one get caught in those of another. But their feet are sure on these paths of beaten earth for they know those ways of old." But I can't remember the rest. Think my grandmother used to read it to me as a warning not to be too independent or you'd find yourself discontented with life and wanting more.'

'Oh, what a terrible thing.' We laugh.

‘Perhaps there was some book or study stored in the library at Cwen’s Reach, before it was destroyed.’ Then she explains: ‘The Citadel was a great place of learning where the Little Sisters of St Florian gathered all manner of books, wrote down tales big and small, grand and mundane. Perhaps it’s something they recorded. But the Citadel fell long ago, its books dispersed or destroyed – but perhaps such a document is in a private library somewhere, mouldering on a shelf, eaten by moths, or lying in a ruin. Perhaps it’s just a wish or a memory.’

‘Even where I’m from the Fall of the Citadel echoed,’ I say mildly, carelessly.

‘And where’s that, Mehrab?’ She gives me a sly look, which I ignore. She harrumphs and asks, ‘Why do you think the hind-girls leave their lives, Mehrab?’

‘Why does any woman walk into the woods and never return? It all becomes too much? An existence one sought or inherited is not what one wants in the end? Escape? Sins you can’t survive by any other means? Exhaustion? A thirst for freedom? A song that leads you away? Any of those things. Any number of others.’ I scratch my head.

‘But the antlers? The feet?’

‘Spend long enough in a new and strange environment, you either adapt or die. Those that adapted needed horns for self-defence, toughened feet to walk those forest paths. They changed, survived. Or perhaps the result of mating with stags? Fauns?’ I tilt my head, thinking. ‘I wonder if they ever die, though? I’ve never seen the body of one, nor even read of one.’

She shakes her head. ‘No. Nor me.’

I shrug. ‘Perhaps they simply aren’t found. Perhaps the

herds take them somewhere, some sacred place. Somewhere they can remain free.'

'What a nice thought,' Rhea muses softly.

'Are you ready to join them when next they pass by? Abandon your shoes?' I grin.

She looks at the boots by the door, their soft leather now scuffed with wear. The pretty blue pair she arrived in lie in the clothing chest in her room, beside the blue silk dress wrapped in tissue with sprigs of lavender in its folds. 'I don't think I'm ever going to be a barefoot girl with horns. Too hard to do my hair.'

'I suspect hairstyles aren't the prime concern of women who walk away from everything, Rhea.' I shrug. 'Never say never, my girl. You can't know what life will give or take and how much of you it'll take with it.'

'Is that why you left your home far across the sea, Mehrab? What did life take from you? And how much of you did it take with it?' she asks quietly, gently.

I rise. 'Goodnight, Rhea. Sleep well.'

19

'Mehrab? Mehrab. Someone's here.' Rhea's peering out the window, careful to not tweak the curtains aside but simply looking through the lace as I showed her.

'What?' No one should be wandering – everyone should be preparing for tonight.

I'm exhausted. We're all exhausted; even Arlo seems to slump on the seat Rhea's set him at after our final harvest day. Summer's last day, our last harvest, and soon the cold will begin nipping at our heels. This morning, I hitched Rosie to the cart (such indignity!) and hauled the sacks of wheat to the village, left them with Sanne for her attention over the next week, scheduled in with everyone else's harvest. And instead of returning Rosie to her owner as I surely promised, I turned the cart right around and came home because I couldn't bear the thought of answering questions as to why I would not attend the harvest-messe.

So, I bathed and scrubbed every skerrick of sweat and dirt from my skin, from under my nails, washed my hair, rubbed the roughness from my feet, slathered lavender cream on myself to put some moisture back in, then went to sleep for long luxurious hours and left Rhea to her own devices. Late in the afternoon, I woke and slipped on a pretty dress which sits in the back of the wardrobe most of the year and went down to begin preparing our own little feast. Harvest homes, these last years, have been spent just myself and the summer husband of the moment, a sweet night because it's one of their last, though they don't know it.

This evening on the village green all of Berhta's Forge will be gathering for their harvest-messe, eating and drinking and toasting each other, giving wishes and blessings to be safely brought through to spring, burning the finest first fruits and vegetables and selected meats, gifted back to the earth in gratitude, in fervent hopes of warding off any ill will from the old gods.

Harvest home, a signal for those born here that they belong – they participate in the life of Berhta's Forge, till its earth, grow its food, husband its livestock. They can rely on the protection of the community. The one and only time I attended, my first year here, I watched the dancing, the flirting, the feasting, and for the first time in a very long while I felt lonely. Where I'd come from, after the high sorceress found me, took me in, I had belonged. She'd given me a place, and I *grew* there until, almost twenty-five years to that very day, the very night, I had to flee, enemies at the gates, the city burning, and my final act as her *creature*…

'Mehrab, it's a handsome someone.' Her gloating tone annoys me.

'Confine your lechery to men of wood, child,' I snap, then

step outside, shutting the door firmly behind me, and take long strides to where my visitor waits by the barn.

'Good evening, Mehrab.' The blacksmith, dressed in fine green linen trews and a shirt white enough to almost glow in the dusk, is mounted on a tall ebony stallion, so comfortable-looking it's as if he's grown there. Behind him, an even larger horse, a young bay feather-foot, tethered to the rail of the enclosure where Rosie is nuzzling him as if checking his bona fides. And… and Faolan appears to have red flowers woven through his beard. 'You're a vision.'

'And you're a long way from home this eve, Faolan.'

He nods gravely. 'Drawn to this den of iniquity by a vile crime. A horse thief resides here. I saw her this very day drive her cart to the mill, then depart the long way around so she did not pass by the smithy.'

I resist grinning. 'Could hardly have got a cart home without a horse to pull it, blacksmith.'

'Aye, that's true. True.' He grins. 'Still, a thief.'

Which isn't the first time such an accusation's been flung at me, but I don't react because for all my other sins, that's not one of mine. I nod towards the bay. 'Hard to give her up, that Rosie-girl. But I note you've brought a friend?'

'This is Eadig, out of the Beck Stables' finest mare.'

'He is very handsome.'

'And well-trained. Biddable.'

'Expensive, no doubt.'

'Very.'

'Faolan…'

'I'm willing to negotiate.' He raises his eyebrows.

'Gods forfend, I'll get my purse.'

'Ah, don't be so obdurate, old woman! The horse is yours! Both the horses are yours – Rosie would have run home first chance she got if she didn't like you.' He holds out a hand. 'Only come with me to the harvest-messe, it's all I ask, so small a thing.'

I look at his enormous hand, at its calluses and scars, think of how it feels to be held and lifted and caressed; then quietly I reply, 'Not afraid of your wife's unhappy ghost, Faolan?'

The hand does not waver although his expression shifts to pain. 'Mehrab, she's been gone all these months. I cannot imagine she'd remain here after escaping, not even to punish me.'

How unhappy were they; why did no one tell me? Not even Reynald? But I know. This is precisely the sort of gossip no one would share with me. The habit of not speaking to me of my once-upon-a-time lover too ingrained, something I, after all, have trained them in over the years. So my tone is sadder than I would like when I ask a question I wish I'd swallowed, 'Why didn't *you* come to me sooner?'

He speaks softly, with neither heat nor hurt. 'And say what? How could I come to you after all that had happened between us? After what I did? I regretted it the moment I tried to manipulate you into marriage – I felt sure you would change your mind and live happily ever after.' He snorts. 'But I'd not thought you'd be so stubborn.'

'Had you even met me, Faolan Alderson?'

'I was sorry and knew what I did – marrying Helvis out of spite – and while I wasn't the worst husband, I wasn't the best. Felt guilty all the time at what I'd done. Not sure I was any better as a father. And I miss her, I do, after so many years together, and she tried her best. She loved me in spite of myself.' He shakes his head. 'But I have years left to live. If you would try again? If you'd find it in you to forgive me? I offer no chains, I will take whatever crumb you're prepared to give.' He grins. 'And even if you can't bear the thought of me for longer than a day, would you give me this one night, if I beg? C'mon, for the cost of two horses, surely it's a bargain.'

There's no thought in my mind when I take the hand he's held out all this time, and he's so strong, the horse so sturdy, that he swings me up behind him without effort. I wrap my arms around his waist, press myself against his broad back and hold on for dear life as the horse takes off at ridiculous speed. Briefly I curse myself for giving in – it's the second time in my life I've made such an impetuous choice – then I embrace it. The wildness, the recklessness, the moment when my heartbeat begins to hammer in time with the horse's hooves and every so often I think I see sparks fly up from where they strike the earth. A sense of danger, yes; a sense of threat, no. No fear of falling, of the beast losing his footing. Utter, headlong certainty of my safety in this at least.

When at last we slow, I can't help but feel disappointment rising; I'd have gleefully continued on in this fashion for hours, perhaps days if it were possible. But the horse is lathered in sweat and breathing heavily. Through the trees is the green, laid out for the harvest-messe, meal and ritual, the villagers laughing, mingling, children playing – Faolan's lad talking to Tieve by one of the trestle tables; I smile at their awkwardness, cannot imagine myself like that, not when the high sorceress taught me how much power lay in me. No sign of Anselm or Gida or Ari, but they might be anywhere in the milling of bodies; the Peppergills are at the head table, young Matthias in his mother's arms being fussed over, the child's stare a little blank. Tiredness, no doubt, shyness.

Suddenly the thought of all eyes upon me (*us*), of anyone staring, sniggering that I'm stepping into a dead woman's bed is too much – and I'm as nervous as those youngsters I just grinned about. Madness to think I'd move easily among these people who seek me only when they need to, who show respect out of fear, who tolerate me for the memory of Yrse who was one of them. No, I'd not given it a thought to this moment, but now… now it's all I can think about and, as he makes to dismount, I lean forward and whisper, 'Not yet. Wait.' He obeys, obedient as the beast beneath us, unmoving.

The sun is sinking behind the trees, leaving a golden corona of fire splashed against the clouds. The giant corn-doll waits at one end of the green, a ring of offerings at her feet. In the hands of children I see the miniatures, awaiting their fiery fate. Thaddeus Peppergill strides forward, a lit torch in hand; I spy Reynald in the crowd, watching anxiously – it's his accelerant that will ensure a perfect and thorough blaze. The brand touches the kindling at the feet of the wheat-wife. The villagers take up a chant and their voices rise and rise with the flames. Children, encouraged by hands on shoulders, gentle pushes, dart forward to throw their own corn-dolls onto the fire.

I can't help but flinch as the woman-shaped thing goes up in a *whoosh* of orange-gold and blue. Faolan feels me do so; we're too close for him to miss any twitch or breath from me, or I from him. He puts one hand over my clasped fingers, still tight around his waist. Without a word, he turns the horse and takes us deeper into the forest, where shadows are growing longer and darker, far away from the songs of harvest home and the buzz of chatter and laughter and feasting and all that will come later.

* * *

The glade is quiet and cool, small and sacred with an altar covered in ivy, not neglected exactly, but ancient, perhaps forgotten; the full moon casts a silver glow over the grass and trees and the flowing river. He dismounts, lifts me down, and we leave the horse to graze as he will. Faolan sweeps me up like a bride, carries me closer to the water, lays me down in the thick, soft grass and covers my mouth with his. There's a clever, cold part of my mind that says this is a foolish idea, the height of idiocy to trust him, that to even partake in this congress either with promises or without is folly. The other part of me commands silence; the part of me that's lonely and has been so for year upon year as each fosterling moved on, as each summer husband met his fate, as every contact in my life proved ephemeral. The part of me that's come to love Rhea's company, even as I've resented her taking a – *my* – summer husband, yet what is such a husband when only for a season?

One I don't have to tolerate for long or compromise for; one that has his function built in so that he can only satisfy the limited expectations that puts upon him? Not human, not unpredictable, not fallible or liable to disappoint – till this year. One that can be controlled.

That's the part of me in ascent as Faolan looms over me,

covers my body with his, removes our clothes so cleverly it seems like magic or some sort of melting away. The lines of him, so familiar, that scar on his torso, and the one on his back, almost as long, healed and raised like a fault-line. The sweat of him, the silk of him, the hardness and the tenderest of tongues; not an inch of skin is untouched, untended, until I'm biting my lip to stop the primitive screams that press up and out of me, until he kisses me, laughing, and I scream into his mouth, wondering if it makes his head ring, his brain shake in his skull, then the screams are gone, replaced by moans and kittenish whimpers and sighs on both our parts.

He curls around me and it's as sweet as it once was, that first year, the second, part of the third.

I think about all I'd lost, all I'd run from, from my old life… To find him so soon after landing in the Great Forest, to love him, be loved by him, seemed a miracle. It seemed as if all I'd done had been or might be forgiven. For a while it *seemed* that my luck might hold. And I have wondered, over the years, if what I felt for him then was merely gratitude; false affection. Pure lust that I mistook for something better. Still, I don't know.

Held by him, I push those thoughts away, tell them *hush*, that this feeling is all I have right now. No plans, no future, no promises. No memory of what I did in the wake of losing him to try and stop the pain. As I'm dozing off, I think I see something pop up in the dark waters of the River Ayda, almost like a head, but it disappears so fast I tell myself it's a fish, catching the rare nocturnal insects that flit too close to the surface for their own good.

I will not speak of things that stalk the forest paths, that have sent me dreams and tried to lure me out. I'll not let my mind pick and pull at every thought and word and deed. I will lie here, warm and sated and, for however long it lasts, loved.

* * *

In the morning, when dawn wakes us, we do it all again. Lying beneath the open sky, we talk, roaming from one topic to another until I ask if he was happy these past years. If he'd been a good husband to Helvis; last time we'd touched on it he'd been somewhat ambiguous in his reply.

'I tried to be. Since I'd chosen her – since I'd hurt you to do so – I tried. I hope I succeeded. It wasn't her fault she wasn't you. Where I failed was with the boy. Gods help me, Mehrab. He was what I'd wanted – children, the whole reason I broke with you – and she gave me that child and I… I couldn't – can't connect with him. Or I just didn't. Don't. Nothing he did was good enough. Even now… I hear myself speaking to him as if he's annoying me. It's my own guilt, I know it, but… my boy… is grieving his mother and I can't make it better.'

'What was your birth father like?' I ask, because our parents inflict our very first wounds, sometimes without us ever realising it. I ask, also, because back then such topics remained shallowly discussed when passion was at its height – and we missed the years when we might have grown together and spoken of deeper hurts. A slithery, hissing part of me wonders if his dislike of Orin stems from the lad not being *mine* – I do recognise that as sheer egotism.

'I don't recall. When I wandered into Berhta's Forge, when the Aldersons took me in, I was already grown and had no recollection of myself *before*, nor of a family. Just a… just the sense memory of a blinding flash, of incredible pain – pain that dogged me until you worked your magic. The only father I knew was Zeb Alderson, and he was kind and respectful – but I was already a man grown. He never had to parent me when I was an infant, child, youth. I was already fully formed, if broken. I didn't learn enough from him, clearly.'

'Then how are you different with Orin? Why?'

'Impatient. I'm always impatient with him. And every fault I know or fear in myself, is one I see in him.' He runs a hand over his face. 'Whether it's there or not, I fear some *lack*.'

'Sometimes,' I say delicately, 'what we consider a failing in ourselves – what we suffer for – we think at first to save others from, to warn them about it. But if you can't accept a fault in yourself, you won't be any more forgiving of it in another – and you can find yourself punishing them for continuing to show you what you loathe or fear. Sometimes you have to like yourself better in order to repair that other relationship. Lest you spend all your time teaching someone you should love that you think they're not good enough. Constant criticism makes for hatred.'

He doesn't reply, just kisses the top of my head and holds me tighter.

* * *

Later still, we bathe in the river, eat the remains of the small feast he'd brought in a saddlebag (suspecting I might baulk at other company), then succumb to each other again and bathe some more until I insist I must return home. He agrees. Asks if I will see him again or permit him to call. I tell him I will come to him but make no promises as to when. I'm no young maid in the first flush of youth; nor a fool to run at his beck and call. He knows better than to push and it pleases me to see him honour (so far) his word. When he delivers me back to the cottage, the last kiss is lingering and it's all I can do to keep myself from pulling him down with me.

I walk to my door, resisting right until the very last moment the urge to glance over my shoulder. There he sits, astride that great black horse, smiling gently. A single incline of his head and he turns for Berhta's Forge. I open the door, bruised and grazed in the best of ways, tender in mind and body and heart, with a stupid wide grin on my face.

20

‘Where were you?!’

As soon as I’m in the door, Rhea strides from the kitchen, shouting. The volume and the distress hit me like a slap.

‘I—’

‘How could you? Just leave like that and not come home?’

‘I am home—’

‘And staying out all night, leaving me all alone.’

‘Arlo—’

‘Disappearing with a man I don’t know. I waited all night. I didn’t sleep.’

‘Rhea—’

‘I wouldn’t have even known where to look for you, where to find your body, who to even ask—’

‘Rhea—’

‘How could you desert me like that?’ Her pitch has risen to a scream, hysteria brightly limning it. Part of me realises she’s terrified, on my behalf, but mostly on hers. A child sent forth from the only home she’s ever known, fleeing men who’ll harm her. A child who became a murderer rather than a victim – and that's a heavy burden, for women are taught to be victims first. A child who found a new home, yes, but will ever live beneath the uncertainty of discovery. Her imagination has run wild with every awful possibility, and the worst one for such a child is abandonment.

And I should be better. I should be the adult about the whole situation – after all, I can see the tears in her eyes, hear the distress in her voice. I should remind myself that she's not an adult, not properly, after all. But because I know she's right, that I was selfish and inconsiderate – how difficult would it have been to tell her where I was going and with whom? Faolan would have waited those thirty seconds – and because I know myself in the wrong after a night of such sweetness, my mood so good and so quickly taken from me, I lose my temper.

And I lunge at the girl standing in front of me.

And I make a noise that might come from an animal in pain.

And I have a hank of her golden curls twisted in my fingers for the shortest of moments before I'm lifted off my feet and flung across the sitting room, against the stone of the fireplace, ribs bruised by a strength no true man could muster even on a good day.

And all at once, there we are: Rhea crumpled by the door, me fetched up with the metal of the tongs and poker pressed hard against me, and Arlo the summer husband standing somewhere between the two of us, voiceless but able to make his feelings clearly felt.

* * *

When I visit Faolan in the days that come, I keep my clothes on when we mate so he can't see the bruises, doesn't ask difficult questions. Our couplings are fast and fevered, hidden from prying eyes, though I'm more polite to him than I have been in years, and perhaps some note that I no longer avoid the smithy. One day, however, the buttons on my shirt are torn in some over-enthusiastic movements, and he slips the fabric down and down before I realise. He swears, asks, 'Was this me? Did I do this? Too rough?' and I must lie, tell him I fell, that I lost my footing and make myself sound like an unsteady old woman. He's so tender after that I want to pull his hair, bite him, to get a rise out of him, to make him stop treating me like porcelain. Like a fragile thing. In the end I swear at him that if he doesn't fuck me hard, I'll never visit again. He does as bid.

* * *

'Where are we going, Mehrab? It's so cold.'

It's three weeks after our fight. After Arlo's attack on me. Our words have been brief and stilted; I've given her instructions for the summer husband each day and not much else. There have been no lessons and I've made my own meals as I have done while alone, left her to feed herself. Anything she needs, she must ask for as I refuse to think in her favour. And I've been waiting to see if she shows any sign of voluntarily doing what I told her she must all those months ago. She has not.

Autumn feels more like winter today and we're both wrapped in jackets and scarves; warm caps would have been wise. It's not cold enough quite yet for the fur-lined coats or the fox-fur inserts in our boots, but it feels as if the weather turned bad immediately after harvest home. Usually there are some more warm weeks at the start of autumn; not this year.

The sky is very grey, almost as if threatening snow so soon. I want to be home before nightfall, but she's moving slow and sluggish. I wonder if she's realised why. Yet this has to be done, no matter how uncomfortable or cold. I made sure we both wore our talismans, that the sprigs of lavender and sage in our hems were refreshed, just in case.

'Mehrab, why are we out here?'

'We're out here so you can see what happens when you don't listen.'

We're out here because this morning when I asked her outright to do what must be done, she refused.

'Mehrab, I'm sorry about Arlo, truly I am. He didn't mean to hurt you. How many times must I apologise?' She's not yet apologised to me for having screamed and yelled like a spoiled brat, though, and even now, my ribs still ache despite all the poultices and tisanes I've brewed. Arlo, it should be noted, is *not* out here but locked in the barn, not heading towards a place I've avoided for so very long. Arlo, who should not be in existence still.

'I told you his purpose. I told you why. I told you what to do.' I shake my head and forge on. Not far now, even though I've not set foot in this part of the woods for almost seventeen years – I'd know the paths, the trees, anywhere. For a moment I think I hear something, a familiar moan, and my heart rabbits along, a double thump with a shot of adrenaline that makes me feel sick. But it's just the wind.

Just the wind.

The land is rising and I start to puff a little; my ribs protest the exertion. 'I told you what would happen. Haven't you noticed? How he's slower?'

'But it's cold, we're all slower.'

'Haven't you noticed, when he walks, how his feet adhere to the ground?'

She's silent at that; she's noticed.

'That's because he's putting down roots. It always happens when they're left too long. Why do you think I call them "summer husbands"? He's well past his season, Rhea.'

'But he's barely beyond a youth!'

'Time moves differently for one such as he. His life is… a gifted thing… a stolen thing… he's not real in that way.'

'But… I love him… he loves me…'

'A voiceless husband is a tempting thing, isn't it? No one to gainsay you, no one to give you orders. There are reasons, Rhea, why I've made most of them without speech.'

'I wonder what he'd say, if he could…'

She's prone to a child's romantic imaginings. I think I know what he'd say too; he's not looked at me the same since the day we came to blows. I know what he'd happily do to me but for the fact that Rhea forbade him from hurting me any more than he already had. I know what I'd happily do to him, but he's not *my* responsibility. And if I take it out of her hands? She'll only resent me more – it's a matter of degree, it hardly matters now, but by the gods I will not clean up her mess!

We come to a wall of trees, old growth, very tall, almost impenetrable so closely they've grown together, but I find a break. Before I slip between I stop, wait for Rhea to catch up. The gap will be tight for her but there's no choice, I'll pull her through the eye of a needle if I must. 'Let me show you…'

She struggles but manages to follow me, and we step into a clearing. There, in the middle, *he* stands.

'This is what I did,' I say, very quietly.

'What? Where?' Her tone is sharp, until she follows the direction of my finger to the thing that might have become a mighty oak, once, if I'd not interfered.

His face is rough, as rough as a first-time effort, 'prentice work. But you can still see it in the trunk of the stunted thing he's grown into: half-tree, half-man, perhaps ten feet tall, anchored to the earth by years and deep-delving roots. I can still see, if I peer closely enough, the marks of my knives and chisels. He's not pretty, just as I told her so long ago; he's only primitively human-looking to be frank, just as he was when first made. But he was *mine*. And I loved him and he loved me in return. He was a salve for a heart broken by Faolan. And because I loved him – because I had so much love that had to go somewhere or become entirely hatred and I didn't want that – I did a terrible thing.

'I let him live… let him live beyond his time until I had to pry his feet from the floor of my cottage and put him in a wheelbarrow to push as far away as I could. This was the copse I'd taken him from; I'd liked the oaks, how tall they stood, how strong they looked, how dependable they seemed. When I discarded him, I brought him back *home*, into the depths of the forest so that I might not see him, might not stumble upon him. And in all those years I've never set foot here again. You need to understand that I made him, and I didn't give him his proper end. I left him there.'

I don't go too close, and I speak low, bite back the sobs.

His wooden lids are closed, perhaps open just a slit beneath the lashes I'd carved so carefully.

'But—'

'Hush,' I say, holding up my palm. 'Don't wake him.'

I can't bear if he sees me, knows me, if he moans my name, or even simply tries with that mouth surely grown stiff with age, with *treeness*.

'I gave him a tongue – my first mistake – so that when I left, he called for me. I could hear it for the longest while even after I was finally beyond the range of his voice.'

Rhea approaches, tiptoeing across the sparse grass. *Don't touch him don't touch him don't touch him*, I think but don't say. Then she makes a decision, stops before she gets too close, retreats, coming to rest next to me. She puts a hand on her belly as if feeling queasy.

'What are you going to do?' she asks breathily.

'What I should have done a long time ago.' Setting an example is the only way to convince her to do what she needs to do. I slip the hatchet from my belt, heft it, wonder if I can actually do *this*—

—but I don't get the chance to find out. I'm hit from behind by what feels like a plank. For the second time in three weeks I'm sent flying, along the dirt and grass; I feel the skin on my face graze, feel pebbles tear the canvas and flesh, feel blood blossom; I think I feel ribs crack this time, and I know at least one of the bones in my left forearm snaps. I cry out, forgetting my fear of being heard for it shrinks beside my fear of dying.

Arlo has followed us. Somewhere in his sleepy tree-brain he decided Rhea wasn't safe with me. I imagine he's broken from the barn, followed Rhea with that unerring instinct, determinedly moving while his feet try to set down roots. I'd almost find it admirable, except for his expression, which is murderous to say the least. He moves faster, with less difficulty than recently, fired by rage. I look past him, past my fate, and see Rhea's face and the terrible truth there. She might never admit it, but it's clear: she told him to follow us. Was she afraid of me too? Did she slip the bolt on the drying-room door? The barn? Or could she simply not bear to be parted from him, even for a day?

Over my own whimpering I can hear two things: a sort of rhythmic grunt pushed from lips that no longer open properly, and Rhea screaming *No, no, no!*

But her summer husband doesn't listen, merely continues to come at me; I can tell from the way he's balancing, measuring his steps, that he's going to kick me, wherever he can. It will probably be enough to finish me. I take a shallow breath, the only sort my agonised ribs will allow, begin to curl in on myself in a feeble hope of minimising the damage, but then there's a third sound.

Unexpected but not necessarily unwelcome.

The whoosh of fire igniting, swallowing air like a greedy child.

Behind Arlo his mistress has a great handful of blue flames; she only hesitates a little before she throws it.

The summer husband goes up like a torch.

In the usual way of things, he'd be given a hemlock potion to make him sleep, then would be beheaded with a single axe blow and fed to the hearth on the first night of winter, serving his final purpose. His body was to have been used throughout the season, for its composition means it burns long and very hot, saving on other materials. But this…

…this is witch-fire and it incinerates like no other; it is fast and consumes utterly.

When Arlo is no more than a pile of cinders, Rhea helps me up. Together we limp out into the wider wood where snow has begun to fall, just little eddies, back towards the cottage and away from the howls of my sin (by no means the greatest), the old summer husband.

21

Rhea's refused to speak to me for two days, lying on her bed in the same clothes she wore to the fateful grove. Refused to eat. And to be honest, I've wanted to stay in my own bed and nurse my own wounds, the hurts the summer husband visited upon me, but I don't. I can't. If I take to my bed, I might not get up again, might allow the despair of this awful pass to overwhelm me. So, I swallow my own potions, I put poultices on my bruises and ointments on my scratches and scrapes, and I keep breathing, working, tending – there's livestock needs feeding, the fields needing final prep for winter, and an orchard in need of proper pruning. Mind you, when I reset and healed my own arm and rib, I almost passed out from the pain of the remaking; if I didn't truly understand before why folk resent healing that hurts, I do now.

Still, I've been watching her carefully these past two days and she's going to need my help soon. Whether she wants it or not. The girl burned her beloved to save me – which might simply mean she's going to hate *me* for what *she* did. There's every chance she'll depart this forest soon, prepared or not for what comes next; I admit I'd be sad to lose her. She's sacrificed something valuable for me, so the most valuable thing I can give in return is a truth, when the time comes.

But, for the moment, I'm content to let her grieve, to ignore me, and I can do with respite from the sound of her guilt-ridden breaths. It also means that when there's a knock on the front door, I'm fairly certain she won't come down, won't want to be anywhere near me, so I don't need to worry about her being seen. I half-expect Faolan to be on the threshold, but that hope is soon dashed.

* * *

Thaddeus Peppergill is a dark-haired, dark-eyed man of faded handsomeness, medium height, mostly trim, still striking but his best days are well over his shoulder. I've never felt tempted by him, but enough women (and a few of the men if Reynald's gossip is to be believed) have thought him worth a turn; in addition to the offspring from his recognised mistresses, there are sufficient children in Berhta's Forge bearing little resemblance to their own fathers, and an embarrassingly strong stamp of the Peppergill features. At my kitchen table, he's opted for a glass of honeyed rum – early in the day, but the weather's sufficiently chilly that no one would raise an eyebrow, unless they're like me and can smell the scent of alcohol already on his breath. I cobble together a ploughman's lunch to soak up the excess and hopefully keep him from tumbling off that very fine roan horse tied to a post by the barn. I've treated him more than once over the years for mildly embarrassing conditions, done my best to ensure he doesn't pass anything on to his partners. Still, not the worst of men.

‘To what do I owe the pleasure of this visit, Thaddeus?’ I sit across from him, begin picking at my own plate of meat and cheese, pickles and bread. ‘Is Matthias well? No ill effects of his adventure?’

‘The boy’s well. Well. But…’ There are shadows under his eyes that hint at stolen sleep, the skin beneath his chin is slack, like that of an even older man. ‘And I thank you for finding him, Mehrab. Deva and I are so grateful. But…’

‘Neither of us is getting any younger, so I’d suggest you spit it out.’

There’s a flare of irritation in his eyes, just briefly, and I know he’s not used to anyone talking to him this way. Of course, I’ve never spoken to him any other way, so there should be no surprise on his part.

‘Come, come, Thad. Speak plainly.’ I think, *I know too much about you for you to play coy.* Then he manages to surprise me.

‘More children are missing, Mehrab.’

The bread in my mouth is suddenly dry, tastes like sand and I can barely swallow. I gulp down my water, wishing I’d opted for rum. It’s a few moments before I can say, ‘How many? Whose children?’

‘Five. All young, seven or eight, all of them under the charge of Widow Wilky.’

‘Shit. When?’ Why hasn’t Tieve come to tell me? The widow’s not a bad sort – a little grumpy, but that’s no crime – and she provides for those children whose families die and leave them unable to care for themselves. She did so even before her wife died, and she herself became ‘Widow Wilky’. Gods know

I've kept an eye on her myself for years, just to make sure she's not a monster in disguise. But the orphans she cares for return to help her after they've left, invite her to weddings and name-days, some call her "mother" or "aunt".

'The last few days – and before you shout, remember that some children disappear for several nights in a row before they return, tail between their legs, begging her charity again,' Thaddeus warns. 'But these ones… well, the widow's experienced enough with children to know whether they're the wandering kind, and she's adamant these were not.'

It's true. Not all want to live under another's rules. Some think they've escaped such tyranny when a parent or parents shuffle off their mortal coil. Some run, heading for other villages or settlements. One or two have settled themselves in the woods, becoming foresters, hunters, small croppers, returned to trade with the village. But all have been trackable, all have been traced.

'And no adults have gone missing?' I ask; he shakes his head. 'What are their names? The children?'

'Uh. I—'

'You didn't ask. Just took the numbers.'

'Mehrab, what can we do? There has to be something. We can't just lock them all up, watch over them night and day. Not indefinitely. Work must be done, life must go on.'

I rub my face, trying to feel less tired, less fuzzy-brained. 'Salt. That is the easiest thing I can think of on short notice: pour a thick line of salt around the village, make sure there are no gaps.'

He sits back. 'That's a lot of salt.'

'A lot. I'm sure there's a good supply of it in your emporium, Thad. Think how grateful folk will be to know you generously donated your own stock to help keep their children – and yours, of course – safe.'

'Is there nothing else you can do? That's a huge expense,' he whines. 'Something more… witchy? You wouldn't want people to think you were—'

There's an implied threat in his words, that the witch in the woods might be responsible or held accountable even if she's not, and I think it's best for both of us that he doesn't finish that sentence. 'Do you know what's happening, Thaddeus?'

'No.'

'Well, nor do I and I am going to do my best to find out – but I doubt I'm clever enough to discover that this very day.' I point at him. 'A ring of salt around the perimeter, that's the best interim measure I can suggest at this juncture. You're welcome.'

After that he can't leave quickly enough. As I watch him through the window, mounting the roan, dangerously close to tipping off, and then finally trotting away, I think about this new development. Children still, no adults. And nameless children this time – or rather, less nameless and more easy-to-forget. Children with less parental oversight, for who could keep track of forty orphans, let alone Widow Wilky in her seventies. I think about the tales of spectral huntsmen preying on little ones, taking the most vulnerable in a herd. I think about that man-thing of shadow and bone at the Black Lake that night, waiting for me to swim to the shore, about the grey creature that stalked me as I hid inside a tree and the grotesque offerings on my doorstep as if I were a dark god. Connections and questions and no proof.

More questions I have no answers to. More matters to deal with. The one issue I can deal with immediately is upstairs, weeping into a pillow, and my natural urge to fix, to solve, kicks in. With a sigh, I turn towards the staircase.

* * *

'Once upon a time,' I say to Rhea's back, 'there was a woman. I wish I could say she was a girl, that she was too young to know better, but she wasn't. She'd already turned thirty, some might say old enough to have a modicum of wisdom at least, but that's not the way of such things. We learn from experience, or most of us to varying degrees, and this girl – woman – hadn't had the sort of experiences needed to soften certain of life's vicissitudes. Many things had come easily to her, though her childhood was a rocky shoal. But she had certain abilities which had lifted her from poverty and deprivation, gained her power and influence, and yes, fame of a certain sort for rather a long time. Then it all fell apart – you don't need those details. They aren't relevant, not really to this story, so don't ask, just listen.

'When everything fell apart – quite literally, the fall of a city, of a dynasty, the erasure of history – she found herself traipsing mountains and plains and deserts and swamps, drifting down rivers in small boats then onto large ships and sent across seas, and finally into the hands of a Visiting Sister. Her name was and is Fenna. Under her watchful eye there came more traipsing, more travelling, more of the fleeing witch divesting herself of who she'd been, her last possessions and personality, hiding her power and working so very hard to cover the haughtiness that had made the people who'd bowed before her for long years forget that she'd been born in a slum. As they moved from place to place, she felt she left something behind with each step, each stop; replacing it with something that felt ordinary, until she didn't recognise herself. Until no one who'd known her, she was certain, would ever recognise her.' I clear my throat, watching for a sign that Rhea's taking any notice. The girl remains still, facing the wall.

'The Visiting Sister left her at last with an old, old woman who'd married a woodcutter and lived in a cottage, made a name for herself as a henwife, not a true witch, not threatening, but folk would come to her for curatives and charms. Her remedies were small, her magics barely more than wishes. The younger woman felt herself abandoned and she was scornful of the old one's smoke and mirrors and nonsense rhymes. She, after all, knew what *she'd* once done, what she could still do if such a thing wouldn't bring undue notice to her, if such an act wouldn't result in her death were she to be found. And she wanted, more than anything, to live.

'Ultimately, the younger witch began to make a sort of peace with her keeper; she grew bolder and began to visit the village, taking messages between the old woman and her patients, ferrying medicines and payments back and forth, wearing the paths to and fro down a little more each time. And she met a man who took her fancy, then her heart.'

A tremor in the body on the mattress, a twitch as if resisting the urge to roll over and stare.

'That man was broken – he'd come to the village some years

before, terribly injured and been taken in by the old blacksmith and his wife. They treated him as their son, cared for him, his body healed as well as it could, he learned the ways of the forge and how to work in spite of his injuries.'

'What were they? These injuries?' Her voice sounds strange after so long a silence.

'An arm terribly broken – the bones shattered – a shoulder and ribs and hip much the same, and healed badly, so his shoulder and back hunched, and he walked with a painful limp. He was clever and handsome, had no pity for himself, and all the confidence in the world.' I smile at the memory. 'And he had no fear of the witch, which was something new for her. And she knew… she knew that she could help.' For long moments I can't speak, can't get it out.

'Is it that man you were with on harvest home? Who whisked you away on that great horse?'

I keep speaking as if she'd asked nothing. 'And she *knew* what she could do. So she offered and he accepted. She'd warned him it would hurt, it would hurt horribly because that's what her gift was like, but he said yes, no matter what. One night they went deep into the forest where no one would hear him scream. And…' I'm choking a little now, my ears ringing with his shouts and cries, sharp to begin with then hoarse and weakening the longer it went on, subsiding to moans and whimpers. But he never pulled away. Never said stop. 'And when she was done, he was whole again, or as much as he would ever be.'

'Why aren't you with him?'

'Everyone was delighted at the miracle. We told them he'd wandered far and gotten lost, that he'd come to a great oak and fallen asleep there after pouring water on its roots to beg its protection for the night. That when he'd woken he was healed; that he'd woken but not where he'd laid down and try as he might he could not find that place again. We're in the Great Forest – folk are willing to believe that such miracles happen. While there's magic in the world folk will believe anything. Even when, I suspect, magic dies and leaves us? Folk will still believe what they want to.'

'But you've healed others since – you helped that man not long after I arrived. That Lutetia woman's son.' Rhea rolls over, onto her back, staring at me with something other than despair or hatred.

I nod. 'And in the years since, it's become less important to keep the secret, and more important for me to be able to help people. Broken bones are the biggest injury I encounter here. When I first arrived, there was a real chance I might be found; however, as the years have moved on my fear of that, the likelihood, has lessened.' I shrug. 'And it's never wise to let anyone know the full extent of what you can do.'

'What happened? Why aren't you with him?' she asks again.

'Will you come down and eat something? The rest of the story in return for a few mouthfuls.' She's reluctant but she's also very hungry and this, I imagine, feels like she's not giving in but rather purchasing something she wants: the end of the tale. I help her to her feet and down the stairs.

In the kitchen, the pot of stew on the hob is ready and the fresh loaf of bread on the counter is still warm. When we're both seated, her meal in front of her, she looks at me expectantly. I say, 'A mouthful of food first. If you starve much longer you really will be ill. You need your strength. Chew slowly, swallow carefully.'

Obediently, she takes a bite of the buttered bread, then a mouthful of stew.

'Yrse warned me. She told me it wouldn't last, not to trust him, that he would break my heart.' I shrug. 'She was right.'

'What did he do?'

'He wanted a wife. Children. Asked me. I said no – I liked how things were between us, liked the freedom to come and go. That had been my life, after all, before it all changed. Freedom. He waited almost two years – not so long in the grand scheme of things – then announced if I didn't want what he did, there was nothing to keep us together. He took a wife and I… By then Yrse was dead, the cottage left to me, and I had no one to confide in, not even to say *You were right, old witch.*'

'And then?'

I swallow before saying the words that have never before passed my lips. 'And then I made the first summer husband. I told myself it was pragmatic – a labourer to help with the hardest of chores, but,' I shrug, 'well, he became something else. Something more. And he was my first so I didn't know what would happen, how short his season would be. As I told you, I kept him too long. Watched him turn back into a version of what he would have been if I'd not interfered. And I… I loved him in my own sad and desperate and aching way. He filled the abyss that Faolan had left. He was loyal, lived to please me, was obedient. That's potent, as you know.'

She's silent.

'And I think that you found that as intoxicating as I had. Your experience of the prince of Lodellan, a suitor with no care for your desires or liberty, nor your voice. Yet here was a creature that thought only of you, protected you and pleased you – and did not have a voice with which to gainsay you. How wonderful, all those things together.'

'I loved Arlo,' she says plaintively.

'I know. And he loved you – but they are such short-lived things. They're not meant to live as men – it's a tiny breath of a moment that they are pulled from their intended cycle. It's as I told you, he began to slow, for his feet to put down roots, for his mouth to stiffen, the words to be less articulated and identifiable. But I couldn't bring myself to… do what needed to be done. Not to him. He'd filled a void and it felt like I'd be killing the last part of me that could feel.'

'Did you name him?'

I nod, but don't tell her what I called him and she doesn't ask.

'So you took him back to the forest…'

'Yes.'

'Then you made others.'

'Yes.'

'And you didn't want me to make the same mistake.'

'No.' I hold my breath for a moment. 'What I do, Rhea, with the summer husbands? It's for a purpose. It maintains my life out here. It's a season. They are tools. When their time is finished, they become firewood – they become something they'd likely have become anyway. The season is sweet. I make no excuses. I do what I do in order to have this life. And this time, if you'd not been here, if I'd not been distracted, then matters would have proceeded as normal.' I raise a hand. 'It's not your fault. It wasn't your fault. It was simply luck, ill or unfortunate or otherwise.'

'Mehrab—'

'I'm glad you had him. I'm glad you had joy and knew something better than you had. I'm grateful for my life and that you chose to save it. But now, Rhea, you must prepare yourself for what comes next, it will not be easy.'

Her eyes widen. 'What do you mean, Mehrab?'

'You've been feeling sick in the mornings, haven't you, even before what happened in the woods, even before you stopped eating?'

She nods slowly.

'I'm sorry to say the child will not live but at least you don't have to wait nine months for it to come to term. These are strange children, born of wood and flesh, blood and sap, and they simply do not take a first breath – too eldritch this mix of mortal and plant. They're not meant to last any more than their fathers are. When you're up to it, choose a resting place. The rose garden is good because it's easy to visit them. That's why I chose it…' I know I sound cold, untouched. I sound monstrous. I *am* monstrous. 'But at least you won't be alone during labour, Rhea, I'll see you through it. When all is done, you may leave, if you wish, you may not be able to bear the sight of me or this place. You're free to go then but remain here where you are safe while you wait. I'll not let you go and bleed to death in the woods.'

She stares at me for a very long time. 'I can't believe you're so kind and so monstrous.'

‘One can be both. I am monstrous. Or I’m simply practical because I know that life is what happens when you’re dreaming of another existence. You’re free to hate me, and free to leave, but only when I know you’ve been safely delivered of this child.’

22

Conversation between Rhea and I remains scarce but at least it's not the pressurised, compacted abyss after Arlo's burning. We move about the cottage companionably enough, and there's sufficient space that we don't need to be near each other if what's unspoken becomes oppressive. We're both careful, I think, to keep a safe buffer. And I think we both know I could have said, 'Now, Rhea, are you listening? He was always going to die. Maybe not so painfully, but that's the result of not doing what you're told.' But I didn't say *that*.

She's already moving more slowly, her belly grown larger and larger, but I think there's still a while yet, just a little. Rhea often rests her hands on her stomach, arching back as she helps around the house, although there's fortunately little to do on the holding now, nothing I cannot manage alone. The apple trees will need pruning soon to see them through winter, she can help with that. If this baby was human? I'd have her doing useful busywork, cutting swaddling cloth, stitching small clothes by the fire, knitting booties and jumpers and tiny caps, all the items a winter-tide child might require. But there's no need for anything more than a shroud.

I'm mostly mended despite the extra bruising. When I'm good and ready, when I'm strong enough, then I must go deep into the forest again. Back to the grove to do what should have been done a long while ago, with hemlock and hatchet and fire. I'll pay my debt to that first summer husband and perhaps somewhere a notation will be made in some grand ledger so that my good deeds might begin to outweigh my ill. And I vow, no matter my loneliness, no matter my losses, I'll never make another summer husband again.

* * *

Outside, early morning, I'm taking a few minutes on the bench by the rose garden, surveying the uneven earth, all those vague little mounds the grass rolls across. It's very quiet and cool, and I adjust my scarf, wonder if my coat is thick enough. Yes, I decide, the ride will warm me up. Rosie's saddled by the barn, reins looped over a fencepost. I'd have started out later, especially with autumn-gloom upon us – but it's lifted. I'll not go out in the darkness until I know what's afoot, what's taking the children, and I'll be certain to return home well before dusk. As long as the cottage wards hold, as long as we're inside by nightfall, we're safe. I am, however, very aware that I seem to be the one and only adult who's felt followed. Rhea has never seen anything nor sensed herself stalked; no one in Berhta's Forge has mentioned it either.

I should find it – I *will* find it, but I need to know *more*.

I cannot forget the image of the huntsman that night, spectral and malign, the most likely suspect.

But *what* is it?

Where does it rest?

And where has it come from and why now?

I shake my head. There are safe boundaries within which we can live for the moment. I will tell Rhea, in a few days, about the huntsman – thus far, I've kept that knowledge to myself. Why? Fear. Fear of being thought mad. Fear of having anyone ask why would such a thing appear to you? What in *you* would call to *it*?

No. Let me find it first. Let me discover its nature. Let me concoct a plan before I mention this to anyone else.

'Mehrab?'

She's wrapped in the thick colourful quilt around her shoulders, but her feet are bare, her hair a wild golden halo, the skin beneath her eyes puffy, and her complexion ever so slightly greenish. A trick of the light, I think, because when she sits beside me it's gone or so subtle I can't see it any longer.

'You'll catch cold like that,' I say, and she gives me a look that says *How much worse can that be?* I cannot fault her.

'You're going into the village again?'

'There are things we're going to need when – when the time comes.' I shake my head, say without thinking, 'Things I'd let run out because my time for such things is done.'

She nods slowly. 'You said… you said that's why you'd chosen the rose garden. Easy to visit. This happened to you, that's why you're so certain of everything, of course.'

I don't have the energy to lie. 'Yes. That's how I know how fast it comes and that they never live.' Tears heat my eyes too quickly and begin to spill, though my voice remains steady.

I nod towards the five little mounds scattered around the spot where Yrse lies. 'Why do you think I spend so much time out here?'

'Mehrab—'

'Each time I've given birth, I've been alone. It's always terrifying. At least you won't go through that. I won't allow it.' I don't look at her but feel her hand on mine. We don't say anything, and I cry. When I'm done, I look at her at last, then pull my hand from hers. 'Oh!'

In her hair blossoms are sprouting, white and pink, thickest along the hairline and around the shells of her ears. 'Oh.'

'What's wrong, Mehrab?' And the girl – she's a child after all – sounds scared.

'It's all right, don't fear. You're blossoming – quite literally – it happens. It happens. It's just sooner than I thought.' I laugh, gently plucking one of the flowers to show her. I don't say that some of mine are pressed between the pages of a book. Her look of shock dissolves, replaced by wonderment, and she giggles.

'I'm a meadow!'

'A meadow, a garland, a bouquet, whatever you wish.' I rise. 'But it means your time is closer than I thought, and I must get moving.'

She holds the horse's head as I mount, stroking the velvety nose. 'Will you visit the Widow Wilky? Ask about her orphans?'

'Eavesdropper.' She'd not mentioned my conversation with Thad Peppergill until now, but I should have known. 'Yes. I'll see her. Now promise you'll not stray from the holding. Stay in the warmth, eat well, drink a lot of water – you will thank me – and don't answer any knocks at the door.'

Her brows lift, her head tilts. 'Anything else, Mother?'

'Awful child. I'll be back before nightfall.'

* * *

It might be time to start bringing Rhea with me when I go into the village. Or soon. After the baby comes and goes, when she's well again. It's been months since Fenna brought her to me, months during which the likelihood of pursuit has faded. It wouldn't hurt for her to become acquainted with our nearest neighbours, find younger folk to talk to so I'm not her only company. Meet men not made of wood. If she stays, of course. If she stays.

I make no plans, merely consider contingencies. If she stays, she can take over some of the village errands; it won't hurt me to do less. It'll be healthy for her to engage with humanity again. At the very least, she should meet Reynald, do some lessons with him because he knows things I do not, has greater skill in his field.

If she leaves, it won't matter.

Abruptly, Rosie whinnies and stalls, dancing sideways. I gentle the skittish beast, trying to see what's bothered her. I took the river path today, a change of scenery, just a slightly longer route – up ahead, there's something lying in the middle of the way. I dismount, keeping hold of the reins but letting them play out as far as I'm able. The horse isn't so keen, snorting and tossing her head as I get further away, but she stays put despite her disapproval.

I'm careful in my steps, sweeping aside any leaf matter

as I go, making sure there's no wolf-pit been dug here for the unwary or a metal trap, hidden, full of gnashing teeth, and no raised earth to say a penitents' path like the one that caught me all those months ago has been laid here. Nothing. And when I get near enough, I laugh out loud. Then I look closer.

A knitted bear of golden-brown wool. Wracking my brain, trying to recall why it's familiar, it finally hit me: I last saw it clutched to the chest of a sleeping Matthias Peppergill at the foot of the tree in his parents' garden. What's it doing out here? Has the boy gone a'wandering again? I pick up the bear and cast around for any sign of the child.

There's nothing. No footprint, no discarded shoes or scrap of fabric torn from a coat or breeches. Nothing disturbing the earth or leaves except for me in my overabundance of caution. From the corner of my eye, however, I'm sure I see something to my left, bobbing in the river. The moment I turn my head, it's gone, no sign of it, and I'm left with an impression of something definitely too small to be a child. *If* there was anything there in the first place. Hyper-alert, I stare for long moments at where the water runs quickly over a small weir, froth and foam as it hits the lower liquid.

No. Nothing.

I go back to Rosie, hold the toy out for her inspection. She sniffs at it with suspicion. Snorts, tosses her head again; disdainful rather than distressed, but she won't go forward, not on that path, so I find another, parallel and narrow and about ten feet away, and she's content to take it. Whatever she can sense on the other, I'm not fool enough to try and ride her over it. The path of least resistance has its appeal. I must be getting old.

* * *

The first thing I notice on arriving at Berhta's Forge is that there's no line of salt been laid around the village. I look carefully and can discern absolutely no evidence of one. There's been no rain, no snow, no sleet, nothing that might have washed it away in the days since I told Thaddeus Peppergill what to do. I can only conclude that he decided the expense was too great, that the loss of other lives was a risk he was willing to take. I wonder if I'll find such a boundary, however, around his mansion alone?

The second thing I notice is that Faolan's with the mares, currycombing the white who's still pregnant. Sorrel and Blister are accompanied by long-legged foals who come straight over to me as I dismount and lean on the fence. They snuffle and nibble at my hands; they smell very new.

'Good morning, old man.'

'And to you, old woman.' He keeps working, but grins at me over his shoulder. 'What brings you here this fine day? I warn you I've no more horses to spare.'

'Hush. Visiting Widow Wilky.'

'What's she done to draw your ire?'

'Oh, how brief was the sweetness of your tongue…'

'My tongue's plenty sweet and I'm happy to demonstrate—'

'I had a visit from Thad Peppergill yesterday.'

'You do know how to kill a mood.'

I shrug. 'He said some of Widow Wilky's orphans have gone missing.'

He stops mid-brush and the mare snorts her annoyance. 'I've not heard that.'

'I don't imagine he's been spreading it around. I don't imagine he's told too many folk and he's probably asked the widow to keep it quiet, lest he have to deal with complaints. Have you heard anything else? Has Anselm mentioned Ari? Have there been any occurrences out of the ordinary? A strangeness in the woods, signs of… incursions in the village?'

He shakes his head. 'Incursions, Mehrab? What sort?'

And I can't bring myself to tell him, though I'm unsure why. The words won't come, cannot find purchase on my tongue, will not push past my teeth. I shrug. 'I don't know.'

'Then why did you come to me?'

I smile.

We drift into the house and as soon as the door closes behind us, clothes are peeled away in that mysterious and effortless fashion, flesh meets and melds, mouths and lips and tongues and teeth go everywhere, tease everything. Hands and fingers transmit desire and heat and he kisses my bruises, the old and the new. Somehow, we find the bed and when he's in me, the pleasure is so intense it feels like I could reach up and touch both sun and moon, reach through time and hold past and present and future in the palm of my hand and freeze them in this moment of pure intensity. There's a second, though, when as my head turns from side to side in ecstasy, I think I see a shape at the door. Gone too quickly, I can't be sure. A shadow, just a shadow from the movement of sun and trees outside the window. And my attention's dragged back to what's being done to me, what I'm doing, and I feel like I might never separate myself from him and I bite at his shoulder to stop myself from screaming like a fox in heat.

In the quiet afterwards, I half-doze, running my fingers along the lines of his scars while he strokes my hair. My mind, never still, picks at the idea that if I'd made a different choice years ago, this bed would have been mine, that I'd not be a visitor here in a house decorated by another woman. That if I'd wanted a child, there might be a lad or lass who looked like me wandering these rooms. That if I'd wanted a constant companion… But perhaps we'd be bored of each other. It happens. No one's proof against it. The irony is not lost on me that though he got no child on me, the summer husbands did, some of them. And that I, each and every time, instead of ensuring those pregnancies did not come to fruition… let nature run her course. That for a time, I had hope and a wish, though I cannot say why. I'd have been a terrible mother.

Abruptly, I sit up, swing out of his arms, out of bed, and gather my clothing despite his protests. I don't snap, I'm gentle, and kiss him tenderly and deeply, tell him I'd laze with him all day if I could, but there are things that must be done, and I'll let myself out.

The truth is that I cannot stay in that bed when it's so crowded by my past, and his.

23

When I knock at the Peppergill house it takes a longish while for someone to answer, and it's only as I'm about to start shouting up at windows that the front door slowly slugs open as if terribly fatigued. The serving maid stands in the doorframe and I can't help but think it's almost as if she hangs there. I shudder and it loosens the illusion so I can concentrate on her face. Dark shadows beneath her eyes, she looks utterly exhausted.

'Oh. Cylla. Are you quite well?'

She nods, then shakes her head. 'I'm so tired. No one's sleeping well.'

'Why? Bothersome noise of neighbours? Creatures in the roof? Nightmares? Is someone ill?'

Her fingers are white at the knuckles where they clutch the edge of the door. 'I can't say. Everyone's restless – or rather, I should say, we all sleep and deeply, but *not well*. I keep waking to find Matthias standing by my bed in the night. He's in such an ill humour, keeps breaking his toys. Does that make any sense at all?'

'It does.' I think about Thaddeus and his day drinking, the shadows beneath his eyes – did he seem overly tired? 'Have you tried camomile tea before bed? Or valerian root, which is stronger?'

'Anything and everything the apothecary can conjure,' she says with a sigh, as if she's answered the question too many times. 'Don't have anything stronger do *you*?'

I do but nothing I'll share; the results are too uncertain, a mix that might drag one down to a slumber one likes too much. I think of my own nightmares and their banishment, my evening ritual. 'The quality of sleep would seem to be the issue. Under each pillow, put a small cloth purse with a handful of graveyard dirt and another of dried lavender. In the morning, try a tonic of honey and ginger mixed with lemon juice and apple cider vinegar. Add a little water if you find it too strong. That should help.'

The girl gives me a weary smile. 'Thank you, Mistress Mehrab. We'll try that tonight. And how may I help you today?'

'Is Thaddeus about?'

'No, he's away for a few days, gone to Asher's Brook to inspect some oxen on Diegan Commerford's holding. Mistress is resting, I can—'

'No, no. Don't disturb her.' Typical that Thad would leave both family and village at such a time and not bother to lay down the line of salt that might afford protection to those he's meant to have care of… I reach into my pocket. 'I found this on my travels this morning, by the river path. It belongs to Matthias, yes?'

Cylla stares blankly, not taking it from my outstretched

hand. 'That can't be his. He sleeps with it, indeed I put it in his arms not an hour ago when his mother took him up for a nap. And yet… it's exactly like his.'

She reaches for it now, plucks it away, turns it this way and that, examining it with bewilderment.

'I can take it – perhaps it belongs to another child, surely there can be more than just one of them.'

She shakes her head. 'No. His mother made it for him.' Cylla lowers her voice. 'Mistress Peppergill isn't the most able of knitters, but she made that with her very own hands, unwinding every mistake and fixing it with care. It was the longest time anyone has ever taken to knit a toy, Mistress Mehrab.'

I suppress a laugh.

She smiles. 'Perhaps one of the other mothers made this one. I'll ask around and if no one claims it, it won't hurt to have a spare if the lad loses his – gods know he'll scream fit to bring the roof down and we'll get even less sleep.'

* * *

There are planks of wood nailed over one of the windows of the apothecary's store, so only half of the lettering can be seen. The shop window has ever been Reynald's pride and joy; no one else has such lovely gold lettering, most still have their signs with hand-drawn illustrations even though illiteracy is low thanks to the school and Widow Wilky's efforts (two extra hours of enforced reading every night for her orphans). The door's unlocked though, and the bell rings as I push in.

'What's happened? Your beautiful window…'

'Fucking children. Fucking, fucking children.' The shock

caused by Reynald's swearing is second only to that caused by the fact that he's clearly been crying. Red-rimmed eyes, sniffling into a handkerchief; on the floor a broom, scattered shards of glass abandoned mid-sweep. 'Yester eve, I heard laughter and then the shattering.'

'Did you happen to see which children?'

He shakes his head. 'I was out back, ran out and saw them bolting away. Little shits.'

Without thinking, I blurt: 'Might you have done something?'

He looks so shocked that I realise it sounded like an accusation. 'I don't mean on purpose! Sorry! I just mean... anything anyone might have taken as a slight even though it wasn't?'

He shifts like a bird with ruffled feathers, calms down a little. 'Nothing like this has ever happened.'

'No.' I bite my lip. 'Anything strange at all the last few days? Are you sleeping well?'

Reynald looks at me strangely. 'Well enough.'

To make up for my rudeness, I help him clear up the glass he couldn't bear to deal with last night. I also buy more than intended – aromatic oils and face creams I can make myself – above and beyond the pads of absorbent moss, and bandages treated with a resin that numbs wounds and reduces bleeding, powdered ginger to ease a nauseous stomach, a concentrate of sage to help dry up Rhea's milk so she's not left with a constant reminder of what was lost, peppermint oil to get the same result but for topical application, and extra powdered yarrow to stop bleeding. The coin seems to have helped.

It'll take an age to replace the glass; it will need to be

purchased elsewhere and brought via a nerve-wracking cart ride. It will be very expensive. The planks will remain in place over winter, letting the cold air creep in. There's a little stove in one corner, but I don't envy Reynald the experience he's going to have.

Before I leave, I try one last time, though it may be unwise. 'The children – was one of them the Hadderholm girl?'

Reynald shakes his head slowly. 'No. No, I think they were all boys, but…'

I wait silently.

'But a few days ago that other little girl, I think they were friends before, ran in here to hide. And I saw the other stalking past in her red cloak. You don't think—'

'No. Just wondering. Her father said she's been in a mood. But don't say anything, I beg of you, it's just a child's whims and nothing she should be punished for – I'm sure it wasn't her. You said all boys, after all.' He nods, and I hug him as I leave.

Yet I think of Tieve saying how Ari only played with the meanest sort now, those she could manipulate. I think of the spite that seems to be flowing through the girl, and if she even suspected Reynald had given Tieve shelter she'd have done this nasty little thing – or caused others to do it.

* * *

Anselm Hadderholm opens the door only marginally more quickly than Cylla did, and he looks entirely worse. Indeed, it seems he doesn't recognise me for a long moment and when he does, he appears resentful.

'What do you want?'

'I came to ask how you are, but you've answered that. Not

sleeping? Or sleeping too deeply?' He blinks. I continue, 'The Peppergills are suffering restless nights. May I come in?'

He nods, pulls the door wide, saying, 'Gida and Ari aren't here,' as if that might influence matters.

In the kitchen, on the tall stools, he offers no refreshment, merely slumps on his chair, hands hanging between his knees, a portrait of defeat. There's something stale about the scent of the place, like a rot beneath the yeast and flour. The smell of baking bread is hours old, not fresh like it usually is.

'And how is Ari? Has she settled back in?' I tally the weeks since the girl's return – two months? Almost? Or more by now? 'Her behaviour?'

'Worse. Worse. Swears and steals. We've a constant stream of parents at the door saying she's made their children cry, pinches and slaps them, scares them with tales that have them screaming in the night.' He shoots me a look. 'You were no help.'

'You didn't send for me,' I remind him. 'Just like you didn't come to me when she first disappeared. You left it for days, Anselm, don't you recall? And I told you after she returned to tell me if her behaviour didn't get better. But you didn't, did you?'

Reluctantly, he shakes his head.

'Too lazy to walk into the woods, man. I'll not take responsibility for something that's not my fault. I have my own life and concerns, baker; I am not your mother, nor the mother of this village. And I'm not, as I am oft reminded, from here.' I breathe through my nostrils, bullish, yet keep my tone low and even. 'What else can you tell me? Anything out of the ordinary, apart from this temper and nastiness?'

‘She still watches us. At night, only now if I wake and see her, I can barely breathe. I can’t move.’

‘What of Gida? What does she say about all this?’

‘She just gives the brat whatever she demands. I…’ The baker licks his lips as if to make the words come out more easily. ‘If I’m honest, Gida didn’t even like the child that much before. Resented her, poor mite.’ He clears his throat. ‘I was the same, I admit. But now… history’s been rewritten; it’s as if this was a longed-for child.’ He puts his head in his hands. ‘She says not to tell *you*.’

I think about Tieve, wonder if the girl’s been left alone; she’s not been to me to say otherwise. I hope she’s kept hold of her little poppet. ‘Have you spoken to Tieve?’

‘Only briefly a fortnight ago. She said Ari’s been trying to get her to go into the woods. Luckily Tieve’s mother doesn’t like my daughter – didn’t before, definitely doesn’t now, won’t let her in the house.’

‘But Ari wasn’t an unlikeable child, not before, right?’

He shakes his head again. ‘No. Entirely likeable, cheerful. Better than we deserved. No temper to speak of, didn’t complain. Biddable.’ A sob. ‘Something’s wrong with her, isn’t it?’

Something’s definitely not right, definitely more than childish resentment. There’s her following Tieve through the woods, there’s the tormenting of her parents, there’s the disappearing orphans, and there’s the matter of a hunk of flesh wrapped in a bright red cloak left on my doorstep seemingly so very long ago now…

And yet…

It's hard to make accusations against a child. Less hard to make them stick, but hard to make them when you're from a group that's always had lies flung at them, lies that are taken for truth without proof. And I, who did not tell the Hadderholms that their child's flesh had been left as an offering on my doorstep, would need to admit to the omission, and my reasons for not doing so were entirely self-serving. No. Self-preserving. It wasn't just my safety, but Rhea's. Ari's a child, but children can be dangerous; turn your back on them and they'll slide a knife between your ribs, just as lethal as any grownup and generally less conscience-stricken by such a deed.

And what can I say? The child's not a witch, no. Something else? Yes – but what precisely? There's research I need to do before I can do anything definitive, but I don't tell her father that; the less he knows the better. 'Be patient, don't draw attention to yourself, don't draw her ire.'

'Will you help? Can you help?'

'I'll try. Don't say anything to Gida, and certainly not to Ari.' Before I go, I mix him a tonic from everyday ingredients in the kitchen: lemon and ginger, some honey, a pinch of the recently purchased sal-volatile from my satchel. 'Has Ari said anything about the apothecary?'

'What? No. Why?'

'His shop window was broken last night.'

Anselm gazes at me morosely. 'I don't think I can say with any authority what my daughter would and wouldn't do anymore.'

I pat his shoulder. 'Well, don't mention it either. Nor my visit.'

‘No fear of that. They both hate you.’

No surprise there.

Before I leave Berhta’s Forge, I find Tieve’s house and, feeling like a wandering tinker, knock politely. Immediately her mother’s there, shouting at me to go away and slamming the door shut. I’m not sure she even sees me properly – but I spot Tieve’s small face in a window, tense and pale, eyes huge. I know better than to knock again, but at least I know the child’s safe indoors, and I can understand she couldn’t get away to bring me news of the orphans’ disappearance. From Anselm’s comments, the mother is unlikely to let her out on her own, and I suspect Tieve won’t want to go out either. Not ideal, but I’ll take what I can get.

The reception at Widow Wilky’s is marginally warmer but she doesn’t let me inside her large three-storey house – in no way luxurious, but solid, warm and clean, enough rooms for her collection of other people’s offspring. Doesn’t want to admit any of her charges are missing either, until I advise that Thaddeus Peppergill has already told me. Her voice is faint as she says, guiltily, that she’d not been worried when the first three went missing – tearaways all, two girls and a boy, though she has hopes of redemption – had assumed they’d either return from an adventure or not. It was the other two that set off an alarm: good lads, kind and gentle and polite, clever. Of them she expected greater things, maybe even travelling to one of the university towns in years to come. But no, she couldn’t say what had happened, or even when, really – over the week of the disappearance, the lads were there all day, were tucked into bed and gone by sunrise. She’d noticed nothing strange any of those days. I urge her, without much hope, to let me know if she thinks of anything else.

* * *

The ride home is untroubled, but the second I step into the cottage I know something's wrong. The pungent smell of blood and sap, a puddle in the middle of the kitchen floor. Water broken. A groan tumbles down from the attic room. I wonder how long since it started, can't believe she heaved herself up all those stairs instead of lying on the sofa (although part of me is relieved she did). So fast! I thought we had days yet. None of mine have ever been so quick. I rush up the steps, calling the girl's name as if she's my own child, my own flesh and blood, my own future.

Rhea's half-on, half-off the bed; the coverlet has been discarded, balled up on the floor. The window's open, the little hearth fire's out, and the air is cold but I don't have time to worry about that. Rhea gives me a wounded look as if she'd never expected it to hurt like this. I'd assumed her mother had told her this at least, but it seems not. Again, I thought we'd have another month, that this would be a deep-winter birth, and I've been reminding myself to dig a grave now while the earth is still soft enough to allow such a thing. Make a resting place for it in the rose garden, beside my own little losses.

'How long?' I ask. Rhea's kneeling as if praying, top half against the mattress, a bright sheen of sweat glistening on her face. She looks uncomprehendingly at me. I begin to unlace the back of her gown – no point being entirely uncomfortable during the most uncomfortable experience of one's life. 'Rhea, how long since your water broke?'

'Not long, not long,' she moans. 'Mehrab, it hurts so much, will I die? Why didn't you tell me it would hurt?'

'Oh, love. Did you think it would be any other way? And no, you'll not die.' Not if I have anything to do with it. 'It hurts, Rhea, I know. It hurts, but I've medicine to take the edge off the pain.' I remove my satchel, begin to rifle through the contents. 'Now, lie down for a bit while you can. You'll want to walk but I've found it's best to rest when you can. Crouching is good but for the moment, lie down, so I can see how far along you are.'

'Oh, you're not going to look at—'

'Trust me, I don't want to be down this end either but—gods!' Which, given the circumstances, is not the most helpful thing I could say, and as I shout, she begins to yell in pain.

Another contraction; the crown of a small dark head, which was already between her legs, is joined by narrow shoulders, a torso. So *fast*! I say 'Push!' and she does, and she makes a noise that I've made myself more than once, a scream of evacuation, an incantation to rid yourself of this heavy tearing burdensome agony.

The little thing – skin the slightest blush of green, hair black and studded with wet blue blossoms, cupid's bow lips, delicate features. A quick inventory shows ten fingers, ten toes, a little girl, nothing out of the ordinary, except the eyes – green, green, green – are open which none of my babies' have been and that little mouth splits to issue a protest at eviction from its warm wet home into the world beyond.

* * *

A little while later, after I've wiped Rhea's brow and cleaned her up as best I can, placed the moss pads and bandages around her bruised core, given her a tisane to make her sleep, to help dry up the bleeding, and after I've settled the little miracle on her chest so it could feed until sated and sleepy. After I've kindled the fire again and closed the window to keep out the cold. After I've told Rhea how well she's done, what a good brave strong girl she is. After Rhea herself has dropped into slumber, only then do I take the child and wrap her in a soft woollen blanket and carry her to the old rocking chair by the dormer window. I sit, rocking back and forth, telling a story oh-so-quietly, so quietly that neither baby nor her mother can really hear, because it isn't really the right one to tell. I'm telling it because it was the only one my mother ever *gave* to me, meant for *me*, and my tears drip onto the tiny, perfect face and onto those closed little lips.

24

It begins with the tree.

Branches reach towards the sky; the tree is quite straight. Its roots, conversely, go deep into the soil and spread out, consolidating their hold on the earth, making their foundation unassailable.

It is the tree that watches over all. It was here before the people and the house, frosted brown and white like a cake; it will remain after they are dust and ashes. It watches and winds its way through their lives in much the same way as its roots wind their way into the soil; it is indelible.

The tree holds many stories, they lie in its trunk like age rings. Its memory is a long thing. Some years it sleeps, some years it wakes and watches and listens. Some years it remembers the lives it has given and tasted and taken...

There was a woman, once, young and dark and very lovely. Her husband had thought a young bride ideal for the getting of heirs. A more robust girl would have been better, he knew, but her green eyes and black hair caught him. There was nothing else for it but to make her his wife and pray there would be children.

He loved her dearly; she was frail but this did not stop his efforts to plant his seed. The man spent as much time riding his wife as he did his horse and to far less effect – at least on the horse he travelled, conducting business and growing his fortune. His wife, however, seemed to be a barren field, a bad investment.

The juniper tree stood in the back garden. The wife loved its spreading branches and the whispers it made when breezes sang through its limbs and leaves. Of the many gifts her husband made her, her favourite was the simplest. A swing was hung from the strongest branch and on summer evenings the wife would sit and sway, dangling her delicate feet as she hung suspended above the ground, dress catching the air and fluttering behind her. The tree spoke to her and it was words of love she heard, before her husband collected her and took her once again to bed.

One spring, when her husband was away travelling, she told the juniper tree of her fears and doubts, of the rigours of her marital bed and of a husband who loved her sometimes too much and sometimes not enough. She leaned against the trunk of the tree, its rough bark smooth under her soft skin, its lower branches seeming to stretch and enfold her. She sank to the base of the tree, curled between the roots and slept for some time. In her sleep she dreamt of love without pain, of gentle caresses, of a lover who took time enough to ensure she was wanting and ready.

When she woke, there were small tears in her skirt and she was wet as she had never been with her husband. Confused, she retreated into the house, throwing uncertain glances at the tree.

She did not mention anything to her husband. When he was next inside her, she thought of spreading branches and the touch of bark, and clung to him, rising up to meet him as she never had before. He was surprised but pleased.

The wife began to glow and grow, and it became obvious that her husband had at last sown fertile seed. They were happy – he would have his longed-for heir and she a respite from his attentions.

The wife grew still.

Her husband was travelling, increasing his fortune so that he would leave a comfortable legacy for his coming child.

One night when they lay beside each other the wife said:

'If I should die, bury me beneath the juniper tree.'

Her husband, startled by her turn of thought, but certain he would not have to fulfil his vow in the near future, agreed.

The child killed her. The daughter, pale-skinned, streaked with her mother's blood, was handed to her father, who held the child tightly and named her Simah. The juniper tree flourished, new blossoms bursting forth, fed by the wife's fertilising form.

The man was rich, and loved his little daughter, but he was lonely. A warm bed and an obliging, soft body were the only things on his mind. When Simah was five, he took a new wife.

Second Wife had a child of her own, a daughter not much older than the widower's little girl. Second Wife loved her daughter with all her heart and vowed she would love her stepdaughter just as well. She did try (in her heart she knew she had tried), but every time her husband slighted her daughter in favour of his, it grew a little harder. Each snub was a prick and her heart soon became a pincushion of jealousy. She began to take her hurt out on his child, in tiny ways at first, then in larger, more bruising ones.

Simah understood only that her presence angered her stepmother. She grew quieter, tried to shrink so as not to attract the woman's ire. Without conscious thought she began to dim, to fade, until she was a tiny voice that seldom spoke. She would light up only when her father came home or when she played with her stepsister. On the worst days, she fled to the back garden and hid in the branches of the juniper tree, eating its berries, her face turned to the sun and the wind, taking in for a short while the breath of a place where she was welcome.

Second Wife's girl, Marlechina, was fond of her stepsister, and tried her best to protect Simah from the worst of Second Wife's temper. She watched as her mother grew into someone she did not fully recognise. When Simah entered the room it was as if Second Wife darkened. Marlechina did what she could but, ultimately, she was a little girl, no match for the dark worm that curled inside her mother.

When her father was away, Simah was fed less than Marlechina; her clothes became old and worn in spite of her father's wealth; no new toys became Simah's while Marlechina's collection spilled from her room like a flood.

Simah's father loved her in the casual way men love their daughters, affection without attention. And her father, as fathers are apt to be, was blind when it came to his wife. The domestic sphere troubled him not at all – as long as his belly was sated with tasty foods and his bed was filled with an agreeable softness, he did not worry about what happened in his own house.

On one of his trips, the husband sent gifts home ahead of his arrival. A large box arrived. Inside it, Second Wife found a beautiful necklace for herself, a pretty ring for Marlechina, and for Simah, ribbons and the biggest doll any of them had ever seen. It was almost as big as the little girl and looked enough like her to be a sister, with dark curls and huge blue eyes.

The children held their gifts happily and Second Wife looked, the one to the other. All she saw was the size of Simah's gift compared to that of Marlechina's – she did not weigh up the value or even consider that her husband had thought carefully in order to give his stepdaughter a gift she would treasure. She saw it as yet another snub. As she seethed, her own daughter spoke: 'Mother, may I have an apple?'

'Yes, in the trunk over there,' she answered. Simah, glancing shyly over the top of her enormous doll, risked a tentative request.

'Mother, may I also have an apple?'

Second Wife turned on the little girl, a refusal at her lips, then paused and nodded. Simah followed her stepsister to the trunk. The woman shadowed her.

Marlechina drew an apple from the trunk and skipped outside to watch the sun shimmer across the red stones of her ring. Simah leaned into the great trunk to reach one of the rosy red apples lying at its bottom. Second Wife grasped the lid of the trunk with both hands and slammed it closed.

The child's body dropped slowly to the floor outside the trunk, now as still as the giant doll. The woman opened the lid and stared at the child's severed head. Blue eyes reproached her.

Shaking, Second Wife picked up the body and sat it at the table, then plucked the head from the trunk by its dark curls. Using a long purple scarf, she wrapped the neck tightly so the head appeared to be connected. Only a little blood escaped from beneath the silk. Second Wife hid in the parlour to watch what might happen.

Marlechina skipped inside. She looked at Simah so still and pale at the table, her doll lying on the floor beside her.

'Sister, may I play with your doll?' Receiving no reply, Marlechina gently shook her sister, which provoked nothing but a head wobble.

'Sister, I would play with your doll.' Once again, she received no reply and she frowned at her sister's unusual perversity.

'Simah, answer me! I wish to play with your doll!' She reached out and violently shook the little girl's shoulder. This produced a more startling reaction – Simah's head rolled from her shoulders like a pumpkin dislodged from a windowsill.

Marlechina screamed, and her mother, watching from the parlour, charged into the room, demanding to know what had happened. Marlechina wept as she blurted out the story. The mother looked at the sad little body and its severed head and began to weep. Second Wife steeled herself – she was, after all, a woman who had decapitated a child.

'No one must know what you did, Marlechina,' she said. Marlechina shrank, fear and guilt frosting her veins. 'Get me the biggest pot in the pantry. I will put this to rights.'

Second Wife cooked her stepdaughter; she made a lovely stew, with plenty of vegetables and a thick brown sauce. Some of the meat she kept aside, to hang later in the smokehouse to dry. Marlechina stood beside her mother, weeping. Her tears fell into the pot, the salt of her grief seasoning the dish.

When the meat had boiled from Simah's tiny frame, Marlechina took the bones and wrapped them in a cloth. She carried the sad little bundle and the doll to the back garden. She hid them under a thick pile of leaves at the base of the juniper tree, and ran back inside. She did not see the earth move and shift, the doll and the bones sliding into the dirt as if swallowed, taken to a place of safety.

The husband returned, his belly growling as the odour of cooked meat filled his nostrils. Second Wife piled the plate high with tender flesh and he ate ravenously, not noticing that his wife and stepdaughter did not touch the dish, nor that his own child was nowhere in sight. He ate and ate; the more he had the more he wanted and soon the large pot was empty.

When he finally pushed back his plate he looked for Simah.

'Where's my daughter?' he asked, picking slivers of meat from his teeth. Second Wife looked meaningfully at her own child, and he shook his head. 'My own daughter.'

'She has gone,' said Second Wife, her voice rough. 'Gone to visit her mother's sister; she wanted to see her aunt.'

The father grunted, disappointed and disapproving that his daughter had left without his permission, though a stronger imperative had begun to take hold. His belly filled with forbidden meat, he now eyed his wife's sweetly curved flesh.

He sent Marlechina to her bed and, almost before she disappeared from the dining room, he was on his wife as if he would eat her, too. Plates and pot were thrown aside as he lodged himself firmly within her. Second Wife thought her happiness complete.

The woman grew round.

When her husband was home from his travels, she would draw his hand to her swelling belly and run it over the taut skin. She was kinder to her own daughter, gentle as she watched guilt swim in the child's eyes and dark shadows grow beneath them.

But she did not say, It was me.

She found herself thinking of the dead child as she rubbed her belly, blinking away tears and wishing things had been different.

Marlechina thought of her stepsister often. One morning as she played beneath the juniper tree, she heard the most marvellous song. Looking up, she spied a magnificent bird, plumed red and blue and gold. The bird sang and its notes began to sound like words:

My mother she killed me,
My father he ate me,
My sister she hid me,
Now my bones lie beneath the juniper tree.

A shower of colour fell towards Marlechina. She reached out, grasped the rainbow, and found coloured ribbons in her hand. The silk shone, glowing like gems in the sunlight. She looked up again but the bird was gone, only the ribbons in her fingers and the memory of its words remained.

She knew now that she hadn't killed her sister. She knew now that her mother had done it. And she didn't know what to do. She could only watch.

The father, returning from an evening at the tavern,

staggered into the yard. From behind the house he heard a song, beautiful and gloriously lonely. He made his way to the back garden and saw a wondrous bird in the juniper tree. It sang him a song like none he'd ever heard:

My mother she killed me,
My father he ate me,
My sister she hid me,
Now my bones lie beneath the juniper tree.

Alas, he didn't understand a single word. When she had finished her serenade, she shook her beautiful head and dropped him something that flashed in the moonlight.

It was a golden chain and it held, banded in wrought gold, a small bone, like that of a child's finger. The man took it to be a religious piece, the finger bone of a saint, a piece of jewellery picked up by the bird in its travels, stolen because it was shiny. He believed in religion, not magic. He hung the gift around his neck and looked up.

She was gone; she had seen his lack of understanding and disappeared.

Second Wife, hanging out washing, heard the song. She did not understand the words but it sounded to her like the sonorous ring of funeral bells, and it struck at her heart with its pain and beauty. She thought of her little stepdaughter, of the way her head had rolled from her shoulders, and she felt pierced. Tears came unbidden.

The bird, glorious fair, swooped down and hovered in front of the woman. It drank in her pain and her regret, her loss, and saw the empty place where Simah could have resided had jealousy not taken hold. In the bird's beak appeared a juniper berry. Second Wife held out her hand and caught the berry as it dropped. With a flurry of feathers the bird was gone. The woman put the berry to her lips and swallowed, the bitter-sweet flesh and juice leaving their taste in her mouth long after the morsel was gone and she had returned to the house.

She began to crave the berries daily; they hung on the tree's branches, tantalisingly just out of reach, purple and lush. Second Wife stood, heavy and fecund, at the base of the tree and stared upward. The tree shivered and shook, and a hail of fruit fell upon her. She dropped to her knees and began to devour the berries.

When they were gone and her mouth was rimmed purple with their juice, Second Wife raised her eyes, and the tree, sensing she still hungered, shuddered until she was once again showered with berries. This second feast sated her and she curled into the roots at the base of the tree.

The feasting became a ritual; no matter what she had eaten or how much, she craved the berries. In her final months they were all she ate, greedily sucking them into her mouth like a child at the breast, juice dripping from her chin. Gradually her hair began to darken and her eyes lost their blueness, hazing into green. Her skin, once golden, lost its colour even though she sat in the glare of the sun for hours at a time, consuming juniper berries. Her nature, once prone to blazing up, settled to a contented hum.

Marlechina watched her mother from a distance, from the windows of her attic room, fingering the ribbons in her hair, singing quietly.

She gave birth beneath the juniper tree. She'd woken in the middle of the night, pains familiar and strangely comforting, rippling across her abdomen. From the garden she could hear – ever so faintly – the song of the bird. She slid from the bed, away from her husband's snoring bulk, and wrapped a shawl about her shoulders. Her feet took her where her mind did not think to go, a movement without thought but necessary nonetheless.

There was no sign of the bird, but the tree welcomed her. She sank to the ground between its roots, and felt the pressure of a child anxious to enter the world. The smell of juniper berries was strong as her water broke. The child came swiftly.

Marlechina, in her attic room, woke to the sound of birdsong. She looked from the window. The white of her mother's nightgown caught her attention and she left her room, swiftly and silently.

Second Wife looked up at her daughter and wept. She lifted the child.

It was the doll. Simah's doll, streaked with blood and birth fluids, still, hard, soulless. Second Wife sobbed.

The bird perched at the top of the tree. In its beak, a juniper berry once again. It dropped the berry into Marlechina's waiting hands. She knelt and gently squeezed the berry between the doll's ever-so-slightly parted lips.

There was a catch of breath; the doll gasped and moved in her mother's arms. Her flesh became malleable, soft and warm as she squirmed, growing rapidly before their eyes.

Marlechina lifted the child, and found her eyes open wide, deep and knowing. Simah's eyes. The child became heavier. Marlechina had to put her down and within minutes the baby was no more. Simah stood before them, naked, and exactly as she had been on the day of her death. Except for the little finger of her left hand, which was missing. The sisters looked at their mother, now almost bloodless, but smiling.

'Take care of your sister, Marlechina.' As the little girls watched, the earth beneath their mother's body opened and drew her down, to rest beneath the juniper tree.

25

At some point, I must fall asleep because when I wake with a start, night's outside the window. Only the dying embers in the fireplace give any light. At least I still have the infant in my arms; I did not let go of her, did not fail in that task. Her eyes are open, they gleam in the faint glow of the last coals.

'Mehrab?' Rhea sounds sleepy. She sits up in bed, the blankets falling from her. 'Where is she?'

'Safe. Here she is.' I rise and return the child to her mother. No sound from the little one, glade-quiet, and I worry for a moment that she's died in my arms. A brief-lived miracle of a creature, here for a mere breath of time and now gone. But no; beneath the fingers I slip momentarily on her warm throat, there's a vein that gently pulses, untroubled as she seeks her mother's breast. Sighing with relief, I wonder what woke me. Us.

I think twice about lighting a lantern or rekindling the fire. Best for the moment to play possum in a darkened house. I tilt my head to listen better, as if the angle will help. Two things, I think: a rhythmic sound circling the house – hoofbeats – but not the house, no. Further away, around the boundaries of the holding, unable to get past the wards. There's that relief at least. The other noise: a scratching at the front door. As if someone is trying the handle, picking at the lock.

'Stay here,' I hiss and take the stairs almost too quickly in the darkness, the soles of my boots – left on in haste to aid Rhea – slipping. Down here, too, only the glow of the fire in the sitting-room hearth. Striding towards the door, I'm neither angry enough nor foolish enough to open it, instead I grab the cudgel from the wicker basket where I leave a shoe horn, old rags, various walking sticks and my seldom-used bow. I have my knife, but the cudgel will be better for keeping someone alive long enough to ask them questions; the knife is likely to kill them too quickly. Still, it has a use.

The night's as black as a goat's guts and I'll see nothing out the windows. So, I make a little nick in my thumb, and swipe the blood across the lintel, behind where the green woman sits, right over a tiny fissure that leads to the head, and whisper, 'Lux.' My own little invention, an improvement to the cottage after it became mine. Through the lacy curtains, there's a great flare of light, greenish in hue, but it illuminates the yard, rose garden, barn, some of the fields and almost to the tree line. I hear swearing and footsteps, a stumbling run away from the cottage and into the woods. They fade into the night and I'm not fast enough getting the door open to see anything more than a figure practically throwing themselves into the woods; no trace, I note, of a red cloak.

My wards may not keep people out, but they work on eldritch things, oh yes they do! At the edge of the green light pouring from my green woman's eyes and mouth lurks the horseman of shadow and bone, on his mount, stalking back and forth. A good several feet from where I know the ward-line lies.

I wonder if, without the presence of the summer husband, the huntsman thought he might resume his game here. I'm not sure what there was to fear in Arlo, but he'd have done damage, given half a chance – my aching ribs are a testament to that – and no creature that lives by its wits and speed can afford to risk damage, not even the thing that waits. Nor the things beside him – not just the wish-hounds this time, but something smaller, different somehow, like two little wolves? Grey rather than black, circling or running figure-eights, nervous, perhaps fearful – still and all, I'd not be risking a pat.

Without the summer husband in residence and with my sleepwalking under control, is it a coincidence that tonight's when this thing reappears? When some mortal in its thrall tries to break into the cottage? The offerings on the doorstep could only have been left there by a human.

The strange thing on its bone horse could not have done so. Therefore, a mortal hand was behind it. But why?

Behind me, I sense a movement and tense, tighten my grip on the cudgel, but it's only Rhea, babe nestled in the crook of one arm, the other unencumbered, a ball of witch-fire spinning in her palm.

'You should have stayed inside,' I mutter.

'It's my home, too. My place and child to protect,' she says, more strongly than I'd have thought possible at this point. I just nod. She's right. But now I have two children at risk, and I'm afraid for them and myself. I wonder how we look to that thing out there, an old woman and a young one, bathed in green light, all defiance, mostly fury. I wonder if it cares.

At that moment, the lord of the hunt's mouth seems to move – by which I mean the shadowy substance of half his face splits and shifts about – and a command spills out, a word so weirdly dark it seems liquid and flows across my ears in a way that feels like the memory of a slap. The hounds – the little ones, the nervous ones – leap towards the cottage, towards the boundary sown with salt and sage and hemlock, with angelica and ash and thistle, with hyssop and wormwood, my words and blood. A barrier that cannot be seen, but can be felt…

The little wolves hit at the same time and burst into flames with a thunderclap and horrible screams. Elsewhere – from behind the cottage, past the fields, to where the ward-line runs around us – come other howls, other screams. This is why the lord of the hunt has not tried to cross the border of my holding. Nor the wish-hounds – too valuable to him, long companions. But the little hounds? Expendable.

The moment that the huntsman holds my gaze is one of the longest of my life. I'm aware of a force of will behind that stare – it must be immense or how else could such a thing keep itself intact? – and there's a sense that it's still trying to get me to come to it. To cross the ward-lines, walk into the woods, mount behind it on its skeletal horse, as if that bag of bones could bear us both hence. I feel no temptation. At last, it wheels the beast about and takes off into the trees, the wish-hounds hot on their master's heels.

'Mehrab, what was *that*?' Child still in one arm, but she's extinguished the witch-fire in her hand.

'One moment, the green woman won't last all night.' I rush inside, pull two old lanterns from the cupboard, oil swishing around in their reservoirs. Back outside I have Rhea light them with a spark from her fingertips, then hang them either side of the door. Then I collect logs from the woodpile, any rubbish branches I can find, build a bonfire, splash slow-burning oil on it to keep it alive throughout the dark hours, and again ask her for a spark. Only when the blaze is in full roar – too much light for anyone to sneak back up the path, if that fool had sufficient courage – do I herd her back inside, lock the door, push Rhea towards the kitchen table and set about building up the hearth and stove fires (adding handfuls of dried lavender and sage for extra protection), then light every lantern and candle I can find. We need warmth, we need food, we need illumination.

When I get the kettle on the hob, I feel my knees lose their strength, my hands shake, as the adrenaline wears off, and fear floods in to make itself known, irked at having been ignored for so long. I blink until the tears stop threatening. It takes a while before I get my breathing under control, though.

Finally, Rhea says, 'I thought, at first, that someone might still be hunting me.' She adjusts the feeding child, and the little girl makes a discontented noise. Rhea hushes her daughter. 'But I think perhaps I'm not the object of interest.'

'Anyone after you would be a god-hound and they're not so stealthy. They tend to kick in doors and take one by surprise – subtlety isn't their way.' I shake my head. 'But, for once, I almost wish it was sons of the church with pious intent.'

'That thing… You didn't seem surprised.'

'You haven't seen it before? Not a trace?'

She shakes her head. 'But you…'

I tell her, at last, the tale of the Black Lake, all those weeks before Fenna brought her to me. Of that creature of smoke and bone and hunger. I tell her I think it's been stalking me, that it was the source of my sleepwalking. I don't tell her that Arlo, I think, kept it at bay because that knowledge will do no one any good.

'The offerings? The red cloak and the flesh?' she asks.

I nod. 'I think so.'

'What is it?'

I wipe the beads of sweat from my face and neck; now isn't the best time for a night-sweat but there's no way of stopping it. It feels like the bonfire in the yard outside has migrated to the very heart of me. I'd get up, make a red clover tea, but I feel too heavy, too hot, too tired. I reach out to the baby's waving hands and she grabs at one of my fingers, holds it tight. That gives me something to focus on.

'Mehrab, are you all right?'

'A hot flush. It'll pass.' I close my eyes for a few seconds, force myself to a steadier breath, slower pulse. 'She's going to need a name, you know.'

'I'm a bit leery of names at the moment. Someone once warned me against naming ephemeral things,' she says pointedly.

'I think she's here to stay.' I manage a smile, reclaim my finger, settle back into my seat. 'Have you ever heard tales of the lord of the hunt, or the lady? An old god, or a new one, some man or woman so enamoured of the hunt that they can't or won't give it up? And other gods, thinking themselves funny, condemn such mortals to an eternity of the chase?' She nods. 'Cautionary tales to keep folk inside after dark, to not challenge the eldritch things that roam. Sometimes just cruel things – all that killing? Slaughter? More than you could ever eat? Just to feel an animal's terror? Acts that just beg for punishment. I think… I think somehow that's what's been following me. I don't know why, other than it noticed me that night and I got away.'

'And that's what's taken the children? Even though Ari and the Peppergill boy were returned? What about the orphans, though?'

I tell her about my conversations in Berhta's Forge, with Cylla and Anselm, with Reynald and Widow Wilky. I tell her how Tieve's mother behaved, and I do not mention Faolan nor how we spent our time. In the end, she asks me what I can do and I answer honestly that I don't know yet. She doesn't suggest I should hurry up and work it out, but her expression makes that thought quite clear. Rhea does say, however, that I should have shared all this earlier.

I have no answer for her.

* * *

Later, when Rhea's sleeping on the sofa, the little one with her, I watch them and think about the nature of the child, this melding of summer husband – of new oak – and human flesh. My mother's tale about juniper trees was designed to tell me about unloved daughters – to let me know that I was one most certainly. I told it to the baby to let her know she was special, that she'd survived in spite of everything, and that it was my most fervent blessing for her to do so forever.

With a sigh, I rise, search the bookshelves for one of the books Yrse left behind – certainly one of her most valuable – the ancient copy of *Murcianus' Magical Creatures*, which Rhea has put back in the wrong spot. Though not native to my homeland, such tomes are known in certain closed circles there, highly prized. Once, to the great rejoicing of the palace librarians and the high sorceress, a shipment of such books arrived to supplement the knowledge of those in the kingdom who sought after such things. I was not allowed to touch them or read them for a very long time. Those very same books I watched burn as I fled, piled high in a courtyard, the bodies of most of the royal family and scions of noble houses all added for kindling.

I shake my head, try to concentrate. I ponder the stories I told Rhea in that long-ago springtime about changelings and stocks, troll offspring left like cuckoos. Then I think about the huntsman, that broken thing with his wish-hounds by his side.

I open the pages and begin to search for anything that might give answers about both of my problems.

26

Just after dawn breaks, we venture outside to see what we can.

The bonfire has burned down, is nothing but cold ashes which I'll sweep away later. The animals are safely in the barn, and are slow to meander out into the cool air of their enclosures. They seem none the worse for last night's visitations, but then they didn't have to experience them. It's only now that I think on how quiet my livestock were, how all three horses remained calm. I wonder if they simply knew themselves not the target of the attack, or just that they felt safe here. Unusual.

Rhea paces about, jiggling the baby – who has grown much faster than a mortal child, and is clinging onto her mother with a greater strength than she should have at this stage – on her hip, while I check on the hens in their coop – all present and accounted for, each one having laid an egg or two. *Productive.* I set them gently in the pocket of my apron.

'Mehrab? Mehrab, come here.' She's standing just inside the ward-line, staring at something on the ground. As I get close, I realise it's where those small hounds fell and burned. 'Are those… bones, Mehrab?'

And they are. Two mounds. Not beasts' bones, however. Small femurs, pelvises, ribs, scapulae, fingers and toes and skulls. Neither canid nor lupine. Human. Child-sized.

'Widow Wilky's orphans.'

'But they were human. The wards—'

'The wards detect the inhuman. Whatever had happened to them, it didn't matter what they had been…' Nervous, Rhea jiggles the baby faster. I put a restraining hand on her arm. 'You'll turn her to butter if you're not careful.'

She gives a half-laugh, a sad sort of thing. 'My mother told me a story, of how, many years before, children went missing from Lodellan. Then suddenly one day the city found it had a wolf problem at night…'

'Similar but different, I think. The magic of it at any rate.'

'Same effect, though.'

'But we didn't need silver or wolfsbane.' Gingerly, I pick through the ashes, find only some imperfectly incinerated fabric. Clothing beneath fur. No trace of fur. No trace of wolf fangs, just the teeth embedded in the jawbone and skull. 'There'll be three more of these around the cottage. It was looking for a weak point, trying to get through. Testing.'

'They were all just sacrifices.'

'Yes.'

* * *

After we've collected all five and wrapped them in shroud-cloth, we bury them in the hole Rhea shows me – she'd begun digging it for her babe yesterday, before labour pains began. I scold her – I'd never meant her to dig it herself, only to choose a spot. When we're done – the babe in question lying in a basket cooing to herself and playing with her own feet, the horses all mesmerised, heads sticking over the fence – Rhea asks, 'What next?'

'I think… no, I know I need to go into the forest.'

'Mehrab—'

'I'll be careful. But I need to find that trap, that penitents' path – I can't help but feel there's something there, something I wasn't looking for then, but that's part of it. The night at the Black Lake was a few weeks before that – it was accidental, that encounter, but I don't think the trap was. Don't worry, it's daylight and the huntsman can't ride until dark. I have Rosie and she's fast.'

'Why now, though?' she asks. 'After all the years you've lived here why has this happened now?'

I shrug. 'The same reason anything happens – something changed. Unexpectedly. And I need to know what so I can deal with it.'

'What about Ari? She – it – can move around in the daylight.'

I nod. 'It can, so there must be something in there that was the girl, something in her core. But I don't believe Ari's been across the ward-line and I don't believe she can because like the wolflings, she's been changed enough. It wasn't her at the door last night. But I can't do anything until I have some more answers – or indeed any answers at all.'

'Mehrab—'

'And no, you can't come with me. I can't be slowed down by a nursing mother still tender from birth and a little creature that will demand to be fed, that will squall and cry the moment its belly feels empty or its nappy full. I need you to stay here so that I don't need to worry about you.' I hug her to take away the sting. 'But there's one more thing I can do.'

I change into trews and a dark green coat, twist my long hair into a knot and pull a woollen cap over my head for added warmth. Check my satchel and add bread and cheese and a waterskin to the tinderbox and variety of powders in pouches and bandages, and one of the little blue vials with the protective oil I mix myself, because you never do know what you're going to need. I gather the bow and quiver of arrows.

Rosie complains about being saddled and again brought out of her warm stall. The sheep, cows and goats eye her as she passes as if in sympathy that's very much seated in better-you-than-me. The new bay, Eadig, looks hurt to miss out on an adventure and I whisper to him that he should think himself lucky to be excluded. Fyren, my old boy, and wiser, merely chews on his oats with contentment. I fondle his ears, kiss his velvety nose. He's too old, too slow, and I need a mount that's sleek and fast and alert. Just in case I need to flee. Poor Rosie, to fit the bill so well.

'Now, I know obedience isn't your strong point, but this is important. Don't leave the cottage because you might not find your way back. Don't answer the door. Don't open the windows. Read, feed yourself and the child, keep an eye on that cat – they like the warmth of a baby's breath a little too much though they mean no harm.'

'How long will you be?'

'I don't know but no panicking. I've Rosie and will move much faster than on these tired old feet. Don't worry, I'll be home before nightfall, I've no desire to remain out after dark.'

'Mehrab—'

'And, again, don't open the door, don't let anyone in. I don't care if they're begging and pleading for help. I don't care if they're bleeding on my doorstep. Keep yourselves safe, that's my only concern.'

'Mehrab, be careful,' is all she says and hugs me awkwardly, the baby between us.

'I will.'

But before I leave, I walk the boundary of the holding, carrying a small wooden bucket and a spade; it's roughly a rectangle, some lines curving a little to accommodate trees and rocks. At each corner, I stop and dig a hole with a compact trowel, about a yard down, not deep enough to disturb the wards, and scatter in tansy seeds, purple monkshood petals, powdered cherry bark, and amaranth paste, murmuring an incantation as I add a few drops of my blood from a cut in my forearm. I refill the holes and water them from the bucket. Before I move on, I watch until tendrils break through the soil, a strange hybrid of all those plants making its presence known. It will remain until I remove it. Once all are set, all four plants with their thorns and purple-yellow blooms about a yard high, I stand back, a few steps outside the ward-line and take one last look at the cottage. On the doorstep are Rhea and the swaddled baby, Mr Tib close to Rhea's feet.

Then I raise my arms, palms open to the sky, and sing the incantation of invisibility. Across the world, across continents, there are witch huts, hidden places only we can sense, find. Concealed from those who hunt us, from any casual gaze. But *we* know they're there and they're safe houses. The spell not only provides cover but sends pursuers astray. The wards are everyday powerful against eldritch creatures (nothing grander, nothing requiring more blood than I'm prepared to spill), but this is the best way I can protect the cottage and those within from the prying eyes of men.

As I watch my home fades from view and a new wall of the forest appears to grow up in front of it. I blink twice and slowly and can see it again, then blink twice again and it's gone. Only a witch will sense it; see through it.

* * *

As Rosie trots along the forest paths, I turn my mind to the huntsman and what he might want with me. My ego isn't such that I think myself irresistible so I will not regard him – it – as some lovelorn suitor willing to destroy all in his path to win my hand.

I *might* believe that the huntsman is punishing me for the summer husbands, for how I've pulled them out of their cycle, stolen them from the forest even if only for a brief while. Or perhaps in revenge for that very first summer husband, the one I created out of madness and grief as a salve to my own loneliness, the one I abandoned in that grove and did not give the kindness of a proper ending, a proper return to the earth. The one I still owe that debt to… But I don't believe the huntsman's a creature working in favour of the forest.

And the stealing of the children… so many and for so little effect, because all the old tales, including those I read last night, agree on one thing: that the lord or lady of the hunt takes only children who are precious to those who've offended them, who've trespassed on their particular tract of earth.

Perhaps the Hadderholms and the Peppergills might have done something, but the orphans? So new to Widow Wilky's large house, so fresh, with so little time for affection to build? And *none* of the children were connected to me.

I follow, as best I can, the route I took that day, weeks and months ago, when I pursued the hare and wandered into the trap carved in the forest floor. Yet I'm not sure I'd have found it had Rosie not whinnied and stalled. Stroking her mane, making soothing noises, I scan the landscape around us. Familiar, I think, that tree there with its branches twisted up so high it looks like a supplicant, that holly bush with red buds changed from when I saw it in spring, larger and lusher, its prickly leaves notwithstanding. The path to the left that diverges in three directions. And yes, there's that break in the undergrowth, what amounts to almost a low hedge, that I ran right through that day, straight into the trap. I think about the hare that led me astray. How when I saw it, I was filled with hunger or rather a *fear* of hunger. Of going short, of starving, of a life of thin soups and watery stews, of an autumn in which I might die. Fear and hunger drew me into the chase, even though there was no real need. The irrational desire of the hunt, the chase.

Rosie shakes her head when I try to urge her forward. Fair. I dismount, tie the reins to a low-hanging branch, then step carefully into the gap in the hedge, mindful of my footing.

There it is, the maze, the penitents' path, so innocuous, so easy to miss if you're distracted. But since I'm looking for it, since I know it's there, it's easier to spot – helped by the fact that each curving line of it has turned brown as if burned with acid. Poisoned perhaps. I think about the iron knife stabbed into it, all my rage and frustration and will to be free behind it – and I have no doubt my will can be a corrosive thing. I think about how iron is hated by so many unearthly and eldritch things, how inimical it is to their makings.

And I no longer believe this trap is an old thing. Nor that whatever set it is a thing that's old in this forest. That it may well have been roaming elsewhere for a very long time, but it's freshly sprung *here*. Otherwise, its presence would have been noted. It would have been *felt*.

So, where is it now? Spring and summer, now autumn, it's been active. When winter proper comes, what will happen? Hibernation? Or predation, like winter wolves starving, desperate enough to attack isolated holdings, or come into the village, uncaring of the danger, seeking only a meal? Or whatever else it's seeking? And if it can't get me, how many more children will it take?

It – he – only moves about by night, so where does he hide during the daylight hours?

There must be a lair…

I examine the maze again, its burned lines, and notice a trail running off to one side – very thin, very faint, yet a trail of dead brown grass nonetheless, heading deeper into the forest. I unhitch Rosie and walk her around the edge of the clearing – I'm not willing to risk there being some spark of magic left in the circle – until I find the spot where the trail runs under the surrounding hedge and out. The horse protests again; I tug her along.

'I don't like it any more than you do, but this is the way we have to go. And I need you to behave because both our hides may well depend upon it. Steel your nerves, beastie.' She shakes her head at me but quietens down. Or she does until we come to the edge of another clearing, stopping at the tree line to stay concealed. Rosie tosses her head and makes a point of thumping my shoulder with her great skull. 'All right, all right,' I mutter as I stare at where the line of browned grass ends.

In the middle of the new clearing, a barrow, I think, but covered with trees. Yet not trees going upwards but growing diagonally, horizontally, espaliered so they look like ribs over the dirt mound, an unwilling armour for this wound in the earth. And the dirt mound, its maw dark and open, uninviting.

'Oh.'

27

Peeking from behind a thick trunk, I can make out some details. Around the barrow's entrance is a series of stones, and I imagine there's more beneath the greenery that grows over the top of the mound as camouflage. There's a sloping path that leads down into the maw, but there's not much more to see from out here. With a deep breath, I tie Rosie's reins to a branch, leaving her in the shadows where she'll be less noticeable. 'You stay here, Rosie, because if I come running out, we're both in trouble.'

Nervously, I check the contents of the satchel again: nothing's changed; nothing more, nothing less. After a moment's consideration, I leave the bow and quiver hanging on the saddle horn because if it comes to a fight in that barrow, my knife will serve me better. I give the sheath at my waist a pat, then step out of the shadows and into the bright midday clearing.

I move slowly, listening hard. No birdsong here, nor insects, even at this time of the year there's usually some sort of noise; autumn doesn't have winter's crisp clarity, merely a sort of dull echo. Up closer, I see thick roots weaving in and out of the stone walls which look older than the foliage – is that greenery a late addition? At the entrance, there's not a simple forward path inside but rather one that winds to the right and down – it's dark but somewhere further in, further down, there's a glow, so I don't bother with my tinderbox but keep one hand on the damp wall as a guide and support. A few feet more and I encounter one, two, three curtain walls to block the daylight. If this isn't a long-term lair, then it's somewhere that's been taken over in recent times; shifted into by some sort of cuckoo, taking over a husk and repurposing it.

I make my way quietly and carefully to the bottom of the slope, and find myself in a large round chamber, niches cut into the wall, torches lit and throwing soft light and dancing shadows in equal measure. Firelight, not daylight, not sunlight – needed for something other than a nocturnal creature that can see in utter blackness. This illumination, then, is for a mortal. A minion. A thrall. Someone who tried to break into my cottage for reasons unknown. Or perhaps guessable. There are some small tables, rustic chairs, a roll of shroud-cloth like that wrapped around the meat in the red cloak.

Scattered across the stone floor: piles of bones and heaps of fur-covered hide, black as night. Long heavy skulls, large bones. Not small bones, not children's. Wish-hounds? Wish-hounds in the daylight hours, disarticulated, waiting for nightfall, for their master's call to hunt. I'm careful as I make my way between them, as if my presence might rouse them. When they do wake? No doubt they'll smell my scent, recognise it because they've stalked me before. It adds a little speed to my delicate steps, in the interests of getting back to the cottage before darkness.

On the other side of the chamber is another doorway, another corridor, spiralling downwards. But additional rooms run off this chamber and I inspect those first, pulling a burning brand from the firepit; most are unlit and empty of anything except more funeral niches, decayed coffins and urns, cobweb-covered grave goods, the occasional skull (human), until I come to the last one.

A round dais is built up in its centre, and four biers radiate around an enormous throne of stone and bone in the middle of the dais itself. There are two firepits either side of the dais and they're ablaze; their purpose, I think, is to keep the small bodies on two of the biers warm. I drop the burning brand into the nearest one.

I hurry over to the still forms: Ari Hadderholm in a filthy yellow tunic and brown trews – no sign of the remains of her red cloak – and Matthias Peppergill, in the blue pyjamas I found him in that day in his garden. Children who are apparently safe and sound in the village. A quick check establishes both have pulses, dry skin, no trace of a fever, but are also in a very deep sleep – both of them pinched hard, neither waking; I wonder what their counterparts in the village feel? I could lay my hands on them and explore their bones, the truth of their flesh, to make sure they're what they seem, but that would be too cruel – to have them possibly wake screaming.

But Ari…

Ari is not *whole*. Her left shoulder is gone, though the wound doesn't bleed, isn't cauterised; I'm looking at a cross-section of muscle and tissue and bone. I think of that chunk of flesh wrapped in the cloak, the thing I couldn't bear to look at too closely when it appeared on my doorstep, not even to establish if it was shoulder or haunch or whatever. I think about scrying for her, with that scrap of cloak, yet she was here all along – and this barrow, this strange place, was enough to shield her from me…

As I'm reaching out to examine the severing, I feel as much as hear the pounding of hoofbeats from above. Someone charging across the clearing.

I cannot carry them both with me, cannot get both onto Rosie and hold them there while we gallop through the forest, likely pursued. And if I take Ari, I cannot guarantee that removing her from this location – this locus of whatever power it is – won't kill her. And if I take one and not the other… I cannot know what will happen to the one left behind.

It makes sense to leave them here, though the decision is cold and I can feel its chill on my spine. Both are alive and have been for weeks, months. They serve a purpose here. And if my reading last night confirmed anything for me, it's that changeling magic (as opposed to other types of double-goer magic) requires the original to stay alive in order for their copies to continue functioning elsewhere. Ergo, they are safe here for the time being.

I'll return with others. I can return with Anselm and Thaddeus Peppergill and Faolan and as many men and women who want to join us. Any number of other brawny folk will come with me to rescue these children. If I just can convince them that those in the village are nothing more than fetches, doubles.

I think about the Hadderholms and the Peppergills, so sleep-deprived and pale-looking. I think about things that steal energy and life away to feed themselves – not blood, not like the Leech Lords rumoured to be gone from the Darklands now – but spirit and thought and essence. The things in those homes, pretending to be children, have taken up residence for their own reasons, or in the service of something else – something greater. Something worse.

The hoofbeats stop. I pray Rosie keeps her mouth shut, doesn't decide she needs to greet the new arrival.

What to do?

I fish the tiny blue bottle from my satchel, almost dropping it in my haste. I shake a few drops of the oil onto my thumb, then draw a circle on each child's forehead – the oil contains a little of my own blood; hopefully it'll prove as effective as the wards which also have my red price in them. I whisper a blessing and a promise to return, then wait by the doorway of the dais room until there's the distant echo of boots on the stones of the entrance.

I could fight, go on the offensive – but if I die, if I'm overpowered, then these two are lost. And Rhea is left alone in the forest with a child and things clamouring to get in. Hand on my knife, I hold my breath.

The footsteps are coming closer. These are the longest seconds of my life – my recent life – then the incomer paces past, towards where the corridor continues spiralling down into lower chambers. As soon as they're dim echoes, I'm up on my tiptoes, moving as quickly as I can, picking my way back through the piles of wish-hounds, and to the path that slopes upward. I wish I knew how to destroy them, but they're already dead things, aren't they? Concentrate, Mehrab.

What might I have found if I'd gone deeper into the barrow? A burial chamber fit for a forest queen or king, where once royal bones and grave goods lay? Long forgotten, long deserted, and found by whatever sleeps there now?

Outside, I spring across the clearing, duck beneath the trees, unhitch Rosie and lead her away so she's less likely to be heard. My heart stutters when I see something large and red on the other side of the clearing, between the trees, unclear, and I drag Rosie along. Only when we're a quarter of a league away do I dare mount, and urge her back the way we came.

It's a long time before I stop listening hard for any sound of pursuit.

* * *

By the time the cottage is in sight, or rather the place where the cottage should be in sight, it's late afternoon. I can discern the waver in the air, that spot between where the veil is thinnest and easiest to pass. That's not all I notice: a lump of trembling and weeping blue fabric is crumpled on the path. The lump raises its head at the sound of Rosie's approach.

A tear-streaked face suddenly looks like it's found hope again.

'Tieve. Are you all right?'

'I thought you were gone, Mistress Mehrab! You said I could come to you, but I thought the forest had swallowed you.' She rises, dashing tears from her eyes and rubbing a fist over her nose. She gestures towards the absence of a cottage. 'Where is it? Where's your home?'

It was lucky she didn't try to push her way closer or the enchantment would have sent her astray, deeper into the woods. 'What's happened, Tieve?'

‘Ari found the little charm doll you gave me. It burned her palms and she threw it on the fire. And then… and *then* a mark appeared on her forehead, a circle, and she really did scream!’ I think of the oil I used on the slumbering children in the barrow; presumably Matthias has one too. ‘She only left me alone because of that – and Ma came home and kicked her out. And her father… Mr Hadderholm’s dead.’ The child starts crying again.

Poor Anselm. Poor man. So little harm in him, he deserved better.

I look at the sky – it’s heading into the early dark of autumn. The paths won’t be safe for either of us very soon, and if Ari or whatever’s in her place has found the little protection I gave Tieve, then the girl will likely be in greater danger. I reach down to Tieve and she doesn’t hesitate to take my hand; I pull her up in front of me.

‘Close your eyes,’ I say, then I hook the hood of her blue woollen cape over her face to make doubly sure. I aim the horse at the thin space and urge her forward. In seconds, my home is in front of us: cottage, barn, fields, gardens, pond. A quick glance behind shows the outside world, the forest, but wavy and uncertain, as if seen underwater. The barrier remains intact. We can see out, but no one can see in.

I pull her hood back and help Tieve slide to the ground. She looks around in wonderment, distracted only when the front door opens and Rhea appears, the baby swaddled at her chest.

‘Tieve, this is Rhea. Rhea, this is Tieve, she’ll be staying with us a little while.’

28

In the sitting room, Tieve's playing with the baby – who's already lost that typical wizened and shocked look they carry for a few weeks after birth. She – still nameless – is stretching her limbs, exploring the edges of her basket; she'll need a new one of those soon. Tieve, bless her, has never questioned the little one's slight green hue, nor the flowers in her hair; just says how sweet she smells. I reassured Rhea the growth spurt was normal for a child such as hers, even though I don't truly know; none of mine lived and I've no experience to base my promises on, only the memory of hybrid children in old tales, growing quickly, needing to be able to defend themselves against humans as soon as possible.

Rhea's in the kitchen, cutting up vegetables and a chicken for soup. I offered to do it but she said she's happy to be moving around unencumbered again. I suspect she's thinking I look exhausted and old, and though the idea offends me, I can't say she's wrong on at least one count. Her eyes on my face as I told her about the barrow, the children… It's a relief to sit on the sofa after riding Rosie for long hours. Tieve's devoured two slices of plum cake and keeps sneaking glances at the activity in the kitchen; I'm still not hungry although I'm on my third dandelion tea, my third red clover tonic against the hot flushes. Tieve's remarkably serene now she's safe, despite her bad news – the initial bit and what follows.

'How did Ari get into your house?'

'One of my brothers let her in – he was going out, and she pushed her way in. He kept going and she… I'd… I'd been playing with the charm dolly. I know I should have kept her hidden, but I like her so much. Ari said I shouldn't be talking to you, and then she saw the dolly, and swore and threw it in the fire like I told you.' Tieve barely takes a breath. 'But she squeaked because it burned her hands, and then she screamed because of the…' she trails off because I'm nodding, although I don't tell her what I did in that barrow. 'And so I ran here.'

'That was wise, Tieve. You can't trust Ari now.' Or whatever's masquerading as her. 'I think it's best you stay here for a little while.'

She doesn't argue.

'I'll get word to your mother.'

The girl shrugs. 'I doubt she'll notice.'

I choose my words carefully. 'Your mother cares for you, Tieve, or she'd never have forbidden Ari from seeing you, and I know a frightened woman when I meet one. Your mother was afraid for you, she's just not very good at expressing it so it sounds like anger. She's not angry at you, but you're the person in front of her at the time and, sadly, most people look for a target without thinking. Perhaps one day you can talk to her about it.'

She gives me a doubtful look, and I don't push it because

some people are simply awful whether they're worried or not and I don't have the energy to ponder Tieve's mother any longer.

'But tell me what happened to Anselm?'

'They found him this morning – out on the green. He looked like he'd been dragged back and forth across the earth, and trampled, too.' Her voice drops low. 'But no one heard anything last night.'

'Had he left the bakery?'

She nods. 'He was drinking at the inn. I think he's been there a lot lately.'

Small wonder with a changeling child in a home where sleep's become something that drains energy and feeds nightmares. I think about a befuddled Anselm staggering home in the darkness, taking the shortcut across the broad expanse of the green. I think about the huntsman, frustrated at his lack of success at my cottage. I think of all those tales of folk taken by the wild hunt, pursued like game. I think of Anselm, not a terrible man, not the best, but not the worst, and his past months in a house with a daughter that's not his and a wife who's lost herself in guilt.

'He was nice to me, like I remember my father being.'

'Poor man,' I say.

'Poor man,' the other two echo.

'And then as I was leaving,' says Tieve, 'I saw Mr Peppergill return with the priests, dragging that poor woman with them by a rope.'

Rhea and I exchanged a glance. 'What woman, Tieve? What god-hounds?'

'Your friend. The woman with the white streak in her hair.'

She mimes the white stripe that starts at Fenna's widow's peak and runs to the ends of her fading red mane.

'How do you know she's my friend?'

She colours. 'I was in the woods and saw her and her,' she nods at Rhea, 'one day, bypassing the village. I know she's brought girls to you before.'

'This is very important, Tieve: did you hear them say anything?'

'Only when his wife ran out to meet him. He said he had the answer to all their problems. But Mrs Peppergill looked pretty shocked to see the priests.' As well she might; as should any woman in Berhta's Forge who knows that life is better lived without church oversight.

'Where did they take the woman?'

'To the bridewell. I think her leg was hurt, she limped very badly.'

The bridewell is a small building with cells built beneath, supervised by Mawgan Carlyon, who calls himself a bailiff but is really just a petty tithing-man, who collects village taxes to pay for communal repairs and work that benefits everyone. There's little enough crime in the village for him to attend to except for breaking up drunken fights, and he spends most of his time as a supervisor at the sawmill. Several of the men who work as sawyers there are frequently conscripted to shifts in the bridewell. None of them complain as it's far easier and there's a free meal from the inn. That and investigating the occasional theft of chickens and the "borrowing" of horses (not from Faolan, *never* from Faolan), which are generally returned after use. Mawgan's no better or worse than most folk.

'Did you hear anything they said? The god-hounds?'

The child shakes her head, curls her knees up to her chin and wraps her arms around them as if by making herself smaller she'll be safe. But no one's safe anymore.

'Were they riding horses? Or did they have a carriage or cart?'

'Walking, all of them.'

'Did they look clean or as if they cared for their appearance? Had bathed recently?'

She shakes her head. 'Dirty and scruffy.'

'Mehrab, what are we going to—'

I hold up a finger to Rhea, begging for quiet while I think.

With every bit of energy left in me, I ponder these god-hounds, dragging Fenna behind them, a rope around her neck like an old donkey or a dog. Scruffy, walking shit-priests, not even a cart between them, not even a broken-down nag for the first among them to ride. So: low-end god-brothers. A better sort would have made time and effort to clean themselves up each day because they know the value of appearing better than they are – what is a church without its *Show*? Its grand performance?

And Thaddeus Peppergill, headman-mayor-what-have-you of this little speck of a place in the middle of a deep dark forest, a place that doesn't have its own clergy, never has had, and Thad thinking *these* men who drag a witch behind them are the answer to his problems? Thinking their presence will save him the cost of a circle of salt around the place he's meant to protect? Will get him back his sleep? Keep the children of Berhta's Forge safe?

What might Fenna have told them? If she'd given me up,

they'd already be here, trying to find the cottage. The veil is a short-term protection – they'll not be able to get through, but they might set a fire to burn as much of the forest as they think will incinerate me, yet set astray by the wards how much, how far might they destroy? Fenna might yet break. She's still alive and suffering for it. They'll have tortured her, that's the only way she'd have brought them back here. I think about her fondness for her apprentices, those Visiting Sisters who've given their lives in order to keep their silence. I won't judge Fenna for not dying.

And I won't leave her behind.

We're going to have to leave. Through a forest that's become home to something very strange and unwelcome. Something that's intent on pursuing me. With winter coming and a woman with a baby, and a ten-year-old child and a fifty-year-old woman whose bones ache, who burns up and freezes without reason or warning. And a woman in her sixties who I'm betting has been beaten so badly she can barely walk.

'Mistress Mehrab?' Tieve interrupts my thoughts and I frown as I look at her. She's holding up a key, large, a little on the rusty side.

'My brother? The one who let Ari in? He works sometimes for Mawgan Carlyon, cleaning out the bridewell cells. He keeps spare keys coz he loses them sometimes. I thought you might need this?'

We're going to need more horses.

* * *

I try to time it carefully. My desire to not risk being caught by the wild hunt and its master, who move by night, warring with another desire not to sneak around Berhta's Forge in broad daylight where god-hounds wait. It's still dark when I venture forth, but I'm hopeful that I've chosen an hour when huntsman and wish-hounds are coursing back across the forest to the shelter of the barrow, and the residents of the village are still in their warm beds. I have to risk the pre-dawn dark if I'm going to find some shadows to hide in while I do what I need to.

The forest paths are quiet and deserted, terribly cold. Soon there'll be snow to either cover our tracks or give away our direction. Rosie picks our way through the trees, until we can cross the short distance between the woods and the smithy. There's no light of the forge glowing in the last morning darkness but it's very early and no one would appreciate the sound of hammer on metal ringing out to wake them. It's all I can do not to creep into the house, into Faolan's bed, tell him I'm going… but if I do that he'll argue, robbing me of precious minutes. If someone tells the god-hounds that he's connected to me there's no telling what will happen; though I cannot imagine him betraying me, who can say what one will divulge under torture? And this village – what if these god-hounds get a foothold? If they petition the Archbishop of Lodellan to build a church here, to let iron bells ring through this ancient place. What will it become?

He was absent from my life for so long… I can live with that again. It will not kill me. I'll send him a letter later from who-knows-where. Perhaps. I remind myself of the years alone, no matter that he's apologised. So, no. I won't risk others for the sake of him.

I lead Rosie into the stables to wait in the warmth for my

return. None of the mares are pregnant now, but their colts are by their sides. Sorrel, Birch and Blister. They whicker gently at the sight of us. There are three geldings and two other mares, older and calmer. Swiftly, I saddle two of the geldings, both dark mahogany – one for Rhea, one for Fenna. Eadig will be the main packhorse and Fyren will bear the lightest of loads; I won't leave him behind. Still haven't decided what to do about the livestock, but one catastrophe at a time. A cart will be too slow and unwieldy when we go off the paths as we'll no doubt need to, so we'll be travelling as light as possible. Tieve will be passed around between us or perhaps she's light enough for Fyren; if she wishes to come with us, of course. I can't just assume she'll happily leave her family.

Faolan will curse me for another theft, so I hang a purse of gold on one of the hooks where the spare bridles wait.

I kiss Rosie on the forehead, bid her wait for me, then sneak out into the grey morning. Both cloak and boots have been enspelled for quiet movement, but these are little spells meant to help make you less obvious, not perfectly undetectable – that requires bigger spells, bigger magic, a larger blood tithe and ingredients that aren't ones a decent witch will easily or willingly use.

I duck between houses and places of business, sticking to the shadows where and when I can; though still dark it's the paling darkness that presages dawn. I don't have long. The bridewell sits low and squat not far from the Peppergill mansion. There's a front door and out back an entrance with a ladder down to the cellar, and thanks to a ten-year-old's light fingers and foresight, I have a key.

I should be paying more attention to my surroundings but I'm thinking how to get a wounded Fenna out of that cellar. Will she be able to walk, make it up a ladder? I don't want to risk the front door. She'll be slow and will need help. Once I get her back to the smithy and the stables, it'll be easier with the horses, then slipping back into the forest and riding hard for the cottage where the others wait. And I'm thinking about the two children lying deep in a barrow, trying to figure how to get them out and what to do with them when and if I do…

Yes, I *should* be paying more attention but I'm not, which is why someone is able to get their hands around my throat before I even know he's there. Then someone's shouting, 'Tie her hands, tie her hands! Don't let her touch you!'

Kian Arnold, Lutetia's idiot son, he of the broken leg. I recognise his voice; he no doubt remembers the pain of being healed by said hands. Someone else obliges, wrapping rough hemp rope around my wrists so tight it doesn't take long for them to feel numb. Kian and his new best friends, four shifty-looking god-hounds in stained habits, frogmarch me towards the front door of the Peppergill mansion.

29

Not in the parlour of the Peppergill home this time – deprived of my knife, coat and the cell key – but the formal dining room with its long table and many chairs, dark polished wood panels on the walls hung with portraits (varied quality of artistic endeavour) of the Peppergill generations, finely wrought tapestries Thaddeus has imported, and a huge fireplace at one end with flames leaping against the chill. No sign of Deva or Matthias, but at the far end of the table sits the master of the house, sharing a very early morning drink with an especially thin god-hound. To his credit, Thaddeus does not look comfortable. The other four (by name Mael, Alderic, Wilfred, Oeric, although which is which matters not at all) stand by the doorway, not offered any refreshment even after the task of dragging me along, not even the one to whom I gave a bloody nose with my elbow before they got a good grip on me. Kian Arnold is somewhere crumpled outside – my boot caught him squarely in the nuts and I can only hope it was hard enough to either make him expire or never father offspring.

I have been rather unceremoniously thrown onto a chair

opposite the thin god-hound. My ears are ringing from being soundly boxed (that bloodied nose had a price). The one sitting comfortably, sipping from an engraved golden goblet, is clearly the leader of this little band, which means he's got a bit more brain capacity than his fellows, and sufficient ruthlessness that they'll fear and follow him. He looks me up and down.

'I'm Father Loic. I'm told you go by Mehrab. *Mistress* Mehrab.' He sneers as if the title is a joke, a stolen thing.

'"Father" you say?' I let my gaze wander slowly down his robe. 'That seems unlikely since you and your little friends are all wearing the same thing. Those coarse off-white linen robes? Nothing more than the garb of a lowly monk, and the only thing to set it apart from a novice's attire is the band of brown at the cuffs and your black rope belt.' Colour leaches from his already-snowy complexion. 'No. An actual priest would wear a brown woollen habit, his belt would be purple and hung with the tools of office: three little silver vials containing the oils for blessing, exorcism and extreme unction. None of which you have.' I flick a glance back at the others. 'Not a one of you.'

I imagine when young this Loic would have had a sort of strange architectural beauty, all cheekbones, jaw and brow, deep-set eyes. Haunted. In youth, it would have been quite fascinating, romantic-looking, and perhaps if he'd been the sort of man who gave and received love from another person in the usual sort of way – with generosity and kindness and patience – he might have developed a little healthy weight, the kind of softening contentment brings. Now in his forties, I estimate, with neither fat nor kindness to pad out his skin, he's nearly skeletal. Haunted has become starved and insatiable – like there's not enough of anything in this entire world to fill the hole in him. The eyes are sunken, bordered by bruised delicate skin, lips thin as gruel. Lady Death herself might find him a little too famine-touched for her tastes. Beneath his robe, there are hints at sharp bones, all angles; it must hurt for him to sit on that skinny arse. Does one of his minions carry a cushion, I wonder? No, I don't believe they're the sort to lay hands on a cushion unless they stole it.

And he is, even though there's an air of authority about him, as grubby and travel-worn as his four god-brothers – and that air strikes me as brittle. Seeing them confirms my earlier thoughts when Tieve described them. A pack of god-hounds, this far out? Holy hounds, this far from Lodellan, deep in the heart of this forest? They've not come from Lodellan – to get from the edge of the Great Forest to Berhta's Forge (not so far from its heart or so the very vague maps say) is six weeks' worth of travel. Then from Lodellan itself to the edge of the Great Forest? Months on top of that. So they've come from some far-flung rural parish, some arse-end abbey within reach of a pigeon with a note attached to its leg, bearing news of Rhea's crime.

I'm not from this continent, I've avoided having anything to do with the god-hounds, but I know their works and I hate them. And I recognise this type, this *Loic* – no *prince* of the church would be sent so far out. Never a bishop or cardinal or a deacon nor even a lowly priest would keep going this far just to catch one little witch, no matter that she roasted the Prince of Lodellan. No, this one is here because he's got nothing to go back to – not without Rhea in tow. I wouldn't be surprised if this merry band is on its last warning with one of the more remote monasteries, and when word reached it (as it would do), they jumped at this chance – and I cannot imagine their abbot raised any objections. Catching Rhea doesn't merely mean bringing a witch to heel: it's money and power and position, likely a pardon for something done wrong. She and any other witch he can catch will mean his own life clawed back. And he's got enough charisma and or brutality to convince the four with him – all young and stupid – to follow him.

'We've travelled a long way, our possessions have been lost, but I still maintain my righteous authority.' His voice doesn't even waver as he lies; still, Thad's expression is uncertain as he watches the god-brother. 'You're going to be judged, *Mistress* Mehrab. I'll see to it.'

'You're not fit to judge me,' I say. 'You have no evidence against me.'

'Your friend would beg to differ and with the right motivation she became very chatty. Fenna, yes? All her tales of bringing a young murderous witch here, one we've been seeking.' Relieved I note he doesn't mention 'Visiting Sisters', so she has perhaps not told everything. 'Fenna will remain alive until we find where the young one's gone, but there's no trial to be had for you.' He shakes his head with false regret. 'I've heard the stories from these good villagers. How they live in fear of you. That you've seduced them with potions and powders, drawn them in by healing imaginary ills, or binding bones that god has set asunder. Why, this man here tells how not so long ago you brought a bewitched toy to this very house trying to increase the reach of your evil. And these children who've gone missing and been returned by god's good grace? Each one has told, now that I am here to protect them and they need no longer fear you, how you lured them from their homes, into the woods, how you haunt their dreams even now, and how your curse has seared a mark into their foreheads.'

'Oh, you little shit. And *those* little shits. And *you*, Thaddeus Peppergill, how dare you? I helped that child be conceived, I brought him into the world, and you dare tell such lies?' I raise my voice when I would prefer not to, not to give these idiots any reaction at all. He has the good grace to look ashamed. 'How *dare* you!'

'Don't try to intimidate this good man, witch!' Again, Loic shakes his head. 'You're too dangerous to keep alive. You'll be dealt with and your cottage will be burnt to the ground before we move on.'

Good luck finding it, I think with glee and relief that he doesn't know Rhea is there. But I feign fear when I say, 'The girl left weeks ago, heading towards Berrick's Bend to the south. You might yet catch up with her.'

'I thank you for that betrayal. But we'll burn your home anyway – no point leaving sanctuary for another like yourself to take up residence.' He gestures to the other god-hounds, and they move in to drag me away.

* * *

They throw me into a cell, and I've never been so roughly handled in my life. I hit the stone floor with its sparse covering of straw, and I feel my shoulder shift. A cry flies from me before I can bite down on it, hide that they've hurt me. But they hear, those vile little boys, they hear and they laugh. The door closes with a slam and the key is turned in the lock with a finality I don't like, and they tramp off up the steps.

I scramble to my feet as fast as I can and, teeth gritted – I can taste blood in my mouth, a tooth might even be loose – and slam myself into the solid mortared wall, violently snapping the joint back in place. The pain is blinding, and I slide down the wall almost as soon as I've made contact, and into oblivion for a blessed while. As I drift off, I think I hear someone calling my name.

* * *

When I come to it's to a voice crying out for me to 'Wake up, oh please wake up and don't be dead'. My instinct is that I've not been out so very long at all. Opening my eyes, I spot Fenna through the bars of the neighbouring cell. She's unmoving – for they've chained her to an iron ring in the floor, and her right leg is at an odd angle. When she sees me sit up, she starts to weep.

'Hush,' I say, though I know it's sheer stupidity to tell her that. 'Don't let them hear you crying.'

'I'm sorry. I'm sorry, Mehrab, it's all my fault. They caught me outside of Aine's Tor' – just beyond the forest's outer edge – 'I wasn't quick enough and… and they hurt me—'

'Fenna, it's not your fault.' I crawl over, not ready to risk standing when my head's so foggy and I can feel the heat beginning to rise in me. 'What did you tell them?'

'I'm so ashamed, Mehrab. And I'm so sorry. I never thought I'd—'

'We never know what we might do in the worst of circumstances, Fenna.'

'They'll find Rhea.'

'No,' I say with a certainty I don't really feel, 'they won't. She's gone. Months ago. Little bitch and her fancy ways, couldn't bear her any longer.' If Fenna's questioned again, tortured again, I don't want her giving up anything of value. So, a lie might help protect Rhea a little longer. 'Did you give me up? Or her?'

'Her. At first. They just thought you'd be a woman sheltering her – I managed that lie – but when we got here, they talked to that Arnold boy who said you'd touched him without his leave? Then Peppergill and his wife, and the nursemaid you told about that toy? And the woman from the mill claimed you were responsible for her husband's death – that you'd bewitched and seduced him as well as cursing her child? All called you a witch. That you'd ensorcelled the children, lured another five from the orphanage into the forest. That you were sending nightmares into households.'

'My, how quickly they do turn. Now, scootch as close as you can and forgive me, this will hurt.' I find the jagged line inside of my mouth where my teeth cut and worry at it until blood flows again. I spit the red price on the straw and reach through the bars to push her filthy skirts up so I can see the full extent of damage to her leg. The bruising is a terrible mix of purple-black and greenish-yellow, and as I run my hand down its length I feel two places where bone presses against skin. It's a miracle she's been able to walk at all. I press both hands onto the heated flesh, hope there's no infection, that I'm in time to save her. I hope I've given enough blood for this service.

And she screams. She screams long and loud and I wonder

if the god-hounds will come rushing back, fearful that I'm murdering their source of knowledge, that I might prevent them from extracting more information from Fenna, that they might not be able to find more witches to slaughter. Fenna screams until she at last passes out and I'm able to continue my work – sweating and bleeding – in peace.

Yet no one comes – perhaps they've left the building completely unattended. Trusting that even witches can't break out of this bridewell. It must be mid-morning by now? Perhaps they're all at the inn celebrating their victory over evil. Or perhaps just the four minions while so-called *Father* Loic makes himself at home in the Peppergill mansion. I wonder how many of my former patients, those who've been so polite to me, have come to me for help, whose lives I've improved or saved, are hoisting drinks with them? *Ding-dong the witch is dead* – or soon to be so.

Will Lutetia Arnold tell her son how well he's done? Will Deva Peppergill be relieved to have me gone, the person who knew just how infertile she was? Will Thaddeus be delighted not to have me delivering his bastards and knowing exactly how many there are? Will Gida think her daughter will go back to normal, now that I am gone? Will Reynald be pleased in public to save his own hide, grieving in private? Or will he expand his business now there's no one to guide births and deaths and everything in between? Who will hunt for his fungi and herbs now?

At last, I feel everything is repaired, each fragment back in place, vital fluids separated and returned to their rightful locations. Fenna will walk again, but she'll have a limp.

Quickly I check the rest of her, whatever I can reach through the bars, and heal the cuts I can, although the terrible rents on her breasts will never be right, and the scar tissue that grows over them under my palms is slow and struggles to close. But with the leg healed, with the knife wounds closed, she *will* be able to run if she has a chance, if she's clever enough not to let them know she's changed.

I draw my hands back, curl up close to the metal bars. I should be making plans, strategizing, being alert for the return of men-children who only mean us harm, but I'm exhausted in the extreme and cannot fight off the darkness. I fall asleep, promising myself it'll only be for a short while.

* * *

When I wake it's to rough hands lifting me, god-hounds dragging me once again.

I throw a glance at Fenna's terrified face and the youngest one sees. Sneers: 'Not her. Not yet. Still more to get out of her, more rebel witches to find with her help.'

Back up the wooden stairs so fast my feet barely get purchase but I won't give them the satisfaction of seeing me trip. The sun is low in the grey sky; there's no one around except Kian Arnold, not dead, alas, but with a gratifying stiffness and smirking at me as he holds a single burning torch aloft as the dusk creeps in.

The priests herd me to the mill pond at the side of Sanne's mill, and along the little jetty that projects out over the still surface. At the end of that jetty Loic waits. There's no sign of Thaddeus Peppergill. In fact, there's no sign of anyone from Berhta's Forge except Kian Arnold, who, as the god-brothers clamp chains around my wrists and ankles, now looks less sure of himself. That often happens as one gets closer to making bad decisions a reality.

One of the god-hounds – Mael? Alderic? Wilfred? Oeric? – makes me hobble to the edge of the little pier. It's just that short walk – hobble – and by the time it's done Kian's face is stripped of its bravado. I don't care if he's afraid, if he feels sorry now – if I get out of this, I swear I'll skin him.

If I were a witch like Rhea, I'd have burned them all long before this. If I were a witch who controlled water, I'd have drowned them with a tidal wave dredged up from both pond and river. If I were an earth witch, I'd bury them in the soil, a wind witch and they'd be carried over the treetops to land on rocks. But, alas, I'm none of those things.

Loic looks positively beatific. 'You're my one-hundredth witch. You should be proud – I am.'

'Pride is a sin and I'm told it goeth before a fall,' I say, then spit at him, red-flecked saliva adding to the stains on his robe, a souvenir of my death. 'Do you think this will gain you glory? Elevation among the princes of the church?'

'Of course it will.'

'Here's a little thing I know and I don't need to be a witch to be certain of it: you're always going to be an errand boy to those men, bishops and cardinals and archbishops. It won't matter what you do, what you bring them, you'll always be beneath their notice. Why else were you sent out so far? You think fetching Fenna will get you higher office? Your kind never gets beyond parish priest in some little backwater with barely a living. A tumbledown church and tiny rectory with a miserable old woman to cook and clean for you if you're lucky. No princely purple garments for a lickspittle like you, *Brother* Loic.'

He turns red with rage and pushes me, without further ado, into the mill pond.

The water's icy cold and deep as I sink into it. The chains are heavy and drag me down. And I can't dislodge them, can't unpick them or will them to open. I can only struggle as my lungs begin to burn, bubbles popping from my mouth and rising, rising, rising as I sink lower and lower. I've avoided death for so long that this is awfully sudden, and an annoying surprise, to say the least.

When the last puff of breath is gone from me, when there's only water inside, filling my throat, lungs, any cavity it can find, only then do I feel the chains around my ankles and wrists *click* and fall away. I'm no less drowned – no less dead – but those are gone at least. I don't know how. I'm not in a position to question it. The current catches me, a deep coursing that takes me to the weir at the end of the mill pond and flushes me out and over, to join the body of the River Ayda. Body face-up, staring at the sky, something pushes its way up from my chest, into my throat, mouth, out my lips: a wispy roly-poly little thing.

My soul.

My soul riding me down the river like I'm a coracle, my mind trapped inside.

30

I feel…

I feel…

I feel but don't feel the press of water in my lungs, my stomach, my throat. I feel but don't feel the strange weight of my soul as it scampers up and down the length of my body, and finally sits on my chest instead of floating up, of flying wherever souls are meant to go. It takes a moment to examine itself – *my* self – a wispy thing, doll-like, pudgy. No, it doesn't bear too close an examination. Instead, it – *I* – turns its attention to my corpse, cadaver, meat sack, shell, husk.

Canoe.

Floating. Lifted by the water, travelling loose-limbed and uncaring down the river. Behind me, the village – twenty years of life around it – haunted by all those I've saved, called friends of one degree or another. Loved them in my own way. Or tolerated them, but isn't *that* love? Not a one of them to be seen, except Kian Arnold and his open mouth.

And the god-hounds.

All five standing on the jetty, watching the witch go;

watching their good work all done. Their mission fulfilled. They've *saved* Berhta's Forge. They've left the place unprotected from whatever's in the forest and stealing the children from this place. What I wouldn't give to get my hands on their flesh and bones, to remake them like clay, weaving pain into their core.

Soon enough, they're gone; the river's pace picks up and I'm speeding along, a little dead boat without a course, yet the waters are surprisingly gentle; I don't bump against rocks or floating logs, almost like the navigation is carefully plotted. I don't know how long this continues, and at no point does my soul try to leave – perhaps fear of drowning, perhaps fear of flying, or perhaps simple curiosity. Or it just has nowhere to go.

I think of the tales of witches who've escaped, told to me by Fenna and the fosterlings she's brought, by other Visiting Sisters who helped me; tales told because it's important to give hope to those who flee. You can run on fear alone, yet it burns through you, eats your reserves, but add hope to that and you can run forever. The belief that you can be one of those who survives.

There was the girl long ago who summoned a daemon to carry her away from an unwanted marriage to a prince of Lodellan.

A woman who made herself so small she slipped beneath the door of a locked prison cell and made her way to freedom.

The young woman who even as the flames of the pyre rose towards her feet, redirected the river to drown the town and its citizens and dowse the fire.

Three old women who turned into swans and flew away from the rabble trying to arrest them.

Another who, with a flick of the wrist and a whispered word, turned a mob into lemmings and the lot of them scampered over a cliff.

And didn't I escape? Didn't I run from what I'd done, what I'd built? Didn't I flee across deserts and plains, mountains and seas? Didn't I survive a most dangerous voyage and claw back decades of a new life? Didn't I try to do better, be better? Didn't I succeed until now? Didn't I succeed until my luck ran out?

I think about Rhea and the baby and Tieve, all alone in the cottage, not knowing what's happened to me. Not knowing what's to come. I think about Fenna in that filthy cellar, unwashed and broken, self-loathing at her betrayal, her shame a choking thing. Yet I still can't find it in me – not even dead, drowned and bobbing along like sea wrack – to blame her. Or not too much. What they put her through, those men of god, that torment and torture. I cannot guarantee I'd have kept my silence. I cannot claim that I wouldn't have sold the souls of any I'd ever held dear the moment they pulled the first fingernail from its bed or cut the first curse into the skin of my breast, made a window in my ribcage with their knives, taking the very canvas of me to add to their book coverings. How long will she last? Will they drown her too or cut her throat or burn her or let her hang from hastily erected gallows on the green, staining the grass where children play with an unjust death? With something Berhta's Forge has never seen before? A woman put to death as a witch. I was the first – will Fenna be the second? Rhea the third? No. Rhea will be taken to Lodellan, her death must be a spectacle. Prince killer, assassin, witch.

Above me, all those leaves and branches, the canopy of trees with flashes of the plum-coloured blackness oozing across the sky. I think about the other city, the one I fled, about the child I changed who was whisked away crying in the smoke and fire of that last night; about the high sorceress thrown onto a pyre with so many books from her library to make sure she burned a merry blaze; about the last of the loyal men-at-arms who marched me through the streets, many losing their lives to get me to the harbour. Their expressions as they turned away from the dinghy that rowed me out to the ship… no love for me, their duty done, the city falling to ruin… Did any of them survive? To see a scarred princess returning to make a claim?

A gentle violence, now, done to my body by the water and my soul clutches at the wet bodice to stay in place; a set of rapids that I'm tossed down, until at last, I'm spat out into the Black Lake.

Here, I think, here is where I sink and rot. Food for fish. And what of that wispy little soul, when its vessel is gone? I float away from the agitated flow, into the smooth glassy black – so cold, so cold. Bobbing and wheeling, moved in circles as if by another current altogether, spinning starfish-like, no volition.

Except something grabs my feet.

Grabs my ankles and I think I'm about to be eaten while my soul watches, too scared to do anything. Will it – I – be slurped in like some airy treat? Dessert?

Green-tinged hands, lightly scaled, long nails, grasp me and tow me down, down, a'down into the greeny-black depths and it feels like a second drowning. My soul, immortal, smoky, clinging to my chest like a terrified child as we descend.

* * *

How to describe that next journey?

Not just beneath the surface of the lake, not just the obsidian-dark water all around, the sense of its cold touch, almost oily, and not just the fading of the sky and trees as I was pulled deeper and deeper, but then gone entirely as I was dragged into drowned tunnels beneath the forest, beneath the earth, thick roots poking through, scratching at my body, at the skin and hair, the sodden fabric of my dress, but not making the way any slower for whatever was towing me along with a powerful stroke. My certainty I was going to be a meal, but the longer the journey continued, the less certain I became. What kind of creature keeps its larder so far from its hunting grounds?

The end, when it comes, is unexpected. Suddenly, we're out of the tunnels and it's up and up and up until I shoot from the water, high, high, high, then down again to slam onto a grassy bank, narrowly avoiding the branches of a sprawling juniper tree. If I were alive, that would *hurt*. If I were alive, I'd have let out a scream to rival Kian Arnold's when I fixed his broken leg. As it is, my soul squeaks loud and long.

But I'm not alive, am I? What even am I, but a soul clinging to a body turned very cold very quickly. A soul that should have gone by now, wherever it is such things go. But my soul, resolutely not going anywhere, loosens its determined grip on my corpse, and looks around, sightless, eyeless, but somehow seeing.

In the water – a decent-sized pond – not so far from this grassy bank, is what looks like a woman. Long green hair woven with waterweed, slanting pebble-dark eyes that stretch from either side of a narrow, thin-nostrilled nose and back towards her temples, skin scaled and with a luminescent green tinge. Sharp teeth in her gappy smile that widens – somehow, she realises my soul can see her. Those eyes see more than what's easily perceivable, more than the prey swimming in the lake where she lives. Not a mer, for they're generally sea-born and bred, seldom taking to fresh water unless for a very good reason – mostly revenge-related according to the old tales. Not a rusalky, either; long-haired maidens, murdered and refusing to move on, becoming something else instead – but they sing, siren-like, in a river far to the south, around the port-city of Bellsholm. So this one, perhaps, is a mari-morgan; similar, but they sometimes go on two legs, taking mortal lovers, other times by tail. While mer can only gain legs at great cost and favours purchased from the sea hags who tally such things, the mari-morgan can do it at will, and some say they can possess a body if the whim takes them. Not mine, apparently.

'Can't speak, can you?' The voice fair gurgles, tripping from her lips like a waterfall. 'Can't nod either. Never mind.'

She swims closer to where I lie, rears out of the water, straight up, then flops her top half onto the grass an arm's length away. A scaly hand with long sharp nails reaches out and winds itself into my wet greying curls; not to pull them or tear them out, but merely to rearrange them as if my appearance might be improved by the gesture. Then she gives the most phenomenal shout – it sounds like a name if all the leaves in the forest sighed at once. How she gets her ichthyoid mouth around such a noise is beyond me – but then again, I'm a dead witch with a soggy soul clinging to me, witnessing all that's going on, so my definition of "possible" might be too narrow. Around us, a grove with no trace of winter, vibrant colours, trees and shrubs and flowers and vines, many I can't even recognise, and a warm breeze that smells like jasmine and rose.

Anyone would think my expression was one of shock from the way she gentles me, pats my shoulder. 'There, there. It's all right. She comes when she's called. Well, mostly.'

She pats the rest of my hair away from my face, out of my eyes, off my forehead and cheeks; she pushes my slack bottom jaw back up, trying to mend my smile so I look less like a dullard. She frowns as the jaw flops, my mouth lolling open again. So much for that.

'What a waste they made of you. Such beauty a woman has when her autumn's upon her. Silver beginning in the temples, lines of laughter and pain to show the life she's lived, carrying a little more fat to help through hard times – and oh, that temper! Funny, isn't it, how cares fall away with so many memories you didn't need? But the lessons, oh the lessons stick – and you've no patience for any who try to make you do what you don't want to, and you can pick a liar like a rotten berry!' Another grin, wider and wider, and she speaks like a mortal creature, so I wonder if she spent time among us, learning how we are, or if she loved a human woman once. Her amusement seems genuine, delighted; her fondness true.

'What a waste,' she repeats mournfully. 'I saw you that night, by my lake, felt you jump in to get away from *it*. That shadowy thing and his horse of bone and blight. You were in there a long time and I can't say I blame you – I warmed the water, did you notice? Didn't want you catching your death – such fragile things you are. Every time you've come and used my lake for your visions, spilling your blood into the water – is it any wonder I felt your death in that mill pond? All that blood you've given me…'

She laughs again, looks sly. 'And that man of yours! That big man in the clearing by the river, on the night of the harvest moon. Him all over you and in you, god-like one might say, and you enjoying him right back.'

And if I had a pulse, any blood circulating around my body, I'd blush so fiercely at the thought of being watched that night. I think about Faolan, wonder where he was when they took me, wonder if he hid away, too scared to be associated with a witch even as his neighbours bore witness against me. The heart in me, dead and cold, seems to ache but perhaps that's just a memory, a fantasy, a phantom feeling. *Where was he?*

If I could, I'd cry for self-pity. If I could, I'd scream and swear for rage. If I could, I'd march back to Berhta's Forge and take my revenge on the god-hounds, whip them until their blood soaked the green or better yet, the fields of my holding to make them so rich and red they'd never need to lie fallow again, an inheritance for Rhea and the baby. But I can't. I'm trapped here, neither able to haunt nor go beneath nor find a better place to be.

The mari-morgan's hand on my shoulder tightens. 'Ah. Be patient, my friend. She comes.'

31

'What is it?' The voice is so deep it rattles the very earth beneath me, yet also sounds like the breath of leaves, the sough of wind around trunks and through branches. It issues from a naked woman, half my height again, hair a verdant tangle of moss and vines and red-purple berries and white and pink blossoms, even though outside – back in the world or wherever we're not – it's verging on winter. Deep-set black eyes, broad cheekbones, full lips. Up close the greenish-brown skin has the slightest sign of crackles and runnels, like bark. I look for traces of horns on her forehead – because she looks exactly like the foliate head over my cottage door, the green woman, but I can't see anything. I do note, however, that her feet end in things that are almost hooves, the toes splitting and beginning to curl, almost prehensile. 'What have you brought me, Fishwife?'

'Don't call me that, you old log.' Hissing asperity. 'You know I hate that.'

'No sense of humour, that's your problem.' A laugh like a storm. 'What is this dead thing?'

'Not dead, or not quite. See? The shimmering golden murk on the chest? A little like a tree rat or a squirrel, surely you're familiar with those? Her soul. Not gone yet.'

'It will. It's just confused now the mortal meat is done. Ignore it long enough and it'll move on.'

'Why are you being wilfully obdurate?'

'Why are *you*?'

I listen, I watch; I've no other choice.

The mari-morgan gestures to me again. 'She needs to be brought back. The water refused her. She's important.'

'And how do you know?'

'She's the one who comes to my lake—'

'Yours?'

'—*my* lake. You may rule the earth and things that grow, but the waters here are *mine*. Now stop dickering and listen. She's the one who uses *my* lake to see other places, she buys that with her blood. As you know, I usually take tears as my payment, but blood has both salt and water, so close enough. Yet she's never asked me for anything. So many gifts over these years. I owe her something.'

'But I don't.'

'Oh, but you do.'

'Mortal meat,' mutters the woman again.

'*Not* just mortal meat. She is *witch*. And that thing that's been tearing through *your* forest the last half a century, give or take? That thing of shadow and spite, his wish-hounds and that mount barely worthy of the name "horse"?' The mari-morgan points at me – my corpse, my shimmering soul – and grins, all teeth. 'She's resisted its call – and it *is* calling for her, I've heard it. *She* has the power to do something about it. But only if you put her back together.'

The green woman snorts, dismissive, while the mari-morgan continues airily: '*I* can avoid the huntsman and its hounds, thanks to their terror of the water. But you… it's been hunting your kind for a long while now… So very few of you left with its predations across north and east… You've hidden so long in this bower that memory of you is nearly gone from the Great Forest.'

The green woman, grumbling, shaking her head, looks at me again, more intently, squinting so hard that the wrinkles around her eyes make a crackling sound. She stares for an inordinately long time, and gods, I wish she'd make up her mind to interfere or not. To bring me back or to say definitively that I need to wait for my soul to learn how to fly.

'You don't think, do you,' the mari-morgan wheedles, 'that she's not in this odd state, this ridiculous *betweenery*, for a reason? How often have you seen one like this? Hmmm? How often? Ever?'

More grumbling.

'I've had her blood, I know her history. Her early life, plucked from poverty, her power sensed by another, elevated in the court of a far-flung land – precisely the sort I once walked – doing good and ill.' The mari-morgan holds up a finger. 'But even when she did ill? She always thought it in the pursuit of good.'

'There's none more dangerous…'

'I know!' The tone's almost gleeful. 'The things she's done! Changed faces on would-be assassins to let them slip by. Mended bones so poor folk could walk and work and not lose their livelihood – did that without payment or prompting. Changed the faces on some so their own people wouldn't recognize them, would cut them down. Her master's enemies. And the last thing she did, across the sea. The seed she sowed. The mess left behind. Ones such as her don't die like this. They make amends. They must or the whole world is thrown out of balance.'

'She's taken my trees, turned them to her own purpose.' A shiver would run down my spine if it could, if I had any vital reaction left, at that ominous line.

'See? You do know who she is then!' A gleeful *I-told-you-so* from the mari-morgan. 'And I know, I know she is problematic. She loves what she fears and fears what she loves! But men and things shaped like men have done worse in your woods and you've left them be. The things she's done wrong, the worst things… that was long ago. She needs a chance to do better. Be better – and her blood has shown me she's been trying. If you don't give her that chance, you take a light out of the world. And she *is* a light, though sometimes a dark one, but a light nonetheless.' The mari-morgan lowers her voice, but I can still hear when she says, 'And you – we – need a light.'

There are long moments filled with more *umming* and *ahhing*, then the green woman gives an exasperated sigh. 'Whatever she does wrong, *Fishwife*, I'll never let you forget.'

The mari-morgan, having gotten her way, lets that one slide, and the green woman kneels beside me. She reaches one large hand – nails black and obsidian-sheened – out and grabs my soul, which squeaks when it realises it's too late to run, and that enormous hand closes around its ephemeral shimmer as if it's as solid as the dead body it sits on. The other hand pries at my mouth – stiff with rigour, which doesn't seem to bother her – and when the lips are parted, she stuffs the soul inside me, and I can feel but not feel it wiggling down my throat and back to wherever it spends its days. The green woman lays both hands on my chest and that's when the pain begins. I would scream, if I could, if I lived, and I imagine I would sound like those I've healed and hurt over the years.

I'm dead, aren't I? Yet I feel every agony and it takes so long that I pass out, with the vague hope that I'm properly dead.

* * *

I dream of a place I left a long time ago. I dream of a night I've tried to block from my thoughts for two decades. I dream of a deed that will haunt me forever.

Here is the palace that's been my home for most of my life, where I fell into luxury like I'd never known – never would have known but that the high sorceress saw me and knew what I was, what I might become, and took me away from the slums and hardship of my childhood. All because I'd chased the moon that night.

And I do not believe I ever said 'Take me back home' or 'Let me go, return me to my mother.' Not even that first night, nor the second nor the third, nor any after that. I said 'Thank you' many times because I could never imagine the life I'd have had in the lower city – or rather, I could imagine it far too well. And I never saw my mother and sister again – or perhaps I lie, perhaps I did notice them once, as I was carried through the streets in a sedan chair (because what simpler way to show folk that you're better than them than by making them carry you?). Wherever I went in that city, I would give out alms because I never forgot what it had been like to be poor and hungry, how a single brass coin could be the difference between a meal or a hollow gnawing pit in your stomach. Perhaps that was why, when the time finally came for revolution, no one looked too hard for me even as they threw the bodies of the royal family and the high sorceress on that pyre fuelled by books.

When, in the early days of my tenure in the palace, the high sorceress said, 'You belong here, little one,' I never contradicted her. I called her *Mother* when she bid me to, I obeyed her wishes even when I questioned them, when they seemed wrong. I held her head when her magics made her ill, when the darkness in them threatened to eat her from the inside out. And I laid hands on her each and every time she seemed to be too close to death, and I mended whatever was ailing within her body though her screams echoed in my ears.

Then *that* night…

I all grown, but still her obedient child…

When she came to me, dragging another child behind her. A little girl, perhaps eight or ten, terrified, a daughter of some kitchen-maid or other, tunic torn, dried vomit in her hair, the red imprint of a hand on her cheek where she'd been slapped to subdue her. Smelling truly awful.

Poor girl, poor mite.

When the High Sorceress Almira came to me and the city was burning, when the gates had been broken down, when those we'd served were already dead or dying – all but one, all but one…

She said, 'Change her face. Make her look like the other.'

And I did.

Oh, I hesitated, just long enough to make the old woman scream. Long enough for her to slap me so that the child and I bore matching hand marks on our faces. Long enough that I could hear doors being battered elsewhere in the palace, long enough to know I was wasting time. But I still did as bid because the habit of obedience was too ingrained.

Because she said it was what was needed. That it would ensure the future. That this night of loss and blood and rebellion would not be in vain, that there would be a return. So I did it. I did it and listened to the screams, which are the worst I'd ever heard before and since. I do not believe they'll ever be surpassed. I watched the terror in that girl's eyes, the pain, her incomprehension that it was bad enough she'd been born into poverty and deprivation in a city where rulers grow more and more heartless and greedy, but then to be hurt like this? To have your own face taken from you?

I wept the entire time, but still I did it, and my tears earned me nothing except the hatred of a child. And when I was done, the High Sorceress Almira handed the weeping girl over to the heavily disguised Chamberlain – the last noble still breathing – and he hurried the child away and into the night. Not long after, the throne room's doors below were broken down; my surrogate mother cried, *Flee!*

And I did, around the viewing balcony that looked down on the throne room, while she remained in place, too old to run, too proud to do so, and awaited her fate. And when I paused, oh-so-briefly, when I turned back it was to see her body in all its finery thrown from the balcony, down onto the room below, her head connecting with the great throne itself of marble and silver and gold and gems – that noise! the echo! – and then I ran even faster, found the entrance to the secret passages that honeycombed the palace, into the ways beneath the rock upon which the city was built. Found my escort waiting, followed them to the harbour…

Sailed and ran and trekked far away. Found another ship, to another continent entirely. Into the hands of one such as Fenna to help me onwards, then another and another Visiting Sister, until Fenna her very self took me to another life, handing me over to Yrse. But always with the old burdens carved upon me, the screams of a child the heaviest among them.

Running and fearful of being hunted, found, though no one could have known where I'd gone. To the realisation that I'd outrun everything but myself. Doing my best to forget, to suppress, to be and do better. Finding Faolan, loving him, thinking I'd been forgiven perhaps – or that maybe my sins hadn't been noticed – and then losing him. Making a life here, hidden. Knowing my secrets were my own.

And now, a mari-morgan who apparently knows everything.

32

The sense of oneness, of being enclosed in meat again, is very distinct.

The ground beneath me is soft, my head rests on a pillowy tuffet and I'm covered by a blanket of moss, warm and slightly damp, earthy-smelling. Every part of me aches; apparently, resurrection is less perfect than I'd prefer. I'm both grateful and smug – when I fix someone (after the initial agony, of course) they're *properly fixed*. However, I'm not about to say that to the green woman sitting cross-legged in front of a small crackling fire. Staring at me.

'She said you'd be cold,' that voice, that rumble.

Sitting up slowly, I nod. 'Thank you. Where is she?'

'Gone. Short attention span. She says you're worth saving.'

'I heard. I heard it all.' I cross my legs, feel the grinding in my hips, stretch before settling into place.

'Good.'

'Do you mind if I ask…'

She raises a brow that's a feathery leaf.

'I thought, was led to believe, that you – your kind – didn't exist. You are a green woman, yes?'

'Do I look *illusory*? Shall I give you a splinter to convince you I'm real?'

'No, thank you. Quite enough pain has already been had. I believe you.' I hold my hands up in surrender. 'I just… I've seen the carved heads on houses but never seen *you* or anything like you. Not a living thing that I can say *Aha! There's the source.* Well, except the hind-girls, although I don't think they're the source of the foliate heads. I think they're an offshoot, perhaps, of you?'

She smiles. 'Such wonderful little things, aren't they? My nieces, I suppose.'

'I've seen them dance through the woods. There are many tales of them.' I shake my head. 'But they're women and girls. Mortals, or started out so.'

She shrugs. 'Nieces in spirit or blood, all the same. They wander from lives they've grown tired of, the spirit of the forest inhabits them. The desire to be lost. A retreat to hooves and horns, leaves and branches, either's a means of escape.' A smile. 'I do like the horns.'

'Ha. So, what are *you*?'

'A green woman.' She sounds impatient, a little offended. 'The spirit of this forest, I – we – watch over all the seasons, the growth, the death, the slumbering trees and plants, the soil, those who live in this place whether they're animal, vegetable or mortal.'

'There were more of you – why have you become legend?' I ask. 'Because, even hidden away, surely the witches would know of you. But Yrse, who was here before me, never mentioned you. She was a little hen-wife, no great magics but a green witch nonetheless. She'd have *known* of you. Where have you been?'

The big woman narrows her eyes, says nothing. So I go on: 'The mari-morgan said you had a problem. That's why she brought me to you, and that's why you brought me back – because you think I can fix it.' Still nothing. 'I'm grateful for the grace you've extended, but I will need answers if I'm going to help.' Then I amend: 'If I'm going to be *able* to help,' because perhaps I'm a little bossy for someone so recently returned from the dead and she might consider putting me back the other way.

It takes a while for her to speak, as if she's picking through what to share. 'I'm *a* green woman. I'm the one who belongs to this part of the Great Forest. Others are scattered through the woods, and each forest has their own green women. Once, there were many more here, but something happened half a century ago, and then some *thing* began hunting us.' She throws another twig on the fire. 'For some while, too long, we did not know. We thought the sisters who disappeared had gone to sleep, in earth or tree, beneath rock or water. That they would reappear when the time came, as is our wont. However, we began to find bodies and parts of bodies. Torn apart by wild animals when nothing in the forest would attack us like that. Neither wolves nor bears would do such a thing, those creatures bow as we pass.'

She clears her throat as if this story is hard to tell. 'And we began to hear, at last, a tale the humans far to the north of the woods were telling by their firesides, for you mortals collect such things, write them down, carry them in your minds, and speak them whenever you can, passing them on and forth.'

She sighs and when she speaks again, her voice has changed, sounds more human, like a storyteller, with cadences learned at foot and knee from grandmothers and old nurses, in the same notes for rumour and gossip, the fastest and best way for something to travel.

'There's a tale of the god of the hunt – a horned thing – whose greatest joy was the pursuit of stag and boar and sometimes man across moor and dale, through forest dark and valley deep. There's the whisper that, once, heedless, he rode off a great cliff and when he hit the rocky ground, a part of him broke off. There's the story that, injured but not quite dead, he rose and returned to the heart of the woodland to recover, hibernating for a very long time – but he was always a broken thing after that. And the piece left behind? It found its own way to dark places, hollows and barrows, fed on whatever it could find, small blood and large, calling living things to it so it was thus furnished with meals. Whatever it looked like when first it was birthed – shattered and sheared from the horned god's body – it took on, at last, the appearance of a man.'

And I think about the huntsman, the creature of shadow and will and spite on his steed of bone and ligaments and scraps of hide. I wonder how long he's been a half-thing, a broken thing. I wonder why he's appeared only now in my forest (the green woman's forest), and why Berhta's Forge has been free of his attention – apart from the children he's taken. Yrse never mentioned him in those nights when she regaled me with tales; those first nights I was here, when I'd not yet met Faolan, when I sat in the cottage and half-listened while I fought against the memories of who I'd been. But the mari-morgan said he'd been north and east of the forest, hunting, clearing out green women. And a long time to heal before that, to pull himself into a shape that he could hold some of the time with will and malignancy and threads of night.

'I've seen it. Him,' I say. 'By the Black Lake. The shadow half, the master of the hunt, whatever remains of the broken god. You think that's what's been stalking the green women of the Great Forest for all these years?'

'What did you think it wanted of you? When you saw *him*?'

I pause. 'To be honest, I don't know. I don't think I was doing much thinking that night. Nothing good, I suspect. Perhaps I'd have been torn by the wish-hounds or thrown over his saddle and taken to the barrow where he sleeps.'

'You know where he sleeps?' She raises a feathery brow.

'I found it.'

'It's called Night's Barrow. The burial place of savage queens and kings long dead.' She nods slowly. 'I wonder if he knows *what* you can do… what the Fishwife said you can do…'

The breath leaves me as if I've been thumped on the back. *And how might it know that?* 'Maybe. Maybe. But I couldn't do *that*. I can't heal anything that doesn't have bones, no solid body. The shadow half is… shadow. And I cannot resurrect the dead.' I rub my hands up and down my arms, trying to generate a bit more heat, but suspect the cold is internal.

'I've given much thought to this, and I suspect that what it is, really, is the part that adores the hunt. The part that thirsts for blood and flesh, desires only the kill. If it somehow knows what you can do, might it not want to be whole again?'

‘Believe me, I know my limitations and there’s nothing for me to work with.’

‘It wouldn’t know that. It would only know – or suspect – what you can do to other things, people.’ She looks hard at me. ‘Perhaps you might be able to take advantage of that desire? To get close enough to it to do something?’

Destroy it.

‘How do you kill a shadow? I’d be lucky to get past the wish-hounds.’ A thought occurs. ‘Oh. The wish-hounds – they’d have obeyed his orders. If he wanted the green women torn asunder, the wish-hounds aren’t under your purview. Not natural things, are they?’

She shakes her head. ‘Not at all. But, if it – *he* – wants something from you, I’m sure he’d call them off.’

‘That’s a very big *if* to hang my newly resurrected arse on.’

She raises a hand in acknowledgement. ‘But what if? What if under the guise of healing, you destroy what’s there?’

‘I’ve never tried that.’ Of all the things I’ve done, I’ve never done *that*. ‘You’ve picked over my life with the mari-morgan, you know that I’ve healed people, changed them, but I’ve never pulled them asunder.’ That idea? The very thought of deconstructing a person, bone by bone, muscle by muscle, artery by artery? Like disarticulating a doll from the inside out? *That* thought is simply too awful. ‘I… I wouldn’t know how.’

The green woman shrugs again. ‘All things might be sundered, you just need to find where the joints are.’

I wonder if she was so nonchalant about pulling things apart before her sisters were hunted down. Does it matter, though? What she was like before she was wronged? In danger? She resurrected me, whether or not she would be able to recruit me. And she's not the thing posing a threat, not the thing stealing children from Berhta's Forge and leaving changelings in their place; not the thing using orphans as fodder to try and break the ward-line of my holding.

'It's been stalking around your home, Mehrab.' She leans against the tree trunk, stretches out her long legs. 'How long before it finds a way in? Somehow. Do you think it will simply give up, go away? It's been killing my kind, stalking and hunting us for decades across the entirety of this enormous forest, wiping us out with such efficiency that we're barely even a myth now. How long before it finds its way into this bower? How long before it – *he* – takes your little cottage apart and the girl and her strange and wonderful child as well?'

'How do you know about Rhea?' I've not given blood to the Black Lake since before Rhea came.

'Resurrection allows for some… access. Forgive me my trespasses.' The corner of her mouth lifts.

I glare at her. 'I don't know how to do *anything* to him.' I cover my face with my hands, am shocked by how cold they are. 'Am I really alive? Properly? Because this chill—'

'It will take time to come back properly to yourself. For the blood to warm itself once more. Be patient.'

I sigh. 'There are books in the cottage, perhaps there's something in there. I… must think on it.'

'You're inventive,' she says. 'Why, look at what you did to all those oak saplings. You adapted your powers to that end. I'm sure you'll be able to figure something out.' And there's a threat of *if you know what's good for you* underneath all that.

'More than one life is resting on what you do next. Because imagine what happens when it runs out of strange things to hunt and looks at the mortals.'

All the old tales say the god of the hunt is happy to pursue folk, men, women and children unfortunate enough to be caught up in the wild reel of the chase through their parents' sins. But there have been no rumours, at least that I've heard, of other villages in this forest being attacked, no stories of deserted little hamlets mysteriously cleared. And Berhta's Forge… there's been no sign of him actually *being* there. The missing children have wandered, it seems. And Anselm, trampled to death. Poor Anselm – why him?

'I must go back.'

'Where precisely do you want to be?' asks the green woman.

Briefly it's on the tip of my tongue to simply say *Anywhere but here* except who knows where that might get me. Gods, especially very old ones, can be literal and capricious; who knows where I might end up? And I've no doubt the green woman *is* a god and I have obligations.

'Berhta's Forge,' I say. 'Thank you for everything you've done.'

'Remember your promises,' says the green woman, as if I might forget the moment I'm free. I could tell her I've never forgotten a thing in my life, least of all my promises, even when they've been likely to lead to worse trouble.

'I'll remember.' I nod and she returns the gesture.

'Are you ready?'

'I'm ready.'

And the world falls out from under me.

33

Somehow, I think it will be the blink of an eye, a simple thing to be in this beautiful bower one moment, returned to the green of Berhta's Forge the next. No. The ground opens beneath my feet, and I go down as surely as falling off a cliff. At some point the descent stops and I'm jerked sideways, shifting horizontally, quickly, through dirt and darkness, watching roots and rocks, earthworms and buried bones, pockets of water and fire as I go, terribly fast, terrifyingly strange. When I'm travelling vertically again – I think I'm going up, gods, I hope it's up – I hurtle, hurtle, hurtle until I finally pop out of the earth as if being born.

Dirt on my skin, some in my mouth, sticks in my hair, brilliant red beetles on my skirts like decorations, but at least I'd dried out in the bower so it's not all mud. I jump, spitting and shaking myself so the majority of detritus and bugs falls away. Only then does it occur to me to look around. I'm in the bridewell, down in its cellar and thankfully not in one of the cells. Clever green woman.

A single lantern throws soft light over the empty cells and

the one with an occupant. Cool down here but still warmer than outside. Warmer than the river.

It doesn't smell any better than when I was last here, and the ragged bundle in a corner doesn't appear to be moving. Heart in mouth, I whisper, 'Fenna?'

Nothing. I say a little more loudly, clinging to the bars: 'Fenna?'

The jerking of someone startled awake, pulled from the refuge of sleep.

'Who is it?' She's at least still got the wit to keep her voice low.

'It's Mehrab.'

'Mehrab's dead. The boy said they drowned her,' she mutters. 'Are you her ghost, come to haunt me?'

'I'd like to think I'd have better things to do, were I a ghost. Now, move your arse if you want to get out of here.'

Slowly, she rolls up to sitting, peering at me through the gloom.

'Can you walk?' Oh. The key.

She climbs to her feet, slowly and stiffly; the hours – days? – I've been away have given her time to heal properly and she limps to the bars, grasps my hand tightly. 'See? Very real, very solid.'

'How?' she asks, eyes very round.

'More lives than a cat, me.' I don't quite feel like explaining at this very moment that I did not in fact survive. I'd prefer to simply get us both out of here. 'Do you know if anyone's here? Upstairs? I'm assuming that's where the key is likely to be…'

'I think just the lad?'

'Which one?' I'm trying to be patient.

'Kian? He brought me that.' She nods towards the bowl of half-finished gruel and what smells like beer on the floor of the cell. There's a bruise on her left cheek, dried blood around her nostrils.

'Did they question you again?'

She nods. 'Their hearts really weren't in it, though. They'd drowned you, seemed like they'd had their fill of violence for the night.'

'They didn't chain you again?'

'That was the lad. Made me promise not to tell – as if! He was crying a lot.'

Whatever's made Kian Arnold have a change of heart won't be enough to stop me throttling him. I'm half tempted to experiment with *deconstructing* him. Perhaps his balls still hurt. 'Just him upstairs, then?'

'I think so. The others are likely at the inn, celebrating their great victory.' She grins. 'May they choke.'

'Agreed. But first things first. Wait here.'

'Where else am I going to go?' She raises her brows.

'Good point.'

I creep slowly up the stairs towards the door at the top, hoping for all I'm worth that it's not locked. Thinking hard, I try to recall the layout of the little entry room where whoever's on duty sits and waits until relieved by the next sawyer-come-jailer. A desk. A chair. A cupboard for storage, a row of hooks for hanging coats and cloaks and hats – and a smaller one for keys.

I try the doorhandle – unlocked! Now to pray that the hinges don't creak.

My luck holds, and I'm able to peek into the room. There's Kian Arnold, asleep in the chair, boots on the desk, head thrown back, snoring lightly. And there's *my* cloak hung on those hooks, and my knife and tinderbox and the spare key on the shelf beside it, and on the smaller rack? Smaller keys, for the cells.

I wrestle with my conscience, think seriously about putting my knife to the lad's throat and drawing it across – then I think about his mother and how she will feel. Lutetia is kind and I'd not willingly hurt her. So I fasten my cloak, put my reclaimed possessions into my pockets and I'm reaching for the cell keys when I hear a whimper behind me. I turn slowly.

Kian Arnold's white as a sheet, bottom lip trembling, swollen, red-rimmed eyes filling with tears. His voice quivers. 'Are you here to kill me, ghost?'

This time I'm tempted to play the spectre, but I resist. 'Not a ghost. I'm here to save my friend.'

'You died. I watched. I saw. I was the only villager to do so, and I've had to keep telling them, all night and all day. Had to tell my mother and she asked how could I? How could I stand by?'

'Surely they all knew. They told the god-hounds I was a witch, the crimes I'd committed.'

He shakes his head. 'They… everyone answered questions, but we didn't accuse you of anything, Mistress Mehrab. You must believe that. No one wanted you murdered. I didn't want you murdered, just wanted you… frightened. That's all. We didn't… didn't know how the god-brothers would…'

'That's what god-brothers do, Kian.' My desire to kill him has cooled. 'Where are they?'

'At the Fox & Crow, drinking. They've all taken up residence at the Peppergill house, and Cylla said they're not welcome, but showing no sign of moving on.'

'And what are you going to tell them, when they return?'

'Only that I saw a ghost. I swear.'

'Not a—' I start forward to touch him, and he shrieks. 'Or perhaps I am. Tell them I'm a phantom and I'll be seeing them very soon.'

* * *

Back down in the cellar, I unlock Fenna's cell, then relock it as soon as she's out; that'll give them pause as long as Kian keeps his mouth shut. May it make them soil their holy robes. I'm not done with them. Fenna grabs my hand again and whispers urgently, 'Don't let me be caught again. Kill me before that happens.'

'If there's no other choice, certainly, but don't give up so easily. It shows a lack of faith in me when I'm already back from the dead.'

Rather than take Fenna out the front door – too brazen even for me – we use the ladder to exit, and sneak into the woods. She's weak from lack of decent food and ill-treatment, but she can move under her own steam; I, on the other hand, am having one of those rare surges of energy when I think I can do anything. Or perhaps that's simply the resurrection. Fenna's canny enough not to try and have a conversation, just follows me as I pick my way towards the smithy and Faolan's horses. With any luck, they're all still saddled and ready to go, but that might be wishful thinking. Surely he's found them today, put them back in their stalls. The horses will give us a better chance of getting home unscathed, or at least more quickly than on foot. I'm delusional, I suspect, if I think it'll be easy to outpace a horse made of bone and ill-will and wish-hounds that travel on the night air, but a woman must believe in miracles if she's to survive this world. And, at the moment, escaping the god-hounds is more imperative than avoiding the huntsman.

We're almost across the open ground between the tree line and the smithy, so very close but not close enough, when the moon comes out from behind the clouds and the doors of the inn across the marketplace open and all five god-hounds come staggering out, stumbling down the steps. For a moment, I think my cloak might save us – Fenna's has been lost somewhere along her journey as a captive – and perhaps for a second, two, three, it might. But Fenna sees the god-brothers and all her fear bubbles up, comes out as a half-scream that she tries too late to swallow down.

And we've got their attention.

They don't start running towards us, however, not immediately because, I can only assume, I'm a ghost and terrifying. Part of me is delighted to have the chance to stick a knife in at least one if not all of them, and I hear my blood beginning to thud, thud, thud in my ears.

Then I realise it's not my blood, but the sound of hoofbeats, accompanied by an unearthly baying. I push Fenna towards the smithy, get her in the stables, and pause only long enough to see the shadow half on his skeletal steed, and the wish-hounds bounding towards the now-shrieking god-brothers.

In the stables, Rosie remains, whickering softly to greet me, and the two geldings, still saddled. I don't question it, just urge

Fenna onto Rosie, then grab the reins of all three mounts and lead them back out into the night, into the trees, praying the huntsman is too busy toying with the god-brothers to notice us. The screams seem to support my hopes.

Once we're well hidden, I mount up and kick the gelding into a gallop. Rosie follows as does the other horse and we plunge away into the darkness.

* * *

The moon appears at random intervals, peeking from behind clouds when we need her most – perhaps to make up for her recent betrayal. The forest itself moves to allow our passage and I think the green woman must be looking out for me in her own way. I hope it won't cost her, that the shadow half won't sense her power, won't be able to track her to the bower as a result. That makes my task all the more urgent.

I don't know how long the huntsman and his pets will take with the god-hounds, whether they'll die quickly or slowly. I can't help but hope slowly, especially *Father* Loic. He'll never get his hands on Rhea, never drag her back to Lodellan to be presented to its archbishop and an ecclesiastical court. For that I'm grateful.

Eventually I slow the geldings to a walk and Fenna moves Rosie up beside me while we're on a broader path. All the horses are lathered with sweat and I feel we've used all our luck in not having one of them stumble into a rabbit or fox hole. Another miracle. A time of miracles, this day and the last, and such things can cease at any moment.

Fenna asks: 'Did you see that thing? All of those things? Am I mad?'

'Yes. And no, not mad.'

'They told me they'd drowned you.' She clears her throat. 'Did they?'

'Yes. And I'll be delighted to tell you more about it all when we're safely home, Fenna. My advice is to keep an ear out for pursuit.'

'You need to know what I heard, after they… drowned you. The Peppergill man was shouting at them – a lot of folk were shouting about what had been done. None of them were happy. They didn't, as far as I can tell, let anyone know what they planned. Only that idiot boy and he's all regret now.' She shakes her head. 'That little shit Loic told Master Peppergill that witches are patient, they play a long game. Like all cancerous growths they lie in wait, hibernate for a long time before doing ill to their host. That you'd show your true colours eventually and he was doing the village a kindness by destroying you sooner rather than later. But, Mehrab, you need to know that you have friends in that village.'

I grunt.

The shadow half terrifies me, but this evening's work has taken care of one problem at least. The god-hounds will not report back to Lodellan, and I doubt anyone will be looking for them. Nobodies, embarrassments to the church, sent on the road to get them out of the way. They'll not be missed by their superiors or the world in general.

'What happens next?' asks Fenna.

'Back to the cottage, rest a few days before we travel now that the god-brothers are no longer likely to try and burn us. Then southwest, I think, towards one of the bigger harbours, take ship somewhere. Away from here. Somewhere Rhea's baby can grow safely.' But what if that child, so linked to this land, this forest, can't thrive elsewhere? Or do we stay? Is it safe? What are the odds of other god-hounds following? Am I being overly cautious, uprooting us all? For the moment, I have enough problems to contend with.

'Rhea's baby?'

'Oh. Oh, you couldn't have known. Yes, a little girl. Something else to discuss once we've eaten, bathed, made plans.' How will I tell them about the green woman? The mari-morgan? Will I tell them at all? Later. Later. A decision for later. I'm starving and so very tired. Not so long ago dead. And in those days of rest, I must work out what to do about the huntsman and his wish-hounds, about the two children who lie in a deathly slumber in a barrow in the depths of the forest.

'Tomorrow, Fenna, all the answers tomorrow. I need to rest, as do you. We'll be safe within the bounds of the holding for a few days at least,' I say as we round the bend where the cottage lies. A few days' rest. *I hope.*

'But where is your holding? Your cottage? I thought…'

'Shrouded. Tomorrow, Fenna, tomorrow, I'm done with questions.'

And behind us, I hear the thud of hoofbeats again. It makes my heart hammer, but there are the two elms and I urge the geldings at the space between them, tug at Rosie's rein so she keeps up. The sudden baying of the wish-hounds is horribly loud – then we're through the veil, over the ward-line and the next sound to be heard is whimpers from the wish-hounds as they try to pull up in time before the enchanted boundary, and the scream of frustration coming from their master.

I wheel the horses about, and smile at the sight of the cringing hounds and the rearing horse and its raging rider. Safe for now. Safe for now. The huntsman takes off into the trees, the dogs trailing behind. I turn back and dismount, help Fenna down.

In front of us: the cottage, lights ablaze, the door thrown open and Rhea and Tieve rushing out, shouting my name.

34

My relief at seeing them is short-lived.

Their shouting takes on an edge of hysteria and fear that makes me look back over my shoulder, certain the shadow half has circled back, found a way through the veil. But no. There's nothing out there beyond the ward-line, nothing but darkness. There are, however, two weeping girls rushing towards us, stumbling over their words and sobs and steps. It irks me that they're so unhinged. I prop an elbow under Fenna's shoulder though she grumbles she's perfectly fine. Except she's not, she's worn out and I can tell.

'What is it?' I ask, trying to keep the impatience out of my tone.

'The baby,' Rhea yells. 'The baby is gone.'

Oh. The words don't make sense. My mind can't take it in; it's had quite enough these past few days, thank you very much. No more, no more. Then the loss hits me and I feel as if my chest makes a hollow sound when Rhea leans against me, shuddering. I thought the little one would stay, was not so weak as my poor babies. I was so sure she would live, that this one would survive.

Perhaps if I'd been here, perhaps if I'd not died myself, I might have kept her alive. Guilt adds its weight to my heart. I wrap my free arm around her. 'Oh. Oh, Rhea. I'm so sorry.'

Then, to my utter confusion, she says: 'We have to go after him.'

'What?' I gently push her away so I can see her face. Angry. Enraged. Not grieving, or not so much as the fury.

'That boy! That shitty boy took my daughter!' And as she shouts, flames snap in her palms.

'What boy?'

'The one she let in!' A howl and a finger pointed at Tieve, whose wailing reaches a pitch to hurt the ears.

'Tieve. Who was it?'

'Orin! It was just Orin Alderson. He's my friend.' She sniffles. 'I thought he was my friend.'

Gods help me. Faolan's boy. A deep breath to calm myself; a wave of relief: kidnapping is an easier problem to solve than death. 'Right, you lot. Inside, all of you. Stop yelling.'

Rhea looks fit to defy me, to charge off into the night. I grasp her shoulder tightly enough to let her know I mean business. 'Inside. It's too dangerous to go now. We need to plan. No point everyone rushing off to die when I'm expending so much energy to keep you all alive. Tieve, stop howling. You're not in trouble.' Not yet. 'Now help me get the horses settled first. Many hands make light work.'

* * *

In the warmth of the cottage I set about restoring order or some semblance of it. I send Fenna to the bathroom for a good and fulsome wash. I send Tieve up to my room to pull an old warm navy serge dress from my clothing chest; it's from my younger days but will fit the half-starved older woman better now. I make Rhea set the table for a meal, send her down to the cellar to retrieve cheeses and salted meats, preserved fruits. There's a rabbit stew on the hob that she must have made earlier, and a loaf of bread, a day old. I saw it into slices, and when Tieve returns I instruct her to sit by the open fire and make toast. I deliver the dress and a fresh towel to the bathroom.

Rhea finishes her tasks and comes to stand in front of me as I relax, briefly blissful, on the sofa. I need a bath too, although less desperately than Fenna, having spent entirely too much time in water, and then in dirt. Mostly, I can smell horse and my own sweat. I pat the seat beside me. 'Sit, Rhea.'

She does, a rebellious gleam in her eyes. 'Mehrab—'

'I will find her. I will bring her home. But I need you to be calm and tell me exactly what has happened. The huntsman is lurking – you heard him?' She nods. 'None of us can go out there until daylight.' As she begins to protest, I hush her, 'It just attacked Berhta's Forge – openly, which means it's grown bolder.'

'But—'

'It doesn't want her, Rhea. It doesn't want her. She's just a lure.'

'How do you know?'

'Because it wants me.'

She stares at me as if trying to work out if I'm to blame for all of this. 'Why? Why does it want you?'

'Maybe because of what I can do. I'm not sure.' I reach out and take her hand; she doesn't resist. 'I promise I *will* get her back, I promise faithfully. But we need a plan. I'd also like to get out of this alive.' *This time.*

And I can see her maternal instincts warring with the good sense of what I'm saying. 'I want to go with you. I can help. I'll burn that thing alive.'

'Nice thought. But I don't know if it can be burned – so much of it's smoke and spirit. You might burn away the last of its sinews and flesh, sear its bones, but the other parts can't be touched by fire. And,' I hold up a finger to forestall argument, 'can you honestly say you can be rational about this? Not rush in the moment you hear your child's cry?'

Rhea looks angry but defeated, hugging her chest; without the child to breastfeed, she's going to be in discomfort very soon. She knows I'm right, that without the child she was already impetuous; with her she's more likely to be reckless. 'Your daughter has a better chance of surviving if I go alone. If you run off into the night? The huntsman's got three hostages against me – and I have more than one soul to protect.'

She looks around slowly, at Tieve and at Fenna who are waiting, watching, then back at me. She nods but her voice shakes as she says, 'You promise?'

'Faithfully.' I touch my forehead to hers. 'But I need you to be kind to Tieve. Think of every stupid thing you did as a child – and adult – and be kind to her. Don't let the guilt and grief she already carries grow any bigger. It's not fair to who she might become. Understand?'

'Yes, Mehrab.'

* * *

After a welcome meal, after Fenna's spoken of her capture and captors – confirming for me that they were indeed outcasts from their order, sent forth from their monastery for a variety of sins with instructions that the only way they'd be welcomed back would be to find Rhea and return her to Lodellan. They knew, Fenna said, that it was a fool's errand, the likelihood of them finding such a needle in such a haystack spectacularly unlikely – but what good luck for them (and bad for her) that there'd been reports of a bright-haired girl and an older woman with a distinctive stripe of white hair travelling months ago by the village of Teind's Tor, and that they'd seen her in a tavern in Belvidere's Lot, taken her after a struggle. How she'd told them where she'd left Rhea, how by chance they'd run into Thaddeus Peppergill in Asher's Brook and joined him on the road home.

Then Tieve, shooting nervous glances at Rhea the whole while, told how she'd seen Orin outside the ward-line, looking confused and searching for the cottage. He was her friend, after all, had been kind and she had no reason to suspect otherwise, so she'd called him in, told him to close his eyes and walk towards her voice. She'd noticed the effect of the veil seemed less in the centre and directed him that way – the child's too smart by half, observant. That will need managing, directing for better purposes. She'd brought him inside, introduced him to Rhea. He'd been polite, deferential, then asked to use the privy – and taken the child from her basket while the other two were preparing a meal. It was a miracle Rhea managed not to run into the forest *then*. Another miracle. There's hope for her yet.

And I… I tell them of my drowning death. Of the mari-morgan dragging me along the River Ayda like salvage. Of the green woman and her tale of a slaughter of her sisters, of a horned god broken and split, of a huntsman of shadow and spite ravaging the Great Forest at his leisure for so many years. I tell them of the promise I made, what I must do – figure out how to do. And when they've all gathered their breath again, their wits, their calm, I announce I need a bath.

Once in the tub, water rushing hot and loud, only then do I let myself weep. Despite the voice inside shouting that I'm wasting time, the other part of me knows that if I don't regroup, if I don't let this out, I've no hope of formulating a plan to save us all. No hope of carrying it off. No hope of anything.

Focus, Mehrab. Examine the pieces.

A huntsman roaming the forests, ravening, wanting something of *me*.

Ari and Matthias, lying on stone biers in a barrow while changelings feed on their families – and this surely of benefit to the huntsman, feeding in turn on all that energy and emotion channelled from his creations. Feeding, in this case, not on flesh but on the ephemera of mortals.

Five orphans stolen away, turned into wolflings, used as fodder trying to break through my wards.

And Orin Alderson. Orin walking freely around Berhta's Forge, nature unchanged or showing no sign of it, not like Ari or Matthias. Faolan hasn't mentioned any change – although with the distance between them, would he even notice? The lad drifts between the horses and the smithy, and playing with other children on the green; plenty of time to get into mischief, plenty of time to wander the woods. A motherless boy with a father who can't or simply doesn't communicate with him – one of the most dangerous things in the world. Orin luring Ari and Matthias from their homes, leading five orphans into the woods, stealing a baby from her mother.

Ari away for so long – 'prentice work while the huntsman poked and prodded and experimented to produce the changeling? Then Matthias, the second attempt, so much quicker. The wolflings, needing only to be bitten…

My mind flips back to Rhea's baby and all the tales about strange children, hybrid children, born of forests, fathered by juniper trees, springing from the earth and putting down roots, hibernating, even of summer husbands and how they might be turned to other purposes. How rare they are, how extraordinary. How their very flesh and blood might have magical powers, containing within them the essence of creation because they have come from the impossible mixing of two very different beings.

What if, used in the right way, they might become alchemical ingredients themselves? The essence of *remaking.*

What if, in telling Rhea the huntsman doesn't want her child, I'm very wrong indeed?

If the shadow half wants me to remake him, but he's only part of something else – something that's lost – then perhaps there's not *enough* of him to work with. But what if…

An infant with the essence of creation within her.

A witch with the power to change the very fabric of a being.

All the energy the changelings are siphoning away.

Might he be made anew, solid and real and entire?

What if?

* * *

It's very late when I send them all off to bed and set about banking the fire in the sitting room. We've made plans for what Rhea and Fenna and Tieve will do tomorrow while I'm making my way towards Night's Barrow. Selecting and packing foodstuffs that won't spoil on a long journey, ensuring the warmest and toughest clothing they can find in the chests and cupboards is in good repair, sewing gems and jewellery into hems and between linings in coats and cloaks because that will act as coin if our purses become empty, and checking the saddles and tack and that the horses are all fit for a long journey. Where? I don't quite know yet; perhaps Adestan's Harbour or St Mortimer's Landing or Windermere's Break or Tredwine's Haven. Perhaps none of them.

Rhea's loitering, her fingers tightly clasped in front of her skirts. I understand – how to sleep when your child is…

'Mehrab?' she says quietly. 'I… I haven't even named her. I was too afraid and now, please let me—'

'I *will* bring her home. Have a name ready for her and it'll be the first thing she hears upon her return.' I reach out, cover her hands with my own. 'But I need you to remain here while I go. Protect Fenna and Tieve, this place – if by any chance something gets in, your fire will be the only thing standing between them and the grave. And I must go alone because I can't be distracted. Once I leave the safety of the holding, I can only look after myself. I don't have a power that can be used from a distance. Wait for me. Trust in me.' I don't tell her to leave without me if I don't return by tomorrow night because that won't instil any confidence.

She nods, hearteningly quickly, dauntingly quickly.

That night, I dream of women as cauldrons, of them remaking the world.

35

Rosie rolls her eyes as soon as she sees me the next morning, which is never a good sign from either man or beast. I apologise as I handfeed her a small apple before saddling her. I check the contents of my satchel, hook the bow and quiver (the arrows dipped in the same mix I use to lay the wards, since it's been so effective against him) over the horn, tighten the laces in my boots and check the knife tucked into the right one, pat the knife on my belt, and make sure said belt is firmly cinched in the loops of my trews. I've chosen a coat in place of a cloak today for ease of movement, less likely to get caught on twigs and other inconvenient obstructions.

At last, I lead Rosie out to three mournful faces. I've reminded them yet again that they've promised to stay here, and manage not to say 'If you follow me, you're on your own' because those are less than reassuring last words, hardly a rousing battle cry. No one cries, although Tieve indulges in some suspicious sniffling and I call her over.

'Tieve, I've made a very large assumption that you want to go with us, but you don't have to – you can return to the village and your family or stay here, make the cottage your home. You're certainly not being kidnapped. The choice is yours.'

She says, 'I'll come with you. If you'll have me,' and sneaks a look at Rhea, all hurt and yearning and guilt.

Rhea catches the glance and, to her credit, she nods. Touches Tieve's shoulder, very quickly like a butterfly's flit, and says, 'You are welcome.'

The child bursts into tears, Rhea follows suit and even Fenna.

Wonderful. Time for me to go.

* * *

I pass out through the veil and don't look back. I cross the ward-line and urge Rosie towards the path we followed not many days since, towards the clearing where the earth-carved trap lies, towards Night's Barrow and all that waits there. Nervous as a cat, I keep a sharp lookout, but I'm also trying to piece together my solution, assess my chances of success, and my worst-case scenario if I don't succeed. What I will do if I can't find a way to pin down a miasmic thing of mist and smoke and darkness. I refuse to consider what to do if anything's happened to the baby. Refuse to consider what I might say to Rhea after all my certainty and promises.

I wonder what might happen if the huntsman were to be caught out of his barrow by daylight. What might that do to him? Something final? An eldritch burning? Is there some way to bring the barrow down on him? Some way to force an opening in the roof? Even if there was, he doesn't sleep in the chamber on the first level – but, I assume, below, in the places I did not venture. I think of the green woman's tale, that it hid in the darkness for years, pulling itself or what remained of it back together into some semblance of a man-shape. It didn't do that in the light. So, it has limitations, weaknesses.

I think of it attacking Berhta's Forge last night when it's stayed away until now. Why? A whim? Or was something – some limitation – removed? If so, what? Wait. Anselm died three nights before. Was that also the huntsman? If yes, why then? Again: a whim or the lifting of a limitation? What changed?

The iron knife broke its trap, left a mark on the earth itself.

It doesn't like water according to the mari-morgan, and I witnessed that myself.

A broken thing, a part of something else. Something snapped off a god of the hunt – perhaps all the drive to pursue and consume? Might that be what keeps horse and wish-hounds, man and god, running other living creatures to ground? Something beyond the need to eat, a greater hunger, a different hunger, for fear and fright? A cruel desire to dominate?

The breaking of a god, such a shattering that unseen things, non-physical things, could be shaken loose. Fractured.

I think about an interesting snippet I found last night before sleep, leafing through one of Yrse's books: that once upon a time, the god, when whole, might sometime leave game on the doorsteps of homes where there was want. Where cupboards were bare, and babes cried. An interesting dichotomy for a thing that reputedly hunted children when the whim took. Then again, different locations, different gods. And, I suppose, those circumstances were different – teaching lessons to the arrogant as opposed to providing for the deprived. Capricious things, gods.

Interesting, too, that the shadow half never sought out its other part.

Or did it?

Was that part lost forever? Did it die? Without that grasping, roaring, snarling, greedy component of itself, was it too soft to survive? What had the green woman said? *There's the story that, injured but not quite dead, he rose and returned to the heart of the woodland to recover – but he was always a broken thing after that.*

Two broken things.

And did that remainder that was neither dark nor violent, or not irrationally and passionately so, did it seek out its darkest part? Or did it forget what it had been? Does it too sleep in another barrow, hibernating, waiting and unaware? Where might it be found?

Did both parts make the choice to stand alone?

What parts of ourselves would we leave behind if we could, slicing them out without consequence? Would the better self root out the dark, the dire, the shameful? Or would the worse self leave behind its conscience and empathy, anything that interfered with enjoyment of the very worst sort? Ordinary folk like to think of themselves as "good", they don't like to admit there might be a part of them that isn't so wonderful, and in refusing to admit it, in refusing to look into their own darkness, they become blind to it, cannot see spite in their own actions. They make of themselves monsters, great and small.

Even gods might do the same. Especially gods.

* * *

Nearly halfway to Night's Barrow, I hear sobbing and rein Rosie in. Ahead of me, a light covering of frost that's not quite melted, speckled with blood. The trail leads off the path. I urge Rosie forward, but don't dismount in case a quick getaway is required. Several yards later, I spy a naked foot protruding from behind a bush. The foot leads to a still-booted foot, and two legs in torn and bloodied trews, all of the foregoing being attached to a weeping, bleeding Orin Alderson. In his lap, the grey head of the lurcher, its side ripped open. Long gone, poor beastie. Still, I don't dismount, just stare.

He looks up at me, cries even harder, and howls: 'Help me.'

'No *please* about it?' Rosie paws the ground, unhappy at the noises the lad's making. From here, I can see cuts and bruises on both legs, and the ankle of the bare foot lies at an awkward angle.

'Please,' he cries, lifting a hand from the dog's head to plead; the other is clamped over what looks like a rip in his torso, red oozing between his fingers, two of which are skewed. All in all, Orin Alderson is in a lot of pain and I can't help but rejoice a little in that. Not happy about the dog, though. 'Please help me, Mistress Mehrab.'

'Where's the baby?'

'What—'

'My fosterling's baby. Small, slightly green, flowers in her hair. You went into my cottage – no, wait, it's worse. You were invited into my cottage by a friend, you betrayed her and stole away a child like some fairy-tale goblin. At the very least, you offended against the laws of hospitality. You definitely offended against the laws of intelligence because you stole from a witch's home. So, young Master Alderson, you'll earn whatever help you want. Where is the child?'

'I don't—'

'I swear I'll leave you here. I'll abandon you as soon as take my next breath and not lose a moment of sleep over it.'

His mouth thins, the lips tightening to keep his secrets in. I click my tongue to urge Rosie onward.

'Wait!' he sobs. 'Help me.' I'm not cruel enough to say that's not convincing, but Rosie keeps moving.

'Please, I'm begging. It hurts.'

I throw over my shoulder: 'Where's the baby?'

'Night's Barrow.'

'Where you took her.'

'No. Not me. I—'

Now, I wheel my horse about, dismount. I crouch in front of the boy and say: 'Orin? You're clearly afraid of someone or something. I'm willing to bet it's the huntsman, but please be assured that at this very moment, the only person you should be afraid of is *me*.'

His pupils are very large and dark, he's in shock; close up I notice his right ear has almost been torn from his head. He looks even younger, face stripped back by pain; he looks very like his father at this moment. I reach out, touch the dangling lump of flesh gently. The lad winces. 'Did the wish-hounds do this?'

He nods, tears welling again. 'They killed my dog. My Merry-girl.'

Poor pup.

I rest a hand on the lurcher's motionless form – she's still warm. Beneath my palm I feel the slightest rise and fall of breath. My own breath catches. She's so far gone, but…

A quick cut on my forearm to pay the red price, then I lay both hands on her, gentle as I can, and feel my way through her flesh and bones and all the broken places, into the warmth and the dear heart of her that loves this idiot boy so, and I begin to knit her back together. It hurts her, I know, I expect to be bitten, but she's quiet, stoic, only giving a yelp at the end, then she sits up slowly – I've never seen a person do that so soon! – and licks her master's bloodied face.

While they have their reunion, I dig around in the satchel for the hunks of bread and cheese and dried meat, tearing into it to get my own strength back because the boy will need mending too. When he's quiet, the lurcher leaning against him, her eyes closed in bliss and his uninjured hand scratching that spot between her ears, I throw questions at him between mouthfuls.

'He set them on you. You're hurting a lot, aren't you?' Another nod. 'What happened?'

He looks around desperately, as if there might be someone else to either render aid or eavesdrop.

'Orin, you're ashamed, as you should be.' I sound mean and I am mean, and the boy deserves it. 'You were happy enough to hand over defenceless children, but you're weeping for yourself. Now, I gave you your Merry-girl back…' I feel ashamed of myself, to use the poor dog so.

'Please help me,' he whimpers. 'It hurts so much.'

'I'm sure it does. But here's the thing: if I help you? It's going to hurt even more. It's going to hurt so much you'll beg for the wish-hounds to return and finish the job, and you'll probably pass out. So, the sooner you tell me everything, the sooner you'll get to the relief of oblivion.'

And he whimpers again.

'So, I'll ask one more time: why did this happen?'

'It – he – told me the baby would bring *you* to him and he needed you. That's what he said…'

'Happy to hand me over too, I see. And then?'

'And when it came to it, after she'd been in my arms, and so small – I couldn't. I waited, thinking it wouldn't find me before dawn, that I'd get a day to plan… But it was out searching, found me in the last of the darkness.'

'You've been doing its bidding for months now. First Ari, Matthias, and five orphans all dead now, but this baby was where you drew the line?' He looks away, and I grab his chin, reef his head towards me; the dog makes no sound. 'What else, Orin?'

'My father…'

'It has Faolan?' I rock back on my heels, hit the ground bum-first and hard. I'd thought he meant that I'd help because of my feelings for his father. But the huntsman *has* Faolan and now there's a pain in my chest. The lad nods, tears making rivers through the blood on his face. 'Why… why would you—'

'I wanted my father to hurt! For every time he's made me hurt! I just wanted him to suffer a little the way I have.' Orin bares his bloody teeth. 'And the huntsman *saw* me! Listened when I spoke, asked for my opinion. Said it couldn't do without me. My da's never said that. Without Mam, there's no one else and he hardly acknowledges me. Then you came along again… Some days I wonder if I exist at all or am I a ghost, the way he stares through me. You don't know what it's like—'

'Oh, Orin.' I think of Faolan warm beside me, skin on skin; remember thinking, *Our parents inflict our very first wounds.* I think of him scarring his son so easily. 'What else did it say?'

'That we'd just scare Da. Just scare him, but it wouldn't say how. Not until…'

'You didn't think it was a bad idea to keep going when it replaced Ari with a changeling? Then Matthias?'

'They're still alive! Just… sleeping.'

'Have you seen Ari? Seen the hunk of her that's missing?' *Oh.* 'It was you. You left the offerings at my door – you're mortal, you could get past the ward-line. You tried to break into my home. You left Matthias in his garden. And it was you and Merry-girl who followed me through the forest that day…' *When I hid inside the tree and saw only a dark grey hide stalking past.*

He mumbles, 'Yes. But I didn't know what that meat was—'

'And poor Anselm…'

'He kept going to see you, interfering…'

'And then the orphans, with no one but the Widow Wilky to watch over them and her attention split too many ways.'

'By then I couldn't… I couldn't…'

'Couldn't stop without someone knowing what you'd done.' I shake my head, lean back, tilt my face upwards to the branches overhead. He didn't take Tieve, though, his friend; tried to stop at last to save the baby; wants to save his father in spite of everything. I speak more gently when I point and say, 'And it did this when you refused to be obedient. But it has your father and the infant?'

'The huntsman said I was a stupid child, that the only way

for me to be free was by my da's death and he would give me that. That he'd be a proper father if only I'd be a dutiful son and hand over the baby.' Orin shakes his head, trembling. 'When the wish-hounds attacked, he snatched her from me.' He sobs again. 'You're the only thing he's waiting on.'

'Well, we'd best give it what it wants.' The small cut on my forearm is still bleeding, so I put my hands on the rent in his torso, where there's most blood. The dog looks at me for a moment, then shuffles away. 'Orin, this is going to hurt.'

And it does, though he's lucky enough to pass out before I get to the broken ankle.

* * *

In spite of being acutely aware of the sun moving across the sky, of my daylight hours bleeding away, I wait a few hours while he sleeps. I build a fire to keep him warm, find his coat and the missing boot, both chewed and bloodied, but otherwise relatively intact, and put them on him as best I can. But I'm also weary from the double healing and my own joints ache in the cold, so I eat more of the bread and cheese, drink water from the flask, and am only a little resentful about keeping the rest aside for him. And I try not to think of Faolan in the hands of the huntsman, because if I do I'll become as irrational as I accused Rhea of being.

At last, I shake Orin awake. He gives me the look they all do when I've had my hands on them, the threads of my magic worming its way through their blood and bone; it's the look you give anyone who's hurt you, no matter that you come out better at the end.

'Have this,' I say, handing over the food and drink, 'and be quick about it. I've still a way to go and no more time to waste on you.'

He sits up gingerly, takes what's offered with a mumbled thanks and then announces with a bravado that doesn't quite work because of the tremble in his voice: 'I'm coming with you.'

'Oh, I know you are. And you're going to tell me everything from beginning to end, and when I go in that bloody barrow, you're coming along too.'

36

Rosie is less than impressed at the weight of two – the lad's slender but he's tall and lightly muscled, like to fill out the same as his father and so heavier than he looks. His arms are around my waist, loose, but he's so close I can smell the blood and sweat of him. It's been a while since he stopped talking, since I stopped asking questions, picking at his story until I thought I'd got all I could out of him. Beside us, Merry-girl lopes along, a little slowly, a little gingerly, but she keeps up.

How, after fleeing a fight with his father, Orin had found himself and Rowan somewhere new in the forest, Night's Barrow, and lost, just as the sun dropped and huntsman and hounds poured out of the earth. How he thought he was dead, but stood his ground, remembering his late gran's tales that if you ran, you became prey. How the huntsman looked at him a long time, sniffed at him as if his scent was familiar, like a horse with a foal, something it recognised. How it had asked for his company, enquired after his dreams, took him hunting – exhilarating! – and then began to ask for favours, small at first, then larger, harder to do, harder to stomach, but he didn't want to let the huntsman down. And I thought how I'd have done anything for the high sorceress, Almira, how the fear of losing her favour was as corrosive as acid. I thought about what I *did* do for her and it's *very* hard to hate this lad now.

A thought hits me. 'You didn't walk out here?'

'He took Rowan.'

'Blister?'

'Only Da calls her that. The huntsman took her so I couldn't leave…'

I grunt. The shadow half didn't want him dead but also didn't want Orin to be able to find help quickly. Does it plan to come back for him?

'My mother hated you,' he says, apropos of nothing. I'm not surprised to hear it. I knew it when she came and begged my help in getting pregnant, knew how she'd eaten her pride like a rotting apple, something that would be sure to leave its mark on her, its bitterness in her.

'Yes.'

'Why?'

'Surely you know.'

'But I want to hear you tell it.'

'What? Am I your storyteller now?'

'Got anything better to do?' he challenges. The little turd has a point.

'Before your parents married, your father and I were friends.' How prim I sound; how stupid I sound. *Friends.*

'Lovers.'

'Yes.' I owe this boy no blushes.

'Like you are again.' His tone is tight as wire twisted

around a bolt. I think about that last time at the smithy, in Faolan's bed, the haze of passion, thinking I'd seen a shadow pass the doorway, thinking myself mistaken. Yet that shadow might have been roughly the height and slenderness of the lad. Orin at the door, watching another woman in his mother's bed, taking his father's affection.

I know I've avoided the smithy and its master for a long time, but in the recent moments I've spent with him I've not seen Faolan interact with his son. And it's to my shame that I've never thought much of it. Orin's not my child, and I'm selfish after so long a separation. Greedy for the man and his time and the illusion of being able to, perhaps, make up for what was lost. To devour whatever days or weeks or months or years we might have left with each other. That was what I wanted for myself, something that for the first time in an age was neither affected nor influenced by consideration for the needs of others. Perhaps if I'd known the lad his whole life – certainly if he'd been my own – then I'd have behaved differently. But for that brief span, I just yearned for something that was mine alone.

'My parents used to fight about you,' he says, and I see I'm the wicked witch of the piece.

'I have no doubt,' I say levelly, 'that your mother was unhappy about me. But to be fair, I knew your father long before she did, and he and I had finished our *business* before they married.' I clear my throat. 'Or close enough.'

'She would scream at him. About you. That he carried you in his heart.'

'Orin, it's very hard for someone to be rational if they

feel insufficiently loved. If they don't think they're first in someone's affections, and if they spend their time concentrating on who came before them. Your father left me for Helvis – had I been her, that would have been a sufficient victory.'

'He thought about you, though, and she knew it.'

'I didn't see him for years, didn't speak to him. Did my level best to not think of him.' *Made a legion of summer husbands to distract myself.*

'When she was sick, wasting away, I told her we should send for you,' he blurts, and I don't reply. 'She refused. Forbade me or Da from doing it.'

'It's no comfort to hear someone would die rather than see me.' But I can't claim she's the first.

'Could you have saved her? If you'd come?'

'If you'd called?' I shake my head. 'I don't know, Orin. I'm not a god. I have some skills, I can heal breaks and tears, but tumours? Carcinomas? They're beyond me. A wasting sickness would likely have defied me, but I could have made her passing gentler.' No point in lying.

'Mam said… that you'd made…' He clears his throat.

'What?'

'Me.'

Oh. 'She came to me because she was having trouble getting pregnant. I was able to help. You're not the only child that's come into the world because of my skills, so don't feel special.'

'I wish you hadn't helped. I wish she hadn't come to you. Then I wouldn't be—' The note in his voice is achingly sad.

'Here? Orin, you were very much wanted – your father wanted you so much he left me, and your mother wanted you so much that she begged the woman she hated the most in the world for help.' Awkwardly I pat one of his cold hands at my waist. 'Your father loves you, he's just very bad at showing it. That's not your fault.'

'It hurts, when he doesn't see you. Stops paying attention,' he mutters.

'Yes, it does.'

'It's like you don't exist anymore.'

'I know.' I'm aware that we're almost at the penitents' path trap; as if I didn't have enough to contend with without giving life advice to a surly teen. 'It's like the sun going away, and your father's affection is very much like the sun. When it disappears behind a cloud you think you'll never be warm again.'

'Doesn't that anger you?'

'Once. Not anymore.' And it's true. It was too long ago and I need my energy for other things. I'm too old for idiocies and what-ifs. 'It hurt at the time but that was a long while ago. And getting mad about it just meant that I made worse mistakes.' *Summer husbands and stillborn babies.*

'Didn't you want a child?'

Why am I answering these questions? 'I wasn't interested, and children aren't toys, not to be got then put aside when you're bored. I'd have been a terrible parent and I never wanted to treat a child the way my mother treated me.' But I don't tell him, just like I didn't tell his father, that I couldn't carry any child, couldn't bear one alive, because that's my pain to hold.

'Then why does my father put me aside?' He sounds so mournful and I remind myself that he is, when all's said and done, a lonely boy who's almost lost his dog, who's crying for his father and grieving his mother, who's become aware of the terrible weight of all the things he's done in hope of love.

'Because men are heedless idiots. All you can do is be a better man than your father, if you have children. Even if you don't, you've a lot to make up to the children you've harmed – those who survive, anyway. I know you protected them, once.' I think about how much little boys adore their mothers until they're taught not to, until they're taught that softness equals weakness, when that softness is all they ever yearn for. How boys grow into fathers who think they must tell their sons that softness is weakness, even though they miss it like a limb. Instead of saying 'I'll not do what was done to me, I did not like it' they repeat and repeat and repeat that awful cutting of heart from soul on their own sons. I clear my throat. 'For what it's worth, I'm sorry Faolan is distant. I thought he'd be better, and you deserve better.'

I angle Rosie carefully past the penitents' path – the trail of dead foliage leading from it looking even blacker, even more dead – and direct Orin's attention to the series of brown concentric circles. 'Did you help with that?'

I feel him shake his head against my shoulder. 'That was him, he made it.'

'But the hare – the hare was possessed, yes? And you'd followed me that morning.' I'm just guessing but he doesn't contradict me. 'And you loosed it near me, and I was caught up in the chase.' My turn to shake my head, but a reluctant laugh pushes its way out. 'You little turd.'

We continue in silence for a while as the air between us settles, and the mood finds its own level that's not quite so heavy, as if something's been lightened.

* * *

There's still some daylight left, but the sky is darkening, heavy with oncoming snow this last day of autumn. We've dismounted and are standing in the shadows roughly in the same place I left Rosie last time, and where Rowan and Faolan's great black stallion have wandered, abandoned. Orin's checked them over, tied their reins to branches, pronounced them hale and hearty with some relief. I think about the red hide I saw across the clearing that last time – realise it was Rowan then too, that it was Orin come to the barrow to fulfil some obligation or other. The boy's examining his torso, the raised pink scars where only a few hours ago he was bleeding. I feel sick to my stomach. I would like nothing so much as to run and hide in a hole in the earth – not the one in front of us, obviously. Instead, I tether Rosie to a tree and Merry-girl with her despite the reproachful look she gives. With an apology, I wrap my scarf around her snout as a muzzle because I can't risk her barking. I hand Orin the spare iron knife from my satchel, then adjust the quiver and bow slung on my back, and am searching for inspiring words when he blurts out:

'What if it's already killed my da?' The lad's face, stripped of all boldness, all swagger, looks achingly young. A little boy deprived of both parents, confused and doing terrible things to wring a little warmth from his life.

'It hasn't,' I say and I'm mostly sure I'm right. I wish I could tell him his father will be safe, that it will turn out all right in the end. What I don't tell him because it will offer no comfort is that I'm fairly sure the shadow half needs Faolan so it won't do anything to him, or at least not without an audience.

That the death of the blacksmith needs to be a *performance*. A ritual. Must be witnessed – because such a death unseen won't have quite the same effect without testimony, without shock. Of course, I'm not sure of anything right now, can't think of anything except the sight of Faolan's scars across shoulder and chest, stomach and hips.

I do the only thing I can and wrap my arms around Orin and hold him tightly until he stops shaking, then say, 'You know what to do. I'm counting on you.'

'Yes, Mistress Mehrab.' His voice is stronger than it has been.

'Remember: Be better. Do better. And if you betray me, I'll get you, I swear.' I grit my teeth. 'You'll wish it had killed you.'

'I won't let you down.'

'If you do, I'll turn you into a frog.'

37

As we step into the maw of the barrow, the storm clouds swallow the remaining daylight, so quickly it's like a candle blown out. I blink rapidly, hoping to get my eyes to adjust. Someone grabs my hand and even though I know it's Orin I have to bite down on a squeal.

'I'm used to the lack of light, let me help,' he says, and leads me down the spiralling path, around the curtain walls one by one. Soon enough I can see the glow from the first chamber below, but I keep hold of his hand and he of mine, and I think we take comfort while we can.

When we step into the large open space, it appears nothing's changed. The same piles of disarticulated wish-hounds waiting for night-proper and their master's command. No sign of the huntsman, nor Faolan nor the baby, but somewhere, deep in the earth, lower and lower, is the echo of crying, a squalling child.

'Where does it sleep? The shadow half.'

'In the lowest chamber. There's another between us and it. I think, from the sound, the child's there.'

Despite the darkness of the snowstorm threatening, we've

still got daytime on our side; the huntsman will be resting until night falls. We can bring Ari and Matthias up into the fresh air, find Faolan and the baby. It might be two trips rather than one, but I pray we've time. Ari's shoulder will need attention; with luck that can wait, with luck she'll remain sleeping for the journey home. We've got enough horses this time, to safely take two adults and three children away, while I wait for night proper to fall.

For the huntsman to resume whatever solidity he can – for there to be something I can fire one of my arrows tipped with the ward-mix into. Whatever lies below is bones and some skin – according to Orin who, unable to resist the push of his curiosity, had crept in there early in his association with the huntsman.

In all my reading, there were many tales of folk who tried to kill gods for whatever reason, but very few who actually succeeded, and a frustratingly sparse amount of detail on the how-to side of things. However, I know the ward-mix has kept him at bay, I know what it did to the wolflings, and the names of two herbs continually cropped up in those tales of the murders of gods: hemlock and hellebore. Black hellebore to be specific. Hellebore – or winter rose or oracle flower – is also meant to be felicitous, and one should plant it in one's garden for luck, which I do.

So, my arrows have been dipped in ward-mix with nightshade and hellebore added. But I need the huntsman to be in a more solid – and therefore dangerous – shape before I can do what must be done. Or try to. Orin suggested that a knife to the ribs might be more effective, but I suggested to Orin that requires closer quarters than I'm comfortable with, hence: bow and arrow.

When we reach the centre of the chamber, I stop, let the lad's hand go. I take off the bow and quiver, place them on one of the small squat tables that litter the room – easier to carry children without those hanging about me. 'Find your father and the baby. I'll get Ari and Matthias. I need you all out of here and away as soon as possible.'

'What about the snowstorm?'

'Better to be out in that than in here when night falls,' I say. I don't say, *Unless I fail and you become prey.* I give him a push towards the doorway to where the corridor continues to spiral down, and watch until he's out of sight, then I turn towards the chamber where the two children lie in unnatural slumber. When they're up and out of here, then I'll descend to the lowest level, to do what I must.

Except.

Except when I step through the doorway all my plans fall apart.

The shadow half sits on the throne of stone and bone, appearing whole and very big indeed. Ari and Matthias remain on the stone biers, still sleeping. There's no sign of the baby, which I take to be the only good sign – or I hope it is. To one side of the throne slumps Faolan, thoroughly beaten and bleeding; a rope around his neck is tied to an iron ring in the floor as if he's some sort of animal. Both eyes are shut, breathing laboured.

How long's he been here? When did I see him last? The day Rhea gave birth? And then… when I went to the stables that morning to acquire horses for Fenna's escape – the first one, the unsuccessful one, the one occasioning my death – it was so early, but surely the forge would have been lit by then in preparation for the day's use? I didn't think much on it at the time, had other matters on my mind, just as I did when I once again went to the stable for horses and a more successful escape. Or was he gone the night before, the night when Anselm was trampled to death? Faolan gone and the shadow half taking free rein against those who displeased him? Two days? Three? Almost four because I drowned and was resurrected, conversed with the green woman before returning to the cottage…

'Mehrab.' The huntsman speaks, and I realise it's the first time I've heard its voice. The first time, really, I've conceived of it as having one despite knowing it had spoken to Orin. Now it's a reality. The voice is… it's like being hit by the first sleet of winter. It's being caught in a lightless abyss. It's the stench of old death, old blood, old shit if sound had a smell. Entirely, deeply unpleasant. And for the longest moment, I believe there is no sound other than this one, that there will never be anything but this forever, enough to make me cut my own throat because I've left the bow and arrow in the central chamber and if I try to run, this thing will run me down.

Then I remind myself that this creature is all *hunt*. All pursuit, all predation, all chase and death. That everything is its prey, and its arsenal is a broad church. Making creatures give up hope makes them easier to pursue, easier to catch. I remind myself that I've cheated death once or twice (or perhaps Lady Death didn't really want me; a ruling is yet to be made) and I take heart: I'm not done yet. 'Hello. Do you have a name?'

'I've gone by many. You might call me by any of them. But you should use *My Lord*.'

'Well, that's not going to happen.' I resist the urge to run and instead move further into the room. The fire has been stoked and I can feel sweat springing quickly beneath my clothing, running down my spine. I stand between the biers, calmly checking the children's pulses. Still breathing. 'But then, I don't think you've had your own name for a very long time.'

'What do you *think* you know, witch?' the huntsman sneers. His head moves as he watches me shift from one child to the other and now that I'm nearer I can make out the part of his face that's more smoke than anything. I wonder how much effort the illusion takes.

'I *think* that you had many, yes. Once. When you were whole. But none since. Only titles: bogeyman, goblin, thief, monster. Half-man.' A growl, animalistic, claws from his mouth and the black smoke of him shifts and curls, shows how thinly he's spread it to appear entire. Holes open, exposing the seat behind him. A lot of effort to hold himself together, then – especially when wrong-footed. Provoked. I am nothing if not provocative. 'How are you awake when the sun still shines?'

It sniggers. 'It's called Night's Barrow for a reason. No light reaches down here, we are removed from that cycle. Mostly I sleep when the sun soars because…' He seems to think better of telling me.

'…because you need your beauty sleep?' *Because keeping yourself together takes so much effort. You can ride the night only if you sleep during the day.*

'You would do well to keep a civil tongue in your head – if you wish to keep it.'

'I'm not some child or maiden to scare so easily, and certainly not by some hermit crab of a thing, stealing husks and homes, scavenging the lives of children.'

'They all have a purpose! Through me!'

'Their purpose is their own, whatever they decide to do with their lives. It's not and was never intended to be fodder for a thing like you.' I point at Faolan, whose breathing seems even more laboured. A rib puncturing a lung? Some organ bleeding inside him unchecked. 'He has a purpose separate to you.'

Its expression goes flat as the surface of the Black Lake, of a shew-stone covered by water before the visions come. 'Do you know then, witch? What else do you *think* you know?'

'That once there was a horned god, who delighted in the hunt, but one day heedless, he rode off a cliff and broke asunder. Broke into two parts, man and ravening hunger. That the man forgot what he'd been, wandered the Great Forest until he found a home. That the other part, the worst part – the desire to hunt and kill unchecked – hid in the darkness until it could at last take on the semblance of a man once more, and then it began to hunt again. And I think with every life it took, it also took energy and force and future from its prey – and it still wasn't enough to make it what it had been.'

I've been thinking about Faolan and his injuries when first we met. How it wasn't a new hurt, but it was so comprehensive it was hard to believe he'd survived. How he could not remember anything but a blinding light and a blinding pain. How he'd wandered the forest until he stumbled into Berhta's

Forge, found a home with the old Aldersons, learned the craft of the blacksmith, became their son. I think how no man could have survived that wounding, think how slowly he aged – and age he did but so very well – and how when I healed him all those years ago he felt *different.* Nothing I could identify then, but nothing I had encountered either before or since.

'I think you're the worst of him. What was left over, the effluvium of a greater thing.'

The huntsman looks away from me, stares down at Faolan's form sprawled on the stone floor beside it. 'I have killed lesser gods at my whim. I have amassed such power that the forest trembles at my tread. And what has he done with his time? Tinkered away with metal. Laboured like a *mortal.* What worthy thing has he done?'

'Become better. Lived as a man. Loved as a man. Cared for those around him – even though he didn't remember what he'd been. While you wasted your kill, when winter made food scarce in the village, he would hunt and share his game, leave offerings on the doorsteps of the poorest. What he'd done as god of the hunt he continued to do as a mortal.'

'I sent offerings to your doorstep, but you weren't grateful, were you? The boy said you burned it all.'

I ignore that, deprive him of a reaction. 'Why, in all these years, have you never sought him out? Your other part?'

'What? And be re-joined? Tethered to all that conscience? All those rules? When as I am I can do as I please?'

'I think you didn't know where he was, at first. I think it took a long time for you to look anything like a man, for you to pull your horse back together, for you to pull yourself together enough to stay in the saddle.' I stop, turn, go back the other way. 'I think you forgot yourself too. Perhaps as you ranged across the forest one day you got a sense of another thing, a part that chimed with your being. But you never entered the village until the first night Faolan was gone, the night you killed Anselm, then the morning when you—'

'Did you enjoy watching what I did to the sons of the church?'

I don't tell him I did.

'I think you're afraid of him, your other half. But you need him alive.'

'And why do you think that is?' It sneers and I begin pacing around the room, so its attention remains on me.

'You found Orin, used him to get a foothold in Berhta's Forge. To spy on Faolan, and to feed off the energy of these children, their families. You didn't want Faolan to see you lest he know you – you didn't realise he'd forgotten what he'd been. But you're tired of being this way.' The substance of him shifts as if in discomfort. 'And while you don't want to be rejoined, you do want a form that has strength. That you don't have to continually hold together like a bride's nightgown. But what do you think I can do?'

'The boy told the tale of how you healed his father, how you've done it more than once. That you could remake broken things.'

'But why the baby?'

'It brought you here.'

And I realise that this creature hasn't thought about her nature as a strange hybrid thing. Hasn't actually thought to use her as raw material or paste or glue or part of some fermentation process, a greater piece of alchemy that will get him a new body. It just thinks I can remove whatever is Faolan in the body and then it can move in like a hermit crab. I change tack, trying to distract it while I'm furiously thinking. 'How did you get him here?'

It laughs, nods towards the still form of Ari. 'Sent her little mimic to tell him I had his boy and he came without hesitation.'

'You're a fool. I can fix things that are broken – bones, limbs, organs – but I can't remove one soul from a body and put another in. I can't hold death back, which is what needs to be done in order to do that.'

The silence is heavy, the shadow half suddenly less chatty.

I continue. 'And if he's dead? I can't just stuff you into the meat sack – it's not that simple.'

I'd swear that, if I didn't know better, it's breathing heavily, trying to control itself against my mocking tone. Better men have tried and failed.

'You're nothing but the shadow of him on a weak watery day. You're the ferment he burps. The fart that creeps out at night. You're the worst of him, and slaughter as many animals as you will, you still can't stand without him.'

For long seconds it remains in place, but then I think my sheer obstinacy has worn through a creature already quite *thin*, its ego pierced if nothing else. It rises, hisses, and dives at me. Its hands go around my throat and, although I really didn't want to get this close, really would have preferred the bow and arrows, I'm glad I rubbed the ward-mix on the blade of my iron dagger too. Just in case.

The grip is tight, tight, oh-so-tight for a thing that's made of mist and smoke, but malice is a leaden weight. Doing this means it's solid for however long and that's all I need. I slip the knife from my belt and plunge it into the mass of the shadow half's body. It screams, its claws loosen, but it's shocked and slow – how long since it's felt physical pain? – and the iron piercing its flesh has the effect of anchoring it. The nature of the metal is such that it forces ephemeral eldritch things to become "real" and I'm able to wrap a hand around the huntsman's wrist and pull him with me to where Faolan lies, barely breathing now.

And I drag the struggling shadow half towards his fleshy counterpart. I remember the green woman shoving my soul back into me, and feel the crimson tithe trickle from the cut I made earlier in my forearm, as I place my other hand along Faolan's scars – those ley lines that I laid down when I healed him all those years ago, and which I unpick now to press the shadow half back into the solidity of the blacksmith. Both halves now screaming as I put my magic to work in remaking a god from two halves.

It is, I reassure myself, just another form of healing, then give myself up to instinct, to believing I can do something I've never done before, melding spirit and muscle, blood and will, bone and breath, ropey black shadows with the solidity of *meat*.

I do not unmake the shadow half, do not leave Faolan as a mortal man, tempting though it might be. We are all light and dark, and I don't know if he would live without his shadow – separated though they've been, but still in the world. And the lord of the hunt has his function too, leaving food on the doorstep of those in need, watching over the forest much as the green woman does. As much a guardian god as a hunter. The two halves together are greater than apart.

Finally, it's done.

No more struggling.

And Faolan's chest is heaving as he drags in air; his eyes are open and they're really the only thing that I truly recognise. The face is differently shaped, the jaw more square, the lips thinner, the cheekbones broader, the skin darker. And while he was a hulking man, the figure lying on the floor in front of me is twice as large again, with antlers growing from his forehead. Still handsome. He's going to have trouble getting through doorways. There is, however, something not quite solid about him, and I think he will need time to heal, to hibernate. Perhaps that was the shadow half's plan, for his transformation to be done here at the end of autumn so he might spend winter sleeping and mending.

'Da?' Orin is behind me, the baby in his arms – he's failed to flee with her as I told him to. On the biers, the other children begin to cry and Ari's pitch heads towards a scream. Her shoulder.

I rise, pat Orin on the back. 'Talk to your father.'

From my satchel, I pull the leather wrap of vials and powders wrapped in paper, select the one I need and fair pour it down Ari's throat, follow that with the warm slosh of water left in the flask. She's out like a light and then I can work, but before I do, I wolf the last of the bread and cheese, hoping it'll bolster me for this fourth healing: dog and lad, god and girl. Regrowing muscle and meat, veins and blood vessels, capillaries and bones, takes longer than remaking a god. Who knew? But at least in the presence of the god, the residual magic the shadow half used to keep Ari alive despite her grievous injury seems to still work. I cannot knit her a new cloak, but I can remake her flesh and bone.

When I am done, when we leave here, I don't think Faolan will be coming with us. When we leave here, Orin and I will take Ari and Matthias to their homes; he will tell how the master of the dark hunt had stolen them away, and how Faolan had died to bring them safely back. With the huntsman's will defeated and no longer fed by the children's energy and nightmares, the changelings will be gone. When we leavc here, I'll return to my own home and bring Rhea's daughter to her.

My home, while I remain there.

When spring comes again, I will leave it behind and do the things I should have done long ago.

38

We spend wintertide hibernating like all wounded creatures.

Fenna's injuries have healed but I worry about the scars left in her mind, on her heart, for she still hasn't forgiven herself for crumbling before the god-hounds. I tell her that what was done to her was inhuman and no one should be subjected to such treatment, that no one should ever have that visited upon them let alone by men claiming to be representatives of the church. I tell her that I do not blame her and nor does Rhea; that she did not ask to be tortured; and reiterate that I'd have done the same thing in her place.

'But you didn't,' she replies. 'You didn't give up Rhea. You healed me when you could have left me to suffer and die. You didn't do those things. You died instead.'

'To be fair, that was never my intention. If I'd thought about it, I might not have antagonised Brother Loic quite so much. It was almost worth it.'

She looks at me shrewdly. 'You *did* die and I can see the darkness limning you, Mehrab, it's like a scorched silver, almost like blurred lightning, a mark left behind after a burning. I can see where you've been.'

I shake my head, lower my voice. 'I didn't *go* anywhere, Fenna. Yes, my soul slipped out but it stayed on my corpse until it got stuffed back in.' I don't tell her about that terrible fear, that I'll never be able to leave this body behind ever again – that there'll be no release for me, that Lady Death will never turn her gaze on me.

In the end, I tell her that she has to set her pride aside – that it's made her vulnerable. She had assumed she would never give away the secrets she kept, but she'd also never been hurt like that by such men, never been tested in that way – and you cannot know what you will say until someone is stripping the skin from your back and breasts. Her apprentices who'd chosen death had their own bravery, certainly, but they'd not been tortured. She who has lived through that and keeps living, takes the opportunity to be better? No greater bravery than that.

Ari and Matthias are well, although Gida and Deva tell me they still wake screaming some nights. I tell them it will fade with time. I had a Very Serious Conversation with Thaddeus Peppergill one evening in his study; he asked if the rumours were true, had I died? I asked if he felt more comfortable talking with a witch or a dead woman and he couldn't quite decide. But he did agree that there was no place in Berhta's Forge for god-hounds. Apparently Brother Loic had told of his plans to build a church in the village, to create his own personal parish rather than go on hunting for Rhea. Why undertake a wild goose chase when one could settle in such a lovely spot? How fortunate then that the huntsman had dealt with the god-hounds and what little remained of them had been buried deep in the woods. There will be no god-hounds in Berhta's Forge, and the witches in my cottage in the woods will not be bothered or harmed.

Tieve visits weekly. Her mother agreed, eventually, that her daughter would do well from an apprenticeship and Reynald, although initially sceptical, tells me he's impressed with how quickly the girl picks up new skills, retains knowledge. She and Ari are rebuilding their friendship, slowly. That, like all things, will take time for such connections are fragile things and can be snuffed out unexpectedly. She brings news of the village when she comes and tells how Orin fares, running the smithy in Faolan's place aided by another blacksmith who worked with Faolan when the workload peaked. She says that the blacksmith is sorely missed by his friends, his good deeds frequently recounted in the inn of an evening, and the mothers of Berhta's Forge have set up a roster for bringing food to Orin's home at least until he can arrange for a housekeeper.

Tieve says that some nights she's seen him saddling his father's stallion and setting off into the woods despite the snow, in the direction of Night's Barrow. And I see the lad there some nights too, when we're both visiting someone we love who's changed forever. It's not very exciting, what with Faolan's hibernating, lying on one of the biers, eyes closed, unmoving, but breathing. There is much involved in mending a god. The lad is, I think, doing better; he is trying to be better. Some nights I arrive after him, and hear him speaking to his father, words I hope Faolan can hear, that he will recall when he's awake. Those nights, I sometimes leave without disturbing them. Other times, I make a noise before I enter to give him a warning, then Orin and I talk about how he can best make amends and re-earn the trust he'd squandered. And I hope he realises that although no one can replace his mother, I've come to care for him. I hope he understands, at last, that he's loved.

The baby, now glorying in the name of Flora, does well. Very well indeed, though her growth has slowed, thankfully, to a more reasonable pace. She's the size of a two-year-old now, but her temper remains sweet and serene. If she finds herself watched, in her cradle or bouncer, or crawling or doing her best to take her first wobbly steps, she will laugh, a great raucous sound, and flowers bloom in her thick brown hair, a riot of colours. I wonder if this will continue through her life or it's something she'll be able to control when she's older. For now, it's a delight and with no witnesses other than us, it's harmless enough. One day, perhaps, Rhea will take her to the Black Lake, ask the mari-morgan for them both to be taken to the green woman because Flora shares blood with that old god. If I have returned, perhaps I'll go with them.

And Rhea herself has changed from the scared, sulky girl who first came here. She's calm and poised, gentle with Fenna, which alternately moves and irritates the older woman, but they get along well enough together and the cottage is harmonious if a little cramped with four of us in it. Soon this will not be a problem. Rhea delights in her child, but I sometimes catch her watching the girl with an alertness I think all mothers wear when they realise their daughters are not their doubles – nor are they meant to be. And, knowing what a fearsome thing it is to live as a woman and a witch, their fear for their offspring is so much stronger. I wonder, some days, whether this contributed to my mother's feelings about me – not *for* but *about*; that I was so different from her, and my sister, from the simplicity their lives had because they were without magic. Perhaps she was simply afraid of me, of what my life might be. Afraid for me, perhaps. She might say, if she were to learn all I have done, all I've become, that she was not wrong in her fears. But Rhea, I think, will not be like that. I think she will not be inclined to try and crush her strange, glorious, blooming daughter into a safe and ordinary shape. Whenever she leaves the cottage or enters it, Rhea touches the face of the green woman above the door, and lifts Flora up to do so as well.

One day, I go alone into the snowy forest. I ride the feather-foot bay, Eadig, with a sled dragging behind him. I take an axe and a flask filled with a hemlock draught. In that grove, I at last do what I should have done years ago: I pour the hemlock on his roots and sing his secret name as he drifts off to sleep. He does not wake when I use the axe. I turn him into firewood, weeping the whole time, then load up the sled and deliver one or two of those long-burning logs to each home in Berhta's Forge because to leave him to rot in the grove would be wasteful, a desecration, and the green woman would never forgive me. This way, many households benefit. I do not feel better afterward, but at least I don't feel worse.

I have not unshrouded the cottage. Maybe I will and maybe I won't, but I know Fenna can cast the veil if need be. And I like to think that the god of the hunt will keep a watchful eye on the place. I believe they'll be safe. But there are horses enough if they have to run, there's funds hidden away if required. They have the maps I drew for them. They have Rhea's fire. They can call on the green woman, whom I've seen some nights when I roam, moving through her Great Forest once more, unmarked and unmolested. Not a word of thanks, but a nod of her head, and after all perhaps that's enough when she gave me another chance at life.

I talk, one night, to the mari-morgan by the Black Lake. I scry, one last time, for the city of my birth to see what I might learn. And I ask the mari-morgan what she might know, for all the waters of the world are joined.

And at last, on the first day of spring, I saddle Rosie and fill a pack. I say my goodbyes and trot into the forest. There are things I must do, mistakes I must unmake, and a long way to go before I begin.

* * *

Weeks later, I at last lead Rosie to the edge of the forest and find myself staring at the demarcation line between the old past, the recent past and the future. Between making and unmaking, old and new. It seems such a small thing, so thin that line, yet now it's here, so hard for me to lift my foot and cross.

And this forest, home for so long; or perhaps not home, not truly. Perhaps merely a refuge, a place to mark time? Until I was prepared to render my tithe. Either way, it's time to pay the piper. I take a deep breath of woodland air – *this* woodland, my last for a while – and prepare to step out.

'You didn't come to find me.'

I spin about, looking for the source of the voice, but it's not as if he's hiding himself, not now. Mounted on a horse that's taller than my head, a great grey-brown beast woven of vines and leaves and branches, the reins living things that writhe and snap (no less eldritch than the bone horse, but certainly more beautiful), he is whole again, clad in animal skins.

I can see the shadow of the man he was when I first came here, met him, mated with him; and also the shadow of the dark half, the killer god. Both of them in there, in the eyes, but they're wrapped within a different man. A different *being.* The hands holding the reins no longer have swollen arthritic fingers, the veins in them less obvious, although the top joint of the left little finger is missing. Not precisely youth coursing through him, but a younger vitality certainly. No less beautiful.

'No. You were sleeping. Mending.'

'You knew where I was.'

'I visited when I could – visited on cold nights when my old bones should have been abed. Did you expect me to climb up beside you on that stone bier? Sleep with you there?' I won't admit to him that I'd thought about it.

From his expression, he *did* expect that but knows it's foolish. Unreasonable. He sounds a little plaintive when he asks, 'Didn't you know or even suspect? When we were together? What I was?'

'Oh. You didn't even know yourself. And while your fucking was certainly efficient it was hardly godlike…' I remind myself this isn't the man of the last two decades, with his patience; I remind myself that gods are petty, jealous things, quick to take offence. But he laughs. He laughs and the part of him that was mine, that found joy in small things, shines through. 'I will miss you, Mehrab. I'll miss you, old woman.'

'And I you, old man, or parts of you at least.' We grin at each other like idiot teenagers, and for a moment I yearn for him, to touch him again, taste him, smell him, feel every part of him. But mortals who mate with gods seldom do well in the bargain.

'You didn't say goodbye.'

'No. I'm not overly fond of goodbyes. But look after your lad, he needs you. Be kind.'

'I'm trying.'

'And keep an eye on my little family – do try not to marry one of them.'

'Stay with me, Mehrab,' he says. 'Stay. Be my consort. You remade me, let me give you what gifts I can. I'll make you a goddess.'

And I'm tempted for the briefest of moments. My skin smooth and taut again, my breasts high, my hips a little narrower, my waist a cinched-in thing. The love of a deity, perhaps offspring, the thrill of the hunt, watching the world change as civilisations rise and fall beyond the forest, watching generations of folk who worship us come and go, watching those who bear a little of our blood do brave and terrible deeds. But I have tasks, things to do, other obligations weightier than rolling in the bed of the god of the hunt.

I smile and shake my head with genuine reluctance. 'I have atonements to make, old man. Liens on my soul longer than my connection to you. Apologies and amends to commit. And leagues and leagues and leagues to travel before I do so.'

'Then come back. Promise me that, old woman. Surely you can give me that.'

'Perhaps,' I say and smile, then turn and step over the border, out of the tree line, from the cool darkness into the bright and terrible light.

AUTHOR' S NOTE

I've been describing this as my "grumpy menopausal witch in the woods novel" since I first started it. Probably because for a while the menopausal and grumpy factors were featuring so largely in my own life. I was also determined that it wasn't going to be a book about the end of a woman's "productive" life because that's not what menopause is. Some members of society might think we're no longer useful because we can't bear children anymore and we've no longer got the patience to put up with everyone's crap, but this is the time when life is finally *ours*.

I'm not saying it's fun. The hot flushes, the sudden emotional floods, the joint aches, the hairs on the chin, the brain fog, the white-hot fury at the slightest obstacle. There are hurdles to get over, sure.

However, we've got so much experience under our belts that we can deal with any problem we feel like tackling – and if we don't feel like tackling anything? Well, we've also got a field of fucks that's completely barren. We're not yet crones, we're not at the end of our time. We have a lot of power if only we're prepared to realise it, to claim it and use it, to no longer worry about whether we're liked or not. We can smell bullshit and gaslighting a mile away. We don't care if men pay attention to us anymore, and it's a relief to stop worrying that your only value is beauty because that shit loses value faster than bitcoin.

This book isn't just a rallying cry for women in their third season (of four – we're not done after three, oh no), but maybe a translation device between younger women and older. The message for all of us is that menopause isn't the end. It's not shameful. It's not something to whisper about. It's a strengthening through fire and sweat and tears and rage. It's a path we all walk, so don't be afraid. You come out the other side of the inferno, forged and tempered like metal.

Talk to each other. Don't judge. Don't be envious of youth or contemptuous of age – because as long as things proceed in the usual fashion, we all start with one and finish with another.

Here endeth the rant, with just a few story notes:

The meditation on the swan and the dragon is an answer to a page in Ray Bradbury's *Dandelion Wine*, wherein an older woman laments that she was a swan in her youth, then swallowed by the dragon of old age. Which irritated me.

The phrase 'Be bold, be bold, but not too bold' is from the old English folktale *Mr Fox* – a tale which I love, however I'm not overly fond of the limitation built into "but not too bold". I always want my characters to push past anything that limits a woman's actions. Mehrab is one of my favourite characters, and I think Rhea, Tieve and Fenna provide excellent foils representing the four ages of womanhood, as well as one of my favourite motifs, found family.

Finally, a huge thank you to Terri Windling and Wendy and Brian Froud, who invited me to work on a secret project. In writing my contributions for that, I was able to think more deeply about my green woman in *A Forest, Darkly* – to consider her as more than a set-aside god or a hidden one, and to ensure the thread of her works runs through the whole novel.

ACKNOWLEDGEMENTS

I am as ever very grateful to:

- My family, natal and found;
- The team at Titan, in particular my editor Cath Trechman, and publicists Katharine Carroll and Bahar Kutluk.
- The incredible Hayley Shepherd for her copyediting prowess.
- And a huge thanks to Natasha MacKenzie for yet another glorious cover.

ABOUT THE AUTHOR

ANGELA 'A.G.' SLATTER has won multiple awards and her work has been translated into many languages. She is best known for her Sourdough Universe novels and short stories, including *All the Murmuring Bones*, which was shortlisted for the Queensland Premier's Literary Awards Book of the Year and the Shirley Jackson Award; *The Path of Thorns*, which won both the Aurealis and Australian Shadows Awards; *The Briar Book of the Dead*; *The Crimson Road;* and *The Cold House.* She has a PhD in Creative Writing, is a graduate of Clarion South and the Tin House Summer Writers Workshop and has judged both the World Fantasy and Aurealis Awards. She lives in Brisbane, Australia, with a superannuated beagle and a TBR pile which will likely be the death of her. Find her on her website angelaslatter.com and on social media @angelaslatter.